Also by Michael Crummey

Arguments with Gravity
Hard Light
Salvage
Flesh and Blood: Stories
Newfoundland: Journey into a Lost Nation
(with Greg Locke)
River Thieves
The Wreckage

MICHAEL CRUMMEY

A NOVEL

Galore

corsair

Constable & Robinson Ltd
55–56 Russell Square
London WC1B 4HP
www.constablerobinson.com

Published in Canada by Anchor Canada,
a division of Random House of Canada Ltd., 2010

First published in the UK by Corsair,
an imprint of Constable & Robinson Ltd, 2012

A copy of the British Library Cataloguing in Publication
Data is available from the British Library

ISBN 978-1-78033-618-3

Printed and bound in the UK

1 3 5 7 9 10 8 6 4 2

for Arielle, Robin and Ben

{ PART ONE }

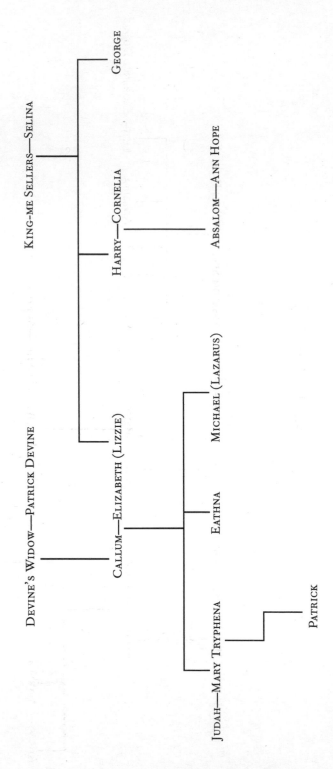

{ PART TWO }

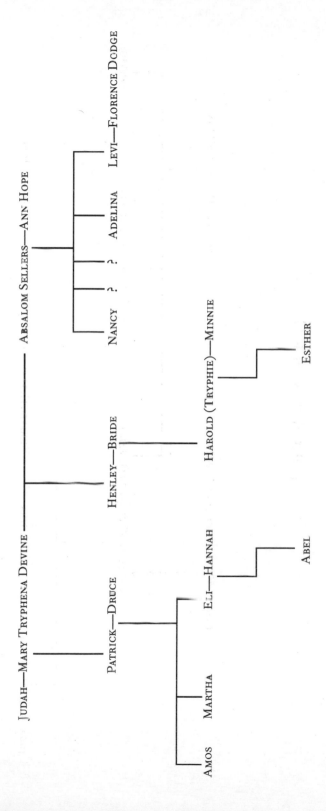

JUDAH—MARY TRYPHENA DEVINE

ABSALOM SELLERS—ANN HOPE

HENLEY—BRIDE

PATRICK—DRUCE

NANCY   ?   ?   ADELINA   LEVI—FLORENCE DODGE

HAROLD (TRYPHIE)—MINNIE

ELI—HANNAH

AMOS   MARTHA

ESTHER

ABEL

The invincible power that has moved the world
is unrequited, not happy, love.

GABRIEL GARCÍA MÁRQUEZ

I will bring my people again from the depths of the sea.

PSALMS

{ PART ONE }

HE ENDED HIS TIME ON THE SHORE in a makeshift asylum cell, shut away with the profligate stink of fish that clung to him all his days. The Great White. St. Jude of the Lost Cause. Sea Orphan. He seemed more or less content there, gnawing at the walls with a nail. Mary Tryphena Devine brought him bread and dried capelin that he left to gather bluebottles and mould on the floor.

—If you aren't going to eat, she said, at least have the decency to die.

Mary Tryphena was a child when she first laid eyes on the man, a lifetime past. End of April and the ice just gone from the bay. Most of the shore's meagre population—the Irish and West Country English and the bushborns of uncertain provenance—were camped on the grey sand, waiting to butcher a whale that had beached itself in the shallows on the feast day of St. Mark. This during a time of scarcity when the ocean was barren and gardens went to rot in the relentless rain and each winter threatened to bury them all. They weren't whalers and no one knew how to go about killing the Leviathan, but there was something in the humpback's unexpected offering that prevented the starving men from hacking away while the fish still breathed. As if that would be a desecration of the gift.

They'd scaled the whale's back to drive a stake with a maul, hoping to strike some vital organ, and managed to set it bleeding steadily. They saw nothing for it then but to wait for God to do His work and they sat with their splitting knives and fish prongs, with their dip nets and axes and saws and barrels. The wind was razor sharp and Mary Tryphena lost all feeling in her hands and feet and her little arse went dunch on the sand while the whale expired in imperceptible increments. Jabez Trim waded out at intervals to prod at the fat saucer of an eye and report back on God's progress.

Halfway along the beach King-me Sellers was carrying on a tournament of draughts with his grandson. He'd hobbled down from his store to make a claim to the animal as it had gone aground below Spurriers' premises. The fishermen argued that the beach in question wasn't built over and according to tradition was public property, which meant the whale was salvage, the same as if a wreck had washed ashore. King-me swore he'd have the whale's liver and eight puncheons of oil or the lot of them would stand before the court he ruled as magistrate.

Once terms were agreed upon Sellers had his grandson bring down his scarred wooden checkerboard and they set out flat stones for the pieces gone missing through the years. His grandson was the only person willing to sit through a game with Sellers who was known to change the rules to suit himself and was not above cheating outright to win. He owned the board, he told the complainers, and in his mind that meant he owned the rules that governed it as well. His periodic cries of *King me*! were the only human sound on the landwash as they waited.

Mary Tryphena was asleep when the men finally rushed the shallows, her father shouting for her to fetch Devine's Widow. She left the beach as she was told, walking the waterside pathway through Paradise Deep and up the incline of the Tolt Road. She crossed the headland that rose between the two coves and carried on into the Gut where her grandmother had delivered Mary Tryphena's brother that morning. The landwash was red with blood by the time she and the old woman made their way back, a scum of grease on the harbour's surface. The heart and liver already carted up to King-me's Rooms on fish barrows, two men harvesting chunks of baleen from the creature's jaw with axes, the mouth so massive they could almost stand upright inside it. Women and children floated barrels in the shallows to catch the ragged squares of blubber thrown down to them. Mary Tryphena's grandmother knotted her skirts above the knee before wading grimly into the water.

The ugly work went on through the day. Black fires were burning on the beach to render the blubber to oil, and the stench stoppered the harbour, as if they were labouring in a low-ceilinged warehouse. The white underbelly was exposed where the carcass keeled to one side, the stomach's membrane floating free in the shallows. The Toucher triplets were poking idly at the massive gut with splitting knives and prongs, dirty seawater pouring from the gash they opened, a crest of blood, a school of undigested capelin and herring, and then the head appeared, the boys screaming and falling away at the sight. It was a human head, the hair bleached white. One pale arm flopped through the ragged incision and dangled into the water.

For a time no one moved or spoke, watching as if they expected the man to stand and walk ashore of his own accord. Devine's Widow waded over finally to finish the job, the body slipping into the water as she cut it free. The Catholics crossed themselves in concert and Jabez Trim said, Naked came I from my mother's womb.

The body was dragged out of the water by Devine's Widow and Mary Tryphena's father. No one else would touch it though every soul on the beach crowded around to look. A young man's face but the strangeness of the details made it impossible to guess his age. White eyebrows and lashes, a patch of salt-white hair at the crotch. Even the lips were colourless, nipples so pale they were nearly invisible on the chest. Mary Tryphena hugged her father's thigh and stared, Callum holding her shoulder to stop her moving any closer.

King-me Sellers prodded at the corpse with the tip of his walking stick. He looked at Devine's Widow and then turned to take in each person standing about him. —This is her doing, he said. —She got the

very devil in her, called this creature into our harbour for God knows
what end.

—Conjured it you mean? James Woundy said.

It was so long since King-me accused Devine's Widow of such
things that some in the crowd were inclined to take him seriously. He
might have convinced others if he'd managed to leave off mentioning
his livestock. —You know what she done to my cow, he said, and to
every cow birthed of her since.

It was an old joke on the shore and there was already a dismissive
tremor in the gathering when Devine's Widow leaned over the body,
flicking at the shrunken penis with the tip of her knife. —If this was
my doing, she said, I'd have given the poor soul more to work with
than that.

King-me pushed his way past the laughter of the bystanders, saying
he'd have nothing more to do with the devilment. But no one followed
after him. They stood awhile discussing the strange event, a fisherman
washed overboard in a storm or a suicide made strange by too many
months at sea, idle speculation that didn't begin to address the man's
appearance or his grave in the whale's belly. They came finally to the
consensus that life was a mystery and a wonder beyond human understanding, a conclusion they were comfortable with though there was little comfort in the thought. The unfortunate soul was owed a Christian
burial and there was the rest of the day's work to get on with.

There was no church on the shore. An itinerant Dominican friar
named Phelan said Mass when he passed through on his endless ecclesiastical rounds. And Jabez Trim held a weekly Protestant service at one
of Sellers' stores that was attended by both sides of the house when
Father Phelan was away on his wanders. Trim had no credentials other
than the ability to read and an incomplete copy of the Bible but every
soul on the shore crowded the storeroom to soak awhile in the scripture's balm. An hour's reprieve from the salt and drudge of their lives
for myrhh and aloe and hyssop, for pomegranates and green figs and

grapes, cassia and cedar beams and swords forged in silver. Jabez married Protestant couples, he baptized their children and buried their dead, and he agreed to say a few words over the body before it was set in the ground.

Mary Tryphena's father lifted the corpse by the armpits while James Woundy took the legs and the sorry little funeral train began its slow march up off the landwash. There were three stone steps at the head of the beach, the dead man's torso folding awkwardly on itself as they negotiated the rise and a foul rainbow sprayed from the bowels. James Woundy jumped away from the mess, dropping the body against the rocks. —Jesus, jesus, jesus, he said, his face gone nearly as white as the corpse. Callum tried to talk him into grabbing hold again but he refused. —If he's alive enough to shit, James Woundy said, he's alive enough to walk.

Mary Tryphena stood watching the pale, pale figure as the argument went on. A man delivered from the whale's belly and lying dead in his own filth on the stones. Entrance and exit. Which should have been the end of the story but somehow was not. Froth bubbled from the mouth and when the corpse began coughing all but the widow and Mary Tryphena scattered up off the beach, running for their homes like the hounds of hell were at their heels.

Devine's Widow turned the stranger by the shoulder, thumping his back to bring up seawater and blood and seven tiny fish, one after the last, fry the size of spanny-tickles Mary Tryphena caught in the shallows at Nigger Ralph's Pond. Selina Sellers came down to the landwash while they stood over him there, her grandson dragging a handbar in her wake. Selina was a tiny slip of a woman and could have passed for the boy's sister in stature, but there was nothing childlike in her bearing. —You can't have that one in your house, Selina told them. —Not with a newborn baby still drawing his first breaths in the world.

Devine's Widow nodded. —We'll set him out in the Rooms, is what we'll do.

—The cold will kill him for certain, Selina said.

They all stared at the stranger as they spoke, not willing to look at one another. His body racked up with tremors and convulsions.

—There's only the one place for him, Selina said.

—I don't think Master Sellers would be so keen.

—You let me worry about Master Sellers.

They hauled the stranger onto the fish barrow and started up the path toward Selina's House on the Gaze. By the time they angled the barrow through the front door everyone in the harbour was watching from a safe distance. Someone sent word to King-me at the store and he was running after them, shouting to keep the foul creature out of his house. He'd sworn that Devine's Widow would never set foot in the building and no one knew if he was referring to the old woman or to the stark white figure she was carting inside. Selina reached back to bolt the door behind them and they continued on into the house.

Mary Tryphena and King-me's grandson stood back against the wall, lost in the flurry of activity as water was set to boil and blankets were gathered. King-me was pounding at the door with the head of his cane, shouting threats, and faces crowded at the windows outside. Mary Tryphena had never been inside Selina's House but the grandness of it was lost on her. She had the queerest sensation of falling as she stared at the naked stranger. A wash of dizziness came over her and she took off her bonnet against the sick heat of nausea as it sidled closer. King-me's grandson stood beside her and she clutched at the hem of his coat. —You'll remember this day a long while, I imagine, he said. The boy had a fierce stutter—d-d-d-day, he said—and Mary Tryphena was embarrassed to find herself so close to him. She shifted away, though not far enough to be out of reach.

The man she would marry opened his eyes for the first time then, turning his face toward her across the room. Those milky blue eyes settling on Mary Tryphena. Taking her in.

———

There was nothing the like of Selina's House anywhere on the shore. It was a Wexford-style farmhouse with a fieldstone chimney at its centre, polished wooden floors upstairs and down. Mullioned windows imported from the West Country of England, iron-latched doors. Selina was the daughter of a merchantman in Poole and the house was a wedding gift, a promise the girl's father extracted before consenting to the match. She was newly married to King-me and only weeks arrived on the shore when the first signs of the big house appeared, the foundation laid when the frost lifted in June. But King-me lost interest in the domestic project once the fishing season began in earnest. The stones lay naked in the ground for years then, the lumber he'd imported on a Spurriers vessel going grey under layers of spruce boughs while stores and fishing rooms were built and expanded, while boats were scarfed out and floated in the bay.

Selina lived seven years in a plain stud tilt, the rough logs chinked with moss and clapboarded with bark. It had a dirt floor and a wooden roof sheeted with sod and was distinguished from the surrounding buildings only by a surfeit of windows, the one touch of grandeur King-me had managed. She birthed three children in the shelter while King-me promised to build next year, when the fish were yaffled and loaded aboard Spurriers' vessels, when they came on a stretch of fine weather, next year.

On the morning of their seventh anniversary, Selina refused to get out of bed. —I'll lie here, she told her husband, until there's a door on that house to close behind me.

Sellers let her lie a week before the depth of her desperation came clear to him. She wouldn't even allow him to sleep beside her, in his own bed. It seemed a lunatic strategy, the logic of someone unhinged. And in a desperate act of his own he sent a servant to the widow woman, asking her to do something to set Selina straight.

Devine's Widow was all they had on the shore for doctoring. Her Christian name passed out of use in the decades after her husband was buried and only a handful could even remember what it was. She'd seen every malady the fallen world could inflict on a body and seemed to know a remedy or a charm against the pain of them all. King-me waited down at the store to leave the two women alone at the stud tilt where Selina was staging her moronic protest. When he saw Devine's Widow walking home along the Tolt Road he caught her up and demanded to know what was wrong with his wife.

—Nothing a proper house wouldn't fix, she said.

—You were asked to put her to rights.

—If I was you, Master Sellers, she said, I'd set to work with a hammer and saw.

The frame of the building with roof and windows was assembled in the space of a month. The morning Jabez Trim hung the front door, Selina got out of bed and dressed, packed her clothes into a trunk and walked the fifty yards to her new home. Selina's House is how it was known and how people referred to it a hundred years after Sellers' wife was buried and gone to dust in the French Cemetery.

The stranger stayed only one night in those extravagant lodgings. An astonishing stink of dead fish rose from the man's skin like smoke off a green fire, insinuating itself into every nook. Even with the windows left open to the freezing cold the smell kept the household awake. The following morning King-me ordered him out and Selina no longer had the stomach to argue. Two of Sellers' servants carried him on a fish barrow past the houses of Paradise Deep and over the Tolt Road to the Gut, a train of onlookers following behind. The man too weak to do more than watch the sky as he was jolted along.

—He come right out of the whale's belly, James Woundy announced, as if he had been the only one present to see it. —As God is my witness so he did. Just like that one Judas in the Bible.

—Not Judas, you arse.

James turned to look at Jabez Trim. —Well who was it then, Mr. Trim?

—Jonah, it was. Jonah was swallowed by the whale.

—You sure it weren't Judas, Mr. Trim?

—Judas was the disciple who betrayed Our Lord for thirty pieces of silver.

—And he was thrown overboard, James said. —That's how I minds it. Thrown into the ocean for betraying the Lord. With a millstone about his neck. And God had him eat up by a whale. To teach him a hard lesson.

—Jonah was fleeing the Lord God Almighty, Jabez insisted. —God chose him to be a prophet and Jonah had rather be a sailor and he ran from God aboard of a ship. And he was thrown into the sea by his mates to save themselves from a savage storm the Lord set upon them. And God sent a whale to swallow Jonah.

—That's a fine story, Mr. Trim, James said. —But it don't sound quite right to my memory.

—Goddamn it, James Woundy. Do I have to bring out the Book and show you?

—Now, sir, as I cannot read, I don't see how that would go far to clearing the matter up.

—Well you'll just have to take my word for it then, Jabez said.

There was no fuss made at the widow's house. The old woman came out to receive the delivery as if she had ordered it herself, directing the servants through the door. She kept the man on the barrow near the fireplace and washed him down with lye soap and carbolic acid and a concoction made of spruce gum and ash, but the foul smell didn't diminish. He hadn't eaten a morsel since he first appeared and couldn't keep down goat's milk or the tea Devine's Widow made for him. And Mary Tryphena's infant brother, born healthy and famished, became colicky and inconsolable and refused to latch on to his mother's nipple after the stranger was taken in. Everyone drew the obvious connection between one event and the other though no one dared mention it, as if speaking of such things increased their reach in the world.

Even Mary Tryphena fell into an uncharacteristic silence in those first days, spending as much time out of the house as she could. She walked up to the Tolt where she'd first spotted the stranger's whale, trying to puzzle the bizarre events into sense. All her young life she had been ridiculed for asking questions about the simplest things, as if the questions put her childish greed on display. Don't be such a nosy-arse, people said. Shut up and watch.

Mary Tryphena was four years old when her sister was born. She'd been told so little about life at the time, she didn't even know her mother was pregnant. Her father walking her into the backcountry as far as Nigger Ralph's Pond one morning, showing her how to catch spanny-tickles in the shallows with the dip net of her palms. The infant girl asleep in her mother's arms when her grandmother came to fetch them back to the house that evening. —Who is that? Mary Tryphena asked.

—This is your sister Eathna, her mother said. —Found her in the turnip patch, naked as a fish.

It seemed too fanciful a notion to credit but she had to admit there was something vaguely turnip-like about the bruised and nearly bald head of the child, the vulgar purple and pale white of the skin.

Mary Tryphena understood the difference soon enough and felt she'd been made to look a fool. Watch and learn she was told a hundred times and she began following Devine's Widow to the homes of the sick where the old woman treated fevers, impetigo, coughs, rickets, festering sores. Her grandmother said nothing to discourage the girl's interest but she made a point of going out alone when a birth or death was imminent and the reality of those most elemental passages eluded Mary Tryphena. Entrance and exit. Eathna leaving them the way she arrived: suddenly and not a hint of warning.

There was no hiding Lizzie's third pregnancy from Mary Tryphena and she was obsessed with the full bowl of her mother's belly. She considered the entries and exits of her own body and there seemed no reasonable resolution to her mother's predicament though she felt ready to stand witness, at nine years of age, to what promised to be an ugly, brutish struggle. But Devine's Widow insisted she stay out of the birthing room when her mother went into labour and Mary Tryphena left the house altogether, wandering up onto the Tolt to sulk.

She felt she'd been delivered into a universe where everyone's knowledge but hers was complete and there was no acceptable way to acquire information other than waiting for its uncertain arrival. She stared out at the water, the endless grey expanse of ocean below reflecting the endless grey nothing of her life. The nothing stretched for miles in all directions, nothing, nothing, nothing, she was on the verge of bawling at the thought when the humpback breached the surface, the staggering bulk rising nose first and almost clear of the sea before falling back in a spray. Mary Tryphena's skin stippled with goosebumps, her scalp pulling taut.

The whale breached a second time and a third, as if calling her attention, before it steamed through the harbour mouth of Paradise Deep and drove headlong onto the shallows like a nail hammered into a beam of wood. Her throat was raw with shouting and running in the cold when she came through the door.

—You've a new brother, Callum said, trying to lead her to the bedroom where the infant was squalling through his first moments of life. But Mary Tryphena shook her head, dragging her father outside.

It was a childish conceit to think she was to blame that things stood as they did now, that her greed to know the world had brought the stranger among them and caused her brother's illness. She felt her nose was about to be rubbed in something she'd have better ignored altogether.

The condition of both the stranger and the infant grew worse every hour, and the baby's mother finally begged Callum to make away with the creature she considered responsible for the child's turn, to take him out to open ocean and send him back where he came from. It was only Devine's Widow that kept Callum from doing just that.

No one understood the old woman's concern for the stranger except to say it was her way. In her first years on the shore, a chick with four legs was born to one of King-me's hens. The grotesque little creature was unable to walk or stand and was thought to be a black sign by the other servants, who wanted it drowned. But Devine's Widow removed two of the legs and cauterized the wounds with a toasting fork before daubing them with candle wax. She kept the chick near the stove in a box lined with straw while it recovered. Raised it to be a fine laying hen.

That story was offered up in the wake of every strangeness that followed in the widow's life, as if it somehow explained the woman. And she was happy to let it stand in this particular case, telling no one about the dreams that troubled her before Lizzie went into labour, of delivering infants joined at the hip or the shoulder. She used a gutting knife to sever the children, slicing at the flesh in a panic and holding the two aloft by the heels, blood running into her sleeves. Both infants perished in her hands and she woke each time to the conviction that it was the separation that killed them.

The widow refused to let Mary Tryphena watch the delivery when Lizzie's time came, expecting the worst. But the baby was born healthy and showed no obvious mark of her dream. And that absence disconcerted her. As if something more oblique and subterranean was at work in the child, something she was helpless to identify or treat. She couldn't escape the sense now that the twinned arrival of her grandson and the salt-haired stranger was what she'd foreseen, the fate of one resting with the other. And she was relieved to have the foul-smelling thing under her own roof.

It was the widow woman's property and there was no arguing with her. But when Lizzie threatened to take herself and the children back to Selina's House in Paradise Deep, Callum sacrificed an outbuilding that was used for hay rakes and scythes and fish prongs to make a bunkroom for the stranger. The change didn't improve the condition of either the child or the sick man, and for a time Devine's Widow doubted herself, seeing they might both starve to death.

Jabez Trim walked out from Paradise Deep and stood in the widow's doorway to speak with Callum. The child was still unbaptized and there was no expectation of Father Phelan returning before the capelin rolled. There was little chance of saving the infant's life, Jabez said, but they had still to consider the soul. He was a tree stump of a man, limited in his outlook but rooted and unshakeable in his certainties. A decent sort and no sober person had ever disputed it. —I'd offer what we have on our side of the house if you have a need of me, Callum.

—What about the other one? Devine's Widow asked.

—He'd as like be baptized already I imagine, if his kind were so inclined.

—He don't deserve to die out in that shed like an animal, Jabez.

Jabez Trim didn't understand what was being asked of him, though he could see the widow was at a loss and grasping. —There's not much else I can think to give him that you haven't tried already, Missus.

—We could bring him to Kerrivan's Tree with the little one, she said.

Jabez glanced up at Callum to see what he thought of the bizarre suggestion but the younger man only shrugged. —If you think it might be some help, Jabez said.

The dead on the shore were wrapped in canvas or old blankets for burial, but Callum couldn't bear the thought of settling the child so nakedly in the ground, so unsheltered. He built a tiny coffin of new spruce before the baptism, tarring the seams with oakum, and the box hung from a peg in the children's room to await its permanent occu pant. Jabez Trim performed the sacrament in the house and they walked with their neighbours to the far side of the Gut where Kerrivan's Tree stood. Lizzie carried the child while James Woundy and Callum carted the stranger on the fish barrow, James insisting on taking the head. —I'll not stand below that asshole again, he said.

The apple tree was marked with a rock fence, the bare branches hanging low and reaching nearly to the circumference of stones. Sarah Kerrivan brought the sapling from Ireland a hundred years before but it had never produced more than crabapples too sour to eat. Last year's frostbitten fruit still lay on the ground where it had fallen months before. The tree would long ago have been cut down but for the fact that Sarah Kerrivan and her husband William were never sick a day in their lives, sailing unafflicted through the outbreaks of cholera and measles and diphtheria that burned through the shore. Their transcendental health conferred an aura of blessedness on everything in their possession, including the tree Sarah had carted across the ocean. Every infant born in the Gut and many born in Paradise Deep during the last half century had been passed through its branches to ward off the worst of what the world could do to a child—typhoid and beriberi, fevers, convulsions, ruptures, chincoughs, rickets. No one considered youngsters properly christened until they had travelled that circle.

It was a ritual usually carried out with laughter and shouted blessings, but there was only a melancholy silence among the gathering as the sick infant made his way over their heads. Mary Tryphena stood outside the low stone fence with Devine's Widow, watching Callum and Lizzie weep as if the child were passing from their hands directly into the hands of the dead. And then the awkward negotiation of the white-haired stranger among the branches, the man so much like an infant in his mute helplessness. Skin the white of sea ice. The fish barrow caught up on an angle that threatened to topple the stranger onto the ground and he had to be held by the shoulders while they disentangled his sickbed, the men shouting at one another and swearing. It seemed a travesty of something sacred and Lizzie walked away with the baby newly christened Michael in her arms. When the barrow was extricated from the maze of branches, the nameless man was carried back to his shed and set down on his bunk, Devine's Widow sitting silent in the doorway to keep him company. To watch him die, is how she spoke of it afterwards, a note of satisfied wonder in her voice, to say how impossible it is to predict the direction events will run.

The summer that followed was uncharacteristically warm and dry and Kerrivan's Tree produced apples sweet enough to eat for the first time in its purgatorial century on the shore.

It was a month after the baptism before Father Phelan showed his face, coming to the widow woman's house before anyone made their way to the Rooms on the landwash to start the day's work. Devine's Widow and Lizzie sat at the table with Callum, the kettle boiling over the dark fire, a single tallow candle making a cave of the room. —Come in Father, Callum said. —We were just about to say the rosary.

—You're a shocking liar, Callum Devine.

Devine's Widow said, We've been looking out for you, Father.

—Only just made it in, he said.

It was Father Phelan's habit to arrive at night and no one knew how he managed his journeys, whether he travelled by land or sea. There were no roads anywhere on the shore but the Tolt Road and the rough paths to freshwater ponds and berry barrens in the backcountry. It was impossible to credit he walked the distances he claimed through wild country and less likely again that he went alone by boat around a coast as savage and unpredictable.

—How did you find your way back to us this time, Father? Callum asked.

—By the grace of God, the priest said.

He'd travelled over half the world as a boy before taking religious instruction. He often spoke of his time in the West Indies and the Sandwich Islands and in Africa and no one understood why he had given up the warmth, the trees laden with fruit, the women lolling nearly naked on the beaches, for a place where his trials were eclipsed only by those of Job. The Catholic Church and its practices were outlawed when he first came to Newfoundland and Phelan heard confessions in safe houses on the southern shore of the Avalon, celebrated clandestine Masses in the fishing rooms of Harbour Grace and Carbonear, offered the sacraments and last rites in the kitchens and bedrooms of the Irish scattered the length of the coast. He'd escaped arrest by the English a dozen times, once by slipping down the hole of an outhouse while soldiers searched a parishioner's home thirty feet away. He told the story with a kind of manic glee, how he stood up to his knees in shit, praying that none of the English be taken by the call of nature.

Devine's Widow thought him a fool and made no secret of her opinion. But she knew years on the coast without liturgy or sacraments and was happy for those comforts now, despite the package they arrived in. Father Phelan claimed she was the only person in the new world he lived in fear of, which she dismissed as base flattery. —You'd be a half-decent priest if you gave up the drinking and whoring, she told him.

—Half-decent, he said, wouldn't be worth the sacrifice.

He was lean and mercurial and abrupt, the sort of man you could imagine slipping through an outhouse hole when circumstances required it. He was fond of quoting the most outrageous or scandalous confessions from his recent travels, he named names and locations, adulteries and sexual proclivities and blasphemies. He had no sense of shame and it was this quality that marked him as a man of God in the eyes of his parishioners.

—I hear you've blessed the house with another Devine, the priest said.

—He's sound asleep back there, Father, Callum said. —Not a peep out of him all night.

They spoke English for Lizzie's sake. She had enough Irish to discipline her youngsters and make love to her husband but lost her way in any conversation more general. She got up to fetch the infant from the children's room and Mary Tryphena climbed out of bed to join the adults around the table.

—Let me look at you, the priest said, holding her by the wrists and leaning back to take her in all at once. Her face pale and sunken and the eyes dark with congenital hunger. —Is she spoken for yet?

Mary Tryphena pulled both hands clear. —No, she said.

—Now I'm not asking you to marry *me*, girl.

Callum said, We were thinking she might take communion this visit, Father.

—Well now. That's a step no smaller than marriage.

—Stop trying to scare the girl, Devine's Widow said.

Mary Tryphena watched the steady flame of the candle on the table, pretending to ignore the conversation, and the priest obliged her by turning his attention to the infant. He made the sign of the cross and offered a blessing.

—Jabez baptized him, I understand.

—We thought we were going to lose him, Father.

—Jabez Trim is a good man.

—I see you got the news from Mrs. Gallery, Devine's Widow said.

Father Phelan nodded, the habitual blankness of his face unperturbed. —I managed to slip in for an hour's rest when I got here.

— And how's Mr. Gallery?

—I keep expecting him gone every time I come back. But so far, not. And he haven't changed one jot all these years. Still won't make confession.

—It might be him not being Catholic, Lizzie said, smiling into her bowl.

—That haven't stopped others, Mrs. Devine. And not a one of those in the same need as Mr. Gallery. How are the fish this year, Callum?

—Please God we won't starve, Father. That's as much as can be said for the fish.

They carried on with the old introductory conversation awhile to settle back into relations as they stood when the priest left the shore months before.

—Is it true now, Father Phelan said, what Mrs. Gallery tells me about your sea orphan?

—Depends what it is she's told you, Devine's Widow said.

—White as the driven snow, she says he is.

—And the fiercest stench on him, Father, Lizzie said. —Would make your hair curl to smell it.

—You saw him born of the fish, Missus?

Devine's Widow nodded. —Delivered him from the guts myself.

Callum took a breath, half afraid to speak. —Is it God wanting to tell us something, do you think?

—God give up talking to such as we a long time ago, the priest said.

Devine's Widow stood up from her chair. —I'll take you out to him, Father.

Mary Tryphena slipped off Callum's lap and followed them along the side of the house. The stranger seemed to glow in the dark of his windowless shed. He was half sitting with his back to the corner, a square of canvas pulled to his waist as a blanket, watching them with the indolence of a creature that's spent all its days tied to a stake.

—Is he a Catholic, do you know? the priest asked.

—He's neither fish nor fowl, this one. But he could use a blessing, Father.

Phelan stepped into the fog of the tiny room. He leaned over the man, made the sign of the cross and prayed awhile in Latin. He took a brass vial from an inner pocket and anointed the white forehead with oil. He came back into the open air and shook his head to clear it. —Mrs. Gallery says there's some would gladly have that creature drowned in Nigger Ralph's Pond.

—There's some would gladly have you drowned in Nigger Ralph's Pond, Father.

The priest turned to Mary Tryphena. —Your grandmother is a miserable witch, do you know? He closed the door of the shed without saying another word to the man inside. —I'll hear your confessions now. Callum will want to be getting out on the water.

Mary Tryphena still thinking about the man's skin, the shimmer of it, his face like the flame of a candle you could snuff between your fingers.

———

Callum crewed a half-shallop with Daniel and James Woundy, an open boat decked at both ends, with twenty foot of keel. There was a poor sign of fish again that summer, and the men travelled further and further along the coastline and out into the Atlantic to search for them. They left hours before daylight and rowed ten or twelve miles into the currents, as far as the Skerries or Monks Ledge or Wester Shoals, where they drifted with hook and line over the gunwales, waiting.

They spoke of the days of plenty with a wistful exaggeration, as if it was an ancient time they knew only through stories generations old. My Jesus, the cod, the cod, the cod, that Crusade army of the North Atlantic, that irresistible undersea current of flesh, there was fish in galore one time. Boats run aground on a school swarming so thick beneath them a man could walk upon the very water but for fear of losing his shoes to the indiscriminate appetite of the fish.

It was true that a cod would swallow any curiosity that strayed by its nose and a motley assortment of materials had come to hand in the process of gutting them over the years. Lost jiggers and leather gloves and foreign coins, a porcelain hat brooch. A razor strop and half a bottle of Jamaica rum, a pinchbeck belt buckle, a silver snuff box, a ball that King-me claimed was used for a game called lawn tennis in France. The prize above all others was Jabez Trim's Bible, recovered from the gullet of a cod the size of a goat. It was bound in a tight leather case but the pages were wet and stuck to one another and it took months of careful work to separate the leaves. There were portions so distorted by their soaking they were barely legible, but for many years it was all they had of the Word of the Lord among them.

Jabez once read the story of Abraham and Isaac during a Sunday service, Abraham leading his son into the mountains to sacrifice him as God demanded, but the verses that followed were blurred beyond reading and Isaac was left with his father's knife poised above him. James Woundy was so taken by the truncated tale that he still retold it on the long trips to and from the fishing grounds, adding his own version of what he considered the inevitably gruesome conclusion. Jabez tried explaining that God gave Isaac a reprieve at the final moment, sending an angel to stay his father's hand, but James was skeptical. —That don't sound like the God we knows out here, he said.

Daniel was almost twenty years older than his half-brother, married with youngsters of his own by the time James came into the world. Everyone agreed James was slightly touched, a childishness about him he seemed unlikely to grow out of. Their mother was the oldest bushborn living, a woman more ancient than Devine's Widow. Sheila Woundy had given birth to seventeen children by three different husbands, the latest of whom wasn't yet fifty years of age and was only thirty when they married. She was rumoured to be the daughter or granddaughter or niece of an Indian woman herself and she spoke a pidgin of Irish and scraps of some other language known only to the bushborns. Some said it was Indians kept the bushborns alive when they first wintered on the shore with nothing to eat but salt fish and winkles and the bark off the trees, there was talk of marriage and children between them before the Indians disappeared off the coast some shadowy time long past. Though Daniel and James took offence at the suggestion and wouldn't allow it spoken of.

The crew stayed on the water until they struck enough fish for a boatload, sometimes drifting three and four days without coming ashore, wrapping themselves in a square of canvas sail to sleep for an hour. The weeks of fatigue and hunger had them hallucinating voices and shapes and figures on the horizon or in the ocean. James Woundy came out of his skin one morning before the moon had set, shouting and pointing at the fugitive outline of a merwoman skimming beneath the surface near the boat. Golden surf of hair and naked arms as long as oars, a trail of phosphorescence in her wake. He had to be held back to keep from going over the side after her, Daniel and Callum pushing him onto his back in the bilge water. Daniel sat on him until he came some ways back to his senses.

They'd been out nearly three days and hadn't had a morsel of food in twenty-four hours. Their fresh water was all but gone and they'd be forced to start the haul back to shore now, with or without fish to show. Daniel was staring off at the landless horizon from his seat on his brother's chest. He looked to be near tears.

Callum said, I know he's blood to you, Daniel, but that youngster's a goddamn fool.

Daniel shook his head. —I saw her too, he said. —I saw her there.

—Sure fuck, Callum said. —So did I. But I'm not ass enough to go overside to try and grab her tit now am I?

The cod had never been so scarce, not in living memory. Even the capelin and squid and bottom-feeders like lobster and crab seemed to have all but disappeared. A season or two past they consoled themselves with talk of times before their own when grass was boiled and eaten and the dead were stripped of their rags to dress the living before being buried at sea. But those stories cut too close now to be any comfort.

By mid-July it was clear the season was beyond salvaging, that no one would clear the debt incurred in the spring to gear themselves for the fishery. Most were in arrears from one failed season aboard another and King-me forced the most desperate to grant him a mortgage on their land estates as a surety. He'd already taken possession of half a dozen fishing rooms and seemed determined to own both harbours entire. The spring's whale meat was long gone and some families were surviving on winkles and mussels dug up on the beaches or the same meal of herring served morning, noon and night until a body could barely keep the fish down. The summer not half over and already there was talk of winter and how many would starve without help from God.

Father Phelan had little solace to offer on that question and tried to make himself useful as a drinking companion, offering reminiscences of the women he'd bedded on the southern shore of the Avalon or details of the sexual dysfunctions of the English monarchs through

the centuries. He sang songs he'd learned from darkies in the West Indies, taught "native dances" from the South Sea Islands that had men leap-frogging one another with underpants on their heads, oinking like pigs. A night without worry was all he had to give them, a taste of God's Heaven on earth.

He came to see Mary Tryphena once a week to school her in the catechism and the finer points of the faith. He was always miserably hungover and they sat in the open air on the shady side of the tilt. The shed where the stranger slept stood behind them, the pale face glimmering in the dark interior when the door was ajar. The man had lately found the use of his legs and for a few days he'd wandered about the Gut, peering in windows or standing to watch women hang out their wash or hoe the potato gardens. They chased him off when they saw him, brandishing rakes or sticks, and children followed after him, flinging rocks at his head. He didn't leave the shed at all in daylight now, and Father Phelan expected he'd be dead if not for Devine's Widow.

The priest stopped at the shed door before leaving and nodded to the man inside. He talked for a while about the fish and the strangely fine weather and his time in Africa, without knowing if a single word was understood. —Well sir, he said finally. The heat did nothing to help the man's odour, the priest could hardly catch a breath for the reek. —There's some people talking of making away with you, he said. —They think you're bad for the fish, is what it is. It's most likely just talk. Although there's no telling what people might do if times get bad enough and times are not good. Father Phelan glanced over his shoulder to see if any of this news registered on the man's face, but couldn't make out his features in the gloom. —The peace of the Lord be with you, he said before he left.

They came for the stranger eventually, as the priest expected they would. Two dozen men drunk and armed with fish knives and hayforks and

torches and rope, a ragged medieval tapestry descending the Tolt Road in the dead of night. Devine's Widow shaking Callum awake. —They're coming for him, she told him.

—Who?

—Get up, she said.

He heard their racket then, the men shouting to one another as if the dark affected their ears as well as their eyes. Lizzie put a hand to his arm, begging him to stay inside, and Devine's Widow went out on her own while they argued. She was standing in front of the shed door when they arrived, her shawl across her shoulders, grey hair loose about her head and her sunken face trenched with shadows in the torchlight. No one was surprised to find her there and it was Devine's Widow they'd gotten drunk to face. There was nothing to the woman but sinew, her body like a length of hemp rope. But she'd brought most of them into the world and delivered their children as well. She sat with the dying and washed and laid out the corpses. She seemed a gatekeeper between two worlds whose say-so they were helpless to carry on without. Someone at the back of the group asked her to stand aside, the deference of the request so comical in the circumstances that she laughed.

—I spose you wants a cup of tea with that, she said.

Callum came around the side of the house and walked up beside his mother. — What is it you wants? he asked.

The same polite voice from the back of the group said, We only wants to have a word with your man in the shed.

—The idiot haven't got a word in he's head.

—We'll burn it down if we have to, Callum.

The door opened a crack then and slowly wider and in the light of the torches Mary Tryphena looked out from the shed to tell them the man was gone.

The mob forced their way past her and then into the house and they carried out a drunken search of the nearby bushes before heading to the waterfront. Callum stood watching the light of the torches dip in and out of the fishing rooms before he went back inside. He sat on the edge of the children's bed to speak to Mary Tryphena. She'd had a dream that woke her, she said, and went outside. Saw the lights coming and had gone to warn the man away, shooing him off as if he was an old cow trampling the garden.

—You went out to pee, did you?

—No, she said.

Callum shook his head. He didn't know if the girl meant to say she'd dreamt the event before it happened or if it was simple coincidence, and he couldn't bring himself to ask. He'd always thought Mary Tryphena had too much of the widow in her. Precocious and grasping after life in a way that made him afraid for her. Eathna had been his girl, gregarious and unserious. Dimples and a head of red curls and a lovely voice to accompany him when he sang around the house. He'd never felt the same ease with Mary Tryphena. There was more to the world than what could be seen or heard or held, he didn't doubt the fact. But it was an invitation to trouble to put too much stock in such things, to cultivate them. —What else are you after dreaming? he said, but she only stared at him with a pitying look.

Lizzie was still awake when he came to bed and they lay that way the rest of the night, both of them rigid and fearful. She was angry with him for going outside, though he didn't see how he could leave his mother to stare down a crowd of drunkards bent on murder. —She needs no help from heaven or earth, Lizzie said. A note of disgust in her voice, as if the old woman's fortitude was something to be despised.

Callum was ten years older than his wife. He'd loved her from the time she was a child and spent much of his adulthood resigned to a life without her. It was thanks to some murky intervention by Devine's Widow they were together now though they'd never acknowledged the fact. Lizzie wasn't used to being in anyone's debt and she never made peace with the notion.

It was still dark outside when he rose from the bed two hours later, the morning calm and warm as all mornings had been since summer began in earnest. The sharpest sliver of moon like a fish hook over the Tolt.

Devine's Widow stopped him at the door as he left. —You'll have a good day out there today, she said, and he nodded without looking at the woman.

Daniel and James were already on the stagehead. No one mentioned the night's events and they climbed down into the boat carting buckets of bait and jigging lines. They loosed the moorings and shoved clear into the still water of the cove. James and Daniel sat to the oars and rowed through the narrows on the high tide while Callum cut and set the baitfish on their hooks. They were an hour out before they realized the standing smell of offal and fish guts from the splitting room was still with them. The stink drifting back from the bow. They found the stranger curled into the fore-cuddy under a bit of canvas sail, a half-naked stowaway. They guessed he made his way to the fishing rooms from the shed the night before, the only place in the Gut where his own stink wouldn't give him away, slipping into the boat to hide when the torches came for him. —Which means he's something more than an idiot, Daniel said. The three men argued about the wisdom of keeping him in the boat, about the time that would be wasted rowing back. —He's a goddamn jinker, James insisted. —We'll all be drownded out here with him aboard.

Daniel suggested they just send him overside and be done with it, but Callum couldn't see what would stop him being carted ashore in the belly of another whale and they'd be back where they began. The stranger hadn't moved a muscle since being uncovered, only his eyes flicking back and forth between them, and he was staring at Callum now as if waiting for a verdict.

—I'll tell you this much, James Woundy said, I'm sick to death of carting the bastard all over God's green earth. I'll not row another stroke with him in the boat.

—What about it? Callum asked the stranger. —You want to take a turn at the oars? He held out his hand as a taunt but couldn't refuse when the man reached to take it. James and Daniel both retreated to the stern as he made his way to the taut and set the oars, rowing cross-handed toward the new sun as if the sun was his destination.

They passed a handful of other boats that were having no luck at the fish. There was pointing and shouting when they saw who was at the oars and by the time the sun had come full into the sky there was a tiny flotilla in their wake, following at a discreet distance. Some among them men who carried torches into the Gut the night before. The stranger rowed on without a glance over his shoulder, shipping the oars on a nondescript bit of shoal ground known as the Rump.

—Now what? Callum asked. —You wants a spell, is it? But the man tossed the grapple and turned to the wooden buckets where the lines and jiggers were coiled. He looked to Callum a moment before letting a line run through his fingers over the gunwale and then began jigging, a rhythmic full-arm heave and release that he repeated and repeated while his floating audience watched silently.

—What do you think, Daniel? Callum asked.

—He's off he's head is all.

James said, I'll bet the fucker won't row us home out of it either.

The stranger struck in then, hauling the line hand over hand, arms straining with the weight. The first pale glove of flesh let loose a pulse of oily ink as it broke the surface. —Fucking squid, James shouted. —He's into the squid. The creatures kept coming out of the dark water, the air webbed with strings of black that fouled the clothes and faces of the men in the boat. Every line in the skiffs around them went over amid a bustle of shouting and it took time in the confusion for Callum to make sense of what was happening. The squid on the line were coming aboard in an endless march, already piling up past their ankles and it was impossible he could have hooked so many in one haul. Callum lifted one out of the bilge water but they rose in a chain, one squid attached to the tail of the next. He looked back to the stranger and could see he'd dropped his line altogether and was bringing the squid in hand over hand in one continuous string, mouth to tail, mouth to tail, mouth to tail. He looked around at the other boats where men were jigging furiously although no one had managed to strike. Daniel had put out his own line and was having no luck either. Callum called to him and pointed. Eventually everyone stopped to watch Callum's boat fill, the weight of the squid lowering the gunwales to the water.

Jabez Trim rowed in close and asked if he might have the chain when they were done and Callum cut it clean, handing it across the open water. —Don't drop it for jesus sake, Jabez said. When the second boat was full the squid were handed on to a third. By mid-afternoon every shallop and half-shallop and skiff in the flotilla was weighted and the crews blackened and fousty with ink. The chain came back to Callum and he tied it to the stern with two half-hitches before they began the slow row back to the Gut, keeping head-on to the waves to avoid swamping in the swell. Callum thought of his mother's words to him before he left the house that morning and a chill passed through him to think she'd foreseen such a thing. He was struck by the sensation she'd made it happen in some way, that his life was simply a story the old woman was making up in her head. They stopped to let other crews take their fill as they made their way home and by the time the last squid came over the gunwales every boat on the water had taken a full load aboard.

The coffin built to bury Michael Devine was whitewashed and fitted with rockers and used as the infant's crib during the warm summer months. He was an uncommonly pleasant child after his baptism, never crying for more than hunger and sleeping through the night by his second month. He was known on the shore as Little Lazarus, the child rising each morning from his casket with a smile on his face, untroubled by dreams.

The albino stranger came to be known as Judah, a compromise between the competing stories of who it was in the Bible had been swallowed by a whale. Jabez Trim complained that Judah was a country in the Holy Lands and not a sensible thing to call a person but he abandoned the argument once it was clear the name had taken hold.

In the weeks after the chain of squid was brought ashore the cod reappeared in vast numbers and no one could keep ahead of the fish. They couldn't remember a time when cod were as plentiful or so eager to be hauled aboard and everyone credited Judah's presence for the change. Boats followed in the wake of Callum's skiff, staying as close as they could to their good luck charm. The fish seemed to float along beneath Judah's feet as if they were tied to the keel by a string.

Jabez Trim closed a Sunday service by reading the story of Jesus instructing fishermen to put their nets down where all day they'd come up empty, how they came away then with more fish than they could haul, and no one failed to think of Judah. By the end of the summer they were calling him the Great White or St. Jude for the patron saint of lost causes. Catholics began crossing themselves in his presence as they would before the altar. The sick sought him out for a laying on of hands if all other cures had failed, sitting with Judah in the poisoned air of his shack and placing his hand against what ailed them. There was talk that one person or another had returned to the blush of health after an audience with St. Jude.

Despite it all, Lizzie refused to allow him across the threshold of the house. Devine's Widow made a show of arguing he should be invited in to eat but the smell of the man was enough to stifle the appetite of a pig. He took his meals sitting on a stump of wood in the open air and Mary Tryphena studied him when she thought she wasn't being watched. His brows and lashes so white his eyes seemed bald, like the lidless stare of a codfish. There was something at once stunned and slightly menacing about the man.

He recognized the name he was called by and followed simple orders or requests, though his life and work were so governed by routine that the simplest of hand gestures or a nod of the head communicated all he needed to know. Most were convinced he understood not a word of English or Irish. When boats worked close to Judah on the water, people spoke about him as if he were deaf.

—Shits as much as the next person, Callum said in response to their questions. —Eats like a Spaniard. Sleeps like the dead. Haven't seen him kneel to pray or cross he's self the once. And he got the smell of a Prot on him.

—You miserable bastard, Callum Devine.

—Now Jabez, he said, I'm only having you on.

—Have he ever spoke a word to you?

—You can't squeeze blood from a turnip, Callum said. —But he's not a fool.

Jabez nodded. —That one's as deep as the grave, I expect.

At the end of that summer there was a confirmation service at Kerrivan's Tree. The Mass was said in Latin and the rest of the service in Irish, although most English on the shore attended for the indecipherable pageant of it. Mary Tryphena and Floretta Tibbo and Saul Toucher's ten-year-old triplets took their first communion as the sun dropped below the hills above the harbour. The triplets were identical and indistinguishable even to their parents but for Alphonsus who'd won the single pair of shoes between them by lot. He slept in the boots to keep them to himself, though his brothers took it in turns to claim one or the other was Alphonsus and the boy wearing the shoes had stolen them from their rightful owner. The shoes and the name travelled from one boy to the next in an endless round and not even the triplets could recall anymore who had been the original Alphonsus. When Father Phelan announced before the sacrament that we are all one in Christ Jesus, the three brothers seemed deflated, as if they'd had enough of such arrangements.

After the service a more secular sacrament was celebrated on the Commons above Kerrivan's Tree with jugs of spruce beer and black rum and shine passed around. Men and women and not a few children besides got drunk there, the moon come out and the mosquitoes and blackflies fierce in the dusk. King-me Sellers and Selina and their grandson made a brief appearance and a handful of people caught sight of Mr. Gallery circling the clearing to watch the festivities. A bonfire of driftwood and green spruce and dried dung from the goats and sheep that grazed the meadow burning at the centre of the field. Jabez Trim's three-string fiddle and a wheezy accordion played by Daniel Woundy led a dance of dark shadows tramping the grass flat. Callum persuaded Judah into the gathering where they danced arm in arm, both men polluted with drink. Judah's fishy stink drifted under the smoke of the fire and everyone on the field welcomed it as the smell of abundance and prosperity come among them. Callum knew a thousand tunes and had been a regular entertainment at weddings and wakes and he was coaxed into singing half a dozen songs for the crowd. It was the first time anyone heard him utter a note since Eathna died the year before. His voice like the first taste of sugar after Lent, a sweetness that was almost hallucinatory.

Couples disappeared into the alders and berry bushes beyond the field as the night wore on, shifting clothes to accommodate the drunken love they had to offer one another. Shouting and singing and petty arguments flared among the congregation as they staggered toward the collective hangover awaiting them. They were never more content with their lot in life, never happier to consent to it.

Lizzie left for home with young Lazarus right after Mass and Mary Tryphena spent the evening in the company of Devine's Widow. Her first communion was a disappointment, the ceremony tarnished by the sullenness of the Toucher boys who swore under their breath and picked at one another through the service. But the night on the Commons that followed was more to her liking, the firelight and fierce release of it. She walked down to Kerrivan's Tree to hide when her grandmother announced it was time to go home. She took off her bonnet so the white of it wouldn't give her away and she climbed into the branches, clear of the old woman's meddling. King-me's grandson had settled into the upper branches earlier in the night for the same reasons, but he was invisible in the pitch and Mary Tryphena sang to herself as she often did when she was alone. She almost fell from her perch when he spoke to say he liked her voice. —I wasn't singing for you, she told him.

—Still, he said.

Absalom, his name was. He said hardly a word in company, and opinion was divided on whether this was due to his stutter or to losing his parents so early or simply a mark of Sellers' airs at work in the youngster. He was introverted and queer and seemed much younger than others his age, sheltered as he was by living in Selina's House. Absalom reached to pick one of the young apples, handing it to Mary Tryphena after taking a bite himself, and the unexpected intimacy of the gesture made her stomach quiver like a hive of bees. She watched the featureless outline of him in the dark awhile. She said, Do you know who I am, Absalom?

—Mary Tryphena Devine, he answered, stuttering on the D.

She thought he was making fun of her in some obscure way, but his manner was all innocence. Somehow he didn't know her mother was King-me's daughter and Absalom's aunt, that he and Mary Tryphena were cousins. It was a laughable ignorance in a boy his age and she felt a rush of maternal affection for him. The smell of the apple was surprisingly sweet and she bit into the hard fruit before passing it back. They finished the apple together and Absalom climbed past her to the ground then, his hands travelling her arms and hips and legs as he went. From the base of the tree he said, You've the loveliest hair, and she answered good night without looking down.

The bonfire went on burning till the small hours of the night, Father Phelan the last to leave the dregs. He was pleased with himself and with the evening, the children brought to the faith and his homily on the jealousy of angels, the gathering on the Commons and the more intimate gatherings in the bushes at the edge of the field. Life insisting on itself out there in the dark, though times had been mean and uncertain. He found the dirt path near Kerrivan's Tree and followed it through the village, drunkenly blessing each dwelling he passed. He walked the steep ascent of the Tolt Road and stood on the headland awhile to catch his wind before descending into Paradise Deep. The coastline bereft of light for a thousand miles in either direction, the ocean festering below him. While he stood at the cliff's edge he blessed the fish of the sea and the dull coin of the moon sailing behind clouds.

Legal strictures against Catholicism had been lifted decades past and a vicar appointed to govern all ecclesiastical matters from St. John's. But Father Phelan continued to operate outside the bounds of state and Church hierarchy. He lived among his parishioners like a refugee, dependant on the charity of the communities he served. He claimed it was only in the Gut and Paradise Deep that he felt safe to walk about in daylight. The shore was so far from St. John's, he said, so far from the minds of the governor and the vicar, that they were almost forgotten.

The surf was heavy with the tide's turn, the shudder travelling up the cliff and through his body, his head like a bell being rung by a hammer. His order preached primitive poverty and austerity, and Newfoundland might have been created to embody both. He was a lousy priest, he knew, and deserved no better than to serve in such a backwater shithole of Christendom. But he couldn't deny the Lord at work in him, that hammer striking.

He was prodigal with blessings in his drunkenness. He turned to the south to bless the people of the Gut and to the north to bless Paradise Deep. He blessed the figure of Mr. Gallery who had waited near the Commons to follow him home and waited for him now just off the Tolt Road. He opened his trousers and wavered at the lip of the precipice to piss into the waters below. He blessed his shrivelled little pecker before tucking it away to walk into Paradise Deep. He held a number of particular blessings in reserve, thinking of Mrs. Gallery waiting for him in her bed and the archipelago of angels they were about to inspire to fits of jealousy.

Through that fall Mary Tryphena found herself showered with small anonymous gifts, handfuls of partridgeberries in the bowl of a leaf, smooth stones or shells from the beach, the weathered skull of a bird, a sweet apple from Kerrivan's Tree in a square of cloth. There was no privacy in her life and the gifts were placed in public spaces where she would stumble upon them, on the Washing Rocks at the mouth of the brook, tied to the door of the outhouse before she made her last visit of the night.

Occasionally her mother or father or Judah discovered the finger of polished driftwood on the doorstep, the jewel of seaglass on the windowsill. But Mary Tryphena never doubted who they were meant for. She was surprised by Absalom's stealth, by the knowledge he had somehow gleaned about the particulars of her days. It seemed out of character, given what she knew of his awkwardness and insularity, given he had no idea they were cousins.

She hoarded the keepsakes under the roots of an old spruce stump near the house and told no one about the furtive relationship, knowing from the start it was an impossible match. King-me Sellers had disowned Lizzie when she married Callum Devine and the man would never allow Absalom, his only acknowledged grandchild, his sole heir, to follow after her. And it was just as unlikely that Callum and Lizzie would consent to such an arrangement.

They saw each other only when she attended one of Jabez Trim's services or accompanied her father to Sellers' store for winter supplies and Absalom was so withdrawn that Mary Tryphena doubted her reading of the world. There was such an unfamiliar pleasure to the conversation between them, such an adult privacy, that it made her feel sick to think she might be wrong. It wasn't until the heavy snows blew in and the men began spending their days in the backcountry cutting and hauling wood that something definitive came to her, a letter folded and tied with string that she discovered among the blankets of her bed. The boldness of it startled her, that Absalom could come into the house undiscovered.

She carried the paper in a pocket close to her heart for weeks afterwards, unfolding it in her rare moments alone. She studied the note like a botanist in the presence of some exotic flower. She smelled it, she licked the paper and the ink which tasted of oil and berries, she prayed to it as if the words might be coaxed into coming to her in her dreams. She passed her days in a state of irritable exhaustion, she kicked and called out in her sleep. Devine's Widow was convinced only a man could be at the root of her trouble but Mary Tryphena denied it. Her mother came to her at night to ask if there was anything she could do and Mary Tryphena turned away to bawl into her mattress of straw. Lizzie had set out to teach Mary Tryphena her letters as a young child but the lessons were abandoned during the lean years of rough food and exhaustion and she'd forgotten most of the alphabet in the time since. The note she carried was like a page out of Jabez Trim's Bible, the word of God which meant one thing and one thing only, and only those initiated into the mysteries could decipher it.

Jabez Trim, she decided, was her only hope. Through November and December as the temperature dropped and people's lives contracted to the circle of their tiny properties, to their hovels, to the three square feet closest to the fire, Mary Tryphena tried to think how she might steal a few moments alone in his company. By the third week of Advent she'd all but given up on talking to him before spring and the thought of the wait made her surly and impatient. —If we don't get that girl out of the house, Devine's Widow said, I'm going to poison her.

Lizzie was boiling Christmas puddings in a pot over the fire, dark molasses with dried currants and cherries. —Leave the child be, she said.

—I'll take her with me when I bring the cakes over the Tolt, Callum offered.

Mrs. Gallery had no work of her own and she survived on offerings made to the church by the faithful, an account at Sellers' store for the woman divided equally among the debts of Catholics on the shore. And it was the custom at Christmas to offer some small token to Jabez and Father Phelan for the services provided through the year. The Christmas puddings were an extravagance, a sign of how well the fishing had gone that year.

—We'll walk out tomorrow, Callum said to Mary Tryphena. —It'll do wonders for us both.

But her father was taken with a flu overnight, the fever so high he lay under a blanket next the fire calling out to his dead father, and Lizzie said the puddings would have to wait. Mary Tryphena wouldn't hear of it, knowing no better opportunity would come to her, and Lizzie insisted she ask Judah along, not wanting the girl out by herself with the weather so changeable. She'd take the dog, Mary Tryphena said, sure it could guide her back if a snow squall came on.

—Leave her go, Devine's Widow said finally. —I'm sick of listening to the two of you.

Mary Tryphena's feet were wrapped in cloth inside her shoes and she went out into the day wearing an old blanket as a shawl against the cold, strapping on her father's snow rackets at the door.

Judah heard the voices and peeked out at Mary Tryphena as she walked the path toward him. He was still living in the shed and had taken to sleeping with the dog under the covers against the freezing temperatures. The dog was Judah's only real companion, a black and white mongrel with a barrel chest and the stunted legs of a beagle. Judah stepped into the open air when Mary Tryphena called the dog and he stood watching as they set out, the animal bounding ahead to break trail through the waist-high snow before turning to run to Jude. It was in a state of agitation, whining and barking as it ran longer and longer relays between the two until Judah disappeared into the shed and the dog sat outside, pawing at the door. Mary Tryphena called uselessly

awhile and then turned toward the steep slope of the Tolt Road. There'd
been a heavy fall of snow days before and so little traffic between the
two communities that it promised to be a slog. The dog nudged past her
minutes later and she looked back to see Judah coming along in his
rags, a coat rigged out of a bit of rotten sail, his boots two squares of
brin tied around his ankles with twine. Her heart fell but she couldn't
think how to send him away without losing the dog.

It was two hours of hard travel to make what was normally a
half-hour trip over the Tolt and down to Mrs. Gallery's tilt, tucked
back in a spindly droke of woods above the harbour and away from
the other houses around the bay. The trees were the only ones within
a mile of the water that hadn't been cut for firewood or walls or
stagehouse posts or oars. Their sparse sickliness saved them from the
axe and the surrounding trees made the little building seem confined
and haunted. Mary Tryphena had never gone near it before and she
called to Mrs. Gallery as they approached. She took one of the puddings from her shoulder pouch as if she planned to heave it at the
door from a distance. The dog stopped behind them and barked its
fool head off, running back and forth along a line it refused to cross.
Judah knelt beside it in the snow, trying to calm the animal down.

Mrs. Gallery came to the door in a heavy woollen sweater and a
bonnet, wiping her hands on a grey apron hung over her skirts. —Hello
Mary Tryphena, she said.

—I brung a pudding from Mother, she said and held it out, still
three feet from the door. Mrs. Gallery didn't invite them in or ask if they
were hungry or thirsty. She stepped out and took the pudding. —Your
mother's a good woman, she said. There was a commotion in the room
behind her and Mary Tryphena glanced past Mrs. Gallery to the door.
She had never laid eyes on Mr. Gallery and wasn't sure she wanted to.
He'd killed a man out of jealousy years ago and never forgiven himself,
was what people said. He was a kind of bogeyman on the shore, parents
warning their youngsters away from the woods or playing on the ice on

Nigger Ralph's Pond with stories of what Mr. Gallery would do if he got hold of you.

—I should get back, Mrs. Gallery said. —You thank your mother for me.

It was gone to noon by the time they reached Jabez Trim's house. Jabez ushered them inside and sat them near the fire where they could open their clothes to the heat. He seemed thrilled to have company, calling into a back room to his wife. The Trims had no children, which everyone agreed was a trial for them, though Jabez let it be known the absence wasn't due to a lack of trying. Olive Trim made her way out to greet them on her fists, her emaciated legs swinging lifelessly beneath her. Mary Tryphena was always surprised by the dexterity and grace she incorporated into such an awkward posture and motion. Olive lifted herself into a chair beside Mary Tryphena and took the pudding she unwrapped from the pouch while Jabez served up bowls of fish and potato stew.

It was Judah's first time inside a house since his move to the little shed and the smell of him was making Jabez and Olive's eyes water, but they soldiered through with good humour. Judah removed his brin boots and hung them at the lip of the fireplace to dry, stretching his filthy, blackened feet as close to the flames as he could stand. Jabez asked after the health of everyone in the Gut and Mary Tryphena, who was still following Devine's Widow on her rounds, had plenty of news to offer. But all the while she was preoccupied by her letter. She had pictured a cloistered conversation, just she and Jabez in near darkness, speaking in whispers, but there was no hope of such a thing. Soon enough Olive was urging them to leave, to make certain they'd be home before dark. —Your mother will be worried half to death you aren't back before supper, she said. Jabez was out of his seat with Judah, the two of them tying strings and arranging clothes at the door, when Olive said, Jabez. She was watching Mary Tryphena who hadn't budged from her seat and Jabez came over to stand beside her.

37

—What is it, maid? he asked.

There was nothing for it then but to bring out the letter and offer it to him. Jabez untied the string and opened the paper.

—Behold, thou art fair, my love, he read, behold, thou art fair; thine eyes are as doves. He stopped there, too embarrassed to go on. He passed the paper across to Olive and she glanced through it, shaking her head. —Thou hast ravished my heart, my sister, my bride, she read.

Mary Tryphena had never heard anything like those words. They made her feel exposed and ashamed of herself, she regretted showing it to a living soul.

—Do you know who this is from? Olive asked.

Mary Tryphena couldn't bring herself to speak Absalom's name aloud. She leaned into Olive's ear to whisper it and they stared at one another, Olive looking to see if it could possibly be true. —Do you love him? she asked.

Mary Tryphena was taken back by the bluntness of the question. —I don't know, she said.

—Could you love him do you think?

Mary Tryphena barely heard the question over the buzz in her ears. She couldn't hold Olive's eye any longer and turned away, caught sight of Judah at the door. She'd forgotten he was in the room and was mortified to see she had an audience. Jude seemed no happier to be overhearing the exchange, his fish eyes bulging in his head. —No, she said. She pointed at him and shouted No a second time, and Jabez went across the room to usher Judah outside.

Mary Tryphena slumped into her chair and did her best not to bawl. —Why would he send me this letter and not say a word to my face?

—Who are we talking about here? Jabez asked.

Olive gave him a quick look and then smiled across at the girl. —You know Absalom has a stutter, Mary Tryphena.

—Jesus loves the little children, Jabez said. —Do your parents know about this?

Mary Tryphena grabbed Olive's wrist. —You won't tell anyone, she pleaded.

—Not a soul, Olive said. She folded the note and retied the string before handing it back to Mary Tryphena.

Judah hadn't waited for her but she could see him in the distance and followed in his tracks toward the Tolt. The wind had come up and the blowing snow whipped at her, as sharp as grains of sand. Mary Tryphena was crying by the time they reached the Tolt Road though she couldn't identify the source exactly, whether grief or relief or pity, the sobs shaking through her. Judah pushed on ahead and the dog ran back and forth between the two, whining and jumping to lick at Mary Tryphena's face before bolting ahead to catch Jude. The weight of the stupid animal knocked her into the snow each time it leaped up and at the crest of the Tolt Mary Tryphena refused to get back to her feet. The dog pawed and licked at her but she ignored it, pulling the blanket over her head to protect her face from the massive tongue. She was being lifted up then and surrendered to it, wrapping both arms around Judah's shoulders and she fell asleep in the stink of his arms as they jolted down the Tolt Road to home.

Father Phelan made it back to the shore two days before Christmas. He arrived in the dead of night and made his way to Mrs. Gallery's house in its pathetic grove of trees, whistling outside to wake her before he pushed into the tilt. The fire had guttered down to embers and he could just make out Mr. Gallery in the dark light, his chair pulled up to the fireplace. Each time Father Phelan laid eyes on him after an absence he seemed to have diminished again, fading under the weight of his guilt. —Bless me Mr. Gallery, he said, it's a cold night. The priest stamped the snow from his boots and leggings and then crossed the room to stir up the embers, adding a junk of spruce and standing to take the new heat. Mrs. Gallery called to him from the single room at the back of the tilt. —I'll be along directly, he said.

Mrs. Gallery's bed was constructed in the same fashion as the wharves and fish flakes and walls of the tilts, spruce logs skinned of their rind and nailed lengthwise on one side of the room. There was a thick layer of boughs as a mattress and bedding of ancient woollen blankets and a leathery sealskin and underneath it all the heat of Mrs. Gallery. He lifted the covers and crawled in beside her. Her mouth sweet as spruce gum and the skin of her thighs like fresh cream. Mrs. Gallery spread her legs and brought his hand to the wet of her, a little noise at the back of her throat when he found it. —That's the bowl that never goes empty, Mrs. Gallery, he whispered. —That's the miracle of the loaves and the fishes. His hand rocking slowly into her and he began talking in Latin, his voice rising enough to be heard through the house as she came for the first time.

An hour later there was a commotion from the other room, a clanging as Mr. Gallery kicked at the cook pot on the fireplace crane. —He's only making trouble, Mrs. Gallery said.

—He's cold is all, the priest told her. —What other comfort does he have?

He stepped out of the bed into the piercing frost, pulling on his breeches and worn black vestments before slipping into the next room to add another junk to the fire and Mr. Gallery seemed to nod absently at the flames. —There's plenty of this to look forward to in hell, the priest said.

He and Mrs. Gallery lay awake after they'd exhausted each other's appetites, talking of the news on the shore and plans for the season ahead. It had been years since people had any enthusiasm for Christmas, households far gone into the winter's supplies by December and months of rough hunger still to struggle through. Toward March some families were so weak they hardly moved from their bunks for weeks at a time. A central fireplace with a square wooden flue was the only source of heat in the spruce tilts, and Father Phelan would sometimes find a family huddled around it in silence, their faces cratered and blank. Not a morsel of food among them beyond a pot of watery soup. He went begging to

King-me Sellers on their behalf, coming away with a pocketful of green fish not fit to feed a dog, a bag of brown flour infested with weevils. It was enough to keep them another week or two and stave off starvation until the seals came in on the Labrador ice.

But Christmas this year promised a return to the days when the shore had known something closer to prosperity. Everyone did well enough on the fish to clear their debt with Sellers and set aside a good store for themselves, and the warm summer delivered a historic crop of root vegetables to see people through to the seals. There was an air of celebration in the two communities and Phelan expected that Christmas was the time it would surface in all its glory.

He held Mass in Callum's fishing room on Christmas Eve, the building lit with whale-oil torches, and he had to repeat his homily and offer the sacrament three times to accommodate the numbers who waited outside in the cold. From Christmas Day through to the Feast of the Epiphany the nights were ruled by bands of mummers roaming from house to house in the dark, five or six to a group and all dressed in outlandish disguises, brin sacks and old dresses or aprons, coats worn backwards and legs through the arms of shirts that were tied at the waist as breeches, men dressed in women's clothes and women in men's, underclothes worn on the outside of their many layers. They travelled with spoons and crude wooden whistles and other noisemakers, they knocked at one door after another for admittance and barrelled inside requesting cake and bread and whatever drink the house had to offer. In return they sang songs and danced and in general acted like fools. Their heads and faces were covered by sacks or veiled with handkerchiefs and they spoke ingressively to disguise their voices and they stayed until the inhabitants guessed their identities or until they'd drunk up every drop of liquor on the premises. They were aggressive and rude, they were outlandishly genderless and felt free to grab the ass of man or woman for a laugh, they frightened the children and left a house in shambles, but not a door was barred to them. Father Phelan loved the devilment and followed in their wake, taking up with one group of mummers and then another. There was a mild spell through the whole of Christmas and mummers criss-crossed the two tiny villages till daylight, the priest making his way back and forth over the Tolt Road half a dozen times in a single night.

On the eve of the Feast of the Epiphany he fell in with a group of mummers that included Horse Chops, a man covered in a blanket, a wooden horse's head on a stick before him. The eyes were painted at either side of the head, one black and one blue, the jaws of the horse driven through with nails for teeth and tied with leather strings so they snocked together. Horse Chops was a seer who could answer any question put to him. At every stop a mummer wearing a crown of spruce boughs chose one member of the household as a victim, asking Horse Chops the most embarrassing questions he could dream up. No subject was too lewd or personal, no question was taboo. Secret loves and affairs, unpaid debts, illegitimate children, ongoing family arguments, sins buried and unconfessed, all were fair game.

—This one now, the King mummer whistled, shaking a stave topped with a bladder of dry peas at Mary Tryphena. Horse Chops galloped across the tiny room to stare at the girl, the great jaws flapping loose. In the gloomy light of cod-oil lamps the creature's face looked like something called up from a netherworld. The other mummers were negotiating their glasses under veils and sacks, tipping their heads back to drink. —Horse Chops, is there someone in love with this girl? the King asked.

—There's no such thing, Mary Tryphena said.

Horse Chops pawed at the dirt floor and the jaws clapped once to signal otherwise. The mummers broke into applause and Father Phelan along with them, though his mood was dampened a little to have missed Callum. Callum had spent the entire Christmas season recovering from his fever and the priest was surprised to find him not at home now. He'd gone off on his own hours ago, Lizzie said, to try and make something of the final night of celebrations.

—Is it a man from the Gut? the King asked.

Clap, clap went the wooden jaws to say no.

—A man from Paradise Deep?

Clap.

—A man from Paradise Deep then. Now is this a rich man or a poor man, Horse Chops?

One clap signalled the former.

—Bless you child, a rich man in love with you. And is our rich man one of Father Phelan's flock?

Clap, clap.

—A Protestant? An Englishman? A black?

Lizzie turned to Devine's Widow and said, For the love of God, Missus. It was clear to them both who the King was suggesting, and Lizzie thought the suggestion crossed the line, even for mummers.

—Let it be, Lizzie, the old woman said angrily.

—And now Horse Chops, the King said, the most important question. Will our girl marry her rich Englishman from Paradise Deep?

Mary Tryphena held her breath, trying desperately to look disinterested, dismissive, though she couldn't help but feel some portion of her destiny was about to be laid out for her to see. Horse Chops stepped back and gave two claps and the mummers fell over one another, groaning in despair.

—No wedding, the King said. —No riches for our girl, alack. He turned to the room and said, A song. We'll give her a song and a dance at least.

—And she'll be better for it, Devine's Widow said under her breath. She was watching Mary Tryphena, reconsidering the girl's inconsolable moodiness through the fall. Thinking of King-me Sellers and all she'd done to keep clear of his way, only to find herself these years later, married to it regardless.

The mummers' last stop of the night was Selina's House, the stars almost doused by the first hint of dawn. There was no one up, the house dark and the fireplace cold, but they hammered at the door until they heard movement upstairs. King-me despised the mummers, who treated him as no one would dare without their disguise and the licence granted by the tradition. He only let them in for fear of what they might do if he refused. During his first years in Paradise Deep he barred the door and had his chimney stopped up with sods, one morning found his cow lowing mournfully on top of her shed. He allowed their visits then to avoid worse again, although he was frugal with the food and drink he offered. The mummers ensured they had plenty of snow on their shoes and clothes to leave a mess behind them, as a protest against King-me's lack of enthusiasm for their entertainment.

—King-me! they shouted up at the windows, but it was only Absalom who peeked out finally, his hair flat on one side of his head and still shivering himself out of sleep. —Any mummers 'lowed in? the King asked as they pushed past him into the cold hallway and felt their way along the walls to the kitchen.

Absalom lit a taper from the embers piled under ash in the fireplace and brought it to the candles on the table, then set about getting a lunch of tea buns and old cheese and two pint bottles of spruce beer. The group stamped the snow off their feet and shouted for King-me to join them, though it was clear Absalom's grandparents had retired hours before and the youngster was the only representative of the family they would see. They were all exhausted and half-asleep and finally let the issue drop. Absalom measured the beer into equal portions and stood back against a wall to wait, like a servant dismissed from table.

Father Phelan watched him through a fortnight's haze of booze and sleeplessness. All night he'd been wondering if it was true that Absalom was in love with Callum's girl and had somehow made it known in the world. He had never seen the boy outside Selina's House except in King-me's company, had never heard him string together more than three words. Even if the match wasn't impossible, the priest thought, little Mary Tryphena would eat Absalom alive.

The King was on his feet again, goading the revellers into one more song and he was waltzing Absalom about the kitchen now, the boy stiff as a broomstick. —Horse Chops, the King whistled hoarsely. His voice was ruined by the hours of speaking as he inhaled and it was almost impossible to make him out anymore. —This boy, he said, still waltzing Absalom in a tight circle. —Is he in love?

Horse Chops clapped his jaw once and the mummers gave a half-hearted cheer.

—In love he is, the King said. A rabid blush coloured Absalom's face and he tried to pull away but the King held him tight. —Tell us Horse Chops, is his love true?

Clap.

—A true love, bless you and amen.

Horse Chops shuffled up close to the dancing couple and clapped his jaws wildly into the King's ear.

—Don't be talking so much foolishness, Horse Chops, the King said. The jaws clapped awhile again. —That can't be true, Horse Chops.

—What did he say? Father Phelan asked when it was clear Absalom wasn't willing to take the bait.

The King stepped away from Absalom though he kept hold of the boy's arms. —He claims young Ab here is in love with his cousin.

The mummers offered their chorus of feigned disbelief.

—Is that true? the King asked. —Are ye in love with your cousin?

Absalom pulled to get clear of the King. —I don't have a cousin, he said, stuttering fiercely.

—Do you hear, Horse Chops? He says he has no c-c-cousin to fall in love with.

Clap, clap clap, clap clap clap clap.

The King went still then, staring at the youngster through his veil. —Oh but Horse Chops here says you do, Absalom. You have two cousins in the Gut, he says.

Clap clap clap, clap clap, clap clap clap.

—Little Lazarus Devine, the King said.

—No, Absalom whispered.

—And Mary Tryphena Devine, your intended. A child of your own aunt. Lizzie Devine is your grandfather's daughter, Absalom.

The boy tore his arms free finally and left them there, his feet on the naked wooden stairs echoing down to them in the kitchen. The mummers sat in a drunken silence awhile afterwards and some of them removed their brin veils and hats to allow their faces the open air for the first time in hours. The details of the room beginning to rise to the day's first light. The King sat heavily in a chair and Horse Chops settled his rump into the King's lap, leaning on the stick that held the horse's head. —Well that's that I suppose, the King said.

Callum pushed his head free of Horse Chops's blanket and scrubbed at his sweaty face with his hand. —I expect so, he said, speaking aloud for the first time. He smiled forlornly across the kitchen at the priest. —Morning Father, he said.

The King raised and lowered his knees under Callum like he was bouncing a child. —And how are you feeling now, Callum? he asked.

—Like a horse's arse is how I feel, Jabez Trim.

—As is right and proper, the King said and he nodded under his bushy crown.

The Feast of the Epiphany was the end of the Christmas season and Father Phelan wandered off to another of his ghost parishes on the island within the week. People settled in for the coldest months of the winter, rarely leaving the narrow border of their own tilts and outbuildings.

The first vessel into Paradise Deep that spring made harbour when the ice cleared off in April, a Spurriers ship freighted with salt and hard tack and twine and barrels of nails. When she shipped out a week later, Absalom Sellers was aboard and bound for England. No one laid eyes on him again for the better part of five years.

{ 2 }

BY THE TIME MARY TRYPHENA was fourteen years of age she'd
endured a dozen offers of marriage, serious proposals from men on the
shore who courted through her parents, clean-shaven and dressed in
their least dilapidated outfits. She sat with her mother and father as the
men paraded their virtues, young widowers with a handful of youngsters
and middle-aged virgins and Irish boys indentured to King-me Sellers,
all promising fidelity and children of her own and what little wealth the
coast provided. She won't starve, they said. She'll be looked after.

Mary Tryphena felt peculiarly helpless in it all and wondered if it
was somehow a state of womanhood, to be sought and fought for and
have only the act of rejection to make a mark in the world. No, was her
answer each time, no, no and no. And with each suitor she rejected,
her reputation as the rarest and most unattainable of women travelled
further along the coast.

Devine's Widow suspected the girl's reluctance was fuelled by an
interest in Absalom Sellers and was anxious to see her granddaughter
attached elsewhere. She suggested there were only so many offers a
woman could expect in a lifetime and Mary Tryphena might exhaust
hers before a bud had grown on the bush. —She haven't even got a bit
of tit to be mauled over yet, Devine's Widow said, and she've turned
away half the single men on the shore.

—She'll take the man she's meant for, Lizzie told her.

—Don't be filling the child's head with your foolishness, the old woman said.

The thirteenth and last marriage proposal of her life came from the skipper of a Spurriers ship just arrived with the Episcopalian bishop for the dedication of the new church. The skipper was an Englishman named John Withycombe who had been making the trip to Paradise Deep long enough to know everyone on the shore by sight if not by name. He himself had carried stories of the raven-haired Irish girl pursued by half the men on the coast to bars and kitchens through Conception and Trinity and Fortune bays and old country ports like Poole and Waterford. He had no personal interest in the child at first. He was in his fifties and had married as a young man, but it was said of him that he didn't stay ashore long enough to wash his clothes and dry them on a line. He hadn't laid eyes on his own wife in nearly twenty years and had spoken of her as though she was dead for so long that everyone thought her so. He had no interest in anything that tied him to the land and relieved his physical needs on the tired beds of the whorehouses that occupied so much waterfront real estate in his ports of call. But as he repeated and refined his story of the unattainable beauty that half the island of Newfoundland was heartsick for, the notion took root in his mind. —Imagine your life, he would say at the conclusion of each telling, in the bed of such a creature.

Eventually he lost his taste for food and drink to imagining just such a thing. He slept poorly or not at all and spent all his waking hours with his vision of the Irish maid. He forsook his regular visits to prostitutes so as not to sully the image of the girl he carried. His shipmates let him know what an arse he was making of himself but their ridicule only strengthened his resolve and he set himself to have Mary Tryphena Devine when next he sailed into Paradise Deep.

He left the vessel after the vicar disembarked that morning and walked over the Tolt Road with the whistles of his crewmates echoing derision off the hills. He found the girl working in a potato garden behind the stud house and made his intentions known before he so much as told her his name. He was standing with a tricorn hat in his hands, turning and kneading it like bread dough as he waited for her response. —You won't starve, he said. —And you can stay on in the Gut if you like, next your kin.

They had never been introduced, though Mary Tryphena knew something of John Withycombe by reputation. She smiled across at him, already at ease with the particular agony of a man in love, and the smile unnerved the sailor completely. The girl was not at all the picture he'd carried in his mind since the previous fall. She was tall for her age and pretty enough but her frame was still a boy's, slender and tough as a whip of alder.

—What kind of a life would that be for me? she asked. —You off on the water most of the time?

It was all going askew. Before answering her question John Withycombe asked if she was the Mary Tryphena who was grand-daughter to Devine's Widow. —I'd have thought it would be just the sort of thing a woman might want, he said then. —To have a man and her life to herself besides.

The notion gave Mary Tryphena a moment's pause and that pause inflated the man's hope she might be considering him. She was thinking of her grandmother who lived by no rules but her own, who could claim the land their house sat on and the fishing rooms on the water, the privilege of ownership granted only to men and their widows. A life to herself. She smiled again at the ridiculous old sailor. —You'll live too long yet to suit me, she said.

The Englishman kneaded his hat, perplexed, trying to comprehend the content of her refusal. —I haven't been well is the truth of it, he said finally. He coughed into his fist, looking down at his feet. —On death's door is what some says.

A rock struck him square in the chest and he startled backwards, dropping his hat to the ground as another sailed by him. He looked past

the girl toward the stud house where her brother Lazarus was in mid-
stoop, searching for another stone. As practised as his sister in brushing
off her unwanted suitors.

—You little bastard, the Englishman growled.

The youngster had an arm on him and was surprisingly accurate.
He whipped a rock that clipped the old man's ear. —Fly the fuck out of
it, the little one said.

—Michael Devine, Mary Tryphena shouted and she went on yelling
at the boy in Irish, chasing him around the corner of the house and all
the way to the tiny outbuilding that had been given over to Judah. They
both fell through the door and onto the bunk Jude slept on, rolling around
with their hands over their mouths to stifle their laughter. By the time
Mary Tryphena gained control of herself and tiptoed back to the house
the Englishman was gone, though he'd left in such a muddled passion
that he'd forgotten his hat where he dropped it. She picked it up and
turned it in her hands. It was made of wool felt, a rosette cockade with a
pewter button on the left side. She turned to Lazarus who had followed
behind her and placed it on his head. It fell around his ears, covering half
his face. —You little bastard, he said in his best West Country accent.

Mary Tryphena could see her father's skiff coming through the
channel, the gunwales low to the water with fish. Devine's Widow
already making her way to the Rooms from the big garden to help gut
and salt the cod. Mary Tryphena took little Laz's hand. —Come on
then, she said. —See if you can't make yourself useful.

When they came up from the fishing room hours later, the
Englishman's abandoned tricorn hat was on Judah's head, Lazarus sitting high on the Great White's shoulders, the dog going before them
like a horse drawing a cart. Lazarus had come to love the animal and
Judah in the same proprietary fashion. Before he'd learned to walk he
began following one or the other around, pulling at the dog's fur,
clinging to Jude's trousers. He crawled to the shed whenever his
mother's back was turned and Lizzie found him at Judah's feet or on

his lap and she dragged him out by the arm, slapping the youngster's backside to warn him away from the man. But he rose from each savage trimming like the Lazarus he was, more determined than ever to follow his own inclinations. Judah became a kind of pet to him, a mute, good-natured creature who suffered the boy to ride his back or poke at his belly with a stick or force-feed him handfuls of spruce needles.

Lizzie swore the child was being corrupted by the company he kept, that he was growing wild and strange in his thoughts from spending so much time with Judah. Callum walked the thin line of defending his friend without drawing his wife's anger squarely down upon himself, repeating generalities about the wonders wrought on the shore in the time since Judah had come among them—the fishery's unprecedented run of luck, the steadily growing population.

Almost three hundred souls were settled on the shore by this time and each spring Spurriers' ships brought planters and their families and young men and women who took positions as servants before striking out on their own. The abundance of Judah's first year continued, though for most newcomers his talismanic appearance and stench were little more than oddities, the tales of his arrival and influence on the fish an entertainment. It seemed more likely the story of the whale was born from Jude's strangeness than the other way round. Even people who had witnessed the events began downplaying the evidence of their senses, and each season saw Judah's status dwindle slightly in the minds of fishermen who preferred to think their success the result of their own cunning and skill and hard work.

King-me Sellers' operation expanded to meet the demands of the unexpected prosperity with a cooperage and smithy and a handful of new stores and warehouses, and additional clerks to keep account of the credit given to fishermen in the spring and the quintals of salt cod used to pay off their debt in the fall. A young Englishman named Barnaby Shambler opened a public house where he sold India ale and dark rum from the Jamaica trade. Some of the local planters—Callum among them—had done well enough that they were cutting and milling lumber each winter to build real houses with wooden floors and stone chimneys. A Church of England minister had finally settled in Paradise Deep, a flagpole out front of the new church in the absence of a bell, St. George's cross raised to call people to Sunday worship morning and evening. All of it thanks to Judah, or so some believed.

—I don't know how you can call that Reverend Dodge a good thing, Lizzie said.

—Now Lizzie, you can't blame Jude for the preacher.

—If you can credit him for the fish, why can't I blame him for the minister?

There was no talking to the woman, he thought.

—You aren't going over there tonight are you, Callum?

—What, and miss the bishop's parade?

Lizzie made a face. —Someone is going to get killed before this is all over, she said. She caught sight of Judah and Lazarus and the dog coming up the path from the Rooms, the tricorn on Jude's head. —Where did his nibs get that hat? she asked.

—Lazarus brung it down to him this afternoon, Callum told her. —Said he found it on the ground.

—Found it on the ground, Lizzie said dismissively. —A little liar you're raising, Callum Devine.

Mary Tryphena was just outside the open doorway, carding wool in her lap. She considered telling Lizzie how the hat came to hand but decided it was better to stay clear of the argument. She was planning to take in the celebrations as well and wasn't willing to risk her mother refusing to let her attend. After the parade there was a garden party planned at Selina's House and Mary Tryphena had yet to lay eyes on Absalom since he'd sailed home in the spring. Twenty now and a man to look at, is what she heard. She'd hardly thought of him while he was gone though each new proposal forced her to reconsider his letter and the autumn of gifts he'd treated her to. She was nostalgic for the innocence of the exchange, considering herself a worldly woman now. And she was interested to know, in an idle way, if he had thought of her at all in his years away.

King-me Sellers had lobbied the Church of England to send a minister to Paradise Deep for almost a quarter century. He felt the lack of a church was a mark against the village he'd built from nothing and saw as a mirror of his own success in the world. When he first settled on the shore he had visions of the place as a rival to St. John's or Harbour Grace, and the church was simply one more benchmark in the progress of his ambitions. Jabez Trim was getting on in years, Sellers wrote every year for twenty-five years, and there was no telling when they would be bereft of even the amateur ministrations he provided. For twenty-five years the Church ignored him. It wasn't until, in the flush of recent prosperity, Sellers promised to underwrite the expense of building a permanent sanctuary in Paradise Deep that they relented.

An archway of var branches decorated with wildflowers was built for the Reverend Eldred Dodge to walk beneath as he came ashore and the entire population turned out to welcome him, Protestant and Catholic alike. He'd been seasick the entire three-week voyage from England and the misery of it was clear in his ashen face. He was six foot tall and thin as a stick, his hair was wispy and sparse which made him look that much sicklier. The archway, which had been built to accommodate people of a more subdued height, confused him. He considered stepping around the thing before King-me directed him forward with a hand at his elbow. He staggered as he ducked beneath it, trying to steady himself with a hand to the flowered arch, and it tumbled to the wharf on top of him. It took King-me and Jabez Trim to get him to his feet and he leaned on Jabez's shoulder all the way up the path to Selina's House. As he stepped off the wharf a massively pregnant girl took his hand to touch it to her belly and the bizarre intimacy of the gesture made him flinch away.

—He won't last here long enough to shave, Daniel Woundy said.

At Selina's House, Dodge was put to bed in Absalom's room like a child. He woke the following morning to the news that young Martha Jewer had passed away overnight while giving birth.

—It was a breech, Selina explained to him. —She was there yesterday, Reverend. Did you see her?

He nodded. —Is the baby with the father, then?

—It was a moonlight child, she said.

Dodge looked to King-me Sellers who was staring down at the table.

—A moss-born, Selina said, trying to elaborate. —A merrybegot.

—The child is a bastard, King-me said bluntly.

The minister nodded again, contemplating a funeral for a woman of loose morals and a baptism for a bastard. He had a moment of real doubt then, not simple misgiving or hesitation but a profound fear that he'd been mistaken about himself or about God. He would live a long life—all of it from this day forward in the one and only parish of his ministry—before he experienced another like it.

—The little one will have to trust to Providence now I suppose, Selina said.

—Providence takes care of fools, Dodge said, trying to rouse himself to a challenge. —Where is the child?

King-me had an Irish servant show him to the Gut where the infant was in the care of Devine's Widow. Dodge had to bend nearly double at the waist to get under the lintel and the ceiling was too low to allow him to stand upright inside. Sellers had offered a brief sketch of Devine's Widow before he set out and he'd planned to stand over her during the visit, but his stunted posture in the low room was too ridiculous to make a proper impression and he took a seat when it was offered. The baby was in Mary Tryphena's lap and she was feeding him goat's milk pap through a tit made of cloth, sneaking a furtive glance up at the minister now and then. No one in the room looked at him directly and there was the air of a smirk about them, as if they had just left off making fun of the pallor of his face when he stepped onto the wharf the day before.

—You slept well I hope, Devine's Widow said. She was a crone of a woman, as Sellers said, her face withered and fierce. She was missing all the teeth on one side of her mouth which made her entire body seem to list when she spoke. He didn't answer the pleasantry, asking instead if he could have a moment alone with her, and she said a few words to Mary Tryphena in Irish. The girl placed the infant in Lizzie's arms and went through the door without so much as a curtsy in his direction. Lizzie stayed in her chair and made no move to join her daughter but Dodge decided to let that go.

—You've picked a busy time to come ashore, the widow woman said.

—I am the Lord's servant, Dodge offered. —I'm told there is no father.

—You don't think she found herself in this condition without help, Reverend?

He couldn't believe the gall. And the woman holding the baby seemed to have fallen asleep while he sat there. He raised his voice, hoping to startle her awake. —Do you know who fathered this child?

—From what I seen of the world, Reverend, motherhood is a certainty, but fatherhood is a subject of debate. Some say it was Saul Toucher or one of his young fellows. But that's what some say whenever there's blame to be cast.

Dodge leaned away from the woman to collect himself. He looked about the pathetic shack, taking in the meanness of the lives it held. The sand on the floor was raked smooth and someone had used a stick to trace a pattern of ocean waves where the traffic of feet wouldn't scar it. There was nothing else on view that suggested the slightest interest in elegance or beauty.

—There's worse off in the world, Devine's Widow said as if she could see his thoughts. —What we have is ours.

A witch, Sellers had called her, and there was certainly an argument to be made. Dodge said, That child will be raised in an English home.

—The Lord's servant you are, Reverend. We were wondering what would become of him. Devine's Widow stood to take the child from Lizzie who was still dead asleep and she plopped the bundle into his lap. —His mother is being laid out at Shambler's, she said. —You'll want to look in on her.

Dodge had the Irish servant he'd come with carry the infant back over the Tolt and he went immediately to Shambler's premises, stood over Martha Jewer's body on a wooden table in the back room. She was wearing her one filthy dress, her chin tied up with a length of twine and her feet bare. —She wasn't fourteen, Shambler told him. —An orphan girl.

—Was it one of the Touchers fathered the child?

Shambler shrugged. —It's all fellows out at Toucher's, nine or ten of them but for Saul Toucher's woman. They're like a pack of dogs, that crowd.

—That hardly answers my question.

—It might mean the question's better left, Shambler said.

Reverend Dodge placed his hand briefly to the belly where the day before there'd been a child. —I should like to see the cemetery, he said finally.

It was a thirty-minute walk up the Tolt Road and then further into the backcountry to the Burnt Woods where there was a meadow of soil deep enough to accommodate a body. Reverend Dodge was accompanied by King-me Sellers who went ahead of him to show the way. It was called the French Cemetery, King-me told him, because the first people buried there were sailors drowned when a French ship wrecked on the Tolt a hundred years before. Or because the land once belonged to a man named French who buried a wife and child during a typhoid outbreak before he was cut down himself. Sellers seemed to have no idea which story was the true source of the name and no obvious preference for one over the other. There was no fence to mark the graveyard, just a scatter of wooden crosses and three tall stone markers placed side by side. The meadow was high enough they could see the ocean and the boats of the fishermen on the grounds, and all the graves faced outward to the sea. —That's a long way to carry a body, Master Sellers.

—Every decent bit of ground is planted with potatoes, King-me said, or used to graze goats and sheep. This is all stone and boulders and plates of shale, not fit for growing. You gets two feet down into that and you're liable to believe the land don't want us here, alive or dead.

Dodge leaned forward to read the stone markers. Sellers, each of them said. He straightened and looked across at his host.

—All mine, King-me said.

Dodge read more closely. Two sons and a daughter-in-law.

—A ship headed over to England, Sellers said. —They'd gone with the youngest, to find him a wife. Harry's woman was from Poole and anxious to have a visit and they made a trip of it. They had Absalom, he wasn't two years old at the time, and Selina kept the youngster here. Told them she wanted to have something to make sure they'd come home to us. King-me smiled at his feet. —You say all sorts of things the world makes you regret, I find. There's nothing in the ground there, being as they were lost at sea. Spent a king's ransom to have those stones shipped over from Devon.

A cold rain was falling, the wind picking at their clothes like the hands of beggars on a city street. Please sir. Please sir. Dodge wandered along the uneven rows of crosses, names scored or painted on the wood. Spingle. Codner. Bozan. Harty. Devine. Hussey. Toucher. Snook. Brazill. Woundy. Protestant and Catholic set down in a mash. He turned at the far side of the cemetery and shouted across to Sellers. —We will have a fence. The earth beneath him was solid enough but he felt as if he was still at sea, adrift on a grey expanse without demarcation or border. He was shaking with a rage that he mistook for certainty.

—Before another body is set in the ground there will be a fence, and the ground will be consecrated.

They built a riddle fence of narrow poles around the graveyard and Dodge himself spent hours each day helping to dig post holes and fix the logs in place to ensure it was completed before Martha Jewer was buried. The funeral was held in King-me's largest storehouse to accommodate the same crowd of people who had come to meet the minister on the shoreline three days before, both Catholic and Protestant. Dodge stood before them on an overturned puncheon tub, decked out in his Episcopalian vestments, determined to turn the tide of local sentiment where he and the Lord were concerned. —Brothers and sisters in Christ, he began.

King-me lost all interest in building a church after Reverend Dodge took up residence on the shore. The minister spent three years trying to wheedle the money promised for the project and he had to threaten to leave to get it. The foundation was laid the summer before Absalom arrived home from England and it was in use for holy services by Christmas, the building complete but for the stained glass shipped from Manchester and stored in St. John's over the winter. It was scheduled to arrive with the bishop when he travelled to the shore for the dedication.

Everyone expected there would be trouble of some sort during those ceremonies. Along with the bishop, Skipper John Withycombe had transported a Navy officer and a handful of soldiers who were meant to keep the peace, or at the very least ensure the vicar wasn't stripped of his vestments and thrown buck-naked into the harbour by drunken Irishmen still nursing their resentments.

At Martha Jewer's funeral Dodge announced that the French Cemetery would be open only to the remains of Episcopalians, starting with the corpse laid out before them. And further that all sacraments in the Church of England would be made available only to those confirmed in the faith. People tried to shout him down but he pressed on with the funeral. Chairs were thrown. Half the congregation walked out in the middle of the service. The funeral procession was pelted with stones and curses, as was every Protestant funeral procession in the year that followed. Mourners were forced to carry wood staves and fish forks to defend their clergyman and brawls often erupted between the two groups on the way up the Tolt Road.

Away from Dodge and his pronouncements most people did their best to carry on as they had, but the sectarian feuding spilled over from the funeral altercations. Boats and equipment were vandalized in a spiral of retaliation. It might have ended in bloodshed but for Peter Flood's corpse being stolen in the confusion of a brawl one April morning. Flood had married a Protestant woman twenty years past but converted to the Church of England only weeks before his death, when Dodge threatened to dissolve the union and declare his children bastards. The thieves buried Flood in the new Catholic graveyard in the Gut without ceremony or prayer and his family were forced to disinter his remains at night, spiriting him away to the Burnt Woods for a proper burial in the French Cemetery. Every week or so the corpse was moved again, carted back and forth from one graveyard to the other. The bizarre tug-of-war went on through the spring and no one could say for certain where Peter Flood finally came to rest. But the episode engendered a revulsion so general that the funeral processions became quieter affairs and some semblance of peace returned to the shore.

Dodge took it as a sign of God's favour that the new church hadn't been burned to the ground before the first services were held. The men who designed and raised the sanctuary were all boat builders and the structure looked like the hull of a ship flipped face down on the Gaze. The eight-foot stained glass window arrived on the vessel bringing the bishop, and Jabez Trim spent the day installing it behind the altar. Dodge had chosen the motif himself: the disciples hauling their nets under the watchful eye of Jesus.

The vicar, the Right Reverend Arthur Waghorne, was an amateur botanist. He barely glanced at the new church before wandering off into the fields behind the building where he spent the better part of the day sketching and collecting specimens on the Gaze. He was accompanied by two soldiers who sat in the grass below him, speculating on their chances of bedding a woman before returning to St. John's. Arscott was a fifteen-year-old private from Devon, a virgin who laboured under the illusion that no one but he knew the truth of the matter. He was next to useless as a soldier, clumsy with his weapons, naive and harmlessly sycophantic in his relations. Arsewipe was his nickname among the enlisted men. Corporal Kinnebrook was four years the boy's senior. —Paradise Deep, he said. —What does that make you think of, Arsewipe?

—Heaven, is it?

—No, jesus, Kinnebrook said, swiping at his head. —A man of your vast experience on the battlefields of love, Arsewipe. Tell me that doesn't make you think of fucking. Paradise Deep, he said with a note of reverence. The name alone had given Kinnebrook high hopes for the expedition, but everything he'd seen of the place so far promised disappointment. —I expect we'll have to jump in the harbour to wet our dicks in this shithole, he said.

By the time Reverend Dodge came up from the church to collect them for the parade the two soldiers were asleep on the grass. —His Majesty's finest, the vicar said as he kicked the men awake.

The parade began at the steps of the new sanctuary and wound its way through the footpaths of Paradise Deep, past the stores of Spurriers' Premises as far as Mrs. Gallery's droke and back again to Selina's House where food and drink was set up on long tables in the garden. The Reverend Waghorne was at the head of the procession on King-me's piebald mare, Dodge walking at the horse's shoulder. The Navy officer, a mutton-chopped Scot named Goudie, marched directly behind them. The clergymen led hymns for the people in their wake.

Olive Trim aboard her truckley at the rear, holding Martha Jewer's orphan boy in her lap, the wooden cart pulled along by a Newfoundland. The soldiers were marshalled in two groups at either side of the procession and they kept a wary eye on the Catholics gathered in clusters to watch the parade. They followed at a discreet distance when the turn was made for Selina's House and watched their manners, not willing to miss a chance at the spread laid on for the celebration.

A pig and two sheep turned on spits over an open fire outside Selina's House and new potatoes roasted in the coals. There was partridge and rabbit stew and vegetables dipped in flour and fried with butter, roasted goose and turr, boiled puddings with raisins and fresh berries with cream for dessert. There was no fish of any description to be had and that absence was another sign of their newfound prosperity. That eating the bounty of the sea was a choice rather than a necessity.

Reverend Waghorne said grace and people lined up in orderly rows to be served. The vicar turned to Dodge. —Your fears seem to have been overstated, he said.

Dodge smiled at his superior. It was early yet, he felt, to judge.

—I half expected, Waghorne said, we might lay eyes on the priest you speak of in your correspondence.

—You can trust Phelan won't show his face anywhere an English soldier would see it.

—I had a most curious visit from the prefect vicar apostolic before I left St. John's, Reverend Dodge.

—The Catholic archbishop?

—It seems the Romans are as anxious to be rid of Father Phelan as yourself.

—Well, they make a poor showing of their anxiety.

Waghorne pursed his lips. —He's a rogue, I'm told. Defrocked by the Dominican Order after he was ordained. And gallivanting through the country all the years since as if it was ceded to him by God.

—And how exactly does the archbishop plan to deal with the man?

—As you are aware, Reverend Dodge, the Romans are not keen to discuss their internal problems. I'm surprised he spoke to me at all.

—He must have wanted something?

—Just an eye, Waghorne said casually. —A line or two now and then to say when Phelan is here, what he's doing. Who he's closest to.

Dodge turned to set his plate on the table. —I hardly thought when I was ordained, he said, that I would be asked to spy on behalf of the Catholic archbishop.

—Come now, Waghorne said gently. —Think of it as a neighbourly gesture. A Christian duty.

A tall girl wandered by with an empty plate, offering a cursory bob in their direction as she passed.

—Mary Tryphena Devine, Dodge whispered.

—Is that the young one half the men of Newfoundland are heartsick for?

—The same.

Waghorne tilted his head in appraisal, his lips pursed. —Well, the girl has fine posture, he said dismissively.

—I expect you will have noted the relative lack of female company about you.

The vicar glanced around the yard and even by that casual assessment he could see the women were outnumbered at least three to one.

—Hunger is the best sauce, Your Worship.

After Mary Tryphena had taken her fill from the tables she heaped a plate with food for Olive Trim, then entertained the baby so the woman could eat her meal in peace. Happy to be distracted from thinking of Absalom who was still nowhere to be seen. Olive was leaning back on a pillow of straw in her truckley beneath the weight of her belly, finally pregnant with a child of her own after taking in the orphan they'd christened Obediah. She was only days from delivering and looked like a creature trapped under some obstruction she was helpless to move.

—Jabez is certain it's a lad we're having, Olive said. —Wants to call him Azariah.

Mary Tryphena looked at Olive to see if she was meant to laugh at this. —Obediah and Azariah.

Olive said, Too many hours with his head in the Good Book if you want my opinion, may God forgive me. She shifted slightly, reaching a hand to change the position of one of her lifeless legs. —Don't know how I'll manage to chase two of the little buggers around.

Mary Tryphena was watching Selina's House distractedly and only nodded.

—Have you seen Absalom since he's been home? Olive asked.

Mary Tryphena smiled across at her and shook her head, embarrassed to be caught out. She saw Judah and Lazarus wandering through the crowd with the wood dog at their heels and she called them over to show off the youngster. Lazarus took the tricorn from Judah to place it full over Obediah's head and the filthy darkness set the child to bawling. Mary Tryphena thought to say something to Olive about the ridiculous proposal from the sailor she'd turned down that morning but didn't see how she could avoid more discussion of Absalom with the subject and let it lie. She took the hat off the baby's head, tossing it back to Jude, and he offered up a fool's dance to try and quiet the youngster.

Captain John Withycombe almost missed the garden party altogether, retreating to his quarters following the disastrous proposal to Mary Tryphena, shutting himself away with a chair against the door and a bottle in his lap. He'd sat there in a daze, unable to understand what had made him behave like such a goddamn fool. He felt as if he'd been living under a spell the last months and before long came to the conclusion that his condition was the girl's doing, that she'd bewitched him somehow and used him for her sport. He took his first drink before noon and did not stop until he'd fallen into a near coma in his hammock. By the time he was roused by a hammering at the barred door he'd all but lost the day's events in the fog of sleep and drunkenness.

His shipmates guessed how things had unfolded by his face when he first came back over the Tolt that morning, and they left him to his misery. But they were drunk themselves by suppertime and insisted on offering some distraction. He'd missed the parade, they shouted through the door, and he was in danger of missing the food and drink as well. He didn't know what parade they were talking about. A sense of disquiet and offence pricked at him but he was damned if he could name its source, and the rush to deliver him to the party at Selina's House pushed it aside.

He saw the girl as soon as they reached the garden, sitting in the grass beside a pregnant cripple, and the morning rushed back to him, the bile of it closing off his throat. She was smiling up at a tall white bastard who was wearing John Withycombe's tricorn and acting out a dumb show that could only have been at his expense. Mocking him with his own fucking hat. The captain's legs shaking with a mortified rage and he started yelling over the noise of the crowd that his hat had been stolen. The man ran off when he saw the captain pointing him out, with young Arscott in pursuit. The soldier jumped onto his back to wrestle him down while a black and white dog savaged the soldier's stockings.

John Withycombe was buried then in the pell-mell confusion, tramped upon by the shoving crowd and half deafened by the cursing and the screams of the women, until a musket fired and the Irishmen scuttled for the hills. When he pushed himself up he could see his hat trampled to ratshit and the dog lying dead on the grass beside it. Arscott sat cupping a wound in his gut that leaked like a Portuguese trader, the poor little shagger as good as dead now, a virgin still and forever and ever amen.

There was no prison in Paradise Deep and Judah Devine was locked in a fishing room, one soldier assigned to guard the entrance.

Lieutenant Goudie interrogated everyone present at the garden party but the mash of conflicting detail made it impossible to settle events with any certainty. The dog was shot by Kinnebrook who couldn't force the animal to leave off Arscott in any other way. Arscott died by a wound from his own knife which was found in the grass beside him and which he'd likely drawn to defend himself against the dog's attack. No one admitted to witnessing the fatal blow but Alphonse Toucher's name was mentioned several times as a likely suspect and four soldiers were sent off to arrest him. They came back to the fishing room with all three Touchers in custody, each accusing another of being Alphonse. Lieutenant Goudie brought in their parents and siblings and a handful of people from the Gut who failed to make a convincing case in any direction and he was forced to set them all loose in the end. Which left them with Judah as the principal.

Callum thought a plea of self-defence might relieve Jude of the charge, but Devine's Widow dismissed the notion. Judah was also being held for the theft of Captain John Withycombe's tricorn and had been apprehended while attempting to escape a soldier of the crown, all of which spoke against self-defence.

The subtleties of the argument were lost on Lazarus. He'd insisted they carry the dog back to the Gut to bury him near the Catholic cemetery and he was tormented by the thought of losing Judah as well. No court in Newfoundland was invested with authority to try capital crimes and Jude would have to be transported to England to face a judge, which was no different than a death sentence in the six-year-old's mind. It seemed not to matter that John Withycombe had abandoned the hat of his own accord or that it was Lazarus who retrieved it. He threatened to confess to stealing the hat unless something was done to win Judah's release and Devine's Widow decided to go to Selina's House herself in the end.

It had been years since she'd been troubled by the dreams that preceded Laz's birth, the blood in the wake of that separation, but the memory was still visceral and immediate and she carried it with her over the Tolt Road. She went to the servant's entrance at the back of the building and waited in the kitchen while the mistress was called. Selina beckoned for Devine's Widow to follow her and they went down the hall to the parlour where Lieutenant Goudie and Reverend Waghorne were drinking brandy and smoking. Devine's Widow turned to Selina when she saw the men there.

—I gave you my daughter, Selina whispered. —I can't be any assistance to you in this matter. And she ushered Devine's Widow in to sit with the other guests. —Master Sellers will be along directly, she said.

The vicar and Lieutenant Goudie were boarding at Selina's House while the investigation was carried out and they fell into silence so suddenly the widow assumed they'd been discussing the case. She took a seat near the window and they all three waited for King-me to join them from the office. Selina clearly hadn't told her husband who it was waiting on him and he stopped inside the door as he entered, startled to come face to face with the old woman.

Devine's Widow looked up at him, then glanced around the room. —Just like old times, Master Sellers, she said.

King-me didn't follow her meaning for a moment but he straightened when he saw it. A naval officer, a clergyman and Master Sellers facing her. Devine's Widow put on trial half a century ago. She smiled her lopsided smile at him. It was the wrong way to begin the discussion she'd come for, but the configuration in the room was so unlikely she couldn't resist.

—There's no talking to be done where Judah is concerned, King-me said, guessing the reason for her visit.

—There's no one saw him raise a hand to that soldier.

—There's none will admit to seeing it, Reverend Waghorne said.

—You was there, Reverend, did you see it?

—My vantage point was not ideal, he said defensively.

—Judah had no part in killing that soldier, no more than Master Sellers' grandson.

King-me turned to Lieutenant Goudie. —Pay no attention to this witch, he said.

Goudie was slouched against the arm of the chesterfield, combing a hand against the grain of a massive sideburn. He had a lazy Scots inflection that made him seem disinterested in life in general. —These soldiers, he said. —They're sentimental men, understand. They'll have blood for young Arscott. We might be able to do something for Judah Devine if someone could help us identify the Toucher lad.

Devine's Widow waved a hand. —It was the soldier's own knife killed him, people are saying.

—I'm not at liberty to discuss the details.

—He fell on his own knife trying to get at the dog is what happened and everyone knows it for the truth, whatever else they might be telling you.

The officer nodded thoughtfully a moment. —There was no Toucher involved, was there.

Reverend Waghorne stared at Goudie. —I don't follow, Lieutenant.

—We can't distinguish the Toucher in question from his brothers, Goudie said slowly, still piecing it together. —And there'd be hell to pay if we hang all three. So. It would appear that witnesses named a man they were reasonably sure would not be convicted.

—Judah has no family you'll have to answer to, the widow said. —That's the only reason he's locked up now. He got no one belonged to him.

—He has you, Missus, King-me said without meeting her eyes.

She stared at Sellers standing stock-still at the door, as if on guard. —How long before you leave, Lieutenant? the widow asked.

—We've delayed the Spurriers vessel a fortnight already, he said. —We'll have to sail within the next day or so.

She stood abruptly and left then, not waiting to be shown the door. She stopped in to see Father Phelan at Mrs. Gallery's, the priest half-drunk and delighted by the proposal she made until he realized the widow had yet to broach the subject with any of the principals. She told the priest to be sober enough to perform his office when they came for him and she would look to all other concerns. —A wedding, Mr. Gallery, Father Phelan said to the husband in the darkest corner of the room. —God's covenant made flesh between man and wife. Will you have a drink to celebrate?

The widow said, A priest isn't meant to relish the sufferings of others, Father.

—We choose our own hell, Phelan said, and he smiled at her.

She stopped at the peak of the Tolt on her way back into the Gut. Dark water and ragged patches of pale blue over shoal ground. As a younger woman she often thought of Ireland gone under that horizon and swallowed by the waters. But it had been a lifetime since she'd felt that regret, knowing it was useless to ask questions of the past.

She wasn't much above a girl when she first came to Paradise Deep, indentured to Sellers for two winters and a summer, and she'd nearly worked herself free of him before his marriage proposal led to her dismissal. The harbour settled by a handful of English and all of them tied to King-me's operation, so she walked to the Gut where she expected a more sympathetic welcome among the Irish and the bushborns. The Tolt Road only the barest hint of a path and rough walking with snow still down among the trees. She made a tour of the cove but no one would chance the merchant's wrath by taking her on. Sarah Kerrivan at least offered a bed but she refused to sleep under another's roof again. She fashioned a lean-to of spruce boughs next the Kerrivan's scrawny apple tree, sleeping with their wood dog to avoid perishing in the cold. The following spring she raised a one-room tilt with logs she'd cut through the winter, but she had no better prospects for employment. There were nine or ten men to every woman on the shore in those days and any single man would have wed her if she showed the slightest interest, if it wasn't common knowledge she'd spurned young Sellers who lived in Paradise Deep like some feudal lord, drinking tea with fresh milk from his own cow. No one could imagine what they might offer to turn her head and they left her alone.

The same had been true of King-me while she worked for him. Before he proposed he never spoke a word to her except to give instructions or request a specific meal from the kitchen, though it was clear to her how besotted he was. King-me had no experience or interest in love and he seemed incapable of recognizing what had struck him. He blamed fevers and ague and indigestion for his feeling so out of sorts. He consulted her on a cure for worms he suspected as the cause of his distress. He ordered Tincture of Sage and Essence of Water-Dock from quack physicians in England who promised relief of the sullen headaches, the poor appetite and swollen stomach, the spirits funk. In desperation he had her brew a colonic of molasses and cod-liver oil to clear his system of its bad humours.

In April of their second winter in Paradise Deep, only weeks from losing his right to order her around the property, he came into the shed where she was milking the cow, standing out of sight on the far side of the animal as he proposed. She didn't lift her head from her work, smiling down at the pail. —Marriage, is it? she said.

— You have no husband, he said. —And I need to take a wife.

She could tell he felt it was a simple business decision about property and standing and knew she could never expect anything different of him. The thought of marrying a man so ignorant of his own motives seemed no different than indentured servitude. —You need to take a wife, is it? she said, and King-me nodded helplessly, out of his element altogether. —And I need to take a piss, Master Sellers. Is that for or against we two getting married?

She could simply have said no and they might have carried on as though nothing of consequence passed between them, instead of her being turned out of the house before she could collect her few possessions or her wages. She could have left the premises without raining curses down on his head, half of which she had no memory of now, something about death to his household and the fruit of his loins and his livestock, though she never mentioned the skinny cow in particular. The words were flung about in the fury of the moment and she couldn't have known they would tie her to Sellers as tightly as any wedding vow.

———

As soon as Devine's Widow left the house, King-me slipped out to the barn where the cows were in from the meadow to be milked. He took a bucket off its peg to join the two hired men already at work. He loved the smell of a barn, the rank closeness of it. He sat next the udder of a cow and leaned his forehead against the heat of her flank, hoping it might ease the ferment that seeing the widow brought on.

It wasn't enough that she had refused to have him those ages ago, an Irish girl who'd come from nothing and owned nothing. She had to ruin his livestock and poison half the household besides. The cow shifted away from him as he latched on to the teats and he whispered to settle the animal down. It made him look a fool to blame Devine's Widow for the state of his cows, he knew, but no one had been able to offer any other explanation. The milk of his one milch cow dried up within a week of the woman leaving his employ and she was never the same mild creature, not even after the milk came back in. All his stock descended from that first cow, each one just as unpredictably skittish, kicking down the stalls at the slightest provocation, knocking pails of milk across the barn. —Explain that, he demanded of the doubters.

And he was supposed to think it coincidence, was he, that four of his servants took sick the very month she was dismissed, their faces gone red and puffy after a particular meal of cod, his own head swollen to twice its natural size? The look of it in the glass like some livid pillow from a whore's chesterfield. He was like to die the better part of a week and knew who to blame for the affliction, but he bided his time, let her think she'd got away with it. There were no magistrates in those days and he had to wait almost a full year before a naval ship stopped into the harbour.

Given the charge, Captain Churchward insisted on having the ship's chaplain present for the trial and they sat in a bare store appointed as the courtroom, the naval officer and his clergyman behind a table, plaintiff and defendant in wooden chairs before them. King-me had no memory of the men's faces, just a vague recollection of the red and black of their outfits. The Irish servant girl who refused him sat her hands in her lap, soft-spoken and polite through the whole procedure, and she still with every goddamn tooth in her head when she smiled. That face still vivid to him, so many years on. The naval officer asked for King-me's evidence and he offered it as calmly as he was able. The milk drying up overnight and he had seen the defendant sneaking away from the property on the evening in question and believed she was there decidedly to take away the milk of the cow by force of witchcraft. The naval officer making notes in a booklet, then leaning to the chaplain to conference in whispers. —Did anyone see the defendant in the presence of the cow, the officer wanted to know.

Not as far as he was aware, King-me told the man, but he suspected no person other than the defendant for the loss of the cow's milk.

The captain pursed his lips, as if puckering for a kiss. —So there is no one who might have seen the defendant placing a spell on the cow in question?

—Never mind the bloody cow, King-me shouted. —We was all nearly poisoned to death by this creature.

—Ah, the officer said.

Fucking *Ah!*

—Do you have any evidence to support this claim, Master Sellers?

—I had my head swell like a pig's bladder and turn scarlet. And most everybody in my employ afflicted to a lesser extent.

—And what makes you think the defendant was responsible for this?

He listed the curses she'd thrown about as she left his property as best he remembered them but there was no one he could call to confirm what was said. Not a soul among the servants who knew the woman would speak against her. He had to haul out of the courtroom and grab a fifteen-year-old taken on the spring he fired the servant girl, a stranger to the witch's influence and more likely to listen to reason. He gave the youngster a quick study in the evidence required as they walked back to the store-room and let him know what would become of him if he refused to give it.

Yes, the boy testified, he'd seen his master's sorry condition and other people ill around him, though he'd not taken sick himself. He looked to King-me a moment before he went on. Yes, he'd seen the defendant down at Spurriers' Rooms of a night before the sickness struck them and she was putting out Sellers' fish to cure in the moonlight. And she was saying some words over the flesh besides to poison it.

The chaplain said, You heard her speak?

—Not that I could understand, sir. She were talking some black language that were beyond me.

The youngster managed an admirable job of it to start, adding the bit about the black language of his own initiative. The captain and his clergyman were whispering on each other's shoulders and King-me had a moment of premature elation come upon him, to see the servant girl at his mercy suddenly, certain the game was won. He straightened in his chair as the captain turned back to them.

The captain said, You observed the defendant place a black spell on the household's fish?

—I did, sir, yes.

—Did you tell anyone about what you'd seen?

The boy glanced at King-me, a look of uncertainty creeping into his face. —I don't believe so, sir.

—Did you or did you not?

—I didn't, sir, no.

—You observed the food of your master being poisoned by a witch and told no one, is that correct?

—I suppose that's the truth, sir.

The captain smiled then and King-me felt the floor fall out of his stomach.

—You allowed your fellow servants and your employer to partake of flesh you had seen being poisoned?

The youngster only gaped. He was shaking so severely King-me thought he might soil his trousers.

—One might conclude from this evidence, the captain said, that you consented to the misfortune that befell Master Sellers.

—No sir, the youngster said.

—One might even argue that you were a conspirator in the event, a party of equal guilt to the defendant.

And with that the boy commenced to bawling. —I never saw it but from a long ways off, he sobbed. —I never heard a word, I was that far off. I don't know for certain if it were she were out there in the dark, that's the truth of it. It might be it were someone else were out there. I might have seen shadows and thought it a person on the wharf.

—Thank you, the captain said. —That will be all.

The officer turned his attention to the defendant after the Irish youngster left the room and King-me stared at the floor, not willing to see the look on her face. She spun some yarn about being owed wages upon dismissal and helping herself to a laying hen as payment while Master Sellers was at his store, but she denied doing anything to cause the cow to lose her milk. She denied curing his fish in the moonlight or speaking black words over the flesh or even setting foot in Spurriers' Rooms after her position was terminated.

—Are you in any wise responsible, the captain asked, for the afflictions described to us by Master Sellers?

There was a pause before she answered and he could feel her staring at him. —If I caused Master Sellers' head to swell twice its normal size, she said, it was through no deliberate action on my part. And I'd wager it was not the head on his shoulders that was so afflicted.

King-me pulled furiously at the cow's teats against the memory of that moment, the milk coming sharp against the pail. Maddening bitch of a woman. Even the chaplain smirking into his chest. Maddening, maddening bitch of a woman. The cow bucked suddenly and knocked him off his stool into the filthy straw and he had to crawl clear of the stall to come away without his head smashed in, the milk spilled over the ground. One of the hired men came to help him but he cursed him away, hanging the empty pail on its hook where he'd found it. Back at the house he offered his apologies to his guests and made his way upstairs to bed.

He stripped out of his clothes and lay naked on the cold board floor of the bedroom, hoping some mortification of the flesh might clear his mind of the woman's poison. There was a time after he'd brought Selina to Paradise Deep that King-me considered himself more or less clear of the widow's trouble, married as he was to a half-sensible girl whose childlike stature suggested she could do him no harm, his work going well and a small brood of youngsters to will the business to.

He should never have gone to her for help when his wife took to her bed and refused to leave it. In some recess of his mind not crammed with ledgers and sums he was sure this request had cost him his children. Lizzie, for certain, a loss he had never rightly recovered from. His girl married to the witch's son, she and her children, his own flesh and blood, living like savages in that woman's house. He'd vowed to let it all lie, for Selina's sake. But this trouble with Judah had simply fallen into his lap. The Great White, sea orphan, St. Jude. He was the widow's work and no one could convince King-me otherwise.

Sellers had paid off a vessel in Newfoundland at the age of eighteen after several years apprenticing to the ship's chandler and he became a small-time lender in St. John's, fronting cash to fishermen and sailors to buy their drink. It was a job that required a minute attention to detail alongside a measured ruthlessness and he was perfectly suited to the undertaking. His success brought him to the attention of the town's merchant community and he took invitations to meals and small entertainments among the quality, but the squalor of St. John's depressed him. Still a young settlement and infested with all the old vices, TB and syphilis, petty crime and drunkenness and an inflated sense of its own importance. He took the position with Spurriers & Co. when he was promised a pristine posting, a merchant operation on a virgin shore that he could set to his own liking. For years they'd been supplying a crowd of bushborns up there and were ready now to make a push into the country. He'd sailed out of St. John's on a May morning with thirty hogsheads of salt, two muzzle-loaders and three Irish servants, a crate of hens, four sheep, a single cow and a bull. A checkerboard that he was assured would help get him through the winters. A fortnight beyond sight of any human habitation he confronted the captain who had been sailing back and forth a wild stretch of coastline for days. —Ten years I been coming out here, the captain said, and the bloody place sits somewhere different every time.

Eventually they anchored in a harbour a full league in length, the bay with fathom and width enough for Spurriers' ships to deliver provisions in the spring and to take on salt fish in the fall. A steep horseshoe of hills rising around them, the densely forested spruce crowding down to the landwash. The silence of the place was implacable, and King-me felt a panic rising through him in the face of all of that nothing, the shoreline a mute angel he was meant to wrestle a name from. He settled on *Paradise* before he'd stepped off the boat, thinking anything less would be an admission of weakness. The bushborns in the Gut knew the harbour simply as Deep Bay and the name was too apt to abandon altogether—Paradise Deep, they insisted on calling it. As if to tell King-me that something of the place would always be beyond his influence.

Watching Judah emerge from the whale's guts, King-me felt the widow was birthing everything he despised in the country, laying it out before him like a taunt. Irish nor English, Jerseyman nor bushborn nor savage, not Roman or Episcopalian or apostate, Judah was the wilderness on two legs, mute and unknowable, a blankness that could drown a man. King-me was happy enough to think of that carted off to England and hung.

His mind was spinning despite the cold board beneath him and he doubted he'd sleep at all that night. It was uncanny how the widow arranged that little tableau in the parlour to mock him, to make him doubt the strength of his position. As if it could all turn her way just at the moment he was certain the game was won. Maddening bitch of a woman. Out there this very minute, he knew, plotting against him.

It was long gone to night at the peak of the tide when the wedding party rowed for the fishing room where Judah Devine was being held. Father Phelan and Devine's Widow in the bow and Callum at the oars, Mary Tryphena facing her father where she sat astern. Lizzie left at home in the grip of one of her spells, and time to weep in solitude at the sudden loss when she came to herself.

They'd walked over the Tolt Road from the Gut to fetch Father Phelan, and Mrs. Gallery stood in her doorway when they left for the waterfront. —Be strong, she'd called. They went along the east side of the harbour opposite Judah's prison and climbed into Jabez Trim's half-shallop where it was tied to the stagehead. The soldier guarding Jude's door was asleep at his post and they made a silent procession across the harbour so as not to disturb his rest.

Callum was watching his daughter's face as he rowed her toward her wedding. She seemed strangely serene for a girl who only hours earlier had no notion of marrying Judah, of sharing a bed with a man. He wanted to offer her a blessing or some encouragement, as Mrs. Gallery had, but he was too ashamed to open his mouth. Jabez Trim's story of Abraham and Isaac was in his mind and he felt himself playing out the scene himself now, about to sacrifice his own child with no hint of a reprieve at hand. Callum held the pilings to keep the boat steady underneath the fishing room, the shimmer of Jude's face appearing at the offal hole as if he'd been expecting them. Father Phelan lifted Mary Tryphena through the hole and dragged himself up behind her, then reached back through to take the hands of the old woman.

Callum waited in the darkness there, the whispered ceremony per-formed overhead by the light of a single candle. The priest and Devine's

Widow climbed down to the boat when it was done and they left the newlyweds to their first night together. The light of the candle was visible in the room's one tiny window as Callum rowed away. He helped his mother climb up onto Jabez Trim's wharf and glanced back across the harbour one last time but by then the light was out.

Lizzie was already in bed when they got home, lying with her face to the wall. Callum placed a hand on her back as he climbed in beside her, his palm snug between the shoulder blades. He sang softly in the black, a song about his love for a dark-haired girl, as Lizzie wept silently, each shudder travelling the length of Callum's arm. —She'll never have this, Lizzie whispered when he was done. —Not as long as she lives, Callum.

—Hush Lizzie, he said. But he knew exactly what she meant and he was awake all night with the thought.

Devine's Widow lay sleepless likewise, thinking of her long-dead husband, preoccupied with his memory for the first time since Callum married. The image of him so vivid it made her hands shake, as if she was the one approaching her first night in a conjugal bed.

After the naval officer declared her not guilty of all King-me's charges and ordered her released from custody she walked the path back toward the Tolt. She felt ill at ease for all she'd seen Sellers put in his place, thinking it was impossible to make a life for herself in the man's shadow. As she crested the Tolt she saw the Irish youngster who'd stood witness against her sitting with his legs dangling over the cliff edge. A moment of black fury rising in her throat, seeing how easy it would be to send him headlong to the rocks below. —You're not thinking of jumping, are you? she asked finally and he started at her voice. He was lank and bone, a boy of fifteen who shaved twice a week and sang at his work and by his own report had been drunk only once in his life. Patrick Devine. —I can't go back to Master Sellers now, he said, on the verge of tears. —He'll throw me out.

The boy was three years her junior, an orphan indentured to the fishery by his parish church in Cork. He had nothing to his name, much as herself. And there was something in that arrangement she found to her liking. She said, You knows how to fish do you, Paddy Devine?

He looked at her as if she'd spoken some bushborn nonsense.

—Would you have a woman in the boat with you?

—I got neither boat, he said.

—One bloody thing at a time, she told him.

They walked together into the Gut and he kipped down in her one-room tilt, crouched in a corner like a stray dog. There was only the one bunk along the back wall and that night she undressed there while he watched what he could in the gloom. She stood before him naked. —We got nothing now, she said, but what we can make together. She could hear him breathing in the dark and he stood up from his seat finally. She said, You don't come over to me unless you plan on staying, Paddy Devine.

There was a long moment's hesitation as he worked through the implications. He said, Are you really a witch then?

—That's no way to ask for a woman's hand, she said.

He felt his way across the room to lay with her, led by his lack of options or led by his cock, she still didn't know which. The time would come soon enough when he could make her wet with a word in her ear, lift her hips from the bed with the lightest brush of a finger, but that first night was brevity and discomfort and doubt, to have the youngster on her and rutting like a dog humping a leg, followed by an awful stretch of silence, both of them sleepless and terrified.

—So we're married then? the boy said finally.

Devine's Widow already working through the obstacles ahead, getting wood cut and dried for their boat, convincing King-me to front them credit for the summer fishery. The opportunity to ruin them completely if they had a poor season was the only angle she could imagine might work. —I expect we are married, she said distractedly. —You and me.

And he must have felt obligated to make an offering of some sort. —I love you, Missus, he whispered.

—Shut up Paddy, she said.

———

Callum was first out of the bed before light the next morning and he and the old woman walked back over the Tolt before the stars disappeared. They rowed across the harbour where Mary Tryphena waited for them at the offal hole and Callum dropped both women on the stretch of shoreline where Judah's whale had surrendered itself, the bones of the creature bleaching white among the beach grass. Devine's Widow walked with the girl to Selina's House then, Absalom answering the door when they knocked at the servant's entrance. He nodded to them both. —Hello Mary Tryphena, he said.

—We need to speak with your mother, Devine's Widow said, and they waited there while Absalom went to fetch her. Selina holding the door only halfways open to watch them, her ancient child's face apprehensive, resigned. —This here is your grandchild, Devine's Widow said.

—I know it.

—You ought also to know she is married to Judah Devine.

Selina stared at Mary Tryphena while she processed the information and the girl looked away at the outbuildings. —Is this true, Mary?

She nodded. —Yes ma'am.

—Are you? Selina cleared her throat. —Are you?

—She is, Devine's Widow said with more certainty than she felt. —And Master Sellers will have them haul the father of her child off to some foreign country and hang him. Leave her a widow before she gives birth.

Selina slammed the door shut before another word was spoken and Mary Tryphena looked at her grandmother. She was thinking of Absalom hearing the news of her marriage inside, of the odd fact he hadn't stuttered over her name when he said hello. —Am I pregnant then? she asked.

—It doesn't matter, child, Devine's Widow said. —We'll just hope for the best.

KING-ME SELLERS REMAINED A BACHELOR years after proposing to the Irish servant girl who eventually became known as Devine's
Widow. The condition had long since taken on an air of permanence
the fall he closed up his tilt and sailed for Poole to find a wife. His one
previous proposal in the New World made him feel safer testing the
waters across the pond and he spent the winter keeping company with
the eligible daughters of merchant families. He told no one his intentions before he left and none who knew the man could have pictured
the taciturn bit of misery attending teas and fashionable dances and
engaging in stilted small talk with young women regardless.

He asked permission of Selina Moore's father over a checkerboard and a glass of brandy on Shrove Tuesday. They settled on an
April wedding and the newlyweds sailed for Newfoundland through
wild spring weather, the masts and sails encased in ice by freezing
rain mid-crossing and the weight nearly capsized the vessel. Wind and
lightning and St. Elmo's fire in the rigging two days short of St. John's
and not a word of complaint from Selina the entire journey.

King-me fathered three children in the next five years, a girl, and
two sons to carry on the trade he was building. The children arrived
healthy and they were intelligent, curious creatures, affectionate with
one another and as well behaved as a parent had a right to expect.

Selina taught them to read and write and do their sums in the main room of their stud tilt until the spring she took to her bed and insisted on the completion of her wedding home. Lizzie was six when they moved into Selina's House, a fireplace in each room, cod-oil lamps fixed to the walls of the hallways. Every spring that followed, the children performed an Easter drama in the parlour for their parents and a handful of friends and servants, a three-act opus penned by Lizzie which she revised and refined each winter in consultation with Jabez Trim and his Bible.

In the spring of Lizzie's twelfth year, John Tom White convinced her parents the play should be performed for the entire community. John Tom was a Harbour Grace man who'd shifted to Paradise Deep after losing his wife to a chimney fire. He worked for Sellers as a culler, assessing and grading the quality of salt fish brought in each fall by the crews on the shore. He bragged often of the seasonal entertainments in Harbour Grace—skits and songs and recitations in the church hall—and he felt Paradise Deep was in sore need of the same. King-me had no interest in the children's play or songs and skits, but the lack John Tom pointed to pricked at his pride. He had the store that once served as a courtroom set up as a theatre, barrels and tools shifted along one wall and an old mizzen-sail hung for a curtain at the far end. Selina helped Lizzie sew costumes, and word made its way along the shore that an entertainment was to be seen at Spurriers' Rooms at the end of Lent.

The whole affair promised to be grander than anything the playwright imagined for her creation. She slept poorly for weeks ahead and anticipation kept her awake most of the night before the performance. An audience of fifty souls crowded into the building and the show went off without a hitch until Mary the Mother of God approached the empty tomb on Easter morning and young Harry Sellers appeared as the angel bearing news of Christ's resurrection. The play's climax was Mary's poem of thanksgiving recited upon her knees and Lizzie fainted dead away three parts through, her head lolling back mid-word and her body slumping to the floor. The audience thought her swoon part of the show until the angel began screaming at the top of his lungs. Even after being shaken awake Lizzie's arms were limp and her eyes vacant and once she came to herself she was unable to explain her brief absence. She was aware of the room and the crowd, she said, but couldn't move or speak. The spells continued in the months that followed, the girl dropping asleep as she brushed her hair or ate or laughed with her brothers. People were divided as to the cause, some suggesting the theatre was a sinful institution and a provocation to God, while others considered the girl possessed by some spirit in need of casting out.

John Tom White came to King-me with the opinion there was a widow's hand to blame, that someone had set the old hag on the girl. John Tom was a walking aphorism with a rhyme for every ripple in the weather, a charm for any ailment. Seven knots in a piece of string worn on your wrist to cure toothache. A potato carried in a pocket to relieve rheumatism. "If the wind's in the east on Candlemas Day, there it will stick till the end of May." It was the queerest case he'd ever seen of someone hag-ridden, he said, coming on so sudden in the middle of the day, and there had to be a witch at the root of it. King-me turned his face away and nodded.

—You wants to set things straight, he said, you got to put a bottle up, Master Sellers.

King-me pissed into a glass bottle and he stuck nine virgin pins in the cork as John Tom instructed.

—That'll block the witch's water up, John Tom said and he hung the bottle in the fireplace to set the liquid to simmer. —She'll come around now the once, he said, begging to be relieved of that.

But the bottle boiled mad and shattered over the flames and a second bottle burst the same. King-me was hesitant to repeat the procedure a third time. John Tom had him place the bottle away from the heat in a corner of the pantry where the liquid came to a boil regardless and King-me smashed the works on the flagstones of the fireplace.

John Tom stared at the mess, running a hand in circles over the bald pate of his head. —You know who it is we're working against, Master Sellers?

—Never mind, King-me said.

—There's one way to escape the sleep hag, John Tom said, has nothing to do with the witch. You hammers nails through a shingle and sleeps with it on your breast. When the old hag comes to pin you to your bed, he said, she squats down on the nails and the fright drives her off.

For the better part of a month Lizzie was forced to wear a board of nails hung round her neck all hours of the day and night. She thought of it as a leper's bell, a physical manifestation of her humiliation, and she refused to be seen wearing it. Eventually Selina threw the contraption into the fireplace. But by then Lizzie had developed an outcast's habits, disappearing in the nooks and crannies of the house, slipping into the woods above the Gaze or out as far as the French Cemetery, solitude her only relief from the affliction that had stolen her life.

Occasionally she went past the cemetery to Nigger Ralph's Pond. Except for the African who'd built a tilt near the waterline and worked there as a tinker, the Pond was quiet, too far a walk to be useful for water or washing. Lizzie pushed through the skirt of alders on the shoreline opposite the black man's property, wading the shallows to catch spanny-tickles in her palms. Ralph Stone never paid the slightest attention to her there and it became her favourite excursion when the weather was decent. She spent hours sitting out of sight across the Pond for the sensation of being completely alone and still enjoying the company of the man pottering across the water.

She knew almost nothing about Ralph Stone. Callum Devine and Daniel Woundy came upon a lifeboat in a bank of fog off the Rump, the black man adrift with a crew of corpses, half a dozen fellows dead of hunger and thirst after three weeks on open water without provision. He was like to have died himself, lips swollen and cracked and his eyes wild, refusing the food and water offered him and carrying on a conversation with his dead companions as the boat was towed into the Gut. On his back by the fireplace, he was fed broth through a cloth tit until he could stomach solid food. Devine's Widow thought his skin burnt or scorched black by the sun and for several days she covered him in a Jerseyman salve of Sea Doctors crushed and mixed with cod-liver oil before trying to scrub him clean with ashes and soap. He stared up at her on the third day, enough in his mind by then to see what she was about. —It won't wash, Missus, he whispered. His name was Ralph Stone, he told her, and were his mates all right, the ones in the boat with him?

No one ever learned where exactly the man belonged, only that he'd sailed the tall ships from his earliest years and had seen the world half a dozen times over. His vessel went down in a storm eleven days out of Portugal and the men in the lifeboat died before his eyes, one by one. For days he had only corpses for company, facing them from the bow while they stared at him like an expectant congregation. His friends. Their faces every hour growing more tortured, more accusing.

He lost his nerve for the ocean after the rescue, refusing to leave the shore and going so far as to build on a piece of land out of sight of the sea altogether. He depended on the charity of others for a time, subsisting on cods' heads and potatoes and wild berries and pond trout. Within two years he was cobbling a living with the cod-oil lamps he built in a tiny workshed and peddled door to door. Half the houses on the shore were lit by the work of his hands and eventually King-me Sellers shipped the lamps for sale in shops from Bonavista to Harbour Grace to St. John's.

There were some who thought his blackness a sign of defilement or witchery and turned their backs at the sight of him. But he was easy to laugh and had more stories of exotic locales than Father Phelan, which made him good company. He kept to himself out at the Pond where the few who counted him a friend could seek him out. He lived in a tilt so poorly constructed a permanent maze of cups and bowls were laid out to catch the rain that sieved through the roof. The single table and chair and his low bed built with board salvaged from the lifeboat that carried him ashore.

Lizzie never laid eyes on him before her excursions to the Pond. From across the water she couldn't make out his face or any features besides the remarkable cast of his skin. If the wind was right she could hear him singing snatches of hymns or drinking songs. She felt herself completely invisible to him and she began sneaking closer to his property to test the illusion. Gold rings in the lobes of both ears, a pale scar on one temple where the tight curls of his hair no longer grew, a missing front tooth like an open doorway.

He was much smaller than her imagination made him out to be from a distance, and older besides. He did little more than tinker out of view in his shop or crawl around on the roof of the tilt to stop up the most insistent leaks, all the while repeating the same three lines of a song. —Some marry for riches, the proud haughty way, some marry for beauty, the flower will decay, but if e'er I get married. He stopped there, seeming not to know how or why he would marry, and skipped back to the head of the verse in an endless loop.

She'd all but decided to give up her game the day he left his workshed, shirtless and walking straight for the spruce bushes where she was hiding. A disgruntled look on his dark face. She jumped to her feet, stars pinging across her vision. He stopped at the trees then and took his cock from his pants to piss.

When she woke from the spell of sleep Lizzie was in his arms and being carted at a run down the slope of the Tolt Road into the Gut. He was slick with sweat, out of breath and whispering some disjointed story about his mother and father, as if trying to keep her entertained during the trip. The strange paralysis that followed in the wake of her sleep made it impossible to nod or call out or ask where she was being taken before he pushed through a door and laid her on a table in front of the widow woman. —She's not dead is she, Missus? he asked. —Tell me she isn't dead.

—What is it you got done to her?

—She was in the bushes up at the Pond, he said. —Didn't know she was there before she hit the ground. Right at my feet she was, he said, what a fright she give me, Lord Jesus.

Devine's Widow peered down into Lizzie's motionless eyes. A crone's features and something ancient about the woman's face Lizzie didn't recognize, a stillness that wasn't calm or peaceful. The widow's stare calling up a mix of fear and distaste that would never fully leave her.

Callum had seen Ralph Stone carry the girl into the house and he came up from the Rooms in time to see Lizzie sit up on the table, looking about herself like she was drunk. She insisted she was fine and refused all offers of help getting home but Callum escorted her over the Tolt Road regardless. He did her the favour of asking no questions about what she had done to give Ralph Stone the shakes. He walked a little ways behind her and he sang to himself as they went, though not in the distracted, fragmented fashion of the African. Most of his tunes were Irish but she had the distinct impression he knew them whole and carried each from start to finish. He stopped behind her when they were within sight of Selina's House to let her carry on by herself and she felt immediately lonely without his voice for company. —I liked your play, Lizzie, he said to her as she went. —You made a fine Mary.

She had to force herself not to look behind.

—That angel of the Lord was some sook though, he said.

She didn't see Callum again until Christmas when he came to Selina's House in the wake of a group of mummers. The children weren't allowed downstairs when mummers invaded the kitchen but she and the boys sat on the landing to listen to their songs and drunken foolishness. She saw him come in, unmasked, and he smiled up where she huddled in the gloom at the top of the stairs. He bowed slightly. —Mother Mary, he said. Not a hint of mockery in his voice. Selina chased the children to their rooms when she found them there but Lizzie could hear Callum sing through the floor. An English air about the love of a dark-haired maid she recognized from their first encounter, and even the drunken mummers fell silent in the presence of what felt like a private moment. He left as soon as the song ended and she crept back to the stairs to see him out. Callum bowing his head again on his way through the door, as if something had been sealed between them.

Lizzie was fourteen when King-me took the entire family to England for her coming-out. During the voyage Selina taught Lizzie the dances that were fashionable when she was a girl. She was outfitted with stays and pannier and open-robed skirts to wear over a pink quilted petticoat, a black silk bonnet with a porcelain brooch, and she was paraded at masquerades and dances and church services, at teas and dinners arranged for eligible young men to have a view of her. She had the tiny features of her mother and a mane of coal-black hair that fell half the length of her back, and there was plenty of interest in her company.

A private audience was requested by a sharp-nosed twenty-six-year-old and they were sent off in a carriage circling a public garden. He did his best to engage Lizzie in conversation about pheasant hunting and French décolletage, his accent and concerns so affected he seemed cartoonish. He made the Newfoundlanders who visited her father with their endless stories of giant squid and shipwrecks and bad drink seem worldly. It struck her suddenly that her father intended her to marry such a one as this fart-faced bore. The notion was so disturbing that a spell overtook her and she nodded off while he talked.

On two other occasions she fell asleep in the presence of suitors and she was stared at and whispered about in the same way she had been at home. Eventually she refused to leave her room altogether. King-me tried threatening her from the other side of the door but it was clear that she'd poisoned her chances at a match in the West Country, perhaps in the whole of England. He and Selina turned their attention to finding a suitable girl to take back to Newfoundland as a housekeeper, so as not to have wasted the trip entirely.

Selina paced the deck endlessly on the voyage home and if the wind was up Lizzie walked with her to keep the willow of a woman from being blown into the ocean. Selina was distracted and melancholy and seemed in no mood for conversation, which suited Lizzie fine. Virtue Clouter often took the air with Selina as well, though she walked several feet behind. A shy sixteen-year-old, she never looked at a person directly and only spoke when spoken to. Lizzie resented the new housekeeper's shadowing them and said little to avoid being overheard. But she couldn't disguise how happy she was to be free of the corsets and petticoats and still single.

—You seem awfully pleased with yourself, Selina said one afternoon.

—I'm happy to be going home.

Selina shook her head. They stopped near the stern of the vessel and stared out at the ship's wake, the empty expanse of ocean between them and England. —Your father, Selina said, won't ever allow it.

—Allow what? Lizzie asked. She glanced back at Virtue standing six feet behind them, her gaze carefully averted. And in that moment it was obvious to Lizzie her secret was no secret now, if it had ever been one.

Her mother reached up to take the porcelain brooch from Lizzie's bonnet. —Mark my words, Selina told her. She weighed the brooch in her hand a moment. —There's your Callum Devine, she said, and tossed it over the rail. —You say your goodbyes now or your heart won't ever be your own.

Lizzie glanced back at the servant a second time but Virtue had turned away.

Virtue Clouter was the only servant in King-me's employ who lived in Selina's House, sleeping in a new room built off the kitchen with its own door facing the outbuildings so she could collect the morning's eggs and carry in firewood. She was inconspicuously competent in her work. She was modestly pretty and her prettiness went unnoticed by all but the most familiar. Harry and George both announced their childish intentions to marry Virtue, and Selina came to depend on her in all household matters. But there'd been no talk of hiring a housekeeper before Lizzie locked herself away in her room in Poole and the timing made Virtue suspect.

In the first weeks after their return Virtue sometimes followed Lizzie when she left the house on her wanders, keeping a discreet distance behind just as she'd tracked behind Selina aboard the vessel. It was a clumsy attempt at spying but Lizzie refused to give her the satisfaction of a confrontation, leading her a chase over half the shore, across rattling brooks that soaked their feet, through the thickest tuckamore on the hills.

Eventually Virtue relented and Lizzie was left to her own devices, though the simple fact was she had nothing to hide. No clandestine meetings in the spruce above the Gaze, no secret trysts on a bed of moss out by Nigger Ralph's Pond. Lizzie was forced to make do with the barest glimpses of Callum sculling in off the fishing grounds with Daniel Woundy or carting a sack of flour from King-me's store down to the harbour. It was her father's meddling that kept Callum at a distance, she was certain, the threat of losing credit with Spurriers which would drive him off the shore altogether. He offered his modest bow if they crossed paths but not so much as a word passed between them.

Months went by in this fashion and years on top of those. Her only reassurance came in rare encounters with Father Phelan, who offered the details of Callum's recent confessions. — Still lusting after a young girl he can't have, the priest told her. —Tormented, he is. The places he imagines kissing the child, it would make the Devil blush.

—But not yourself, Father.

—The Lord gives me strength, he said.

She spent her life in a state of unrelieved anticipation that made her flighty and unreliable and increasingly reclusive. Her family treated her as a kind of retarded child they expected would carry on in the same perpetual half-life. She roamed as she wished and reported to no one and grew wild in her habits, spending days at a time alone with the plague of yellow nippers and blackflies in the woods, snaring rabbits in the backcountry or fishing for trout at Nigger Ralph's Pond.

When King-me's eldest boy turned eighteen, the family planned a return to England to find him a wife. King-me was afraid Lizzie's strangeness would ruin Harry's chances and was relieved when she showed no interest in going. She was left behind with Virtue for company and John Tom White assigned the task of watching out for them.

The two women barely acknowledged one another, even as the winter closed them inside. Virtue attended to the needs of the household and cooked the meals and retired to her own room early each evening. John Tom talked about Virtue regularly while they ate, sitting back in his chair with both hands on his belly, as if he were the patriarch of the house. —That's a good woman going to waste is what that is, he said. —She twenty-three now and so many unattached men in the harbour. John Tom seemed unaware he might be implying the same about Lizzie across the table.

In November, John Tom began bringing a fellow from Harbour Grace along for supper, a single man spending his first winter in Paradise Deep. John Tom introduced him to Virtue and sat back then as if a match had been made. The man appeared to assume as much as well, arriving on Sundays to sit with Virtue in the kitchen while she worked dumbly at the fingers in her lap. He talked of wedding dates and children and cutting lumber for a house in the droke at the base of the Tolt Road. Virtue refilled his tea without offering a word. She assumed she'd said or done something to encourage the man's assumption but could not for the life of her think what it was.

John Tom White was delighted with the arrangement. —You won't find no better man the length and breadth of the country, he told Virtue. —A horse of a man you got there.

He let it be known far and wide the two were engaged and Virtue could only nod helplessly when visitors called at the house to congratulate her and wish her well. She went at her work with a furious energy, scouring the walls and floors and windows, cauldrons of water at a full boil to scour bedsheets and curtains and their clothes, as if all the activity would free her of the obligation she'd somehow contracted.

On Boxing Day, John Tom White organized a dance in one of King-me's stores. He convinced Daniel Woundy and Jabez Trim to play together and word of the entertainment made its way to every household on the shore. Lizzie had no interest in attending but Virtue was in a torment about facing her fiancé in public and begged for her company. —Perhaps your man Callum will be there, she said.

It was a sly tactic that Lizzie couldn't help admiring. She said, Who was it asked you to spy on me, Virtue?

—Spy, ma'am?

—When you first came out here. Following me when I left the house.

Virtue looked at her feet. — I didn't know a soul here is all. I thought maybe . . . But she stopped there and backed out the door. —I'm sorry to disturb you, ma'am, she said.

Lizzie entered the dance arm in arm with Virtue, sitting against a wall while the floor shook beneath them. There was no sign of Callum, but Virtue's intended was waiting and he approached her with his hand extended. He was a good-looking man, there was no denying the fact. Dark hair and most of his teeth still and he looked like he had never gone hungry. Virtue hadn't stepped on a dance floor in her life but he made her look a natural.

Lizzie danced only once, forced to her feet by Father Phelan who seemed to have made a pledge to dance with every woman present. Bowed low when he returned her to her seat. —Your man Callum, he said, leaning close. —He asks you not to wait for him. The priest straightened and looked down on her while she searched his face. —I wish I had news more suited to the season, he said.

Virtue stayed on the floor hours before she took note of Lizzie watching the dancers blankly from her seat against the wall. She excused herself from her partner and walked over to ask if there was anything wrong but Lizzie could only shake her head. Callum had given her up and she wished now she'd gone over the rail of the vessel after the porcelain brooch. Virtue helped her to her feet and the two women slipped out of the dancers' heat to make their way home. The servant settled Lizzie into her bed and left her staring out the window, the stars being choked by frost creeping across the pane.

Virtue's intended came by hours later, begging to be let in. He was drunk and insistent, slapping at the door with his open palm, and Virtue stood a chair against the handle to keep him out. He sang half a love song and then hammered at the door awhile longer. Lizzie came in from the kitchen to ask if she was all right and Virtue shouted out to him that he'd woken the mistress. —The mistress is it? he said. —You sure it isn't someone else I'm disturbing? Virtue begged Lizzie to go back to her bed and he demanded to know who she was speaking to. He cursed her for a lying whore and accused her of taking a stream of men to her bed while he sat demure in the kitchen and talked of marriage like a fool. —Who is it? he shouted. —Tell me the bastard's name.

—You're drunk, Martin Gallery, she said. —You be on your way.

He came to the house the next day, grey with a hangover and remorse. Fighting back tears as he explained it was only love of the woman that made him so heatable, that he had no doubt Virtue was alone last evening and her refusing to let him in proved only her worthy character. He would be a fool not to see she was a Christian woman and he prayed she might find it in her heart to have him still. He was standing near the fireplace, his head bowed in an attitude of abject contrition, and Virtue watched him a full minute, thinking of his hand at her back on the dance floor. It was the first time since she left her home in England she hadn't felt lonely. —You will not drink in our house, she said.

—I will not, he said.

—You will not speak to me in the manner you spoke yester evening.

—I swear to God.

Virtue took a breath. She'd never mustered a tone of such authority in her life and having some say in the affair gave her the impression she'd consented to it all.

After Gallery left the house, Lizzie came into the kitchen. She hadn't cut her hair since she'd heard Callum sing for the first time, when she was still a child, and it had grown almost to her thighs. She'd been proud of the extravagance, the weight of it a constant reminder of him. She set a chair in the middle of the kitchen and handed the housekeeper a pair of scissors. Virtue weeping as the lengths fell away from Lizzie's head, the dark scrolls mounding about their feet. —Burn it, Lizzie ordered before she left the room.

Through January and February and March the foul weather made a prison of the house. Lizzie grew to despise everything in it, her minder not the least. John Tom White drank regularly in honour of the upcoming nuptials he seemed to feel single-handedly responsible for arranging. He was giddy with his little triumph. He came to Selina's House direct from afternoons spent at Shambler's tavern and he treated every meal as a kind of personal victory celebration. —A horse of a man Virtue have got herself there, he told them.

He dropped dead in the middle of a toast in March, striking his head against the heavy table as he fell. Virtue thought he'd knocked himself senseless and she knelt over the bulk of him, laughing at the ridiculous man and shouting his name until Lizzie forced her to stop. —He's not asleep, Virtue, for the love of God.

She held the back of her hand to her mouth and laughed. —He's not dead? she said. And she bit her hand to keep from laughing again.

Virtue was sent to Barnaby Shambler who had become undertaker to the Protestants on the shore. John Tom White had been drinking on a tab for months, Shambler told her, and he refused to add to the uncollectible debt by burying the man. Virtue went to find Jabez Trim and when they returned to Selina's House they found Lizzie sitting in a chair beside the corpse. Keeping John Tom company out of remorse for wishing ill on him so long.

—We got no choice now, Jabez said, but to fetch Devine's Widow from the Gut.

The widow was already gone to her bed when Jabez arrived at the house. Callum woke his mother and he dressed to accompany them over the Tolt.

—You oughten to come, Devine's Widow said.

—And who's going to see you back after you've looked after John Tom?

The old woman watched her son while he busied himself at his boots. —I thought your mind was made up to leave that girl be.

—I'm only coming to keep you company, he said. He was out the door then, shouting at them to get a move on.

Callum hadn't known a moment of real peace since the afternoon he'd seen Lizzie perform in Spurriers' storeroom as a girl. Mary the Mother of God speaking to the gathering as if she'd appeared out of a Lordly shaft of light through the roof. It was a witching he'd never heard tell of, that a child could conjure such a vision, his pulse so fierce as he watched her that each heartbeat rippled across his sight. When Mary fell to her knees at the Saviour's tomb his legs quivered and he thought he might drop where he stood. And then Lizzie surfaced through that likeness of rapture, collapsing up there in his stead. A hush in the room those few moments before the angel began screaming, Callum's cock on end and his throat closed over with reverence and dread and wanting the strange little dark-haired girl for his own.

He'd never learned how to quiet his head during the years without her. He was a regular fixture at Shambler's for a time, trying to muffle the roar of the girl's proximity with booze. But the hours of drunken respite guttered into a bitterness that threatened to kill him and he chose to bury himself in the dredge of all that needed doing instead, taking to it as though to a religious calling. Rinding lungers for wharves and stages, tanning sealskins in the fall, barking herring nets, framing boats through the long winters. He offered himself up to others on the shore, slut for work that he was. He spent several days each spring working on Ralph Stone's pathetic roof. He adopted the childless and aging Kerrivans, helping William haul and split and stack their winter wood, trenching their potato garden and fertilizing it with seaweed or capelin, building a stone fence around the apple tree at the margin of their property. The endless physical labour was a hairshirt he wore next his skin, though it was only Devine's Widow who named it for what it was. —No good ever come of pining, she told him.

Callum had confessed his intentions to Father Phelan early on, but the priest had no patience for his vigil, thinking it an insult to God to live in such denial. He made a habit of plying Callum with drink, offering to take him to the home of a woman he guaranteed would make them welcome, dismissing Callum as a sodomite, a fairy, a eunuch in fisherman's boots when he refused. —Whatsoever thy hand findeth to do, he quoted drunkenly, do it with thy might, for there is no work, nor device, nor knowledge, nor wisdom in the grave. The priest slapped at Callum's crotch. —With thy *might,* you useless tit.

Father Phelan's ridicule never bothered Callum as much as the relentless public speculation concerning Lizzie. Everyone had an opinion about the girl to share, about her spells and the years spent skulking on the margins of their lives, all of which suggested some flaw at her core. Eventually Callum was forced to admit that what people said of her was true, that she was wild and twisted in some fashion. He couldn't help thinking he was to blame, asking the girl to share a truncated life that was slowly deforming them both. And he became increasingly withdrawn and reclusive as that fact came home to him.

On the evening of the Boxing Day dance organized by John Tom White, a crowd came to the house in the Gut, drunk and fed up with

Callum's cloistering himself away. They took his solitariness as an insult to their own company and decided to carry him if necessary to the festivities in Paradise Deep. Daniel Woundy and Saul Toucher and Father Phelan and several others dragged him to the door while he fought like a man being led to a lynching, elbows and knees and cursing, his shirt tearing along its seams. Saul Toucher punched at Callum's ribs to get his hands off the door frame and Callum went down, grabbing legs as he went. The group moved off into the darkness with this strange crablike creature hobbling at its centre. They made slow progress on the narrow pathways through the snow, Callum fighting every inch, and the hill to the Tolt defeated them altogether. Saul Toucher looked up to the night sky, his hands on his hips. —I won't miss the dance for this faggot's sake, Father.

—All right Callum, the priest said. —Do you have a message you'd like passed on to Lizzie at least?

Callum's chest was a knot of pain, each breath like a fist against his ribs. He nodded. —Yes Father, he said. —I do.

It was after midnight when they reached Selina's House, Lizzie still sitting beside John Tom's corpse on the floor. Callum and Jabez lifted the body onto the table. —I'll be getting home to my own, Jabez said then. —If there's nothing more I can do for you here.

Virtue had to fight to repress her laughing fit whenever she was in the corpse's presence, and Lizzie dismissed her. She sent Callum after the servant and he offered his infuriating little bow. —Make the gentleman at home, she said.

Devine's Widow was holding her hand over the eyes of the corpse, waiting for the lids to close for good. —I can manage this on my own, she said.

—I've no doubt, Lizzie whispered.

They began stripping the layers of shirts and undershirts, the foul socks. Rigor mortis still setting in and the head lolled as the body shifted left or right. The old woman pulled the filthy tunic over John Tom's head in one abrupt tug, working with a cold efficiency, as if she were skinning a rabbit. The absence of life in the flesh she was handling made Lizzie's stomach turn. John Tom's chest and belly covered in a thick moss of white hair, the stink of his feet acrid. Callum sitting in the next room. She grabbed the table edge, one of her spells travelling down its black tunnel toward her, and before they managed to remove the man's trousers she was dead asleep on the floor.

The widow woman called for Callum and he carried Lizzie away to the kitchen, her body almost weightless in his arms, her close-cropped head like a child's. Virtue stood back by the fire, the laughter finally choked out of her, and Callum sat beside Lizzie on the daybed while she struggled back to herself. He'd never been this close to her, never had the luxury to simply stare and stare. He'd been right to stay clear of her all this time, his hands shaking now he was close enough to touch her, his stomach in an uproar. He'd given her up and should have stayed at home, as the widow told him.

Lizzie's eyes slurred open, the spell still on her for all she was awake. Callum could see her taking him in, piecing together why he was there, remembering John Tom dead in the next room. He said, You cut your hair, and she managed a half-smile that made his chest ache.

—Miss made me cut it off her, Virtue said, and told me to burn it all. Burn it?

—Virtue, Lizzie said, would you give us a moment.

They watched one another as the housekeeper closed the door of the kitchen behind her. —Even Virtue has a man comes knocking at all hours and won't take no for an answer, Lizzie said.

—I never wanted to see you here, Callum said. —Like this.

— We could have run off.

He shook his head. —I didn't want that either.

—What did you want, Callum?

He glanced at his boots, feeling foolish. He'd known all along that the grudge between his mother and King-me stood in the way of the match, though as far as he could figure the feud stemmed from a disputed hen, a trifle invested with weight by time and pigheadedness. A stubbornness of his own was all he thought necessary to overcome the squabble. Each year on the anniversary of Lizzie's Easter pageant he had walked into Paradise Deep, standing before King-me's desk to ask for the girl's hand, thinking the man would eventually have to acquiesce to the obvious. But King-me's one-word refusals insisted something illicit was all they could look forward to. And Callum was too pigheaded himself to allow the man to force that upon them.

He looked at Lizzie squarely now, her wounded girl's features, the ragged haircut. —I couldn't let you waste your life waiting for your father to die, he told her.

She said, Not even when we marry, Callum Devine, will you decide how I waste my life.

Virtue Clouter gave her notice to Selina after Lizzie's family returned from Poole in the spring. She married Martin Gallery within the week and Lizzie consented to be maid of honour. Gallery had expected John Tom White to act as bridesboy and he asked King-Me to stand in John Tom's stead. Sellers didn't know Gallery well enough to refuse him though he disliked being set in a dead man's shoes. He carried out his duties as the vows were taken, walking ahead of the couple arm in arm with his daughter when the ceremony was complete, and people said it was as close as King-me would come to giving his daughter away. The old man stood straight and true as a navy mast, he looked like he might live to be a hundred. Lizzie caught Callum's eye as she passed, as if to reassure him, her gaze steadfast and certain.

They endured three more years of their peculiar sentence after Virtue's wedding, when another excursion to England was planned to find a wife for George. King-me decided to stay behind, unwilling to leave Lizzie with Callum still set for her and neither John Tom nor Virtue to watch them. Selina was afraid what might happen with father and daughter left alone in one another's company so long and decided at the last minute not to sail. She begged Harry and his wife to leave Absalom with her, the child just weaned off the breast and learning to walk. Harry's wife refused outright at first. But she was pregnant again and the second child would be born in Poole that winter, which Selina argued would satisfy her family's desire to fawn over the offspring. After two days of needling and bartering and naked pleading the mother relented.

They shipped out on the last crossing of the fall and it wasn't until the following spring that any news reached Paradise Deep. The vessel never made port in Poole and was unheard of since departing St. John's. The blinds in Selina's House were drawn, the windows darkened for a period of attenuated mourning, months waiting for some final word though it was obvious there was no hope. For the first time in years stories of how Devine's Widow left King me's employ made the rounds, variations of the curse she was said to have laid upon him discussed and debated. *May the sea take you and all the issue of your loins* was repeated often enough to take on the air of truth and was generally accepted as such by the fall.

At the end of September Selina herself walked over the Tolt Road and into the Gut. She'd never stepped foot in the neighbouring community and had to be directed to the stud tilt where Devine's Widow lived. She refused the offer of tea, refused to sit down. Devine's Widow expressed her condolences and she refused even to accept those.

—You'll leave her be, Selina said. —If I settle things with her father and she marries Callum. You promise me you'll let her alone.

—Mrs. Sellers.

—Your Callum is set for her, everyone on the shore knows as much, and I will see he has her. But you, you bitch. Selina took a breath to steady herself, a twitch about her mouth making it look as if she was trying to fight off a smile. —You will not harm a hair on her head, so help me God.

There was something familiar in the woman's tone, a sickening note somewhere between supplication and threat. The widow's husband had died during an epidemic of measles that burned through the shore twenty-five years before. Seventeen deaths in the span of three weeks, Jabez Trim performing four funerals on one black day alone. Her husband and only child both suffering and Devine's Widow lay awake the last nights of their illness in a fever of her own, offering all she had to offer. It seemed for a time she would lose them both and in her desperation she chose between them. —Spare the boy, she said. —Take my husband but spare Callum.

In a way she envied Selena, believing there was someone other than God to bargain with. —My Callum is a good man, the widow said.

—You give me your word, Missus.

She picked up her apron to wipe at her hands, knowing it would be a cruelty to deny Selina the illusion of safety she was after. Knowing Callum would never otherwise have the bride he waited on. She said, I'll do what I have in me for Lizzie if you settle Master Sellers on the wedding.

—That's no promise.

—You take care of Master Sellers, Devine's Widow said. —Let me worry about the rest.

Callum insisted the ceremony be put off a full year out of respect for the dead. —I've waited too long to marry into grief, he told Lizzie. King-me showed his face at the service long enough to give his daughter away before cutting all ties with her.

Callum came to bed the first night of their marriage with an erection that Father Phelan would have described as a decade in the making. His cock went limp so abruptly after he came that Lizzie thought for a moment she'd damaged or broken it somehow and Callum couldn't disguise his amusement, his whole body shaking when the level of her ignorance came clear to him. —You wanted to marry a slut, did you? she asked.

He said, You haven't ever seen King-me's bull mount the cows, maid?

She had not. She'd never seen anyone, not even her brothers, naked. She avoided the barns and for all her wild roaming she'd maintained a careful ignorance of the most basic facts of life. She'd had glimpses of the act, wood dogs or goats at one another, though it looked like a fight, a sickening intimacy to it that made her look away. She told Callum about the surreptitious trips to the Pond, the game she'd made of sneaking closer and closer to Ralph Stone's shack, the shock of seeing him take a piss only a spruce branch from her hiding place. Nothing at all to hint at the truth of the matter before her encounter with Ralph Stone's pizzle. She was beating at Callum's chest to stop him laughing as she tried to explain herself. —Nothing, nothing, nothing, she said furiously. —And then to come face to face with the like of that.

—From the stories old Ralph told me, Callum said, you're not the only woman he give a mortal fright with that oar of his.

They went quiet then, the man between them a moment, not two years dead. Passed in his sleep days before Jabez Trim walked out to look in on him. A miserable October, three weeks of a steady downpour and at some point after he died Ralph Stone's long-suffering roof gave up the ghost as well. A three-foot hole cratered above him, the steady stream of rainfall soaking the bedclothes and the corpse and threatening to set the very bed afloat, as if the ocean he'd escaped had come to claim him after all.

Lizzie said, We wouldn't ever have come to this if he hadn't carted me down here.

Callum shrugged against her. —I expect that might be true.

They could hear Devine's Widow snoring in the room Callum laid on the back of the tilt before the wedding and Lizzie nestled her forehead into his chest, thinking of the old woman's face when she'd stared down at her, paralyzed on the table. A look of cold appraisal that made her helplessness seem irremediable.

They knew Selina had come to speak to the widow after Harry and George were lost. Within a week King-me offered a tortured blessing to his surviving child and her fiancé. Lizzie and Callum had never spoken about the role Devine's Widow played in that sequence of events, refused even to acknowledge it. They were happier telling themselves love alone was responsible for their union. Love and blind chance. Love and the intervention of Ralph Stone's bladder on a summer's afternoon before they knew one another.

Lizzie reached down to cup Callum's penis, the mysterious little creature spent and still wet, like something half-drowned and just clinging to life. The old woman's snores echoing from the back room. —I hate your mother, Lizzie whispered to him. And she felt her husband's cock stir in her hand.

Virtue Gallery was a woman who blossomed in marriage, as if she'd tapped some vibrant subterranean source of beauty. It was the sign of a happy match, people said. Virtue had never so much as kissed a man before her wedding night but she followed her husband's lead as she did when they danced and she fell in love with him in the act, in the give-and-take of a physical pleasure she hadn't considered possible outside some paradisical realm reserved for the virtuous dead.

The only shadow in their lives was the absence of children. Virtue was embarrassed by her trouble and Gallery, cavalier about the subject at first, was more and more taken up with the idea that his wife was defective. They'd shared the house he built in the droke of woods for five years and had both begun to think they might never have a child. Their discussions on the subject became increasingly unhappy, Gallery talking as if he'd been tricked into wedding a barren woman. Virtue subjected herself to long courses of sour teas and potions of sheep laurel boiled with tobacco and she observed a variety of superstitions that were said to ensure conception. She went so far as to ask Jabez Trim to pray for them, though Gallery scoffed at the notion, given Trim's own childlessness. Virtue suggested they ask a blessing from Father Phelan instead but Gallery wouldn't hear of it. He'd rather cut off his own balls with a rusty fish knife, he said, than have a child on the say-so of a mick priest.

—Oh Martin.

He turned on her with a flash of anger. —You'd love to have the bastard's hands on you, I'm sure.

Virtue got up from her seat.

—No, he said. —It's his mick cock a slut like you is after.

It was the first time he'd spoken to her in such a fashion since the night he'd come to her door at Selina's House. She stared at him awhile, hoping to shame him without speaking, and then she went to her bed alone. She found him asleep on the flagstones of the fireplace next morning, wrapped in a coat. He woke meek and remorseful and newly in love with his wife and the couple enjoyed a period of sexual appetite unlike anything since their first weeks together.

She knew she was pregnant the moment it happened, felt it like a wick lit inside her. But she said nothing until she missed her second period. Gallery hadn't touched a drop of liquor in the house since the wedding, never drank in Virtue's presence and never came back to the droke until he was sober. But at the impromptu celebration for the pregnancy he toasted his wife and the child and his neighbours and returned the toasts offered by everyone else in the room. He was up half the night singing love songs to Virtue where she lay in the back room, pretending to sleep. It was late autumn, after the fall fish was in and before there was snow enough to haul wood from the backcountry, and Gallery carried on celebrating at every opportunity. Virtue felt he'd proved himself long enough to be granted a reprieve and she found small doses of the man when he was drinking surprisingly easy to take. He came to bed asking her if she might show him, once more, if it isn't too much to ask mi'lady, the precise steps she'd taken to sow the infant in her belly. And they lay together afterwards with the impending glory of the child between them.

—Those were all the steps? he asked one night, his hand in the heat between her thighs. —You're certain?

—Each and every one.

—You didn't leave out a step or two?

—Those were all I remember.

—Perhaps we should go over it again to be sure.

She laughed at him, pushing his hand away. —Go to sleep, you fool, she said. And she'd almost drifted off when he spoke again. —You're not leaving out a step are you, Virtue Gallery?

—What are you talking about, Martin?

He sat up in the darkness, struck by a doubt. —It seems strange, is all. Five years we've shared this bed and your belly barren all that time.

—I won't be talked to like this, she said.

—You didn't ask a blessing of that mick bastard, did you?

She let out a long breath, relieved by the ludicrous accusation. —Of course not.

—Well what did you do then?

—I just showed you.

—All the steps? he shouted. He was out of bed by then, knocking around in the dark after another drink, and she found him passed out beneath the board table in the morning, his dancer's legs splayed across the floor. She made breakfast without waking him, too angry to speak to the man, stepping back and forth over the motionless body. He didn't come to himself till noon, smacking his head on the table as he sat bolt upright from the floor. She was carding wool in a chair across from him.

—That's the good Lord, she said. —Telling you it's time to give up the drinking.

He rubbed his temples with both fists, still uncertain where he was. He stood up straight and held the table to steady himself. —All right, he said.

But Martin Gallery was taken with the notion his wife carried another man's child and even stone sober it grew in his mind. Virtue lost her patience with his sullenness and silence and she ignored him as best she could. The child was all she thought of. Their child. The baby's arrival, which she prayed would bring her husband back to himself.

His mood darkened with the first incontrovertible signs of the pregnancy, as if the distended belly and swollen breasts proved his worst suspicions correct. He drank next the fire every evening as winter descended and Virtue stayed in the bedroom to avoid his accusations. When he went out to find drinking company she barred the door and Gallery spent a portion of the early mornings screaming at his wife and her secret lover locked away in the house that he'd built with his own hands.

It was no secret that Martin Gallery was terrorizing his wife during his binges, accusing her of infidelities, threatening to take the lives of Virtue and any man he found in her bed. Jabez Trim once tried to talk some sense to him and succeeded only in placing himself first on the list of Gallery's suspects, so most people avoided the couple altogether. The mummers passed by without calling at the house in the droke that Christmas season and Gallery drank most often with Saul Toucher who treated Gallery's drunken tirades as a bit of harmless theatre. Names of possible adulterers were discussed at length, scenarios which placed particular men in Mrs. Gallery's company were explored. They agreed there was no man on the shore above suspicion, no woman alive who could be trusted completely. Saul's wife was still nursing the new triplets. —How do you know for certain, Gallery asked, those children are your own?

Saul pointed out the cleft of his chin, as prominent as the cheeks of a baby's arse. —They all got the same, he said.

Gallery shook his head. Even that seemed flimsy evidence to inspire so much confidence.

Sheila Woundy's husband found Gallery passed out in a snowbank one January morning on his way into the backcountry after firewood with Daniel and James. He would have walked by the man in the pre-dawn light if his wood dog hadn't stuck his head off the path, his tail wagging furiously. Elias Fennessey couldn't call his dog off whatever had its attention and when he tried to drag the animal back onto the trail he discovered Martin Gallery half-frozen in the bush, hair and eyebrows white with frost.

They strapped a length of twine under his armpits and the Newfoundland dragged him out the Tolt Road to his house in the droke. Elias knocked at the barred door, calling for Mrs. Gallery, and together they shifted him inside and set him near the fireplace, stoking the fire until it roared. Elias didn't want to leave Virtue alone with her frozen husband and he sent Daniel and James on into the woods with the dog, saying he'd catch them up later in the morning.

When Gallery's eyes opened an hour later he looked at Elias a moment before nodding his head in recognition. —Mr. Woundy, he whispered.

Elias was a widower himself when he wed Sheila Woundy. She had married into his name, but the change never took on the shore. Their only son, James, had been christened Fennessey but was commonly known by his mother's surname. Even Elias was referred to as Mr. Woundy and he was too old to take offence. He nodded back at Gallery. —You give us some fright, he said. —Thought you was a dead man.

Gallery looked around the room until his eyes settled on his wife in a chair near the table. —Mrs. Gallery, he said.

Virtue was almost five months pregnant when Gallery killed Elias Fennessey, setting on the man as he walked to the outhouse in the early hours of the morning. Gallery slit his throat from ear to ear with a fish knife that had been stropped to a razor edge, then walked the Tolt Road to his own home, the blood on his cuffs freezing solid in the cold. The door was barred and he climbed onto the roof to lower himself down the wooden flue into the blackened fireplace. He caught Virtue as she was shifting the chair from the door to run, dragging her back into the room by the hair, slashing at her with the knife. He pinned her to the floor until she exhausted herself and lay still. —Please, she said. —Don't hurt the baby.

—I killed him, Virtue, just as I promised I would.

—I don't know what you're talking about, she said. —You're drunk.

Gallery raised himself a little higher as if trying to get a better look at her in the near dark and he spat full into her face. He said, I killed the father of your bastard child.

Virtue turned her head away. —If that were true you'd be a dead man, Martin Gallery, and the world would be better for it.

Daniel Woundy came for Callum as soon as Elias's body was discovered and they gathered half a dozen others to go after the murderer. They went straight to the house in the droke where the door stood open and Virtue lay as pale as sea ice on the floor inside. It was the bitter cold or blind luck that saved her bleeding to death when Gallery lost his certainty or his nerve, leaving her where she was, slashed at the neck and chest.

Virtue hovered near death awhile. Devine's Widow replaced her dressings morning and evening, inspecting the state of the rough stitches she'd sewn in with needle and thread.

—The baby, Virtue whispered each time she opened her eyes. —The baby isn't moving, Missus. I don't feel him moving.

Devine's Widow pinned Virtue to the bed against her panic, trying to keep the stitches in place. —The child is dead, she told her.

Gallery was found floating under Spurriers' premises in the harbour a week after Elias was killed. He'd stripped down to his shirt-sleeves before throwing himself into the ocean and had been dead in the water a long time. But his two hands were still black with soot.

Virtue birthed the tiny corpse on the eve of Valentine's Day and she spent the long months of convalescence in her room off the kitchen in

Selina's House. Absalom Sellers was nearly seven years old and appointed himself Virtue's nursemaid, bringing her water and clearing away her dishes and emptying her honeypot in the mornings. He knew nothing of the circumstances surrounding Virtue's injuries and that particular silence was so familiar to him he thought for a time she might be his mother. The boy was never let alone outside Selina's House, held apart from the larger community of Paradise Deep to spare him stumbling upon the details of his parents' deaths. The slight stutter he'd always suffered multiplied in his isolation, like mould invading an abandoned house, and Virtue fell in love with the boy's articulate reticence, his refusal to ask the first question about her torment. He made a habit of bringing her gifts, a piece of sea glass or an eagle feather or a finger of polished driftwood, and they carried on a subtle exchange after she took up her duties as housekeeper, placing scavenged presents in one another's path through the house. They each found a salve for their separate losses in the other and as the months passed it looked as if they might escape their individual nightmares together.

After the first anniversary of Elias's death Virtue began catching sight of her dead husband as she made her way to the henhouse to collect eggs in the morning, sitting in the highest branches of a tree to peer in the second-floor windows, occupying the darkest corners of a room beyond the reach of Ralph Stone's lamps. She thought she was losing her mind until other servants began telling stories of a stranger on the property who couldn't be seen but in glimpses, and eventually they refused to work alone in the barns or step outside their own shacks after dark. Two Irish youngsters in their first year of service woke to find Gallery standing at the foot of their bed one morning and they lit out for the Gut without putting on their boots.

Virtue went to Selina's bedroom to speak to her in private that afternoon, Selina at her dressing table watching Virtue mirrored over her shoulder. —I thought you were happy here, Virtue.

—It's not that, ma'am.

—Well where do you plan to go?

—There's the house, she said. —In the droke.

—Don't talk such nonsense, Virtue.

—I won't be the cause of him harming another soul, ma'am.

—Who are you talking about?

—Mr. Gallery.

Selina turned in her chair to see the woman true. —Your husband?

—Yes ma'am.

There was a noise overhead and they both looked to the ceiling. —What is that? Selina whispered. She stood from her chair and reached a hand to hold the housekeeper's arm. —Virtue? she said.

Mr. Gallery's feet and legs came through the ceiling first, dangling there a moment before he came crashing through thatch and plaster and landed on the bed in a cloud of debris, a wash of soot drifting out of the fireplace. Selina screamed and ran from the room, shouting the Devil himself had come through her ceiling. Virtue stood where she was, watching her dead husband stand amid the plaster dust. He was thinner than she remembered and there was something nearly opaque about his face, as if the light from the window at his back passed through him. —What do you want? she asked finally, but he refused to look at her, only stood with his head bowed like a servant awaiting instruction.

Virtue went downstairs to pack her few things in the room off the kitchen and left Selina's House for a second time, walking across Paradise Deep to the stud tilt that had been sitting empty more than a year. Those who witnessed it swore they saw the figure of Mr. Gallery following at a distance and disappearing behind her when the door of the house in the droke was closed.

Jabez Trim made a visit the following day, holding his leather-bound Bible to his chest like a shield. He couldn't bring himself to step over the threshold and he called to her from the doorway. —Everything all right here, Mrs. Gallery?

Virtue was in the tiny pantry where she'd been washing dishes unused since she left and setting them back on the shelves. The place was dilapidated and damp from sitting empty so long, broken panes in its one window. The fire burning in the fireplace had barely touched the chill of the place. In the gloom he could see Mr. Gallery huddling as close to the dog irons as a chair could be set. —Mrs. Gallery?

She came out to him, wiping her wet hands on her apron. He looked down at his shoes and whispered, not wanting to be overheard by the figure near the fire. —We've just been wondering, Mrs. Sellers most especially and the little one, Absalom. We were all of us fearful for your safety.

—A year too late for that I'd say, Mr. Trim.

Jabez nodded and motioned with the Bible in his arms. —Is there anything can be done for you, Mrs. Gallery?

She turned to look directly at her husband. —Can you send this one to hell?

—Would I was at liberty to make such arrangements, he said. —What is it the creature wants of you?

—I would have thought you might be able to tell me such things, she said. —You and that Book of yours.

—I am the dullest instrument of the Lord, Mrs. Gallery, and that's the sorry fact of the matter. You don't plan to stay here?

—You can ask Mrs. Sellers to send along what wages she owes me, Virtue said and then held up her hand to ask Jabez to wait, disappearing into the bedroom. She came back, folding a coil of jet-black hair into a square of cloth. —This is for Absalom, she said. —Tell him I meant him to have it when he was older. And Mr. Trim, she said. —If you could find a private moment to pass it on.

Jabez nodded and turned the strange gift over in his hand. —You've precious little wood to keep that fire, he told her.

—Whatever you can offer, she said, I'd be grateful.

The charity of the communities kept her fed and provided enough fuel to heat the house but no one came near the droke other than to drop potatoes or salt cod or a turn of wood in the clearing outside the door. Absalom Sellers occasionally escaped his grandparents long enough to place a keepsake on the window frame or at the door of the outhouse, and that single sign of affection was all Virtue had to sustain herself. Mr. Gallery was seen at times perched like an owl on the roof of the house and people occasionally crossed paths with him on the trails in the backcountry, though he took no note of other travellers, muttering fiercely to himself as if in argument with the universe itself. They crossed themselves or whispered the Twenty-third Psalm and walked as quickly as they could in the opposite direction.

Father Phelan spent Lent and the holy days of Easter in other parts of the country and it wasn't until the Labrador pack ice moved past the coast and the first buds appeared on Kerrivan's apple tree that he came back to them. Jabez Trim searched him out as soon as he heard word of his return, tracking him down at the widow's home. The priest had a weakness for stories of hauntings and unclean spirits and ritual exorcisms, recounting them in all their arcane and nauseating detail. He was full of questions for Jabez, wanting to know what Mr. Gallery was wearing when he saw him and if his features appeared changed and what language he spoke.

—No language what can be made out, Father.

—You buried him, Jabez.

—Myself and Callum there, we dug the grave away out past Nigger Ralph's Pond where no one would have to look on it. Never left a stick of wood or a stone for a marker.

Lizzie said, He's out there looking for his grave is what he's doing, wandering all over God's creation like that.

—Hush Lizzie, Callum whispered. He considered it bad luck even to speak of the man and wished the conversation were going on in someone else's house. Mary Tryphena was in his lap and he leaned down to hum a tune into the child's ears, as if it might protect her from the conversation.

The priest turned to Devine's Widow. —You've an opinion on this, Missus.

—He wants something of that woman, I'd say. And there's no one else alive or dead can give it to him.

—Do you not know what to do, Father? Lizzie asked.

—The dead are more like mortal creatures than we know, he said. —Each one rises to a different bait.

The priest set out early the next morning and walked to the house in the droke. Mrs. Gallery didn't get up from the table, calling him in from where she sat. Her husband occupied his usual chair by the fire, huddling close to the flames, as if against a draft.

—He's forever cold, Mrs. Gallery said. —I think sometimes he might sit his arse right in the fire to try and get warm.

—There's fire galore awaiting him elsewhere, Father Phelan said. —Does he talk to you at all?

—He talks only to himself. And I can't pick out a word of it.

The priest sat at the table and watched the two awhile. It was difficult to say which of them looked lonelier or more forlorn. —Why do you think he's here, Mrs. Gallery?

She slammed a hand on the table and even the ghost startled in his chair by the fire. —Isn't it your job to tell me such things, Father?

He smiled at her. —I don't want to tell you what you already know, is all.

—I won't forgive him, she said. —May he burn in hell, I won't.

The priest walked across to the figure by the fire, crouching to look up into the face. —Would you like to make confession, Mr. Gallery? he said, but the spectre's mouth only went on working at its indecipherable monologue. —It's not forgiveness he's after, Father Phelan said.

—Well *what* then?

—It seems to me, Mrs. Gallery, your husband thinks you know exactly what.

They fucked on the dirt floor beside the fireplace, Mrs. Gallery's skirts hauled to her waist, the priest's black cassock unbuttoned and his drawers at his feet, and the woman's dead husband kicked at the fireplace crane to drown the feral noise of them together, the cast iron clanging like a church bell, his stricken face raised to the ceiling.

—I thought he'd come to kill me, Virtue said afterwards. —To finish what he'd left unfinished.

—He's not here to hurt any but himself, the priest said, watching her straighten her skirts matter-of-factly, as if she were laying a tablecloth for dinner. —It may be a long penance he's after, Mrs. Gallery.

I've no pressing obligation elsewhere, she said.

Father Phelan visited the house every morning and led Virtue through the most varied and perverse acts of love his years of lechery had taught him. Her husband's ghost a tortured witness to it all. Virtue sat over Phelan's cock to take the length of it inside her, reaching behind to cup his balls in her hand. —He used to call you a dirty mick priest, Father.

—Oh sweet Jesus, Phelan whispered.

—Said he'd cut off your nuts if you laid a finger on me.

—Oh Christ help us.

The ghost appeared to weep at times, though the tears were dark as soot on his face.

No one was privy to the goings-on at the house in the droke, though there was plenty of speculation about the rituals being performed to rid Mrs. Gallery of the cross her husband had become. Father Phelan was uncharacteristically reticent about the details, though he stayed longer than was his custom. After two months of parading the basest carnal pleasure before Mr. Gallery, Father Phelan asked again if he wished to make confession, but the spectre simply muttered in refusal.

—He's a stubborn devil, the priest told Virtue. —It could be years of this ahead of us.

—I trust I can count on you to fulfill your ecclesiastical duties.

—I am the Lord's servant, he said, and he paused at the door. He said, It's hard to fault your husband wanting to keep you to himself, Mrs. Gallery.

—He had me to himself, she said.

From that visit forward, the priest stayed at the house in the droke whenever he was on the shore and no one doubted a match of some sort had been made between Father Phelan and Virtue. They were never seen together outside the house, but to Mary Tryphena Devine and every child born after her, Mrs. Gallery was "the priest's woman." And Mr. Gallery took his place in a crowded netherworld the youngsters came to know as well as their own, a realm populated by charms for fetching lovers or curing warts, by fairy lore and the old hollies which were the voices of the drowned calling out of the ocean on stormy nights. They inherited their parents' aversion to the house in the droke, taunting Mr. Gallery as they ran past the little patch of woods or daring one another to sneak close enough to touch the door. That spectral figure on the margins of their lives seemed as ancient and abiding as the ocean itself, and generations after Gallery was sighted for the last time he occupied a dark corner in the dreams of every soul on the shore.

{ 4 }

MARY TRYPHENA DEVINE BORE A CHILD by Judah, just as
Devine's Widow told Selina she would. At the time there was no evidence to support such a claim and Mary Tryphena felt it was the old
woman's certainty that set the world in motion, as if her telling a thing
somehow made it so. —You'll marry Judah, the widow woman said to
her, and that will keep him with us.

Lizzie was the only person with gall enough to oppose the old
witch but she fell into one of her spells as she tried to bar the wedding
party from getting through the door. While they walked over the
Tolt, Devine's Widow asked the girl had she seen the rams mount the
sheep or the dogs on one another. Mary Tryphena nodded uncertainly. —Man and wife, Devine's Widow said cryptically.

Judah helped lift them through the offal hole into his prison on the
waterfront and nodded in assent when prompted by the priest during
the ceremony. But left alone, Judah seemed as doubtful as Mary
Tryphena what should follow. —We're married you and me, she said.
—You know what that means, Jude? The smell of the man was as
strong as ever, though in the company of the room's fishy stink it
seemed less oppressive. Mary Tryphena turned away finally, kneeling
and lifting her skirts over her waist to present her bare backside. Judah
sat motionless and she glanced back at him. —Jude, she whispered. He

was chained to the floor by an ankle but managed to shuffle toward her, leaning to one side to put out the candle. Cock the size of a snail, her father used to say, and she had her own memory of him naked on the beach, Devine's Widow lifting his prick's tiny blue head on the blade of her knife. He was groping blindly behind her and accomplishing nothing that she could tell. Mary Tryphena reached back and latched on to what she thought was his wrist.

King-me's cows woke to the racket carrying up from the shoreline and they kicked at their stalls, lowing mournfully while it went on. The soldier standing guard scrambled away from the door with his musket at the ready, afraid for his life. Father Phelan leaned into Mrs. Gallery's neck as the noise rose and ebbed and rose again. —From the sound of that, he whispered, Callum must have been mistaken about the size of Judah's blade.

Mrs. Gallery shrugged away from him. —You're no better than a whoremaster, she said.

Events unfolded then much as Devine's Widow predicted. The machinations at Selina's House occurred behind closed doors and they could only guess at the arguments presented, the threats and promises made between King-me and his wife, the promises and money exchanged between King-me and Lieutenant Goudie. Sellers called court to session in short order, the charge of capital murder dropped due to insufficient evidence and Judah convicted of theft on the testimony of Captain John Withycombe. He was fined fifteen pounds sterling and taken directly from court to the public whipping post where he received thirty lashes. Devine's Widow soaked sheets in vinegar and strapped them to his back to cover the welts and Judah slept six weeks on his stomach.

Jude moved into the tilt when Callum completed the new house at the end of that summer, though Mary Tryphena and the baby stayed under her parents' roof. Judah seemed to have no expectation that his wife share his bed or his home but he knew Patrick for his own and doted on the child.

Mary Tryphena ignored her husband as much as possible. She was tormented by the thought that everyone on the shore knew what they'd done in the fishing room, the same as if she'd raised her skirts to him in broad daylight on the Commons. She swore at the time it would never happen again and had rarely faltered since. Once or twice a year appetite got the better of her resolve and she slipped from her parents' house in the dead of night to call Judah outside where the open air made the smell of the man less overwhelming. The same stew of release and regret in the aftermath, creeping to her room like a thief, the buzz of simple animal pleasure pulsing through her. The last time, she swore after each lapse. The very last.

When little Patrick Devine was five years old, Father Phelan announced plans to build a Catholic sanctuary on the shore. A cathedral, he said, that would put the modest Episcopal chapel to shame.

The work involved in such an undertaking ran so hard against the grain of the man that no one took him seriously. The bishop in St. John's was steadily carving the country into parishes, resident priests were taking up duties once the province of itinerant clergy, and Father Phelan found himself with less and less territory to cover. He was bored staying so much in one place, people said, and the church was simply idle talk.

Phelan spent hours in the company of the shore's best boat builders and carpenters discussing naves and arches, trusses, beams, windows. He chose a plot of land on the Tolt as the church's location. —The wind up there, Callum Devine warned him, could strip the flesh off a cow. But there were almost as many Catholics living in Paradise Deep as in the Gut by then and the priest insisted the sanctuary sit between the two.

Jabez Trim and a handful of other Episcopalians worked with the Catholic men to raise the frame in September, Mass held within the skeletal walls that first evening. And the entire structure collapsed in a gale of wind before the roof was shingled or a single pew was placed inside.

—It's like in the Book of Job, Jabez suggested to Father Phelan. —God sends trials to test us.

—God is a miserable bastard, the priest said.

Father Phelan had crews cutting fresh timber to rebuild through the next winter, Callum and Judah and young Lazarus, the Woundys and Saul Toucher's crowd. They milled the wood in the spring and hauled it up the Tolt Road to set the church on the foundation of the one recently lost. They timbered the walls like a fortress and anchored the four corners of the building with ship ropes against the trials of God. The altar rail was fashioned from a gunwale salvaged off a Portuguese wreck, an iron cross forged in King-me's smithy fixed to the steeple. The Romans had two months of services in the new building before a lightning strike set the church ablaze. The fire brought every soul to the Tolt, even the shade of Mr. Gallery walking the edges of the inferno.

The main doors were choked off by fire but the side door leading to the sacristy stood open. Callum Devine passed the window nearest the altar as he ran toward it and he saw a man backlit by the flames inside, trying feebly to break the glass. Callum smashed out the frame with his elbow and hauled Father Phelan through, the priest choking and retching, his hair and eyebrows singed. —Tried to get the Blessed Sacrament, he whispered. —From the altar.

The crowd milled helplessly while the roof fell in and the fortified walls burned to the stumps. Lightning had struck a flock of sheep on the Commons as well, five animals lying charred and bloated in the grass, the stink of burnt flesh lending the scene an acrid, apocalyptic feel.

In the wake of the storm the day was calm, the sky a scoured blue. Lazarus and Judah took the skiff out after a load of fish even though Devine's Widow suggested they were tempting fate to go on the water in the wake of such an ill omen. Callum didn't discourage them but stayed in himself and he sat at the kitchen table with the women while they waited. All of them speaking in whispers, as if at a wake for a child.

Mary Tryphena was watching her son half-asleep in Callum's lap, his grandfather running his fingers through the boy's hair. Patrick's features hadn't changed since the day he was born, the disconcerting look of an adult about him even then. After Devine's Widow washed away the blood in a basin he was almost as pale as Judah, the eyelashes and the wisp of hair at the crown rabbit-white. Devine's Widow placed the child in her arms and Mary Tryphena held him close, moving her face across the nape of his neck, relieved to find only the smell of new life there.

Callum looked out the window to guess the time of day by the sun. —They'll be along now the once, he said. He set Patrick on his feet and stood up himself. —I'll send the boy up for you when the fish are in, he told the women. Mary Tryphena caught the faintest scent of Judah drifting from her son as he passed by. She'd refused to let him go out in the boat with his father and during his little tantrum of protest the stink wafted from his skin like a squid's black ink.

It was only days after his birth that Mary Tryphena discovered how a crying jag or a good fright or a fit of infant rage would call it up in him, sour and fierce. She could barely stomach the youngster's presence when he was upset and she felt cheated of something by his affliction. It was Judah or Lazarus he went to when he wanted comforting. And there was a distance between mother and child that felt unnatural to Mary Tryphena, an undercurrent of something like grief.

—You'd hardly believe that, Lizzie said, looking up at the ruins of the church still smoking on the Tolt. Devine's Widow suggested even Father Phelan would have to recognize the fire as a sign from God but Lizzie shook her head. —God give up talking to the likes of us, she said, a long time ago.

Father Phelan was taken to the house in the droke while the church was still burning. Mrs. Gallery stripped and washed him and settled him into bed and early that afternoon she joined him there. They were unusually gentle and patient with one another, staying in bed all that day and through the night that followed. They woke several times in the early hours to start in again where they'd left off, drifting back to sleep in a sticky haze. The priest was first out of bed the next day with breakfast ready by the time Mrs. Gallery joined him at the table. She glanced up from her plate suspiciously. —You aren't after falling in love with me, Father.

—Mrs. Gallery, he said, I am married to the church.

She smiled for only a moment before the thought of the fire struck her. She said, You don't think there's a message being sent you?

—What sort of message?

—Perhaps the Tolt isn't where the church belongs.

—Even Christ was denied three times, he said.

After his breakfast he walked the path to the outhouse. He felt remarkably peaceful sitting there, shut away from the world. He'd always thought of the privy as a holy place, a refuge from all but the most basic human concerns. As a novitiate he scandalized his superiors by claiming it wasn't the church but the shithouse that was God's true home in the world, the pungent effluvium as meditative an odour as incense, sunlight through the crescent moon carved in the door providing the dusky ambience of a monastery cell. He laughed at the thought now. Nearly an old man and more ridiculous with each passing year.

God spoke to no one, he knew that. God was scattered in the world and the word of God was a puzzle to be cobbled together out of hints and clues. He sat far longer than he needed to, pondering Mrs. Gallery's questions. It was the thought of losing the country he'd been fighting against with his sanctuary on the Tolt, the church meant to lay claim to these few of his flock, this one bit of coastline still left him. It was vanity, plain and simple, trying to hold what you loved a moment longer than God granted it. But he'd always been a vain man.

He walked back through the droke of woods and stood a moment staring out at the shoreline crowded with wharves and flakes and slipways, fishing rooms and storehouses and twine lofts. Only the hundred feet of waterfront reserved by King-me Sellers stood vacant, a straggly meadow of uncut grass above it. Sellers satisfied his expansion requirements by foreclosing on the properties of debtors and legally the plot remained public land, but the merchant refused to allow anyone to build on it. A view of the entire harbour from that patch of ground, the meadow a midden pile of fish bones and maggoty cod and broken pike handles, wood scraps too rotten to burn. The whitened bones of Judah Devine's whale scattered about like the ribs of a wrecked vessel. A shit heap of garbage at the head of the bay.

The priest made his way up to the Tolt where a forlorn band of searchers picked through the ruins for iron nails that might be reused. Father Phelan called Judah and Callum up to the chancel and they unearthed what was left of the altar from beneath the cindered remains of timber and shingle. They found the pyx containing the Eucharist in its cubby there, the container unmarked, the wafers inside as white as the white of Judah's face.

—I've seen the error of my ways, Callum, the priest said.

—You're giving up the drink, Father?

—I'd sooner be dead. Call everyone round, he said and he began praying in Latin, the searchers making their way up the blackened nave to receive the last Eucharist ever celebrated on the Tolt.

There were two late-summer arrivals on the shore that season which, added to the loss of the Roman church, made it the most memorable in years.

Ann Hope travelled from Poole to marry Absalom Sellers, sailing into Paradise Deep in mid-August. The two had met during Absalom's years as an apprentice in Spurriers' accounting offices in England and they maintained a correspondence after he returned home, her letters full of books and theatre and politics. She was five years Absalom's senior, sister to a fellow apprentice at Spurriers and just returned from eighteen months travelling on the continent when they met. —I expect I will be a spinster, she admitted in their first conversation. —I am too homely and too intelligent to warrant a proposal of marriage.

It was her nose, he thought, that made her face such a trial to look at. Her eyes beady and wide-set on either side of that imposing cliff, which gave her obvious intellect an unfair whiff of treachery. Their friendship was rooted in Absalom's belief that friendship was all she expected. She was the only woman who failed to reduce him to a helpless spurt of stuttering.

Her letters were Absalom's only link to the wider world he'd briefly known. They filled him with a sick nostalgia he mistook for passion and he'd proposed to her by mail the previous fall. She sent news of her acceptance on the first vessel out in the spring, outlining her plans to leave England at her earliest convenience, but the letter went astray en route.

Absalom assumed from her silence that he'd insulted the woman. As the summer wore on with no word from her he'd even begun to feel a measure of relief at the rejection. No one in Paradise Deep knew she was coming before she disembarked on the wharf and asked to be taken to Selina's House. —Where shall I have my trunks put? she asked him.

King-me took an immediate dislike to the woman. —She haven't the look of someone with the inclination to be a mother, he told his wife, but Selina wouldn't allow him to speak another ill word of her. The wedding promised to be the grandest affair on the shore since the Episcopal church was dedicated, though planning the event was left entirely in Selina's hands. Within a week of her arrival Ann Hope was badgering King-me for space that could be adapted to use as a school. She spoke to Barnaby Shambler and Jabez Trim and Callum Devine and a dozen others on both sides of the Tolt for contributions to cover the materials necessary to such an enterprise. —You see, Selina told her husband, how much children mean to her.

—She's a schemer, King-me said. —She haven't got a maternal bone in her body.

—They've got a school in Harbour Grace, Selina told him. —And in St. John's and in Bonavista.

King-me looked afresh at the woman every time she demonstrated this knack for political maneuver. Cavalry charge or subtle manipulation, axe or razor edge, that and all between were in her bag of tricks and he couldn't help but admire her for it. A school it was then, supposing he had to fund the entire thing himself, and he nodded angrily to signal his defeat.

Days before the September wedding, Father Cunico arrived on the shore. He carried letters of appointment from the prefect vicar apostolic in St. John's naming him priest of Paradise parish. Cunico was sent with instructions to reverse the ecumenism that threatened the extinction of Catholicism on the shore and his first official act was to forbid his parishioners attending the wedding at the Episcopal church. The Italian priest went door to door to present his credentials and make his wishes known, though he spoke no Irish and his English was so heavily accented that people made a show of not understanding him. Phelan dismissed the new priest as a milksop and a zealot, a shameless bootlicker whose grandest ambition was to be appointed arsewiper to His Holiness the Pope. —He won't be with us long enough to shave, Phelan predicted.

Cunico's only ally on the shore was the Reverend Dodge who fed him and found him a place to sleep and provided what advice he could. He insisted the Italian pay particular attention to the widow's crowd, and Cunico spent an evening in Callum Devine's kitchen, trying to bring the family back within the bosom of the true Church. Lizzie was handed the letters of appointment and she read them aloud to the room. She hadn't converted before her wedding and Cunico denounced the union, like Dodge before him. Their children and their children's children were stained by it, Cunico told them. There was a quick back and forth between Lazarus and Callum in Irish and the Italian hammered his walking stick against the floor to quiet them. Before coming to the shore he'd been warned to expect indifference, even insolence, and he was determined to nip it in the bud. —You hide your thoughts from me? he asked.

—Forgive us Father, Callum said.

Cunico looked at Michael Devine, Little Lazarus, the boy almost thirteen and already the height of his father. —And you? the priest demanded.

Lazarus turned to his father to speak again in Irish and Callum cuffed him so hard he fell from his chair. Lazarus smiled as he picked himself up from the floor. He genuflected toward the Italian with an attitude of false deference inherited directly from his grandmother. He left the room and was followed quickly by Lizzie, then Mary Tryphena and the strangely livid child in her lap walked out as well.

Cunico stood from his seat so he might look down on Callum and the widow. —God appoints a man the ruler of his household, he said, just as Christ is the head of the Church.

After he left them Devine's Widow said, He's sent us by the archbishop, Callum.

—I don't know your archbishop, Callum told her and he walked down to the Rooms to be alone awhile. He opened the doors onto the water and sat looking out at the still pool of the cove, the wide flat tables of the flakes on the waterline where the summer's fish had been set to dry. His hand was still pulsing from striking his son and sitting there he was overtaken by a puzzling nostalgia for Eathna. He could barely picture her now, a little redheaded girl climbing into his lap, insisting he pay attention to some childish secret. He used to set her aside, calling to Lizzie to occupy the girl so he could get on with knitting his twine or hear the end of Father Phelan's foolish story. And she was gone now, her childish secrets with her.

There was no neater sum of how life unfolded, he thought, and he was ambushed by a crying jag, sobs tearing through him as ragged and relentless as a seizure. Judah found him huddled over his lap with his arms wrapped about his chest and went to fetch Lizzie, leading her to the Rooms like a dog trying to alert someone to trouble. Callum was as helpless as Jude to tell her what was wrong and in the end she simply stood beside her husband while he cried himself out, a hand to his bowed head, the tangled mat of his hair. Beloved.

—Was this all a mistake do you think? he choked out finally.

—Hush Callum, she whispered. —Hush now.

On the afternoon of Absalom's wedding, Father Cunico stood on the path to the church in his clerical gown and surplice as if standing at the gates of hell, turning Catholics back to their homes. James Woundy and Lazarus and Judah holding Patrick's hand walked past his warnings without so much as a nod. The priest chased after them, waving his wooden stave and shouting like some lunatic highwayman. He came too close to Patrick for Judah's liking and he shoved the priest away.

Cunico was apoplectic to be treated so roughly, swinging blindly with his cane. Jude was struck in the face and spat one of his front teeth into the grass beside the path. The three men fell on the priest together then, dragging him to the harbour where they threw him into the bitter cold, Cunico twisting free of his vestments as he fell. Lazarus Devine standing with the sacred habiliments of the priest still in his hand.

Jabez Trim and one of Peter Flood's youngsters fished the priest out before he drowned and the scandal cast a shadow over the wedding. No one spoke of anything other, not the bride's dress or the extravagant spread of food laid on or the money spent. King-me took a moment before the ceremony to swear in half a dozen constables who were sent to track the perpetrators down while the wedding went ahead.

At the reception Barnaby Shambler told Reverend Dodge the Romans were a crowd of savages who would eat their young if left to their own devices. Dodge suggested Shambler was being unchristian in his assessment, though privately he nursed the same opinion not just of the Romans but of practically every soul on the shore. At times he felt all civilization had been bred out of the livyers by the climate's extremes, by the implacable barrens and bushland and bog. By the ocean's stark. Dodge was no fan of Mrs. Ann Hope Sellers' unwomanly mouthiness, her insistence on having opinions regardless of the topic. But the school she was proposing, he thought, might actually be of some value to a population so unremittingly backward.

Father Cunico took sick after his dunking and lay prostrate in bed a full week with a fever, attended there by Devine's Widow who applied cow-manure plasters to his chest. Judah and Lazarus and James were arrested by King-me's constables and held for several nights in the same fishing room where Patrick Devine was conceived, but they were released after Cunico publicly absolved them. No one doubted they had the widow's intervention at the priest's sickbed to thank, though the cost of the bargain remained a mystery. Cunico left the shore for St. John's in mid-October, citing the need to regain his health and to spend time in spiritual retreat to undo the damage inflicted upon him by the parish.

—That's the last we'll see of that milksop, Phelan told Mrs. Gallery. He was still making plans for the new church and laid them out before her in their bed. The land lying fallow on the waterfront at the centre of his scheme and she shook her head against his shoulder.

—King-me won't ever let that land to you, she said.

Phelan lay still a moment. He and Sellers had never spoken except when the priest was begging food for starving parishioners, the merchant niggardly and resentful of the imposition. —No, he said, I expect he won't. But he devoted the fall and winter to cutting and standing timber to dry for the church, taking a crew of twenty-five men into the bush and working them until dark.

Ann Hope Sellers' one-room school opened its doors in January and three dozen children carried in a junk of wood for the fire and took seats each morning to be taught their letters and sums and the basics of hygiene, and nursery rhymes that they chanted in unison. Even James Woundy came to take instruction to avoid conscription into Father Phelan's work parties. Ann Hope put aside her initial reservations about the man's attendance when she saw he was slow enough to enjoy practising his letters on a slate and reciting the juvenile poems. He fancied himself her assistant and helped keep the students in line if they got restless. She took to leaving him in charge if she was called away from the school, until the morning she came back to find a row of boys standing with their pants around their ankles and James Woundy measuring their hairless peckers with her wooden ruler. The girls writing numbers in careful rows on their slates as James called them out. It was the end of James Woundy's academic career and Ann Hope felt compelled to burn the ruler in the fireplace.

The raw wood for the church had to be hand-milled with saws and axes and planes, and Father Phelan had crews at work as early as possible in the spring, James Woundy entertaining the men with nursery rhymes laden with obscene substitutions. Hickory dickory dock, the louse ran up the cock. Old King Cole had a hairy old hole and a hairy old hole had he. He offered up the details of his going overboard after a merwoman years ago, taking her underwater and the cunt on her as cold and wet as March month, he pissed ice for a week afterwards. James didn't do a tap of work but he was diverting enough to be tolerated.

The finished lumber was laid in the droke behind Mrs. Gallery's house and the priest directed every Catholic man to meet him there before light on the day after Pentecost. The assembly numbered nearly one hundred, and in the first grey glim of dawn the church was carried in planks and beams to the midden above the shore. Mary Tryphena was watching from the Tolt with Lizzie and Devine's Widow and a handful of other women. It looked to them as if a column of ants was marching spruce needles and sticks from one nest to another. The work began in earnest before smoke showed in a single chimney on the shore, the corner posts laid and framed and the floor joists fastened across them. By the time King-me got wind of the project and roused his constables, badgering ahead of them to the waterfront, the wall studs were up and the ceiling trusses all but hammered into place.

The women came down from the Tolt to stand with their men when they saw King-me approaching. The two groups squared off on the waterfront, the priest flanked closely by Judah and Callum and Lazarus, by Daniel Woundy and Saul and the Toucher triplets and a dozen others not at work on the roof of the church. Absalom had followed his grandfather to the shoreline and he watched the faces railed across from him. Every one of them looked ready to hammer the first man to touch the priest.

Lizzie and Mary Tryphena stood at the front, their childlike features set off by the dark bounty of their hair, though Lizzie's was veined with grey now. The shock Absalom felt the first time he laid eyes on Mary Tryphena's bare head pricked at him again. Her hair the same blue-black sheen as the lock Mrs. Gallery gifted him when she left Selina's House. Jabez Trim slipped him the square of cloth when they had a moment alone and Absalom kept it under his pillow, sleeping with a hand wrapped in the coil. He felt it was his life he'd been handed in secret, if only he were able to decipher its meaning. The day they'd carted Judah up to Selina's House from the landwash, Mary Tryphena inched near to clutch at the hem of his coat with her bonnet in her hand and he'd glanced down at the coal-black hair of her head. A lock. A key. He was right to see his own story tied up somehow with the girl's, though he misread the markers childishly, falling in love with her as if the stars themselves had ordained it.

Absalom couldn't take his eyes from her still, her face set and ready to spit on anyone who stood against her men. King-me was directing the handful of constables to arrest the priest but they weren't willing to risk life and limb in the undertaking. He cursed them all for cowards and moved to take Phelan into custody himself until Selina came between them. She managed to talk King-me into relenting to avoid bloodshed and they retreated up off the landwash. Back at Selina's House the old man stood at a window, watching the Roman sanctuary shingled and sided and hung with doors oddly marked with crescent moons. —We'll have the Navy in to haul it down, he said. —And arrest every man jack who stands in the way.

Ann Hope said, I doubt that would do much to improve the situation.

King-me turned from the window to gape at her, but left the room before speaking another word.

A Mass was held in the bare church by the light of Ralph Stone's lamps that evening, Father Phelan decked out in the fine clerical vestments once the property of the Italian priest. When he made his way back to the droke, he found Mrs. Gallery sitting at the fire beside her husband. He went straight to the bedroom and called her to join him but she only came as far as the doorway, her outline dark against the fireplace light.

—You'll get yourself killed at this foolishness, she said. —And I'll be left alone with that creature out there by the fire.

—Come to bed, he said. —We'll make the angels jealous.

She didn't move and he could feel the weight of her considering him. —You're just like him, you know.

—Like who?

—Mr. Gallery, she said. —You think of no one but yourself.

The priest swore under his breath. He'd come to the house pleased with himself and with the events of the day, the speed with which the church was raised, the Romans facing down Sellers and his henchmen, the beauty of the sacrament celebrated within the bare wood walls, and he wanted to toast it all with an evening between Mrs. Gallery's legs.

—Make him go, she said. —Before you leave me, promise you'll make him go.

He was afraid for a moment she might cry but there were no tears in her. It was anger that made her voice quiver and he was surprised to see it, undiminished after all these years, a shape as black and bottomless as her outline in the doorway.

—Promise me, she insisted.

—All right, he told her. —If you'll come to bed. I promise.

She waited a long time at the doorway and he thought for a while she might decide against the bargain. But in the end she stripped out of her clothes and settled under the blankets beside him.

In late June Father Phelan departed to make his annual visit to the archipelago of tiny communities along the coast, baptizing the children born and formalizing the marriages undertaken in his absence, saying a funeral mass for those who'd succumbed through the winter.

Father Cunico returned to Paradise Deep while Phelan was away, sailing into the harbour on a day of cloudless blue sky. The sloop he arrived on was a forty-footer built in St. John's for the archbishop's use. The vicar had spent the first weeks of the summer touring parishes on the Avalon before accompanying Cunico to Paradise Deep. The two men stepped off the vessel under the shade of umbrellas held by members of the crew and stood looking at the church before them. The walls painted with whitewash, the windows in place and a wooden cross fixed to the steeple.

—They've built you a church, Father Cunico, the archbishop said.

Word was passed house to house that the vicar had come with the Italian priest, that a Mass was to be held the next morning, and the church was full an hour before the service began. The vicar was a severe-looking Irishman, a cleric with an air of enthusiastic fasting about him, and he wasted no time in reprimanding the community for its treatment of Father Cunico. He reiterated the Italian's appointment as the parish priest and outlined in detail the cost of defying him. Then he blessed the new sanctuary and held communion and at the end of the service when most believed he was done he opened the Bible to read from Galatians. —Even if we, or an angel from Heaven, should preach to you a gospel contrary to what we have preached to you, he is to be anathema. He listed Father Phelan's crimes against the church then—heresy and schism which spread division and confusion among the faithful, as well as direct violation of the sacramental seal of confession by a confessor. Father Cunico tolled a brass handbell while the archbishop closed the Gospels and snuffed a candle that had been lit upon the altar and Father Phelan was excommunicated from the Holy Roman Church. *Vitandis*, the archbishop informed the congregation and warned them that a similar fate awaited anyone who ignored the Church's will. On his return journey he stopped in every community between Paradise Deep and St. John's to repeat the ritual of exclusion.

Father Phelan arrived at Mrs. Gallery's two weeks later and she offered him the news when he came to her bed. —What does it mean, Father? *Vitandis?*

—Shunned, he told her. —To be shunned. The priest lay quiet a long time and she thought he might have fallen asleep. —Tell me that Italian shite hasn't been saying Mass in my church, he said.

He spent an inordinate portion of the next morning in the outhouse though it offered no solace. He went directly from there to Callum's house in the Gut, the men already back with the day's first boatload of cod and sitting to a second breakfast of tea and bread. Everyone stopped still when the priest came into the kitchen and he looked from one to the other without catching the eye of a single person. Patrick came out of the pantry and ran to greet the priest but Mary Tryphena grabbed him by the arm, lifting him into her lap. —God be with you, Father Phelan said, and Devine's Widow stood to turn her back. One by one the others stood and did the same, Callum and Mary Tryphena and Daniel Woundy. Even Lazarus turned away after his grandmother nudged his shoulder. Only Lizzie defied the old woman. —I'm sorry Father, she whispered.

The priest nodded. —Say me to your family, he said.

The same reception awaited him in every Catholic house on the shore. Doors barred against him, faces turned away, as if he were ringing a leper's bell through the streets of ancient Jerusalem. The hundreds of children baptized by his hand, the dozens of love matches he'd solemnized, the ten thousand thousand sins he'd absolved, and not a soul would so much as say hello. Even the Protestants whose houses he'd once blessed, whose sick and suffering he'd prayed for, did little more than nod, embarrassed by a predicament they didn't understand.

No worst, there was none, and he sat the rest of the day at the fireplace beside Mr. Gallery.

—What will you do? Mrs. Gallery asked him.

—It will pass, he said. —All things pass.

He waited the rest of that summer and long into the winter while Cunico said Mass and offered the sacraments in the church Phelan had built. He walked the paths of the outports, looking to catch even the slightest subversive nod from a parishioner but no one obliged him. Mr. Gallery followed him at a distance and the priest felt more and more that they were one and the same, pale shadows cast on the present by faces from the past. The contributions of the congregation that had sustained him and Mrs. Gallery came to an end and they survived on the charity of Protestants alone. It made the priest feel like a beggar and he refused to eat for days at a time, subsisting on a diet of strong drink and self-pity. He lost his nature and slept beside Mrs. Gallery as chastely as a saint.

At Christmas he roused himself from his funk long enough to put on a mummer's elaborate rags, wearing a veil of brin and a twine belt looped at the waist to hold the layers of dirty clothing and cast-off material in place, and he walked from house to house, taking drink and food and offering a few moments of foolishness before he was recognized and his hosts turned their backs or left the room altogether. Not even a man as apostate as Saul Toucher was willing to make him welcome, and the priest trudged back to the house in the droke to sit by the fire in his filthy costume, drinking steadily. Mrs. Gallery stood behind him but he shrugged away from her hand. —You can't live this way, she told him.

—Pray, what would you have me do?

—There are still people with no priest among them. You say so yourself.

—The back of beyond, he said. —Not even God knows they're there. He took a forlorn mouthful of his drink. —I'm too old to live like a fugitive, he said.

—I will not have the two of you in the house like this, Mrs. Gallery told him. —Do you hear?

—Leave me be, woman, he said.

—I will not have it, she said again.

—You'll heave me out on my ear, will you?

—Mind but I don't, she said. And she left the priest and her husband by the fire to go to her bed.

The sound of an iron clanging woke her hours later, a frantic alarm, and it took her a moment to place the sound. She went barefoot to the main room and there was just enough light from the coals to see Mr. Gallery kicking at the fireplace crane and Father Phelan hanging from the rafters at the end his twine belt. She stood on a chair to cut the priest down and he lay weeping and choking on the frozen dirt while she stoked up the fire. She helped him to a chair and sat him up. —This is not how it will end, she said.

The priest shook his head. —Leave me be, he begged her.

Mrs. Gallery turned and spoke to her husband for the first time since he came through the ceiling at Selina's House. —Kneel down, she told him. —Kneel down, goddamn you.

Phelan looked up at her, then at the faint features of the spectre kneeling beside him.

She said, Mr. Gallery would like to make confession, Father.

The priest leaned over his lap as if struck by cramps and he rocked back and forth in an idiot's spasm, moaning helplessly. Mrs. Gallery yanked him upright by an ear. He wiped the snot from his nose and mouth with his sleeve and tried to tip his head away from her hand. —Please, he said to her. He grabbed the breast of the fool's outfit he was wearing and shook it helplessly. —Please.

She twisted his head far enough he was forced to look at her.

—Choose your hell, Father, she said and then she turned her back on them both.

The priest watched after her a long time, though there was nothing he could see in the black of the bedroom where she'd disappeared. The figure on the floor shook with the cold, and the shivering finally drew Father Phelan's attention. The priest's saviour kneeling there. His miserable little life preserved by one of the damned, the face streaked by its sooty tears. —Would you like to make confession, Mr. Gallery? he asked.

Father Phelan was gone when Mrs. Gallery rose from her bed in the morning and there was no sign of her husband besides, the fireplace black and cold. She stayed on in the droke the rest of that winter before returning to her position at Selina's House a third time, nursing King-me and his wife into their doddering years while Absalom took on more and more of the ramshackle empire his grandfather had wrestled out of wilderness and fog.

Father Cunico lived three years on the shore before the animosity of his Irish congregation and the winters defeated him. He was a solitary figure within his parish, spending long hours writing melancholy letters to his family and the archbishop and his friends at the Holy See, complaining about the infernal Newfoundland weather and the insolence of the livyers that seemed congenital to the place. His only companion and confidant was God, who the priest thought of as an unhappy visitor to the country, much like himself—called to the irredeemable wilderness by duty and homesick for more civilized surroundings.

Cunico was a refined and delicate man in a world where delicacy and refinement were ridiculous affectations. He kept a silk handkerchief in the sleeve of his vestments that he produced to cover his mouth and nose whenever he walked near the fish flakes on the waterfront. The locals found it a chore to take him seriously and the Italian responded to their condescension with a show of ecclesiastical force, instituting a growing list of strictures. He saw the Irish language as a tool of sedition and refused to allow it spoken in his presence or within the sanctuary. He forbade Catholic children to attend Ann Hope Sellers' school, running classes of his own where he taught Latin catechisms and forced students to memorize the labyrinthine hierarchy of the Church. He condemned the tradition of passing infants through the branches of Kerrivan's Tree as a pagan rite, and Catholics, like their Protestant neighbours before them, were forced to carry on the practice in secret. He withheld the sacraments from families of mixed marriages until the Protestant spouse converted to the faith.

Callum Devine stopped attending Mass altogether at that point. He'd never forgiven himself for denying Father Phelan though the excommunication was all that kept Lazarus and Judah and James Woundy out of prison. He'd no doubt Devine's Widow orchestrated the entire thing while she nursed the Italian priest and it was his mother's shadow as much as the Church Callum wanted to leave behind. He and his wife and everyone else in the house but the widow were confirmed in the Episcopal faith and the Devines became the only Protestant household in the Gut.

Those Catholics who had no express argument with the priest had little time for the Italian's manner. Cunico was a stickler for decorum, for religious formalities, as if he were already ensconced in the make-believe world of the Vatican. He became widely known as Father Cuntico in honour of his perpetual state of vexation. At every Mass he listed the congregation's failings in their duty to the parish and its priest and threatened to abandon them if the situation did not change.

He took it as a personal insult when things did not and he left for good on a June morning of steady drizzle, his trunks packed and carried aboard a Spurriers ship bound for St. John's. A small group of parishioners were there to see him off but he refused them a final blessing, offering only his assurance that their community would never prosper again, as if God were departing on the same vessel as His emissary.

Callum felt the story disproved the notion that Father Cuntico had no sense of humour. But in the wake of the Italian's departure there was little enough to laugh about. The quintals of fish taken that summer declined for the first season since Jude had come among them and the extraordinary wet of the year rotted vegetables in the ground. Snow fell on the first of October and an implacable winter settled over the shore, icing in the harbours until the middle of May. Households ran low of provisions by the end of March and people survived on frostbitten potatoes and pickled herring. Selina Sellers passed unexpectedly in her sleep that June and the capelin came late to the beaches.

The price of cod in Europe had been falling for years and dozens of local men had taken to travelling to Harbour Grace and Wesleyville and St. John's in the spring, taking berths on sealing vessels to supplement the fishing. Even Sellers was under strain and he convinced Spurriers to mortgage the Paradise Deep operation in order to break into the market for seal oil and pelts, commissioning a sixty-seven-ton double-hulled schooner. The frame of the vessel came together over two summers in a makeshift shipyard beside the Catholic church, the boards reinforced with stanchions to withstand the ice fields where seals whelped their pups. It was an enormous outlay of money for a venture fraught with risk and the old man lost his nerve as the project progressed. King-me worried a ledger of figures and percentages through the winter but he was unable to torture a moment's comfort from the numbers. —We'll all of us wind up in the poorhouse on account of that goddamn boat, he said, as if it had been someone else's idea. He woke from dreams of the vessel in flames or set with full sail fathoms underneath the ice fields and he was so troubled by these visions that he walked over the Tolt to speak with Devine's Widow.

Lizzie was alone in the house with Patrick when King-me sat himself in the kitchen, saying he wouldn't leave until he saw the old witch. Patrick was sent to fetch the widow from Daniel Woundy's house and he burst in out of breath. Patrick had never spoken a word to King-me Sellers but knew who he was. Mary Tryphena explained his connection to the dead woman and the pew of mourners at the front of the church during Selina's funeral the year before. Three youngsters between Absalom and Ann Hope, King-me sitting nearest the aisle and following behind the casket as it was carried from the church. —Me great-grandda is at the house to see you, he shouted and it took Devine's Widow a moment to get his meaning. —Old Man Sellers? she asked, and he nodded. —Me great-grandda, he repeated. —He wants to see you.

She followed Patrick back along the paths, the boy rushing and glancing over his shoulder to make sure she was with him. Held the door to let her in where King-me sat turning a hat between his knees. The moment the widow came through the door he started in to ramble about some dream that was troubling him, fire he told her and a ghost ship that was sailing under the ice with all its sails set. He was blind to the room as he described the visions that haunted his sleep, offering details from one and then the next and back again, as if they were superimposed one on another in his mind. The widow let him go on talking until he exhausted himself and he looked around slowly, surprised to find himself in their company. He lighted on Patrick standing three feet from him. —Who's this one? he asked.

—You're me great-grandda, the boy said.

King-me turned to Devine's Widow in confusion. He looked half-starved, like everyone else on the shore, the long face staved in at the cheeks and the eyes black as cold firepits, though she knew his trouble was something other than lack of food. His mind rudderless and turning in mad circles and she was surprised he'd survived Selina even this long. —We don't have much time left, Master Sellers, she said.

—No, he said uncertainly, a rheumy film of tears setting his eyes adrift.

Patrick turned to Lizzie and said, What's wrong with him, Nan?

—Mind your mouth, Lizzie whispered.

Devine's Widow glanced at the boy, that foreign face of his. She'd gifted him a set of rosary beads after Mary Tryphena began carting him to the Protestant church in Paradise Deep and she once or twice talked him into reciting the mysteries but the habit never took. Hardly a word of Irish in his head besides. She felt as if she was being erased from the world one generation at a time, like sediment sieved out of water through a cloth. —You spend your days trying to make a life, Master Sellers, she said, and all you're doing is building yourself a coffin.

—A coffin, King-me repeated, nodding his head. He stood from his chair suddenly and stumbled past the boy, Devine's Widow watching after him as he went through the door.

—That's your father, Patrick said to Lizzie, still figuring the connections that seemed as convoluted to him as the Catholic hierarchy.

—Go on outside now, Devine's Widow said. —Leave us women be.

She and Lizzie stared across the table after the boy left. They had learned to travel adjacent to one another in the tiny world they shared, mastering an intricate dance that offered the illusion they lived independently. It was impossible to say the last time they carried on a conversation not mediated by someone else's presence. But they were both struck by the same cold presentiment now and mirrored it each to the other.

—I won't ever speak to my father again, will I, Lizzie said.

The widow shrugged.

Lizzie pushed at her eyes with the heel of her hand and lifted her apron to wipe her face, shaking her head angrily.

—I know you hates me, the old woman said.

Lizzie laughed then. —Yes Missus. I surely do.

—That's all right, maid. It means you'll always carry me with you.

———

King-me's winter-long season of nightmares fed a growing sense in Selina's House that the old man was veering into senility, and the trip to consult Devine's Widow seemed a final proof. He was delirious when he came back into Paradise Deep, claiming it was a coffin they were building next the church and ordering it be left to rot. Absalom could tell that nothing short of a talking-to from Selina would settle his grandfather down. Selina's influence on their world had been subterranean, almost imperceptible, and it was a shock to see the extent of the change when she left them, King-me on the verge of foundering altogether. The old man took to his bed mid-summer and didn't leave it until he was carried from the house in a casket that September.

Absalom resumed work on the sealing vessel and it was completed late the following summer. She was christened the *Cornelia* for Absalom's long-dead mother, sails and equipment and provisions were laid in for a maiden trip to the ice in the spring, and that promise was the one source of optimism on the shore. There were only thirty-odd berths available and men paraded to Absalom's door, pleading for tickets for themselves and their brothers and sons. The fishing had gone poorly for a third straight season and steady rain through July and August ruined the gardens. The winter fell early with heavy snows, the harbours were iced in by Christmas and stayed that way till mid-June, months too late to sail after the seals. Some households had not enough wood laid in to last the length of the winter and they burned furniture and the timber and walls of outbuildings to avoid freezing to death. Even in Selina's House the milk froze solid in the jug and had to be chipped with a knife and dropped in slivers into their tea. By the end of May cows and sheep and dogs were falling to starvation and the foul meat of those animals sustained people until a straggle of capelin finally spawned on the beaches at the end of June.

Judah Devine became a subject of much speculation on the shore through those dark days, Protestant and Catholic alike making pilgrimage to Jude's shack to sit awhile in his presence, as if some of his old luck might accrue to them just by breathing in the smell of the man. For the first time in years his boat was followed around on the water as if he were an Old Testament prophet trailing a retinue of acolytes and hopeful doubters. But the cod seemed to have vanished from the waters and everyone finished the season deeper in hock to Spurriers.

Years of extravagant misery and want followed one on the other. Even the smallest luxuries were beyond them. Men smoked wood shavings or spruce rind or mollyfudge off the rocks for lack of tobacco. What little cod oil they put up through the summer was doled out in spoonfuls to the young, leaving Ralph Stone's lamps dry, and the winters passed in darkness and shades of grey. Snow sifted through fine cracks in the stud walls and people woke to white drifts spread like an extra blanket over their bedclothes. Their shoes so stiff in the mornings they couldn't be put on before being thawed next the fire. The sap of backcountry spruce froze solid and exposed stands shattered like glass in the winter winds, the noise of the chandelier disasters carried for miles on the frost. Ice locked the coastline solid each winter and in March Absalom set a crew to hacking a channel clear for the sealing vessel. But they never managed to reach open water and the ship sat unmaidened in the harbour year after year. In the last months of those winters whole families survived solely on potatoes and salt, young and old occupied with days of dead sleep. And each night the sky alive with the northern lights, the roiling seines of green and red like some eerily silent music to accompany the suffering below.

When the ice finally lifted in May or June, Reverend Dodge engaged Jabez Trim to take him to the outlying tickles and coves. No priest had come to replace Father Cunico, and Dodge added the isolated Roman charges to his travels. The visits had once been pastoral in nature, a celebratory air about them, to be welcomed by people who'd endured months of isolation, to bring the small gifts of news and tobacco and prayer. But it was a grim undertaking to arrive in those tiny outports now, a handful of buildings perched over bare rock and little sign of life as Jabez rowed them in.

They carried several bags of flour from Sellers' stores and soft turnips and carrots scrounged from root cellars for the starving. But at times they found no one to feed. Three children lying in a slat bunk between their parents, all huddled under a raft of blankets and dead for weeks. Dodge could see where they had torn up floorboards to burn when they ran out of firewood. A midden of mussel shells in a corner, the corpses of half a dozen starfish boiled to make a broth. He could hear a shovel rasping earth as he stood in the darkness of the room, Jabez already at work on the grave outside.

—The four of them is it, Reverend? Jabez asked when the minister stepped into the open air.

—Five, Dodge said.

—There's another one born since last summer?

—Born and died, the minister said.

Jabez nodded as he nosed the spade into the ground. —We live in a fallen world, Reverend, he said.

Every autumn, premises were lost to public auction to clear unsustainable debts, and Absalom Sellers, suffering a barely sustainable debt himself, was unable to front provisions to households on the verge of bankruptcy. He organized letter-writing campaigns and once led a delegation to St. John's, badgering the island's governor for a relief program that never materialized. The population on the shore ebbing under the weight of hard times, tilts and wharves abandoned and falling into ruin.

Daniel Woundy had long since taken up with his own youngsters to fish, and Callum crewed with Jude and Lazarus. But in the spring of Patrick's twelfth year Callum suffered an infection in his leg, the limb too swollen and sore to hold his weight. And Patrick took a full share on Jude's boat in his stead.

Mary Tryphena couldn't look at her son that summer without a needle pricking at her heart, the boy's head oversized on his spare frame like a poppy on its stem, the pale face discoloured by hunger's fatigue. A youngster on the verge of becoming a man and there was a faint, lingering smell of decay about him. He was an unlikely marriage of contradictions, introverted and resolute, solemn and studious and the water in his blood besides. Lazarus ridiculed Patrick's interest in Ann Hope's school lessons as an affectation not far removed from Father Cuntico's silk hankie, but the youngster knew how to handle a set of oars and bait a hook. And he was the first one awake in the household every morning, eager to head for the boat.

Devine's Widow and Lizzie saw the men off at the door each morning and Callum hobbled down to the fishing rooms, badgering them about lines and bait and the weather before they rowed out the Gut. But Mary Tryphena refused to leave her room until she knew they were gone. There was a hint of something final in the most casual farewell during those savage days. And despite all she'd seen of the world, she believed it impossible to lose her son if she hadn't said goodbye to him.

Callum puttered around the Rooms awhile after the boat went out, until the leg forced him to limp home and put it up the rest of the morning. He could feel his pulse throbbing in the swell of it, his heartbeat a steady torment. Absalom Sellers had set aside two berths on his new sealing vessel as a peace offering to his estranged blood, and if the ship ever managed to escape the harbour some spring Callum promised Lizzie he would go to the ice to watch over Lazarus. Devine's Widow insisted Laz would be safer with Judah for company and the two women bickered the issue for months. Lizzie still hadn't forgiven Callum giving away Mary Tryphena's hand at the widow's instruction and he felt forced to side with his wife, though his body was a worn thing, a tool held together with twine, cross-braced with wood and nails. He could feel the two women ignoring one another in the tiny house and he sat with his rosary to keep clear of the strife, praying the chain of beads through his fingers.

—You're a fine Episcopalian, Devine's Widow told him. She thought their defection to Dodge's church was a meaningless gesture. —Catholic you're born, she said, and Catholic you'll die.

—In that case, Callum said, it makes no odds where we goes to pray.

The only real religious affiliation Callum knew was a personal one, and Father Phelan's absence cut deeper each season. He never shared Phelan's weakness for drink and women and the sacraments, but Callum was a child of deprivation and there was comfort in the priest's insistence that feeding an appetite was at the heart of a proper life. —The Word was made flesh for a reason, he'd said. Callum thought it was the priest's lust for life he was grieving as his own body faltered. But it was the certainty of Phelan's calling he missed most, its suggestion that the people on the shore were something more than an inconsequential accident in the world.

No one heard anything of Father Phelan but for rumours of his nomadic work in the furthest reaches of the country where the Church held too little sway to bar him gathering congregations of six and seven in a kitchen. The priest living itinerant in the isolated realms of his parish like a thief, baptizing and wedding and burying as he passed through. Callum was years dead on the Labrador ice fields before the only shred of real news reached the shore—that Father Phelan had drowned while travelling among the northernmost islands of the coast. The priest's corpse was found afloat on its back in open seas, decked out in the threadbare remains of Cunico's clerical robes, his arms crossed over his chest. The fishermen who recovered the body found the pyx nestled safe in Father Phelan's hands, the Blessed Sacrament inside it still dry.

{ PART TWO }

{ 5 }

THE DOCTOR WAS SCHEDULED TO ARRIVE via packet boat out of St. John's and the entire population crowded the landwash to watch him come ashore. He was greeted on the wharf by Barnaby Shambler, publican, undertaker and member of the Legislature for Paradise District since elections were first held in Newfoundland thirty years before. Shambler had courted other doctors and nurses to serve his constituents, two or three of whom had made it as far as Halifax or St. John's before illness or belated discretion sent them packing. People doubted his most recent recruit would get any closer and they'd been waiting with a skeptical anticipation. Even Shambler was surprised to see the man step off the boat with his leather medical bag in hand, as if he were ready to see patients on the wharf.

The Honourable Member's official words of welcome were slurred and the doctor thought him drunk at first, the swelling on the right side of his face disguised by the handlebar moustache and beard. —If you would be so kind, Shambler managed, rubbing his cheek.

The surgeon was an American, fresh out of medical school in Baltimore. Harold Newman. Granny glasses on a young face, his smile like a whitewashed fence. —I hope there's no underlying message, Newman said as he pried the infected molar loose, to the fact the district elected a mortician to government.

—Uhnrh uur hhunnrhu, Shambler replied.

Newman's father was a doctor, as was his father before him. —It was passed on to me, Newman told Shambler, like a disease. He preferred fishing, mountain climbing, big-game hunting and sailing to anything he encountered at home in Hartford or in medical school. He'd spent a summer away from his studies in Alaska and almost stayed for good. Not yet twenty-six, lanky and athletic, he'd come to Newfoundland to avoid the stultification of an urban practice, the straitjacket of Connecticut manners and expectations. Days before he left the States he'd broken off an engagement to a distant cousin brokered by his mother. —My parents, he said, have all but disowned me for coming here. He stuffed cotton into the crater that surrendered Shambler's tooth. Wild country was what drew him to Newfoundland, rivers and lakes, caribou and black bear and ocean. Half a world away from his father was also a draw.

The relief Shambler felt after the extraction made him giddy. —A drink, he muffled through the mouthful of cotton. —A drink to welcome the good doctor.

He was working in a corner of Shambler's tavern, a long line of people who followed him up from the wharf waiting their turn at the door. Shambler set a bottle of dark rum on the counter and parcelled out a shot to patients before their turn in the chair.

—You see now how he gets elected, the next in line told the doctor.

Newman had never encountered mouths in such a state of decay and sorry misalignment. Everyone he saw was in need of dentistry and he spent the afternoon packing gums with cocaine before reefing with the forceps, his forearms flecked with blood, white shards of enamel under his feet.

A girl sat in the empty chair and smiled up at him. —I wants them all out, she said.

—All what?

—Me teeth, she said. —I wants them all pulled.

—How old are you, miss?

—Sixteen.

She said some more then that was incomprehensible to Newman, though Shambler laughed and slapped his hand on the bar. She was tall and barefoot, the part in her brown hair as sharp as a blade. Not beautiful, Newman thought, but handsome. Something non-European in the features, in the fullness of the nostrils and lips, the olive skin. —Open wide, he said. The tendons in her neck pulling taut as she tipped her head back. The delicate line of the clavicle. —There's two that may need to come out, he said.

—I won't get out of this chair till they're every one gone, she told him. Or so he guessed.

—There's absolutely nothing wrong with the rest of your teeth.

She went on awhile in response, Newman trying desperately to pick words from the rushing stream. He glanced across at Shambler.

—She says they're only going to cause her grief later on, Shambler translated. —And she'll as like be somewhere she got no one to pull them. The Honourable Member shrugged to say he had no argument to counter the girl's insistence. She got up from the chair an hour later, her mouth packed with cotton and her bloody teeth in a handkerchief.

Shambler called Newman to the counter. —You'll want a little pick-me-up, he said and handed the doctor a tumbler of rum. Newman took a mouthful and shook his head. Startled to have disfigured so pretty a face. —I should have refused her, I suppose.

Shambler spat a clot of blood into an empty glass. —She can watch out to herself.

—She's hardly more than a child.

—Bride was never a child, is the truth of it, Doctor. I minds the time Thomas Trass tried to come aboard of her when she wasn't much above twelve. Trass was drunk and pawing at her and he said, Bride, I'd love to get into that little dress of yours. Shambler ducked his chin to his chest, trying to head off a spurt of laughter. —And Bride said,

Sure there's already one asshole in there Mr. Trass, why would I want another one.

Newman turned his head to the door as if he might catch a glimpse of her still.

—What a saucy little bitch, Shambler said when he'd caught his breath. —It's two years you signed on for is it, Doctor?

—That's right.

—Any regrets now you had a look at the place?

Newman downed the last of his rum and rolled his shirtsleeves another turn up his arms. He felt bizarrely elated. —No, he said. —No, I think I'll be quite happy here.

He took over an abandoned house near the public school, setting up an examination room and a surgery in the front rooms and sleeping on the second floor. Half the men on the shore were away at the cod fishery on the Labrador for the summer and he saw mostly women and old men and children in those first months. He set broken limbs and pulled teeth, he treated swollen glands and apoplexy and typhoid, gangrene and pneumonia and asthma. When the fishermen returned in September he dealt with strains and sprains and boils, water pups, bones rotten with tuberculosis, cuts from fish knives gone septic under a foul poultice of molasses and bread.

The patients he saw were virtually incapable of articulating their troubles, offering only the broadest, most childish descriptions of what ailed them. I finds me side, they told him. I finds me legs. I got a pain up tru me, they said. Bad head, bad back. Bad stomach, which sometimes meant trouble breathing. Even under questioning they had difficulty presenting specific symptoms, which made them sound like a crowd of hypochondriacs, but it was rare to root out a malingerer. People on the shore were unable to distinguish illness or injury from the ordinary strain and torment of their days until they were crippled and it was only the desperate who braved the clinic, and only after they'd exhausted every quack potion and home remedy available. No one had money to spare for treatment. They paid the doctor with potatoes and cabbage and salt fish, with a turn of split wood, with pork hocks and herring and dippers of fresh blueberries and bakeapples, with a day's work on the roof or help digging a well, with spruce beer and goat's milk and eggs, with partridge and turr, with live hens.

Newman's company was actively courted by the town's quality and he suffered their attentions with a curt politeness meant to keep them at bay. He ate at Selina's House where Ann Hope Sellers offered lectures on a variety of political subjects while Absalom and their youngest daughter occupied themselves with the needs of an ancient aunt. Ann Hope was a long-time abolitionist and had written some two hundred letters to the House of Lords and to the Congress and president of the United States on the matter. —You've undoubtedly become acquainted with Nigger Ralph's Pond, she said. The name, she felt, was a black mark on the shore.

—A black mark, Mrs. Sellers?

Ann Hope set down her soup spoon. —You know what I mean, Doctor, she said.

Ann Hope had long since retired from teaching, but she'd devoted the last five years to having the new public school built near the Episcopal church. There was no money for desks or books or fuel to heat the building and she meant to make it an issue in the next election.

The daughter was past thirty, with the guarded look of someone trying to hide a permanent scar. Insular, he could see, but not shy. She taught in the unfurnished school but showed little interest in the upcoming campaign or anything political. Everyone referred to the aunt as Mrs. Gallery. The old woman was suffering the advanced stages of senility and she spent the meal cursing a long-dead husband who haunted her still. The entire household seemed quietly lunatic and Absalom Sellers, who barely spoke a word all evening, offered the doctor a bashful look of apology now and then.

Newman refused all invitations to attend church and let it be known in an offhand manner that he was an atheist. Some thought the assertion would be the end of his appointment, but Reverend Dodge and the Catholic priest let the matter be. Dodge had served the parish nearly half a century, Father Reddigan more than a decade, and neither was willing to see the shore stripped of its sole medical professional. Only the Methodist evangelist took issue with the scandalous claim, pushing handwritten copies of his sermons on the doctor. He'd converted half the local Protestants and a handful of Romans in his two years in Paradise Deep and he considered the atheist doctor a personal challenge. —Since you're too busy to join us on Sundays, he said, pointing to the sheaf of papers he'd laid on Newman's desk. Reverend Violet sported a tidy navyman's beard, black strings of hair combed over the bald pate of his head. There was an agitated optimism about him that kept his hands in motion as he spoke. Newman glanced down at the sermons, the topmost epistle titled *Sleep as the Urging of the Devil*. —I prefer sleep to reading, he said, pushing the pile back across the desk.

He spent what little free time he had in the open air. Half a dozen government roads ran miles into the backcountry beyond Nigger Ralph's Pond, built by destitute fishermen forced to work for their dole during the worst years of the century. They were intended to open up the island's interior where fields of arable land were simply waiting to be plowed and planted, according to Shambler and his like. That mythic Arcadia never materialized and the roads petered out among the same dense stands of spruce and low scrub and blackwater marshes that covered the entire island. The gravel thoroughfares were in constant use by horse and cart hauling wood or bog turf, by berry pickers and trout fishermen and youngsters in search of freshwater swimming holes. Newman walked them all with a fishing rod or rifle in the early mornings and on Sundays when his surgery was closed. Everyone he crossed paths with was civil but a little distant, he thought. They warned him to carry bread in his pockets to ward off the Little Ones who might lead him astray when he tramped through the woods and offered tips on the best rivers for trout and then wished him a good day. They were a people at their best with visitors, he was learning. They would turn their own children from their beds to give a night's sleep to a stranger. But Newman occupied an odd middle ground, an outsider they were beholden to, someone who might very well overstay his welcome, and they were slightly wary of him. He took what kindness came his way and was grateful otherwise to be left alone.

While the weather held through the fall Newman occasionally travelled by foot to the smaller coves and inlets within the district or was ferried along the shore in a bully boat owned by Obediah and Azariah Trim. In his first week of practice he'd removed an egg-shaped fibroid below Obediah's Adam's apple, slipping it through an incision that could be hidden afterwards behind a shirt collar. The trips were intended as payment for that procedure but the Trims carried on with the service for years as a Christian duty. They were among Reverend Violet's first converts on the shore and like all Methodists they were teetotallers who never took the Lord's name in vain regardless of provocation. They quoted the Gospels endlessly and let the atheist doctor know they were praying he be brought to Jesus. Once the snow settled in they carted Newman to medical emergencies by dogsled, harnessing their motley assortment of animals at a moment's notice.

The brothers were chalk and cheese to look at—Azariah a squat tree trunk of a man, his face as livid and sinewy as a plate of salt beef, Obediah nearly six foot, a dimpled chin like the cheeks of a baby's arse—but they were twinned in their dispositions. Newman never heard a word of complaint from either man. They ran alongside the sled and were cheerfully tireless. One or the other would take the harness at the lead when the dogs flagged or the sled bogged in heavy snow, shouting Crow boys! to encourage the team ahead. They never lost their way or seemed even momentarily uncertain of their location. They travelled narrow paths cut through tuckamore and bog or took shortcuts along the shoreline, chancing the unpredictable sea ice. Every hill and pond and stand of trees, every meadow and droke for miles was named and catalogued in their heads. At night they navigated by the moon and stars or by counting outcrops and valleys or by the smell of spruce and salt water and wood smoke. It seemed to Newman they had an additional sense lost to modern men for lack of use.

They worked for Sellers like everyone else on the shore, but had tried their hand at any entrepreneurial opportunity the country afforded, spinning wool and churning their own butter, fur trapping and fishing the local rivers for salmon. They'd built a sawmill that they ran with help from the sons, brothers-in-law and nephews in their widely extended families. They were practical and serious and outlandishly foreign. They described the deathly ill as wonderful sick. Anything brittle or fragile or tender was nish, anything out of plumb or uneven was asquish. They called the Adam's apple a kinkorn, referred to the Devil as Horn Man. They'd once shown the doctor a scarred vellum copy of the Bible that Jabez Trim had cut from a cod's stomach nearly a century past, a relic so singular and strange that Newman asked to see it whenever he visited, leafing through the pages with a kind of secular awe. He felt at times he'd been transported to a medieval world that was still half fairy tale.

He filled his letters to Connecticut with the medical oddities he encountered, providing clinical descriptions alongside the apocryphal or speculative pathology he was offered by locals. He visited Red Head Cove where more than half the population had inherited red hair and freckled skin and hemophilia from a single foxy Irishman. He treated a five-year-old with webbed fingers that were somehow supposed to be a vestige of her grandfather's tryst with a merwoman. Saw a family of seven brothers and sisters in Devil's Cove who were suffering accelerated senescence, their bodies entering puberty within the first three years of life, progressing through middle age by five. Two older siblings hadn't survived beyond a decade and the younger children had no hope of outliving them. It was a widow's curse according to some and the strangely ancient children defied any medical explanation Newman could dredge up. He took photographs of these and other striking cases, idiopathic scoliosis presenting with a forty-five-degree curvature, cleft lip, birthmarks in the shape of animals or continents. A middle-aged brother and sister born bald and without fingernails in Spread Eagle. He developed the albumen plates in his office, bathing the glass in solutions of gallic acid and silver nitrate and fixing the image with hyposulphate of soda.

Newman was on a call to the Gut when he first laid eyes on the startling figure of Judah Devine, throwing rocks into the cove for a black Labrador, the dog retrieving the stones and dropping them at his feet. Newman introduced himself, asking permission to do an examination. There was a boy with Judah who explained the man was mute. Jude sat quiet as the doctor checked his eyes and ears and mouth, and ran his hands against the grain of the white hair to see the scalp. The stink off him almost unbearable. —What's his name? Newman asked the boy.

—Jude Devine. He's me grandfather. The boy had a Nordic look about him, the hair white-blond and his face pale as the royalties of Europe. Eyes a blue so light they were almost colourless. —He was born out of a whale's guts, the youngster said. —That's why he suffers so with the smell on him.

—What do you mean, born?

—Devine's Widow cut him from the belly of a whale with a fish knife, they says. Jude come out of it naked as a fish.

—And you believe that, do you?

The boy shrugged. —He is what he is, Doctor. I got no reason to doubt it.

—Do you think he'd let me take a photograph of him?

—He's not deaf.

Newman wrote his father a long description of the faux-albino of indeterminate age, salvaged from the belly of a whale about the time James Woundy enjoyed his dalliance with the mermaid. Man suffers acute bromhidrosis, Newman wrote, and is completely mute. Eyes, oddly, displaying no lack of pigmentation though the blue is unusually faint. Not a true albino, then, although he could think of no other explanation for the man's appearance. A full set of teeth but for a central incisor lost to some blunt trauma.

His father complained frequently in those early months about losing his son to a backwater of superstition and ignorance, but his tone thawed in the face of Newman's unexpected passion for his vocation, in the carefully detailed histories the letters offered. He responded with advice and articles and requested follow-up on cases of particular interest. There were no questions about his son's personal life or his plans for the future and as far as Newman was concerned, that was just as well.

It was during the long hours of travel with Obediah and Azariah Trim that the doctor learned most of what he knew about the people on the shore. The brothers' knowledge of the coastline's genealogy was biblical in its detail and they offered all they knew in a call-and-return that had the fluency of a catechism.

Obediah: James Woundy now, he was a lazy stawkins.

Azariah: Not quite right in the head, but sweet as molasses.

Obediah: Sweet as molasses and just as slow.

Azariah: He had the one daughter. And James Woundy had all he could do not to choke on his food so there's no telling how he managed it.

Obediah: The child's mother was Bridget Toucher and the Touchers was a hard crowd to grow up a girl among.

Azariah: They was never married those two but they had Magdalen between them. And Bridget Toucher, she finally settled with Lester Flood and they both come to the Lord last year, just before Les died of the consumption.

Obediah: Young Magdalen, James's daughter that is, she jigged up with a fellow name of John Blade.

Azariah: Not John Blade from Devil's Cove now. John Blade from Devil's Cove, he turned Catholic and married Peter Freke's widow and they lives up on the Gaze. The Roman Blades, they are.

Obediah: Magdalen married the John Blade whose father come over from Devon. John and Magdalen have got the three youngsters between them now.

Azariah: There's James and Matthew. And the young one with the webbed fingers, Hannah her name is.

—Yes, Hannah, Newman said, relieved to have a face to cling to. He sometimes used a pad and pencil to map the spiralling connections but even then he lost his way. The roots of each family so intertwined they were barely distinguishable. Obediah's first wife, Sara Protch, died in childbirth and he was married now to her younger sister. Azariah's sister-in-law married her way through the Toucher triplets, the first fellow freezing to death on the ice, the second lost to a bout of typhoid. The third passed away not eight months ago, asleep on the daybed in the middle of the afternoon.

—Identical triplets? Newman said.

—You doubt it, do you?

—One in two hundred thousand. Never seen it myself.

—It was Alphonsus that Sandra married the first time round, Az Trim said. —And she called her husband Alphonsus regardless which one it was in her bed, they were the spit of one another in every particular.

Newman was surprised by their candour. There was no confidence, no family intimacy from the past century they seemed unacquainted with.

Obediah: Adelina Sellers now, she teaches the little ones up at the school. She's the youngest of Absalom's lot save Levi. She was afflicted with warts as a girl, Doctor. Used to walk around in a mourning veil, with her hands tucked up in her sleeves, half the shore thought she was born without fingers.

Azariah: 'Twas Mary Tryphena Devine cured her of the warts. She got the gift for such things.

Obediah: Adelina's sister Nancy, she married a Yank and left for the Boston States. Thirty year ago. The two older brothers followed after her and they haven't so much as cast a shadow on the shore since. Only Levi and Adelina is still with us.

—Absalom inherited most of the shore from his grandfather and once Ab is gone, Levi will have it all.

—He's a hard man, young Levi. Money is all he thinks about. He's married to Reverend Dodge's daughter Flossie but he don't have a thought for a soul except his mother.

—He got no time for Absalom at all.

—Well, I expect he's got his reasons to dislike his father.

—Now Brother, Azariah said and the two fell silent. It was a rare instance that saw the Trims edit the catechism, stumbling on a subject too sensitive or scandalous to mention in the company of an outsider. —Crow boys! Az shouted to the dogs, as a way of ending the conversation. —Crow!

Each time they passed the droke at the foot of the Tolt the dogs bristled and growled at the trees and shied from the path. The brothers averted their eyes and kept quiet until it was well behind them, as if they were holding their breath against some poison in the air. There was a grown-over clearing in the trees and Newman was curious to know who had lived there and why it was abandoned. —You'd do well to keep clear of it, was all the brothers offered.

On Old Christmas Day the Trims carted him seventeen miles up the shore to see a man reported by a son-in-law to be on his deathbed. Newman drunk and running alongside the sled to sober up. Deking off the trail to puke into the spruce trees before catching up the Trims. —You're having a fine old Christmas, I see, Az said.

Mummers had invaded the clinic the first night of the season and stayed until light the following morning. Newman didn't know what to make of them or their antics, swinging him by the arm while music was played on fiddles and accordions, demanding he feed and water them, and all hands taking liberties with his arse as if they were testing the freshness of a loaf of bread. He sat them to glasses of rum and slices of the dark fruitcake patients brought in by the dozen and they left without ever revealing their identities. Each of the next eleven nights followed the same pattern though the troupe of mummers was always different. He guessed some of them from their limps or postures or physical tics and when the rum ran dry he sent around glasses of ethyl alcohol that they drank down honey-sweet.

The clinic was still crowded with mummers when the Trims came looking for Newman with news of the dying man. They left two hours before light and arrived mid-afternoon to find the elderly gentleman sitting with a glass of rum next to a fire. —I was feeling a bit nish when Sally's man come by yesterday, he told the doctor, but I'm the finest kind now. Newman listened to his heart and checked his temperature and reflexes and there was, from what he could tell, not a thing wrong with the man. It was ten hours hard travel to reach him and after a meal of tea and bread and molasses they started for home, arriving after the moon had set and twenty-four hours without sleep for all three.

Newman insisted they stop at the Trims' property to spare the dogs another half-hour hauling and he walked back to the surgery on his own, half asleep on his feet. There was a man sitting in the darkness of the front room when he arrived. —I let myself in, Patrick Devine said and he hurried out the door holding Newman's sleeve. —I hope to God we haven't lost them both.

He led Newman over the Tolt Road to a house in the Gut where a man with a wooden leg met them at the door. —Lazarus Devine, the man said by way of introduction. There was a sombre group at the kitchen table, a woman with an infant in her lap, and Amos Devine, the young Nordic boy he'd seen with the albino. There was a man at the head of the table smoking nervously and rubbing his knuckles across a weak chin. —My brother Henley, Patrick Devine said, nodding to the smoker who had nothing like the shock of white hair on Patrick's head.

—You the father? Newman asked.

—I hope to be, the smoker said. He stuttered on the *b* and had to stamp his foot finally to move past it.

—That's my wife, Druce, Patrick said, pointing to the woman with the child in her lap.

Lazarus took the doctor's arm. —We'll have time for all that now the once, he said and ushered Newman to a back room where the pregnant woman lay unconscious on the bed, her breath coming in long, ragged intervals. Newman turned the girl's face toward the lamplight and saw froth speckled with blood at the corners of the toothless mouth. —Jesus Bride, he whispered. She must have been newly pregnant when he pulled her teeth his first day on the shore.

Mary Tryphena was sitting beside the bed. —The baby was coming along fine this afternoon, she said, but Bride's eyes started rolling back into her head just after suppertime. She had a spell of convulsions then, before this come over her.

Newman swore under his breath. He couldn't guess what kind of distress the baby was suffering but the mother had little chance of surviving the severe eclampsia. He looked around the tiny room and cursed again.

Mary Tryphena said, If swearing was any help, Doctor, Bride would be up and around this ages ago.

The bed was narrow and nailed to the wall and Newman called the men in to help carry Bride to the kitchen, clearing mugs and cutlery to lay her out. Patrick's wife stood rocking her own crying child until Mary Tryphena ordered her home out of it. Amos went with her and Henley was headed for the door as well before Newman called him back. —You'll have to help hold her, he said. He unpacked forceps and a scalpel and pushed the unconscious woman's muslin shift high above her belly, cut the perineum from the vaginal canal all the way to the anus. Newman arranged the family around the table, each assigned an arm or leg. Henley weeping and whispering J-J-Jesus Jesus. Newman picked up the forceps and put one foot up on the table's edge to brace himself. —Everyone hold tight, he said.

By first light the baby was washed and swaddled and asleep in a cradle beside the stove. Bride was back in her bed, drifting in and out of consciousness while Newman stitched the ragged folds of skin together as best he could. Mary Tryphena watching over his shoulder. —Do you think she'll live, Doctor?

—With any luck.

—She've had precious little of that the last day or so. You're a dab hand with a needle and thread, Doctor.

He guessed the midwife's age at somewhere north of sixty. Small fine features, a thick head of grey hair shot through with filaments of the deepest black.

The men were sitting about the kitchen smoking as he came through. The table and floor already scoured clean. Lazarus had removed his wooden leg and Newman leaned over to examine the stump. A rough amputation from another lifetime. —Does it give you any trouble?

—Falls over every time I tries to stand on the bugger is all, Lazarus said.

Newman looked across at Mary Tryphena. His head swimming from lack of sleep and twelve solid nights of celebration. —Send for me if the girl's no better by this evening.

It was a full week before he was sure of Bride and he engaged the Trim brothers for a call to Spread Eagle he'd put off to stay close to her. A day of still cold, clear skies and nearly windless, the sound of the dogs' barking echoing crisp off the hills. They stopped in a sheltered valley to boil the kettle and Azariah said, So you been round to see the Devines.

—I have.

—Mary Tryphena says they'd have lost the girl and the baby both if you hadn't come by.

Newman brushed the notion aside. —How did Lazarus lose that leg?

The brothers glanced at one another and shook their heads. They gave a brief account of the hard times that fell on the shore forty years ago, sneaking up on the details. How many seasons the new sealing vessel lay frozen in the harbour before it was able to make its maiden voyage to the ice. Everyone hungry and in debt and there was a fight for berths aboard the ship. The Devines with only two tickets and Lizzie insisted Laz be accompanied by his father. But Devine's Widow wouldn't suffer Lazarus to go to the ice without Judah, thinking it unlucky somehow.

Obediah said, We two was there when she come to the house to ask for Father's ticket.

—We're all fair gone here, Jabez told Devine's Widow. Olive was lying on a daybed near the fireplace, the young brothers fussing over her like spinster aunts. —That's a payment of cash money if we gets into the fat and enough pelts are taken.

—Jude will hand over whatever he makes on the trip. I'll see to that, Jabez.

—I was never much for living off charity.

—That's fine, the widow woman said. —There's Laz's death if he goes off without Judah, she said. —I'm telling you now.

Jabez sighed and got up to put more wood on the fire. There was no logic to the notion but that made it no easier to dismiss.

—I'd be happier having you home, Olive told him. —We'll manage somehow.

The Devines loaded aboard the *Cornelia* the last of March, their boots hobnailed for the ice, a sealing box packed with salt meat and hard-boiled eggs and pork tongues. The *Cornelia* sailed north for the Front with a crew of twenty-nine men and the entire population turned out to see them off, waving and cheering as if they were at a carnival. And that mood persisted until the weather turned two days later. The harbour was blocked with drift ice pushed ashore by an unfavourable wind and in the first week of April two gales blew down from the Labrador. They heard rumours of ships wrecked by the storms, and no one slept for fear of what their dreams might tell them. By the tenth of April survivors from Bonavista and Conception Bay began trickling through on their way home. As many as fifty sealing ships were ice-bound and then wrecked, they said, the *Cornelia* among them. Some sealers were able to reach Belle Isle on foot but were stranded there without food or shelter for days. Those that felt strong and foolhardy enough struck out over the ice toward communities on the Northern Peninsula and from there hitched rides on coastal boats and fishing schooners that were ferrying them home.

The governor dispatched a vessel from St. John's to collect the sealers still stranded on Belle Isle and eventually it arrived in Paradise Deep with most of the *Cornelia*'s crew aboard. Flags at half-mast and corpses stacked like cordwood on the deck, the bodies still frozen in the postures in which they'd died.

—We was all down on the waterfront to see the boat come in, Obediah said. —And not a sound for all the crowd was there. You could hear the chain let go when they anchored off in the harbour.

Boats were rowed out to collect the survivors and the dead and no one knowing still which of the two was being brought home to them. Eleven corpses all told. Seventeen haggard survivors.

Lazarus went through the ice as they made for Belle Isle and soaked himself to the waist, his feet frozen, and he was forced to lean on Judah the rest of the way. On the treeless island the sealers built snow walls to block the wind and trudged in endless circles through the nights, knowing they would perish if they lay down. Lazarus lost all feeling in his right foot and couldn't walk without help. Their last day out he was too exhausted to stand and Judah stripped him of his clothes, wrapping the younger man under his gansey sweater next to his skin. He crouched under the snow wall then and covered them both in Laz's coat. The rescuers found them there like that, huddled one around the other and Lazarus thought dead by all who looked at him. Couldn't separate the two even after they got them carted aboard the vessel. The captain wouldn't allow Judah to go below with the corpse in his arms so he sat out on the deck with a seal pelt for a blanket, a shroud of April snow settling over them. Lazarus didn't so much as open his eyes before he was carried home to the Gut and set before the fire. Devine's Widow cutting him free of Jude's clothes with a knife.

Azariah said, Laz was frostbite to the ankle and the gangrene set in. It was Devine's Widow took his leg off, a carpenter's saw all she had for the job. Az paused at the thought of it. —That woman was a fierce creature, Doctor. Tied off the leg above the knee and reefed it tight, put a horse bit in young Laz's mouth. Cauterized the wound with a poker hotted up in the fireplace.

—Same as she did with her four-legged chick, Obediah said.

The brothers shaking their heads, struck by the odd coincidence book-ending the woman's life on the shore.

—What happened to Callum? Newman asked.

Azariah emptied the dregs of his tea into the fire and rinsed his cup with snow. —Callum never made it to Belle Isle.

—They left the vessel together, but Callum wasn't with them when they reached the island.

—The weather was blowing and he must have fallen behind, lost sight of their tracks. Or just sat for a spell and never got up.

—He was an old man, is what he was, Obediah said. —That gimpy leg of his. Shouldn't have been to the ice at all probably.

—Lizzie went a bit strange after that. She set Callum's place at the table every meal until the day she died.

—And she doted on young Henley when he come along a few years later. She ruined the boy if you ask me. Still wiping his behind when he was near old enough to vote.

—Lizzie wouldn't have let Bride Freke get near the man, I guarantee.

—Why, Newman said, what's wrong with Bride?

—A hard case, she is, Doctor. Hardest kind. Her mother was a Tibbo from over in the Gut, a bushborn she was. Died giving birth to Bride.

—And her father, Jim Freke, he married one of Henry Jolliff's girls then. Loretta.

—Loll never took to Bride, her being another woman's youngster.

—And a bushborn, Azariah said. —Called the girl a Jackie-tar. Treated her like dirt, if you wants the bare facts of the matter. And Bride, she more or less got raised up by her mother's people in the Gut.

Obediah: They caught Bride trying to sneak off with a bagful of their garden soil last spring, Henley and Mary Tryphena did, and they had a row you could hear halfway to Red Head Cove.

—She was stealing a bag of dirt?

—People holds a bit of soil very dear in these parts, Doctor. Years turning in capelin and seaweed to make earth enough to grow a few spuds. There's been blood spilled over half an acre of garden.

—There was no real blood this time, mind. Just Henley holding on to Bride while Mary Tryphena wrestled the soil away and Bride screaming her fool head off.

—Hard to see how they went from a scrap like that to living in the same house with a child between them.

—Almost as odd a match as Mary Tryphena and Judah, those two.

Newman held a hand in the air. —Mary Tryphena is married to the albino?

—All the widow's doing, that was, Azariah said.

—Devine's Widow?

—The same.

—So, Newman said, trying to slow the conversation. —Mary Tryphena is who to the widow?

The Trims shifted on their haunches but there was no other sign of impatience. —Devine's Widow, Obediah said, is mother to Callum

Devine. Callum married King-me Sellers' daughter, Lizzie. He paused to wait for a sign the doctor was following. —Callum and Lizzie had Mary Tryphena and Lazarus between them. And Mary Tryphena is married to Judah.

—And that was the widow's doing?

—You been in Judah's company, Doctor. No woman in her right mind would have him to wed of her own accord.

—They've never shared the same house, mind, let alone a bed. And you can't blame Mary Tryphena for that.

—Still and all, Newman said. —There's Patrick and Henley between them.

—Well, Obediah said, there's Patrick between them at least.

—Now Brother, Azariah warned him.

The dogs were whining and restless in their traces, anxious to get moving, and the brothers began collecting their gear aboard the sled. They insisted the doctor ride the rest of the way and after a token argument he settled under a fur, watching the country pass. He fell into a light sleep and dreamed again of Bride, of her upturned face as he wrenched molars from the back of her mouth, the dark eyes wide and watching him steadily. Of kneeling between her legs to suture the brutalized flesh, his fingers tatting the delicate folds into some semblance of womanhood while Bride whispered to him words he tried and tried and was unable to recall when he finally came to himself in the cold.

It was the consensus on the shore that the Devine men were destined to live in the shadow of their women. And Bride Freke was too much woman for Henley Devine, even so he was twice her age.

Henley was born with the air of someone mistreated by the world and he was pampered and protected and coddled all his young life. His grandmother devoted her every waking moment to sussing out and meeting the boy's needs. It gave Henley the idea his safety and comfort were the sole purpose of a woman's love and this notion ensured he remained a single man through his twenties.

Bride was exactly the sort Henley wanted no part of in a wife, hard-edged and reckless and spoiling for a fight. He'd no more thought of love and marriage when he bedded her than Bride herself. He was drunk and she fucked him as a kind of revenge, to humiliate the helpless stutterer who held her down while his mother stole away her brin bag of dirt. She led him by his cock like a puppet on a string, left him on his back in the moss with his pants around his ankles. She had him twice more, to reef the knot tighter, before she turned her back. Ignored him or mocked his stutter and considered herself done with the man. Four months later she came to Mary Tryphena's house with all her teeth gone and the pregnancy just beginning to show.

—You know that child is Henley's, Bride?

—I do, Missus.

She don't know that for a f-f-fact, Henley said quietly.

Mary Tryphena turned to look at her son. He was rubbing his knuckles against the little chin he was blessed with, as was his habit during difficult conversations. It gave the impression he was hedging when he spoke, that his actual thoughts were different from the ones he expressed. —If you made your bed, Mary Tryphena said to him, you will bloody well lie in it.

—He lay in his bed, Bride corrected her, and now he'll fucken well make it.

Mary Tryphena removed Bride's stitches two weeks after the baby's delivery. She made no effort to be gentle, jigging the thread clear to make the girl's breath catch. She had no idea what circumstances conspired to bring a child into the world through the unlikely couple, but she had little sympathy for the girl or her own son.

The night Henley was conceived, Mary Tryphena told herself it was surrender to fate, to the stars. That threadbare little lie. Absalom pushing the lamp to the back of the table, darkness settling on them like the shade of the inevitable. Never mind he was married and father to five children, the youngest only hours old and asleep beside his wife in an upstairs room. Absalom's hands under her breasts as he kissed her and she'd never been kissed like that before, not once. She could feel his cock when he pulled her close and they shuffled awkwardly to Virtue's bed in the servant's quarters, struggling with clasps and buttons.

—Go easy, Bride hissed but Mary Tryphena gripped and tugged the stitches clear, furious at the memory. She said, It's time you and Henley got married, my maid.

Bride moved into the house the day she announced the pregnancy, but Mary Tryphena wouldn't allow the couple to share a room until they were wed. The girl was raised Catholic and refused to convert simply to satisfy the self-righteous Reverend Dodge, so they kept to their separate beds. They disliked one another but still managed to screw on the sly when they found themselves alone, taking the sex as consolation for their predicament. Bride straddling Henley's lap while she slapped his chinless face or pushed her fist into his mouth. —You long sonofab-b-bitch, she taunted him and he roared through the gag of her hand, nearly bucking her onto the floor. Their only other interactions were arguments about conversion and marriage. Henley threatened to throw her and the baby out if she wouldn't listen to reason. Bride threw shoes and junks of wood in return, forks and knives, a red-hot iron from the stove. Lazarus Devine was just home from a season on the Labrador coast. He could hear the racket from the house he'd built on the stone foundation of the widow's old tilt next door. —She'll as like kill him as marry him, he said to Judah. Through it all Mary Tryphena carried on without taking sides. —Wait until the child comes, she said, and things will settle out.

She tweezed hold of another stitch and pulled. —You can't have that youngster go unbaptized, she told Bride.

—He'll be baptized.

—And which preacher is it you think will christen him before you and Henley are wed?

Bride felt it was an unfair time to broach the subject, she on her back with her skirts around her waist and Mary Tryphena rooting at her down there. It seemed to give the woman an unfair advantage. —He'll be baptized, never you mind, she insisted.

The baby came down with thrush, his mouth cankered white, and the infection made breastfeeding a torture. It felt as if a hundred tiny blades were slicing at Bride's nipples as the youngster nursed. The sweet head of black hair, the innocent appetite. There was no helping the pain and Bride never shed a tear. —You little *fucker,* she whispered as the baby fed, her hand cradling the soft spot at the back of his head. She knew as she'd known nothing in all her life that she was his, that she would do any- thing for him. Mary Tryphena came through the kitchen with a basket of laundry and Bride said, All right Missus, we'll get married.

—It's the proper thing.

But Bride wasn't ready to surrender all say in the matter and she added, We'll join the Methodist crowd.

—Jesus Bride.

—You tell Henley if he wants to marry the mother of his son.

The wedding took place in the plain board Methodist chapel and after the marriage Harold Callum Devine was baptized into the Methodist faith. Bride nursed the child under a receiving blanket while the service went on with hymns and scripture readings, the latch of his mouth like razors at her flesh, the pain so intense it was blinding, all her thoughts wiped clean of thought. Reverend Violet delivered a forty-five-minute sermon, the hypnotic peak-and-vale rhythm of his voice lulling Henley and the baby to sleep. But Bride took it all in. The physical relief when the infant was done nursing was like a heightened state of awareness, her mind clarified and focused. Parishioners began witnessing from their seats after the sermon and old Clar Bozan stood with his hands raised to the rafters. Bride had seen Clar get the glory while he worked on the flakes or walked along the waterfront and she'd always thought him a fool, his head thrown back, his clothes so untidy they looked to have been dropped on him from a height. —Praise the Lard, praise the Lard, he shouted. —Gonna meet me dear old mudder over there.

She felt only compassion watching him now, a pity that felt biblical and maternal both. She knew as she hadn't known anything in her life. She raised her free hand in the air and startled Henley awake when she wailed *Amen* over the noise of the congregation.

Henley stared at his new wife, leaning away from her in the pew. On the night Harold Callum Devine was born he'd been forced to watch the girl cut from stem to stern by the doctor, blood and shit on the table, the baby hauled clear like a tree stump uprooted with axes and rope. Seeing her so helpless and fouled spoiled the girl in his mind and he felt only revulsion at the thought of lying with Bride as a husband was meant. And he was terrified now, watching her overcome by some foreign spirit.

That night she placed the sleeping child between them as if she were drawing a line and Henley made no attempt to cross it. Bride intended the child as a temporary restraint, too raw still to allow anyone between her legs, her mind too full of the Lord's light to think of more carnal pleasures. But Henley seemed to consider himself released for good. They spent years together in the same bed but the marriage between Bride and Henley Devine was never consummated.

Bride's sudden conversion was as complete as it was surprising. She swore off drinking and cursing, she went to prayer meetings and attended church twice on Sundays, she sang hymns as she nursed and changed the baby, as she worked on the flakes and around the house. She took evening instruction at the church so she could read the scriptures on her own. Laz allowed Bride might bore Henley to death dragging him to the interminable Methodist services, but a bloodier murder no longer seemed likely.

Mary Tryphena knew the couple had been stealing time alone when

Bride was pregnant and thought it a hopeful sign, but for all the couple was sharing in the marriage bed Henley might as well be sleeping next door with Laz and Jude. And the obvious distance between the newly-weds mirrored the lack at the heart of her own marriage. The house was quieter with Bride become such a gentle lamb of God and Mary Tryphena was thankful for that. But she couldn't help feeling lonelier in their company.

Lazarus and Patrick came to the house to see her on a Sunday in April. She was watching the baby while Bride and Henley were at the evening service. Patrick took the youngster up, walking back and forth the kitchen with the baby on his shoulder while Lazarus sat at the table and removed his wooden leg, setting it on a chair and rubbing absently at his stump. Laz took a cup of tea and asked how the infant was sleeping and he speculated on the summer's weather and spoke for a time about their mother's habit of setting Callum's place at the table after he died. When he was almost finished his tea he said, Henley wants a spot on the Labrador crew this year. As if it were just one in a series of unconnected notions floating through his mind.

Mary Tryphena glanced at Patrick who was humming into the baby's ear to say the conversation was of no interest to him. They were like vessels tacking east and west in a contrary wind, travelling north in slow tangential increments. Both men born into the sly indirectness that made her childhood a torture.

Laz shifted in his chair. —He come and asked me straight out to hold him a place.

Judah and Lazarus were the first to give up on the local fishery, sailing for the coast of Labrador each May. They found fish galore there and for the last time Jude's talismanic luck drew men from up and down the shore. Hundreds living the same migratory existence now, away from home all summer. Three decades they'd been making the trip, staying through September or October if the weather held, the Devine women left alone half the year to fend for themselves.

Lazarus drank the last of his tea and picked up the wooden leg, set about reattaching the leather straps. He said, You think it's a good idea, him coming down with us?

—Why wouldn't it be?

—He got the itch for Labrador awful sudden. Never showed no interest before. That don't seem like a particular good sign for a marriage, does it?

It was a dodge meant to avoid stating his real concerns and Mary Tryphena snapped at him. —What would you know about what's good for a marriage?

Lazarus stood up and tapped the floor several times with the peg leg, like he was testing the strength of ice on a pond. There was talk he'd long ago taken an Eskimo bride in Labrador, that there were half-breed children down there christened Devine. —I expect I knows as much as you do, he said, managing it somehow without a hint of meanness.

Mary Tryphena and Judah hadn't touched one another in years by the time Henley came along. Jude arriving home from Labrador in the fall to find his wife pregnant. Henley's birth in late February was a subject of much speculation on the shore, and even if the timing hadn't aroused suspicion it was obvious there was nothing of Judah in the boy. His skin fair but not pale, his little tuft of hair black as sheep shit. There was an awkwardness to the welcome the new child received from family and neighbours, as if he'd been born with a deformity they were studiously ignoring. Jude was civil to the boy but there wasn't a single moment's ease or affection between them. Henley never ventured into the house next door and never found his footing with the men. Lizzie tended to the youngster hand and foot, as if to make amends for sending her husband to his death on the Labrador ice fields, and Henley settled among the women where he trusted he was welcome.

Lazarus was at the door when Mary Tryphena said, What does Judah think of Henley going with you?

He smiled at her, embarrassed to have the issue addressed so squarely. —Jude's not saying one way or the other.

—Patrick will watch out to Henley if he goes, she said. And she nodded at her son, as if he might need to be encouraged in the undertaking.

—All right, Lazarus said.

Patrick settled the child on the daybed when Lazarus left, a straw pillow as a guard to keep him from rolling off the edge. He asked for the tea he'd turned down earlier and sat in the chair Laz had just vacated. Mary Tryphena puttered with cups and sugar and then leaned over the youngster to see if he needed changing. —You're upset, she said to Patrick.

—I'm not upset, he said.

But there was no disguising the whiff, that telltale mark of his father rising up in him. —Don't lie to me, Patrick Devine.

—Henley don't know his arse from a hole in the wall, he said.

—Well if you haven't got it in you to look out for your own flesh.

—Jesus Mother, he's liable to get killed down there. Why are you taking his side in this?

Mary Tryphena couldn't say, other than Henley needed someone to take his side where the men were concerned. Patrick was fifteen when Henley was born, old enough to do the math. He'd married Druce Trock at eighteen to get out of the house, to put that distance between himself and the truth about his brother, building a house on the edge of the Little Garden.

—You didn't put the idea in his head to come? Patrick asked her.

Mary Tryphena looked into her lap. —I'm not that spiteful, she said.

Two hundred local men and boys loaded their gear and provisions aboard a Sellers vessel bound for the Labrador in mid-May. The clergy offered prayers to bless the summer's enterprise before the men rowed out to the ship at anchor in a steady drizzle. Henley facing the ocean as he went, not so much as lifting a hand in farewell.

The American doctor was there to witness the exodus, shaking hands and trading stories and offering medical advice among the crowd. Mary Tryphena was at the waterfront with Bride and the baby, and Newman made a point of stopping to see them. He held his namesake in the air a moment, as if guessing his weight, before settling him back in his mother's arms. —He's as fat as a calf, he said.

Absalom and Levi Sellers were on the docks to oversee the loading of provisions and Mary Tryphena watched them discreetly. Levi stood with his hands on his hips, saying something to Absalom over his shoulder and gesturing out at the vessel where Henley clambered aboard with the rest of the Devines. Absalom staring off in that direction, his head weaving slightly. He turned to the crowd then, searching faces, and Mary Tryphena looked away to avoid him.

The rest of the month and the whole of June was relentless drizzle and fog. The women spent their time clearing the Big Garden of stones turned up by the winter's frost and hauling in capelin and seaweed to fertilize the soil. Bride badgered Patrick's wife and daughter into attending the Methodist services and they took to the faith like ducks to water, Druce and Martha converted by the time the potatoes were set. The three of them singing the seeds into the ground together.

It was gone the end of July before Absalom came to see her, though she'd been expecting him every day since the men left for Labrador. Mary Tryphena alone with Bride's infant child while the other women were at Sunday evening service. He pushed the front door open just enough to peer inside.

—Come in if you're coming, she said impatiently.

Absalom set his walking stick against a chair but refused to sit down, leaning to one side to favour the worst of his knees. He'd been a legendary walker in his prime, earned the nickname Mr. Gallery for the miles he covered on the roads through the country, for the sullenness he turned on anyone who crossed his path. But his legs had crippled up and he could barely walk the length of himself now without a cane. —What in God's name is Henley doing down on the Labrador? he said.

—He asked for a spot on the crew.

—You know he's not made for that kind of life.

—Patrick promised to look out to him.

—Hell's flames, Absalom said, which was as close as he came to obscenity. He limped across the room to look at the baby on the daybed and shook his head. —How Henley got tangled up with the like of Bride Freke is beyond me.

—Judge not, Mary Tryphena said and Absalom winced as if from a physical cramp. They were both embarrassed to be dealing still with their one act of indiscretion, so ancient now it almost seemed to have happened to other people.

Mary Tryphena had never served as midwife to Ann Hope before being called to intervene in Levi's birth. The infant stalled in utero after crowning and she spent half the evening dickering the baby's shoulder past the bridge of cartilage between the pubic bones, Ann Hope so exhausted she drifted to sleep between contractions. Levi arriving blue and frail and Mary Tryphena stayed on to watch him until the moon had set. She left Virtue to keep an eye on mother and son then, making her way downstairs and along the hall toward the servant's entrance. She assumed the rest of the house was asleep but Absalom stood from his chair at the sound of footsteps, turning to face Mary Tryphena as she came into the kitchen. —Did you need something, Mrs. Devine? he asked.

She glanced at the table where he'd spent the night and most of the evening before, flipping through ledgers by the light of Ralph Stone's lamp, feeding wood to the fire to keep the kettle simmering over the dog irons. —I was just on my way, she said. —But for one thing. She walked past him to the cupboards, opening doors until she found what she was looking for, reaching for a teacup placed upside down on the highest shelf. Absalom stared at her with his head to one side. —I thought it might be some help to Adelina, she offered by way of explanation.

—This has something to do with her warts, does it?

—I had Virtue put it up there for me, she said.

—Does Ann Hope know about this?

Mary Tryphena passed the cup across to him. —I doubt Virtue would have come to me without your wife had sent her.

He looked down at the cup, turning it in his hands. —I guess that's one more thing we're in your debt for, he said. —There isn't a mark on Adelina to say the warts were ever there.

The room was close with the fire's heat, Absalom's shirtsleeves rolled to the elbow. They hadn't enjoyed a moment as private since they were children in the branches of Kerrivan's Tree, watching Father Phelan's festival of debauchery on the Commons. Absalom set the cup on the table beside a draughtsboard he'd used to distract Adelina while they sat waiting for news the previous evening. Mary Tryphena reached a hand to fuss idly with the checkers. In a dark room at the back of her mind she could hear Devine's Widow calling her a vain fool to have brought out the cup in Absalom's presence, to be standing in the kitchen still. She stared at the table to avoid his eyes. —Is this King-me's checkerboard? she asked.

—His board, yes. Most of the checkers were missing when I was a youngster. We used to play with stones.

—I remember watching you, she said. —On the beach that time. She stopped there to avoid mentioning Judah.

—I had the missing pieces replaced years ago, he said and held one up. —Would you like to try a game?

—I don't know the first rule of it.

—Child's play, he said. He placed the wart cup on the windowsill and pulled the board toward them, inviting her to sit. —White leads, he said when he finished explaining the mechanics of the game. They made their alternate moves in a slow dance, the white and black drifting into hybrid patterns, a competitive intimacy to it that felt illicit. Mary Tryphena moved a checker the last square to the far side of the board. —King me, she said.

Absalom placed a second checker atop the white, aligning it carefully with his index fingers. —Are you sure you've never played this game before?

—You're letting me win, Mr. Sellers.

Absalom raised his hands in a gesture of surrender.

—I should be getting on, Mary Tryphena said.

Absalom reached out to turn the lamp back, the room settling further into darkness. —You've the loveliest hair, he said.

Bride's baby stirred on the daybed suddenly, the little limbs jerking in a spasm as he woke. Mary Tryphena crossed the room and lifted him into her arms.

—You're certain this one is Henley's boy? Absalom said.

—Motherhood is a certainty, she said, but fatherhood. She was quoting Devine's Widow to make light of the situation, but Absalom only winced again as if she'd kicked him. She said, Henley married the girl, Mr. Sellers, he must think as much.

—Hell's flames, Absalom said, lifting his face to the ceiling. —I wonder if we'd ever married, Mary Tryphena. Would I have killed you or you have killed me?

It was the closest he'd ever come to acknowledging the note he left for her when she was a girl. She was on the verge of asking what possessed him to use those bizarre biblical endearments, but Absalom seemed to regret the mention of marriage. —Ann Hope will be worried if she finds me gone after church, he said.

—As she should be, I spose, Mary Tryphena said quietly. She'd expected the sting of shame would ease over time but just hearing Ann Hope's name made her face burn. The new mother lying with her infant in an upstairs room as she shuffled to Virtue's bed with the child's father, Absalom falling on her with his pants around his ankles. They lay still after he came, both aware of the house suddenly and listening for voices or footsteps. Mary Tryphena's arm was levered awkwardly behind her back and she'd lost all sensation in the limb beneath their weight. —Get up, she said, shifting under him. —Get up, get up. He rolled away and she pulled her clothes together as best she could, wanting out of the house.

He tried to say her name but the ghost of his old stammer had come back to haunt him. It was the first thing people noticed when he returned from England, that he'd all but conquered his childhood stutter. He grabbed her wrist to make her wait, hauling his pants up with his free hand. —I have s-s-something, he said.

She waited in the kitchen for him to come back from his office and he handed her an envelope. A kernel of something hard in the bottom, a stone or a dried seed or what. She shook it out and a shard of white clattered on the tabletop. She picked it up to take a closer look. A little wave of shock and revulsion rolling through her when she realized what she was holding.

—I thought you should, he said. —I don't know. It doesn't b-belong to me.

He placed the tooth back in the envelope and pressed it on her, as if it was payment for a debt, as if that tooth would free him of any claim she might have. He was God's own fool, she thought. The spasm of revulsion galled the back of her throat and the sour flavour stayed with her for days afterward. She could still taste it now as the events played over in her mind, these years later.

Absalom turned away from Mary Tryphena and the baby to retrieve his walking stick, eager to be gone. There was something odd about him, Mary Tryphena thought, a vulnerability she hadn't seen in him since he was a boy, and she felt the need to give him something before he left. —The youngster has your eyes, she said. But Absalom was unable to look at her directly, raising his walking stick in mock salute as he stepped out the door.

He walked with his head down toward the Tolt Road, thinking, as he always did after seeing Mary Tryphena, about that tooth in its envelope. He'd gone looking for it the day after he married Ann

Hope, walking back and forth along the path without knowing he was searching until he spotted it in the grass. Unable to explain that urge to himself even now. Kept it tucked away for years before he pressed it on Mary Tryphena, to make amends somehow. To have something more pass between them than a sordid little tryst in a servant's bed. Her husband's tooth. Hell's flames. He was God's own fool, and if ever proof were needed.

He couldn't avoid feeling watched as he walked to the Tolt but if there were faces in the windows, he was too blind to tell for certain. Only Ann Hope and Levi knew his sight was failing and not even Levi knew how quickly it was leaving him. He'd lately found it impossible to read or make entries in the account logs and he finally had the doctor come see him at Selina's House. Newman turning Absalom's face to the light of an upstairs window, moving a finger across his field of vision. He sat back and folded his arms. —How many fingers am I holding up? he asked.

—Somewhere between one and five, Absalom said. He asked Newman how long he had before he was completely blind.

—Months, the doctor said. —Years perhaps, but not many.

—Don't tell my wife.

—I'm right here, Ann Hope said from across the room.

It seemed to him his body was in open revolt, hot coals flaring in his joints as he walked down the Tolt Road. The path was wide enough now for horse and cart but it was studded with roots and stones and Absalom walked with his head at an odd angle, trying to watch his feet from the corner of his eye. He stumbled on the path, flailing to catch himself, and he felt exactly like the ridiculous old man he appeared. His entire life's endeavour about to pass on to a son who despised him. —Hell's flames, he said aloud.

King-me was thought to be a wealthy man but the truth was he'd nearly bankrupted himself by the time he died, licked out by grief for the wife he didn't know he loved and ranting about the nightmare fate of his sealing vessel. Absalom put little stock in dreams but King-me unnerved him with sheer repetition, with his detailed litany of disaster. He overinsured the *Cornelia* and came through her loss with money enough to finance a larger vessel that enjoyed better luck on the ice. He added a second, then a third schooner to the fleet, and the annual harvest of seal pelts brought in just enough to offset the losses incurred in the cod fishery. It was a delicate balance that a single lean year could sabotage. And there was no way to make more of the operation with most of what the shore produced going directly to Spurriers.

The firm was known as Spurious & Co. when Absalom worked as an apprentice in the accounting department in Poole. Cod prices collapsed at the end of the Napoleonic Wars and the undercapitalized business was kept afloat with one dubious financial sleight of hand after another. Ann Hope's brother stayed on in the accounting office and his letters kept them abreast of the increasingly outlandish maneuvers. Absalom leveraged a purchase of the company's assets on the shore months before a fraud investigation sank Spurriers for good. The transaction made a reality of King-me's charade, leaving Absalom owner and lord of all he surveyed, though it wasn't until the shift into the Labrador fishery that Sellers & Co. managed to post a profit. And by then Absalom had lost three children to the Boston States. The eldest married and gone before Levi was born, the two older sons following in quick succession. And all three lobbied their parents to sell off and come to the States as well.

Ann Hope was uncharacteristically silent on the topic, though it was obvious what was in her heart. Most people on the shore were still dressed in rags, their children afflicted with rickets and consumption, only a handful could recite the alphabet, despite her lifetime crusade against squalor and ignorance. Nancy's letters were full of music and theatre and poetry readings, church bazaars and tea parties, market stalls filled with vegetables and meat of all descriptions. Fresh tomatoes. Pears. Just the words on the page brought a knot to her throat.

But she never so much as hinted at her opinion, wanting her husband to do this one thing for her without being told. It made a sullen walker of Absalom in the last half of his life. To have so consciously disappointed his wife.

By the time he descended the Tolt Road the streets were busy with parishioners on their way home from evening worship. Levi and his wife were at Selina's House when he arrived, seated in the living room with Ann Hope and Virtue while Adelina served tea. He took his seat beside Virtue as if he had just returned from a quick visit to the kitchen.

—How was your father's sermon? he asked Flossie, addressing the person least likely to ignore him.

—If you are so interested in the theological musings of Reverend Dodge, Ann Hope said, perhaps you should have attended the service.

—Fresh air was all the blessing I needed this evening. Walked out the Tolt Road as far as the Pond.

Reverend Dodge arrived after dispersing the last of his congregation and once he was settled with a cup of tea he said, We missed you at church this evening, Absalom.

—I converted to the Methodists, Absalom said. —Like everyone else.

Dodge pursed his lips to say he understood the comment was meant to be humorous.

—I expect you'll be preaching to an empty church before long, Reverend.

—The Lord works in mysterious ways, Mr. Sellers, he said.

Levi was turning his cup in circles on its saucer during this exchange and he waited until he was sure it was done before he spoke. —I've heard reports from several sources this past week, he said. He used his most perplexed and innocent tone. —That Dr. Newman made a call at the house?

—He came to have a look at my knees, Absalom lied.

—They've been bothering you more of late? Levi had his mother's nose and seemed always to be looking down that eagle's beak as he spoke.

—I'm an old man, Absalom said. —Everything bothers me.

—And what miracle cure did the good doctor offer that made you want to walk out as far as Nigger Ralph's Pond this evening?

—Levi, Ann Hope said.

Adelina set her cup in her lap and sighed. Virtue reached to take Absalom's hand and she smiled across at him with her vacant look of affection. The old housekeeper was the excuse he gave when Levi or Flossie or Reverend Dodge raised the possibility of a retirement to the States. Virtue wasn't well enough to leave behind or take with them, he said. And there was enough truth in it to give the claim some conviction. But everyone sitting in the parlour knew Absalom chose to stay for the sake of Mary Tryphena and for Henley, a man he'd never spoken to directly.

Even to Absalom it made little sense, cleaving the family he had for an illegitimate son he couldn't acknowledge. But he couldn't bring himself to leave Henley behind completely, to vanish from his son's life as his own parents had. Thinking an opportunity would come to make things right if he stayed close and waited.

The Labrador crews began returning by mid-September and the Devines arrived home on the afternoon of the twenty-third. Patrick's oldest boy, Amos, had grown half a foot over the summer. Mary Tryphena wouldn't have recognized him but for the white hair and the pale pale blue of the eyes. Henley nodded warily to Bride when they reached the garden and she held the baby up for him to see. At the house the men stripped off their clothes in the yard where the lice and fleas would be boiled out of the seams. Judah stood a little off to himself and Mary Tryphena couldn't help taking him in. He looked almost normal among the group of naked men, their torsos the same cold slug-white under the one change of clothes they'd lived in nearly half a year. The same hum of filth rising from each and every one.

It struck her that Judah had barely changed in the years since she'd first seen him naked on the landwash, his age still a mystery to judge by sight alone. Time had been kind to him, she thought, though the notion was a poor gloss for what she actually felt and couldn't articulate to herself. That something in the man seemed to stand apart from time altogether.

They were all in a fine mood. They'd made a good voyage of it, the fish cured to a high grade. No one was killed, there'd been no injuries beyond cuts and bruises. Amos was given his head with the rum bottle the season's last Saturday and he'd thrown Laz's wooden leg on the fire. And even that event was already reduced to anecdote, a story to amuse themselves and tease the youngster. Lazarus stood naked in the cool September air holding the new peg leg he'd carved during the voyage home, the straps fashioned out of leather salvaged from an old apron.

—D-don't let Amos near the stove, Mother, Henley shouted. —He'll have every chair in the house b-broke up for f-firewood.

Laughter all around. Even Judah managed a tired smile. And Mary Tryphena allowed herself to think perhaps it had been for the best.

Years followed the same migratory pattern. Henley slept chaste beside his wife through the winter and took what pleasure could be found on the Labrador during the fishing season. Even Harold Callum Devine could sense his father's habitual lean northward and he never warmed to the man, as guarded saying his goodbyes each May as when the stranger arrived home in the fall.

Patrick and Amos followed the women into the Methodist fold. —We spends enough time apart, Patrick said, without going to separate churches every Sunday. Martha had inherited Callum Devine's gift and she was a major attraction at the services, singing out over the congregation during the hymns. Her white hair like a saint's halo shimmering with the palest colours of the northern lights, her voice like the voice of a creature only half-human. She and Bride accompanied

Reverend Violet on his summer mission trips along the shore, Bride witnessing to the change Jesus made in her life, Martha leading the motley congregations through half a dozen hymns.

The Trim brothers volunteered their boat as transportation for the mission trips and the American doctor sometimes travelled with them to pull teeth and lance boils on the stagehead. Reverend Violet was leery of allowing a hardened apostate to accompany the evangels, but came to appreciate how physical relief and spiritual rebirth could follow one on the other. Bride became a kind of nurse during these trips, assisting during procedures requiring an extra hand, working with Newman until the service began. The sound of Martha singing "Rock of Ages" or "Amazing Grace" would steal the last of his patients and he followed them up to watch from the doorway. Bride and her youngster taking up a collection of pennies while Martha lifted her face to the wooden rafters. Those raw and unlettered congregations startled by the hint of grace in her voice, half of them in tears to hear it.

Bride's son had long ago been nicknamed Tryphie, in honour of Mary Tryphena's legendary inquisitiveness as a girl. Bride could see Newman found children trying and she did her best to shield him from the boy. But confined aboard the Trims' thirty-footer, there were inevitable interrogations.

—You're American, Tryphie said, staring at the doctor, and Newman admitted he was. The boy wanted to know if the doctor's mother and father were American as well, did he have brothers and sisters and were they American, did he have a dog, a horse, a cow and were they all American? It was exactly the kind of child's questioning Newman found exasperating though he did his best to hide it around Bride. —Yes, he said, my dog is American, my horse is American, my cow is American.

Tryphie nodded his head slowly. —You don't belong here, he said finally.

—No, Newman sighed. —I don't.

—What is it brung you then?

The doctor shrugged elaborately. —I have no idea.

—You been called here by the Lord, Bride offered. —Me and Tryphie is all the proof you needs of that. And she quoted from Psalms. —By thee have I been holden up from the womb, thou art he that took me out of my mother's bowels: my praise shall be continually of thee.

Newman felt the heat rising in his face and he looked out to open water. —Your Reverend Violet is the expert on religious questions, he said.

Bride said, If there was no one calling you, Doctor, you'd have left us for long ago.

—Amen, the Trims said.

Newman leaned in close to Tryphie, desperate to shift the conversation elsewhere. —I have a Spanish pig at home in Connecticut, he said. Five minutes later Bride ordered the boy to stop pestering Newman with questions about the Spanish pig. She said, You may live to regret that fanciful creature, Doctor.

Newman nodded. He thought of *regret* as Barnaby Shambler's word. —Any regrets, Doctor? Shambler asked each time the doctor committed to yet another contract extension.

—Not a one, Newman said and the answer felt more evasive every time.

He lived alone in the clinic, the woman who occupied his thoughts in rare moments of quiet was married and born-again beside, the work relentless and most of what he could do for people provisional or useless. It didn't amount to much of a life, looked at through his father's eyes. He'd travelled home to the States on three occasions in the past five years, touring to raise funds for clinic equipment and medicine, trying to explain the place to industrialists and politicians and professional philanthropists. He spoke at colleges, at men's and women's clubs and churches, in the private drawing rooms of the wealthy. He brought along his medical pictures and wide-angle portraits of buildings perched over the ragged coastline, the images so outlandish they had the air of forgeries, like photographs of fairies in a garden. His audience intrigued and amused by his stories, peppering him with endless questions about the Spanish pig.

He'd been called from the clinic to the shoreline one spring, pushing through a wall of spectators to find Matthew Blade kneeling in the shallows, cradling his intestines against his belly. His brother James was crouched beside him, both boys with bloodied faces. Someone reported the fight had started at Shambler's before migrating to the landwash, as if this explained the state of things. Matthew was scooping careful handfuls of seawater, flushing away the sand that coated his guts when they'd spilled onto the beach. At the clinic Newman examined the intestine strand by strand before packing it into the stomach cavity. The incision made by the knife was almost surgical, slicing through the abdominal wall without causing any internal damage. He stitched the layer of muscle and then set about closing the surface wound. It was a miracle, Newman told the brother, that the intestine wasn't perforated. —Will he live, Doctor? James asked.

—If he stays out of Shambler's and away from knife fights, he might have a chance.

James was nineteen and the older of the two brothers by a year. —I'll watch out for him, Doctor, on my mother's grave.

—Who was it cut him, James?

The boy's face went brick red. —I only said something about his girl as a game, to get his goat, Doctor. He got a fierce temper, Matthew have. I wouldn't have used the knife if I didn't think he meant to kill me.

Matthew nodded out of the ether fog sometime through the night and he left the clinic with James in the morning, leaning on his brother's shoulder for support. Newman found them sitting together when he stopped by Shambler's that evening, Matthew showing off his stitches to everyone who came through the door. They toasted the doctor from across the room and stood him a glass of rum and went arm in arm into the dark when they left the pub.

Hannah Blade came by the clinic two days later, taking her hands out from where they were hidden under her apron. The girl was only seven or eight, her adult teeth just coming in. Red hair and a ribbon of freckles across the bridge of her nose. She held out the eggs to him, two in each hand. —For patching up Matthew, she said.

—Your father sent along half a barrel of salmon yesterday, Newman told her.

She nodded, proffering the eggs again. —They're awful good to me, Doctor, she said. —James and Matthew.

Newman took them from her one by one, the shells still warm from sitting in the folds of skin webbed between the girl's fingers. —How is Matthew doing?

—No worse than James, she said. —Father hauls him out of bed first light every day, sets him to chopping wood. To teach him a lesson, he says. Matthew is only stacking, on account of the stitches.

Newman turned away to hide his smile from the girl. —Thank you, Hannah, he said and she tucked her empty mermaid hands under her apron before going out the door.

Even to Newman, the country he spoke of in Connecticut or Boston or New York felt impossibly remote. Newfoundland seemed too severe and formidable, too provocative, too extravagant and singular and harrowing to be real. He half expected never to lay eyes on the place again, as if it didn't exist outside the stories in his head. A riptide of relief running through him each time he sailed back into Paradise Deep to find Barnaby Shambler with Ann Hope and Absalom Sellers on the dock, Azariah and Obediah Trim, and a choir of Sunday school children singing a welcoming hymn. Judah and Mary Tryphena and the rest of the Devines further up the landwash. Bride with her close-mouthed smile and the curious little one hanging off her dress. No regrets in that moment at least. And the crowd followed him up to the clinic where they presented the afflictions that had befallen them while he was away.

———

By the time Tryphie was six years old Absalom was blind and too crippled to leave Selina's House. Virtue Gallery passed in her sleep two winters before and Absalom lost the heart to fight his own slow decline with her gone. He retreated to his bedroom where he received the few visitors he was willing to see, his legs too weak to chance the stairs. He resigned his position as justice of the peace and gave up the business to Levi's oversee, though he still vetted and approved all decisions. There was a weekly meeting in the sickroom where Levi provided updates on quintals and hogsheads and gallons. It was the only real conversation the two men had managed for years past. And even then there were disagreements, subtle insults, the most innocuous discussion dragged into their long-drawn-out struggle. Absalom could feel his son bristling across the room. —Will that be all, Mr. Sellers? he asked before leaving. Levi had his mother's perfectly English accent, which felt willful to Absalom, one more way their son chose sides between them. He'd thought Levi would forgive him one day or simply grow tired of carrying such a single-minded hatred. But they were running out of time.

Ann Hope tried to talk her husband into relinquishing the work altogether. —The meetings are too hard on you, she said.

—It's bad enough to have Levi trying to rush me out.

—Levi isn't rushing you.

—He can't wait for me to die, Absalom said.

His wife insisted on a weekly appointment with the doctor, hovering in the background while Newman listened to his heart and lungs and inquired about the regularity of his bowel movements, about his appetite and how well he was sleeping. The questions seemed pointless to Absalom and he fired off inquiries of his own in response, as if he and the physician were involved in a wrestling match.

—Why aren't you married yet, Doctor?

—Only death is inevitable, Mr. Sellers.

—An insensitive remark to make to a man in my position, Absalom said. —And a falsehood besides.

—I apologize on both counts.

—A man will marry, Absalom said. —It's in his nature. If not a woman, he'll marry his work. Or the bottle.

—Quite the philosopher you're becoming, Mr. Sellers.

—My mind wanders, Absalom said. —It's all the legs I have left.

—Deep breath. And exhale.

—Have you had a drink already this morning, Doctor?

—I'll do the examining if you don't mind.

—Let me save you the trouble. I'm dying. And you've been drinking. I can smell it.

—One more deep breath, Newman said.

After the doctor let himself out, Ann Hope scolded her husband. —You shouldn't provoke him so. He'll refuse to see you if you carry on like this.

—I'd be no worse off for that.

—Don't talk that way.

Absalom sighed heavily by way of apology. —I married well, he said. —That's as much as a man can ask of the world.

Ann Hope straightened and took a step away from the bed, not willing to indulge him. —Reverend Dodge has asked to come by this afternoon.

Absalom sighed again and turned his face toward the window, as if he might actually see something through the glass.

—You've refused him three times now, Absalom.

Dodge had talked of retiring back to England before he was widowed but appeared to see no point in the notion now. He'd officiated at his own wife's funeral and carried on in the ensuing years with his insufferable single-mindedness, even as his congregation steadily dwindled. Just the sound of his octogenarian footsteps on the stairs set Absalom's teeth on edge, the blinkered energy in them.

—Have you noticed, he asked his wife, how often the reverend has taken to saying the Lord works in mysterious ways?

—No, she lied, I hadn't.

—What was it he used to say? About Providence?

—Providence takes care of fools.

—He's not as bold as all that anymore, Absalom said. —Now it's all the Lord's mysterious ways with him.

—You make him sound like a real livyer, Absalom.

He smiled and reached for her hand. It was the unlikeliest transformation to think Reverend Dodge a Newfoundlander at heart. Though the change made the man no more likeable. —I can't suffer it, he said. —Not today.

The only people Absalom never refused were Azariah and Obediah Trim. The three men reminiscing about the shore when they were young, wandering through the histories their lives intersected at different angles, Jabez Trim's Bible and Judah born from the whale's belly and the loss of the *Cornelia*. Az and Obediah growing up terrified of seeing Mr. Gallery in the droke or crossing paths with him in the backcountry, how they sometimes mistook Absalom in his wanders for the murderer's ghost. Absalom pointed blindly to the ceiling, telling them Mr. Gallery had come through this very roof, feet first and the man dead a year by then. How he'd swept up the plaster dust himself after Virtue left the house with Mr. Gallery trailing behind her.

They had never been close as younger men, but their conversations created the illusion of a shared past that was a comfort to Absalom. The brothers brought Jabez Trim's Bible to read aloud to him as he grew frailer. Obediah made his way through the truncated story of Isaac one afternoon, the child left tied and helpless under Abraham's knife. There was a rare silence among them afterwards, all three thinking of Henley and Levi. Both sons bound in their way by Absalom and neither seemed likely to be spared.

—Father told us James Woundy liked to write his own endings to that story, Azariah said. —All of them bad.

—Perhaps James Woundy was a smarter man than he let on, Absalom said.

After the brothers left, Ann Hope came to tell him Levi was waiting downstairs. Absalom pushed himself into a sitting position, lifting his legs one at a time over the side of the bed as his son came up the stairs. —Hello Levi, he said.

—Mr. Sellers, sir.

—What do you have for me today?

Levi gave a clipped summary of the latest reports from Labrador on catches and weather, the price they might fetch for Labrador green and West Indie in the fall. He said, It's been a wet summer, we're likely to see a quantity of dun fish not worth the salt used to cure it.

—There's no sense worrying about the weather, Absalom told him. —It'll make you old before your time.

—Yes sir, he said.

—Don't patronize me.

Levi turned the hat in his hands in an endless round. —Yes sir.

Absalom took a laboured breath. —You expect all this will be yours soon enough, he said. —The business.

—Soon enough, Levi repeated, yes sir.

—I'm afraid, Absalom said and he lay back on the bed, too tired to sit up any longer.

—You're afraid, sir?

He shook his head on the pillow.

—Should I fetch Mother?

Absalom raised one hand and then coughed a rope of blood onto his nightshirt. Levi shocked into stillness by the obscenity of it.

—What is it? Absalom asked. —What's happened?

Levi left Selina's House after the doctor arrived, asking that any news be sent along directly. He went straight home and shut himself in the office, sitting among his account books and ledgers while he tried to quiet his breath, to stifle the tremor in his legs. His wife knocked at the door. —You look as if you've seen a ghost, Flossie said.

—No, he said. —Not a ghost.

—Would you like some tea?

He nodded and after she left the room he thought on what exactly it was he'd seen against the white of his father's nightshirt. The sight terrified him, but the fear was braided with something murkier—a kind of awe, to see his own heart laid bare before him. It was like a sign that his life was about to begin in earnest.

He couldn't fix in his mind when he learned the truth about his half-brother. He'd singled out Henley for abuse long before the question of paternity arose, the youngster was a sook and a stutterer which made him an easy target. The sting of their fraternal connection came to Levi over time, knowledge he grew into like clothes handed down within a family. The reality of his mother's humiliation, to be teaching her husband's bastard son his letters and arithmetic.

When Flossie returned with the tea, Levi had recovered himself enough to smile up at her. She came around the desk and placed her hand against his forehead. —I'm fine, he said.

His wife was a mouse of a woman, brown-haired and slight. Levi had barely taken note of her before he turned twenty-one, when Adelina suggested they marry. His sister and Florence Dodge were kindred in their insular seriousness, in the isolation that was part and parcel of their families' standing on the shore. It was only in Flossie's company that Adelina was unselfconscious about the warts afflicting her and they swore a sisters' fidelity to one another as children. It was the thought of losing Flossie that kept Adelina from following her siblings to the Boston States and she brokered the match with Levi to formalize the sisterly relationship between them. Levi had a house built in a far corner of the north garden above Selina's House and Adelina moved into a spare bedroom a month after he and Flossie married.

—Where's Adelina? he asked.

—She's upstairs with the children.

—The doctor is at Selina's House, he said. —Perhaps she should go sit with Mother.

By the time the Labrador crews returned in the fall Absalom was said to be on death's door and the business turned over completely to Levi Sellers. Levi revoked credit to the most desperate debtors on the shore and sent constables to repossess what little materials the bankrupts owned. There were altercations and bloodshed and half a dozen debtors were jailed in the old fishing room while they waited for the governor to appoint Levi the new district justice.

Absalom recovered enough by mid-September to eat toast and tea and soft-boiled eggs and to sit at the window with a blanket across his legs, but he heard nothing of what was happening in the wider world. The doctor insisted that visits be kept to a minimum and Ann Hope refused to allow the meetings with Levi to continue. —This is not a prison, he protested. —You are not my warder.

—It's worse than that, I'm afraid, she said. —I am your wife.

The notion was enough to tamp down what fight he had left and Absalom approached the end of his life in a state of enforced ignorance not unlike his earliest years in Selina's House.

Ann Hope catered to his every need through the day and she sat up with him at night, wearing herself thin with the vigil. She refused her daughter's offers to share the load. —You can't carry on like this on your own, Adelina warned her.

—In sickness and in health, Ann Hope said.

There was something fearsome in her mother's sense of duty that Adelina wasn't willing to challenge. But she moved back into Selina's House where she might at least put food in front of the woman, encourage her to drink tea, to nap.

Levi spent the fall leaning his full weight into the business, order-ing his cullers to bump ten percent of the season's catch to cheaper grades across the board. When the Devine men came to settle their accounts they were told two-thirds of their fish was West Indie and vir-tually worthless. Levi and Lazarus yelling at each other across a desk, half a dozen hired men throwing the Devines off the premises. A lamp was smashed in the process, one of the hired men required stitches, and Levi added the damages to the Devines' account.

Levi's vindictiveness was the talk in every household on the coast but for Selina's House where the dying man insulated them from the daily round of news and gossip. When Adelina answered a knock at the servant's door off the kitchen early in October she had no reason to expect Mary Tryphena. —I needs to see Mr. Sellers, she announced.

Adelina retreated behind the door. —You shouldn't be here, she said.

—I'd be happy to wait at the front of the house if you rather, Mary Tryphena told her.

—One minute, she said, closing the door. —Please.

Ann Hope was half-asleep in the chair by the window and Adelina called her from the sickroom in a whisper. She had to repeat herself several times to make Ann Hope understand who was waiting down-stairs. Her mother walked to the hall window and looked down at Mary Tryphena who was facing away from the house, taking in the row of outbuildings and barns that Absalom had put up in the past forty years, the gardens fenced and under cultivation, the sheep pens, the dozen horses grazing in the fields. —Go in and sit with your father, Ann Hope told her daughter.

She stopped at the hallway glass at the foot of the stairs, trying to find a suitable face to present to the woman. Her pulse visible in the pale skin of her temples. She stepped through the kitchen to the back door. Mary Tryphena was still looking out over the property and Ann Hope had to clear her throat to get her attention, then stood back from the doorsill.

They sat at the kitchen table, facing one another for the first time since the night Levi was born. Ann Hope folded her hands on the tabletop.

—I needs to speak to your husband, Mary Tryphena said.

There was something infuriating in the nonchalance of the statement. Your husband. She'd been looking about the property with the same casual innocence while she waited, without the slightest inkling it was all down to her.

Ann Hope long ago recognized that everything Absalom set out to make of himself was for lack of Mary Tryphena Devine. Every quintal of fish, every pelt-laden schooner, every stick of wood in every vessel and building, every calf and foal and lamb, every egg laid by every hen. She thought it impossible the woman could be oblivious to the truth of that. But she saw now Mary Tryphena had no idea Absalom loved her still. Ann Hope felt something give way in her chest, a sudden spring of feeling like milk coming in after giving birth. Little rivulets of anger and despair seeping through her. Somehow Mary Tryphena's ignorance made her betrayal less forgivable.

—Mrs. Sellers, Mary Tryphena said. —I don't expect you'd be happy to see me. And I wish I could have spared the visit, given how Mr. Sellers is feeling so poorly. But I don't know where else to go given what Levi have done to Lazarus and his crew.

—I'm afraid I have no idea what you're talking about.

—We got youngsters will go hungry this winter. Your own blood some of them.

—Not my blood, Mrs. Devine.

Mary Tryphena took three deep breaths. She said, I didn't come here to beg. I come to ask for what's fair and proper. Levi got no right to change the culler's grade of those fish and give us less than we deserve.

Ann Hope stood from her chair. —My son operates his business as he sees fit. I can't help you.

—If I could have a word with your husband.

Ann Hope smiled down at her guest. She was angry enough she thought she might be sick. —Absalom and I did not marry for love, Mrs. Devine, you know that. But I've been a good wife to him. Better than you had it in you to be.

Mary Tryphena stood herself then and walked to the door before turning back to the woman at the table. —We'd been better off if I let you die in the bed, she said, you and Levi both.

Adelina came downstairs when she heard the door and found her mother still standing at the table's edge. She eased Ann Hope into a chair, set the kettle over the fire.

—How is your father?

—Still sleeping.

Ann Hope nodded. She reached for Adelina's hand, ran her fingers over the smooth skin. No sign of the warts that made her childhood such a torture, just the scars of the knife she'd used as a six-year-old to try and dig them free. From the moment the girl was born there was talk she was afflicted by some ancient curse laid on King-me Sellers, which made Ann Hope's stomach churn. It was bad enough Adelina was forced to endure her singular disfigurement, she thought, without adding superstition and dread to the mix. Half a dozen people told her Mary Tryphena Devine might charm her daughter free of warts but Ann Hope dismissed the notion so coldly they felt obliged to apologize for the ridiculous suggestion.

Adelina gouging at herself with a knife then, the sleeve of the child's dress red with blood. It made her daughter's despair so palpable that Ann Hope sat up half the night with Virtue, bawling helplessly. —I know you don't want to hear talk of it, Virtue said. —But I can go over to the Gut and see Mary Tryphena.

—You think this is some kind of curse too, I suppose.

Virtue shrugged. —If there's some relief to be offered the child, why keep it from her?

Ann Hope was about to give birth to Levi and she cradled her massive belly in both hands, shaking her head.

—Mary Tryphena might not even have to step foot in the house, Mrs. Sellers.

The baby kicked against her hands and Ann Hope turned them palm up to stare at them. —You won't tell her I sent you.

—I'll take care of this, Virtue said.

The following evening Virtue made Adelina a cup of tea, as she was instructed. The girl was sent out of the kitchen when she finished, the dregs emptied into the fire and the cup placed upside down on the highest shelf in the cupboard. Ann Hope was standing at the door, watching. —No one touches that cup, Virtue told her.

In the morning Adelina found the warts lying loose around her in the bedsheets, each the size and texture of a raisin. Virtue gathered them up, enough to fill a teacup, and she burned the lot in the stove. Adelina was surprisingly subdued to find herself cured overnight, thinking she might just as easily wake some morning to exactly the opposite. And the relief Ann Hope felt was followed by a stubborn uneasiness. As if she'd surrendered some part of herself to the shore for good.

She went into labour three weeks later, the baby stalling as he crowned, and after several hours without progress Virtue gave her an ultimatum. —I can't be any more help to you or that infant, she said, and I won't be the cause of the child's death, may God help me.

A hired man was sent to the Gut to fetch Mary Tryphena and things went as well as could be expected once she arrived. Ann Hope even managed to feel a grudging admiration for the woman's impersonal effectiveness, her discretion.

She was supposed to lie in a week after the delivery but never could stand the enforced idleness. She hobbled downstairs when she woke the next morning, walking gingerly along the hall toward the servant's room where Virtue was watching Levi. She stopped to catch her breath in the kitchen, one hand on the back of a chair. Saw the single cup on the windowsill where Absalom had set it. She couldn't explain it to herself still, how seeing the cup there told her what she had no other way of knowing.

That evening Absalom came up to the bedroom where she lay with the baby. He stood at the bedside and held out his hands, but Ann Hope made no move to pass the child to his father. —You will not see that woman again, she said.

Absalom let his hands fall back at his sides.

—Promise me, Absalom Sellers, or so help me God.

He took a step back. —I never meant, he said.

—That will be all, thank you, she told him and she settled Levi closer to her breast.

They never spoke of the incident again, though it circled their lives like a moon, its tidal pull sucking at their heels. Henley Devine coming into the world nine months later, his hopeless stammer in her classroom. Ann Hope treated him like any other student, to protect Levi from the truth as long as she could. Strapping her own son when she caught him mimicking the bastard child's stutter.

Adelina put her free hand over her mother's. —What was it Mrs. Devine wanted?

—You don't mention that woman to your father, Ann Hope said.

In the last weeks of Absalom's life, Ann Hope closed off the sickroom to everyone but the doctor. She thought there was something purposeful in her husband's tenacity, something in particular that was keeping him alive. A declaration to be made, some duty unfulfilled, and Mary Tryphena's unexpected appearance at Selina's House filled Ann Hope with dread.

It was a shock still to see herself such a pessimist, so vindictive. She'd arrived in Newfoundland determined to turn the wheel of progress a notch and managed only to grind herself down on the implacable rock of the place. She still spoke the language of reform but she'd lost her faith years ago. Ann Hopeless. Greedy to cling to what little was left her. There were whole seasons of her life when Mary Tryphena never entered Ann Hope's thoughts. But she could see now that every day since Levi's birth had been a fight to surrender nothing more to the woman. She lived in fear of Absalom asking to see Mary Tryphena before he died, but the only visitors he showed any interest in were the Trim brothers. He mentioned them several times a day and eventually she relented, instructing them not to indulge in idle chatter that might tire or upset him.

The brothers spent their time in silence while Absalom slept or read to him from Jabez Trim's Bible. Azariah read the story of Ishmael, prophesied by an angel of the Lord to be a wild ass of a man, his hand against every man and every man's hand against him, and destined to dwell over against all his kinsmen. Absalom smiled grimly up at the ceiling. —That sounds like my Levi, he said.

—He's a hard man all right, Obediah said quietly.

Absalom moved his head on the pillow. —Has something happened?

—Not since, Azariah said, no.

—Since what?

The brothers glanced at one another. —We oughten to trouble you sir, Azariah said.

—It's too late not to trouble me.

The blind man's face twitched as they gave a brief account of Levi's activities, Absalom raising his hand for silence finally, struggling for air. The Trims stood from their chairs. —Go fetch Mrs. Sellers, Obediah said.

Ann Hope set him lower in the bed once he'd recovered himself, the brothers waiting against the wall to say their goodbyes, solemn and regretful, feeling they'd ruined what little time the dying man had left in the world. Absalom passed days in silence, unable to speak a word to his wife or daughter. He felt he must have poisoned Levi somehow, sleeping with Mary Tryphena in the servant's quarters while the youngster took his first tentative breaths upstairs. Half a lifetime then waiting to be reconciled to one son before he could put things right with the other. Even as his life was reduced to this single upstairs room, to the deathbed he lay on, Absalom had managed to nurse the fantasy some miracle would spare him setting them one against the other for good.

When he woke from his fitful bouts of sleep he could tell there was someone in the room, his wife or daughter keeping an eye on him. A difference in the quality of the silence, occupied space. —Who's there? he asked.

—It's Adelina.

—I need to speak to your mother.

Ann Hope came into the room in a rush. —What is it? she said. —Can you breathe? Are you feeling ill?

—Sit down, he said.

She pulled the chair close to the bed and took his hand.

—I need to speak with Henley, he said. Absalom squeezed her hand to keep her close. —I need you to bring him here without Levi knowing.

Ann Hope extracted her fingers slowly, folding her arms across her breasts. —You aren't well enough for visitors, she said.

He reached in the direction of her voice. —I know it's unfair to ask you, he said. He could hear the sound of weeping muffled behind a fist. —But I won't die with this on my head. If you feel anything for me at all, Ann Hope.

She blew her nose and tucked away the handkerchief. —Let me think about it, she said.

His time passed in sleep broken by brief moments of consciousness, the quiet of someone in the chair beside him or an empty room. He had no sense of how many hours or days passed before Ann Hope knocked lightly at the door and announced, There's someone here to see you.

He could hear the man breathing where he stood just inside the door. —Tell him to sit, he whispered to Ann Hope.

—He won't sit, she said. —He didn't want to come at all.

—Give us a moment alone.

Absalom turned his head toward the door when Ann Hope left. —Thank you for coming.

—What do you w-w-want?

Absalom nodded to hear his childhood affliction echoed in his son's voice. He cleared his throat. —You know I'm your father, he said.

There was no response but Absalom could sense the silence in the room shifting, like colours turning in a kaleidoscope. —I don't expect you to forgive me, he said.

—Wh-wh-why am I here?

—I have six children. Three live in the United States and each will receive an equal monetary inheritance. Levi is responsible for my wife and for Adelina and he will inherit fully two-thirds of my estate and business interests. Which leaves one-third for you, Henley.

—I don't w-want your god-d-damn money.

Absalom raised his hand. —My wife will have the papers drawn up, he said.

—F-fuck you, you b-b-b—he stamped his foot to shift the word ahead—*bastard*.

Absalom heard the door. —Henley, he said. But the footsteps were already halfway down the stairs. He tried to call out to Ann Hope but didn't have the breath for it.

He woke hours later, the house submerged in the stillness of early morning. —Who's there? he asked.

—It's me, Absalom. It's Ann Hope.

—Did you talk to Henley before he left?

—He was in rather a hurry. He looked very unhappy.

Absalom repeated what he'd told his son then, outlining the changes he promised to make to his last will and testament. —He claimed he didn't want my money but he'll change his mind once I'm gone. I'll be easier to forgive when I'm dead.

Ann Hope laughed then, a harsh little bark.

—Will you do this for me? he asked.

—I'll have the changes made, if that's what you want.

—We can't use the company lawyers. Go see Barnaby Shambler, have him draw them up.

—All right.

Absalom took a quick breath. He said, I never deserved you, Ann Hope, I know that for a fact.

—Perhaps I'll forgive you once you're dead as well, she said.

Sleep seemed to drift down upon him from some great height, he could almost hear it as it approached, the weight of it like fathoms of ocean above him. He woke to the sound of a whispered conversation. —Who's there? he asked.

—Mr. Shambler's here to see you, Ann Hope told him.

—Hello Mr. Sellers.

—Did you bring the papers?

He could hear the man shifting in his chair. —I did, yes. He said, It's not my place to tell you, Mr. Sellers, but I don't see how this will help matters.

—You're worried what Levi will do when he finds out you witnessed these papers behind his back.

—I'm too old to worry, he said. —And old enough to know that doing the right thing isn't always advisable.

—Spoken like a true politician, Absalom said. He held his hands out in front of himself. —Show me where to sign.

Ann Hope spoke to no one at the funeral. She'd already packed the trunks she was taking to America and she was done with every soul on the shore but her husband who had only to be set into the ground.

The Episcopalian chapel was full to overflowing for the first time in years and the mourners talked of nothing but the length of Absalom's illness and Ann Hope's faithfulness, her unwavering vigil, which would have tried the nerve of a mule. She refused to leave the sickroom to eat or sleep or wash her face the last seven days of his life. Newman stopped in to see Absalom morning and evening though there was nothing to be done, he said, but wait. He lifted the bedcovers to examine the dying man's feet, a mottled purple climbing past the ankles toward the knees. —Hours now, he said. —Days at best.

Ann Hope sat in the chair by the window and waited for Absalom to die. He rarely spoke or opened his blind eyes, but she was with him each time he came to himself. —Who's there? he asked, though he was addled and sometimes uncertain who he was speaking with.

The funeral procession rimmed the harbour along Water Street and inched toward the Tolt Road. There was a carriage for Adelina and Florence and the children but Ann Hope insisted on walking to the French Cemetery. She kept her hand in the crook of Levi's elbow, Absalom's coffin an arm's length ahead of them on the cart. She was still furious, though the anger that sustained her felt more diffuse now, its object less clearly defined. She felt an odd kinship with her husband to be saddled with the weight of an action so irreversible. She had listened outside the sickroom as Levi gave his flawless imitation of Henley's stammer, reminded just how skillful a mimic he'd been in school. The little stamp to shake a particularly stubborn word loose. F-fuck you, you b-b-bastard. That part of the conversation, at least, had been genuine.

All that was left to do afterwards was guide her husband's hand to the bottom of a blank page while Barnaby Shambler told Absalom he was a fool, though he admired the man's moral fibre to be so concerned with what was right and proper. He went through the motion of signing his own name beside Absalom's illegible scribble and left the room with a smile on his face.

It had been appallingly easy to orchestrate, and watching Shambler at work almost undid Ann Hope, his businesslike act of deceit setting a niggle of guilt to simmer in her belly. She came to see something of her husband's long-time prison in herself after the fact and she felt unexpectedly sentimental toward him in those final days. She camped out in Absalom's room, turned him one side to the other every hour, wet his dry lips with a cloth, refused Adelina's offers of relief. Relief was the last thing she wanted.

Hours before he died Absalom stirred in the bed beside her, the dry, cracked lips moving a moment before he managed to find his voice. —Who's there? he whispered. It wasn't forgiveness exactly, but she found herself willing to set him free of what she knew was holding him still. She leaned forward to take his hand. —Absalom, she said. —It's Mary Tryphena.

{ 6 }

ABSALOM SELLERS WAS BURIED in the French Cemetery in November. The following April, Tryphie fell into a barking pot on the beach while the fishermen were curing their herring nets for the season. Fir bark and spruce buds were kept on the boil in a large iron cauldron, the concoction ladled into half-barrels where the twine was soaked before being laid out on the bawn to cure. A handful of boys horsing around nearby, Tryphie and Patrick Devine's eight-year-old, Eli, leading games of pitch-and-toss and tag while the men shouted at them to mind their step, to keep clear of the fire, to shag off home out of it.

The tubs stood only two foot high and Tryphie tipped backwards into the steaming water trying to avoid Eli's tag. The men were spreading their nets on the rocks below and it was only Eli near enough to help. He grabbed Tryphie by the shirtfront and without thinking dipped a hand under his back to pull him out. Neither boy felt any pain, just a sudden breathless shock that was almost pleasurable. Eli led Tryphie up off the beach to avoid having the men see the state they were in and they were halfway home before the scald kicked to life.

Martha was alone when they came through the door. She stripped Tryphie out of his clothes, the sweater still hot and clinging to the flesh of his back. The bald outline of the burn from his shoulders all the way to the left hip and buttock. She sent Eli to get Mary Tryphena while she tried to quiet Tryphie's bawling with a spoonful of honey.

A crowd gathered at the house as news spread, all staring at the naked boy kneeling over Martha's lap, his back lobster red. Bride gathered blankets while the boy's father went after a handbar. They lay Tryph on his stomach and covered him and started out for the Tolt Road, the youngster wailing and begging for a drink of water.

Newman heard them coming and followed his patients outside. Saw Bride half running toward him, one hand under the quilts piled on the handbar, the other holding her skirt clear to keep up with the stretcher. A man at his shoulder said, I 'llow you'll earn your keep today, Doctor.

Tryphie was unconscious when they carried him in. Layers of ruined skin peeling away when the blankets were lifted. There were two dozen people in the room and Newman had trouble locating a pulse amid the babble. He ordered everyone out but Bride and Mary Tryphena. —One-forty, he said aloud. There was severe swelling and capillary dilatation in the damaged areas and the boy's blood pressure was bottoming out. —He's in shock, he said, still talking to himself. —We're going to lose him.

—He'll live, Doctor, Bride said and he glanced up at her. —We got him here to you, he'll live.

There was something distressingly erotic in her surrender to the compass of his knowledge and skill. —You'll have to help me, he told her.

—Tell me what to do.

Newman thought it possible there was a God after all.

There was an extension built onto the clinic with an examination room, a crude operating theatre, and six beds for in-patients. But after Tryphie stabilized, Newman had him moved upstairs in the main house, laying the boy on his stomach in a tent of sterile sheets. He jerried up a wooden frame to keep the sheets clear of the burn, a kerosene lamp under the bed for heat. The sheets and pillowcases were sterilized in gentian violet and at night the lamplight made the room glow like a Sacred Heart, the pale, unearthly purple visible through the window outside.

Tryphie was in a coma for seventeen days. Even after he regained consciousness Newman told Bride the risk of infection made his recovery unlikely.

—He'll live, she said.

—It'll be months yet before he's out of danger.

Bride said, You know we got no way to pay for all this.

—Now Bride.

She raised her hand. —And you got no one here to help.

—Miss Sellers comes by three days a week when the school year is done.

—I knows all about Adelina Sellers, Bride said.

Adelina passed out at the sight of blood, the smell of urine and vomit made her nauseous, she was more nuisance than help. Newman occasionally lured medical students to Paradise Deep for internships and twice an American nurse spent a winter at the clinic, but the dark and cold and relentless work drove them off. Newman resorted to a regular cocktail of ethyl alcohol flavoured with blueberries or partridge-berries to survive the grind alone. Twice in the past year men came by to pay him for birthing children he had no memory of delivering. It was a matter of time, he knew, before he maimed or killed someone.

—Everything happens for a reason, Doctor, Bride said.

The Devine men left for the Labrador in mid-May and Bride moved into the room across from Tryphie, Newman sleeping in an outbuilding with a bunk and stove for propriety's sake. She cooked and laundered and assisted during procedures as anaesthetist and scrub nurse. She had the stomach of a soldier and a nose for the rare shirker or hysteric, culling them from the doctor's lineup with suggestions of an imminent amputation or enema. She saw patients when Newman was away on calls, triaging and performing simple dental procedures, admitting the truly desperate and keeping them alive until the doctor returned.

Tryphie wasn't out of immediate danger until August when the threat of infection passed. Eli Devine started to make regular visits to see him as soon as he was allowed and Newman made a point of examining Eli's scalded hand when they crossed paths in the hall. —That looks to be coming along fine, he said.

Eli helped Tryphie out of bed and they spent the visit kneeling at the window. Tryphie wore a johnnycoat that tied loosely across the back and Eli couldn't avoid the sick sight of it. Ridges of black scab and pus and scarlet new skin. He could guess the torment Tryphie was suffering from his own injury and he did his best to divert his cousin's attention, fabricating elaborate histories for the vessels at anchor on the waterfront. Even the most pedestrian flat-bottomed tub battled storms and pirates and giant squid that had to be fended off with axes and swords in order to make harbour in Paradise Deep.

At first he did his best to make Tryphie laugh as well, before he saw how excruciating laughter was. Eli staring out the window as his cousin bawled through the pain, a sick roil in his gut. It was an intimacy too adult for the boys, layered with guilt and frustration, with affection and pity and resentment.

At the end of that summer Bride asked the doctor when Tryphie might be well enough to go home. Newman had been gathering information from his father on advancements in skin grafting for burn victims which could ameliorate the disfigurement. It was experimental, he warned her, and promised to be torturous. But left alone, the scar tissue would make a severe hunchback of the boy. Bride surprised Newman by crying at the thought of what lay ahead for the child, it was as if she'd stepped out of her clothes in front of him, and he excused himself to offer some privacy. Though he would have cut off an arm for a few moments more in the presence of that nakedness.

He didn't understand how living in close quarters with Bride could make the woman more exotic than she was at a distance. She was pious and demure and all spine, she was peregrine and aloof, a vulnerability about her that she could bury or wield like a stick. All summer he was sick with wanting her and dreading the return of the Labrador crews in the fall. Even if Bride stayed on as a nurse she would move back to the Gut with Henley Devine and that cloud followed him as September descended. He spent his free time in the backcountry with a muzzle-loader and a horn of powder and the thought of Bride in another man's bed. He shot at anything that moved in the landscape, using his surgeon's scalpel to skin fox and rabbit and grouse, beaver and lynx. He slept under the stars to prepare himself for the black void of losing her.

Newman was miles inland on the barrens when the Devines returned from Labrador with Henley's corpse, the man dead since the first week of August. A seven-foot shark took his line as it was set, Henley hauled overboard by a boot tangled in the twine. He was dragged five fathoms under, half-drowned and unconscious when the crew managed to lift him above the gunwale. Henley never opened his eyes again, though he held on three days before he died. Judah Devine built a casket of spruce and they covered his body with the salt meant for curing fish to keep it long enough to be shipped home and buried.

Bride was on the wharf when Laz and Judah and Patrick angled the rough spruce box onto the stagehead. The men silent as they raised the coffin, a bashful look about them, as if they were sneaking home after a night of drinking. —Someone should go tell Mary Tryphena, she said.

The casket was set out in the parlour, doors and windows propped open against the smell. Mary Tryphena stayed with her son while Bride made arrangements for the burial and she felt gutted, sitting with a hand on the coffin, the cover nailed shut weeks ago. She couldn't avoid cataloguing Henley's failings as she sat there, he was juvenile and spoiled, selfish, self-centred, intemperate, he was a lousy husband and father, he was myopic and feeble and solitary. Mary Tryphena had loved him as compensation for all he lacked, fiercely and without reservation, knowing she was alone in her devotion.

Tryphie wasn't well enough to attend his father's funeral and was relieved to be spared the event, not knowing how he was meant to react to the stranger's death. There was more awkwardness than grief among mourners at the church, an embarrassment to feel the loss so little. Judah helped dig the grave and waited alone there during the service, staying to bury Henley after the prayers were said and Bride had tossed her handful of dirt on the coffin lid.

No one spoke of it openly, but the Devine men expected Henley's death would mean the end of their persecution by Sellers & Co. It was a surprise to find themselves screwed over a second time when they settled up their accounts in September. Levi refused even to allow Judah through the office door. —That white bastard stays outside, he shouted down the room.

By Christmas the Devines had exhausted their dried peas and flour and salt pork. They had a root cellar of potatoes and turnip and their fall fish and a barrel of pickled salmon and the charity of neighbours to see them through to Lent. Bride took up permanent residence as nurse and housekeeper at the clinic which offered some relief to the household in the Gut. She prepared Newman's meals and washed his clothes, she cleaned the operating theatre and disinfected the surgical tools and chopped firewood. She studied his medical books to learn as much as she could about adenoid removal, tonsillectomies, abscess drainage, amputation of the fingers and toes. She had the fire roaring before Newman rose in the morning and read three chapters of the Good Book by lamplight each evening before wishing him good night.

Newman lying awake hours in the darkness, wondering how long it was proper to wait before asking for a widow's hand.

There was a general election set for the winter after Henley Devine was buried in the French Cemetery. The shore's Irish population had long ago edged ahead of the English, but Protestant Tory Barnaby Shambler was the only member the district had ever sent to the House in St. John's. The Irish vote was always split between the priest's man and one or another mad-dog candidate, and Shambler rode that divide to victory like Moses crossing between the parted waters of the Red Sea.

But Shambler's margin of victory was steadily narrowing as Father Reddigan took steps to unite the Catholic vote. Reddigan was the first Newfoundland-born clergyman to serve on the shore, with little invested in the politics of the old countries. His nation, he said, was Newfoundland and all Newfoundlanders were his countrymen, his kin. It was an attitude that threatened to make a Liberal candidate irresistible. During the most recent election Shambler felt compelled to surround the polling station with a mob, instructing them not to let Catholics pass unless they swore to vote Conservative. The mob was armed with staves and seal gaffs and Catholics carried the same to defend their right to suffrage. The brawling began in the morning and carried on until the polls closed, with Shambler holding his seat by the skin of his teeth.

Father Reddigan filed a suit with the returning officer demanding that the tainted results be voided, and a delegation from the Gut descended on the officer's house to protest when the suit was dismissed. They cut the timbers and set hawsers to the eaves and pulled the building to the ground before they butchered his five head of cattle in their stalls. As they walked back to the Gut they threw the bread his wife had in rise into the ocean. Seven members of the mob were whipped at the public whipping post and marched in halters to the wreckage of the house where they received twenty lashes more. Reparations were paid. And the shore settled back into some semblance of calm. The genius of democracy at work, Shambler called it.

But the coming election was ruining his appetite. Father Reddigan lobbied for and was granted a separate polling station in the Gut, making Shambler's mob redundant. There were rumblings of dissatisfaction among the Methodist teetotallers. Matthew Strapp was expected to run for the Liberals, a planter educated by Jesuits in St. John's, owner of three flakes and a stage, two gardens and eight head of cattle, twenty sheep and twelve pigs. A staunch anti-confederate, a moderate drinker, father to seven children, he had no enemies, no obvious weakness. Shambler, who'd always been able to make any brawl serve his interests, attacked the Catholic Church itself to hold his support among the Methodists. Anonymous broadsides appeared on the shore decrying the Papist influence on Newfoundland politics, calling the Roman Church a bulwark of superstition, depravity and corruption with no place in the Legislature of the country.

His only other trump card was the considerable influence of the local merchant. Shambler had betrayed blind old Absalom Sellers on his deathbed to keep Levi from crossing to the Liberals. And he was tied to the man now, for better or worse. People often compared Levi to King-me Sellers, but the resemblance was superficial to Shambler's eye. King-me would skin a louse to make a cent. He had no talent for or interest in human endeavour except where he could insinuate some consideration of money and profit. Levi's motives were never quite as obvious. There was an Old Testament ruthlessness about him, Shambler thought, something inscrutably tribal at the root.

Matthew Strapp announced his candidacy in early December and his barn was burned to the ground a week later. The animals were let loose before the fire was set and only the building was lost, but Strapp took the warning at face value and withdrew. No one with Strapp's property and credentials was willing to risk standing in his place and by Christmas it was clear the Tory seat in the Legislature would go unopposed.

The season was a week-long celebration at Shambler's public house, the proprietor presiding till the wee hours with a lecherous generosity, with winks and nudges and knowing looks. Bands of drunken Tories wandered the streets and fell in with the mummers roving house to house. Levi Sellers was not a drinker or a social creature and he waited till Old Christmas Day to make his obligatory appearance, setting his public seal of approval to events as they'd unfolded. He took a seat in a corner, hugging a glass of brandy diluted with water while the room pitched and rolled around him. Shambler had just that fall imported a plate of Wellington teeth from England to replace his own, the set scavenged from corpses on some European battlefield or from the mouths of executed criminals. His cadaverous smile made Levi's skin crawl and he refused to look Shambler in the face when the Honourable Member came to the table.

—I half expected not to see you, Mr. Sellers.

Levi raised his glass an inch. —I wouldn't be so miserable.

—Well if you're in such a fine mood, Shambler said, I've been wanting to talk to you about Selina's House.

—You aren't going to make me regret coming, Mr. Shambler.

—Dr. Newman thinks it would make a fine hospital.

—He does.

—The clinic is too small by half for what the shore requires. And Selina's House is going to rot boarded up so.

—And how does the good doctor plan to buy Selina's House?

—Well now, Shambler said. —Can I get you another? he said and Levi shook his head. —We were thinking it would be a gesture of good will to the people on the shore, he said. —If it's only going to rot there as it is.

Levi stood from his chair and pulled on his overcoat. —I'll give it due consideration, he said.

Shambler insisted he have one more drink before leaving but Levi ignored him. He stood outside a moment to let his eyes adjust to the black, sorry to have come. The indigo glow of the snow under stars all there was to light his way home. He started around the ring of the harbour, the noise of Shambler's muffled by the frost. He turned up Sellers' Drung toward Selina's House which had been sitting empty since his mother left for Boston. He stood below the building in the dark, thinking what a scabrous bastard Shambler was to suggest giving it up for nothing. As if it was something Levi owed. Any debt between them was settled the night Strapp's barn burned to the ground. And he'd see Selina's House fall in on itself before Bride Devine and her son of a bastard moved in there with Newman.

He heard voices coming his way and carried on toward the lamps in the windows of his own house. He could make out a group approaching from the Gaze, mummers dressed in castoffs and rags, their faces hidden under veils.

—Master Sellers sir, the man in the lead said, using that grating ingressive voice. He was wearing a brin sack dress and a crown of spruce boughs and carried a sceptre improvised from a barrel stave.

—Gentlemen, Levi said.

—Have you any drink for a poor mummer, sir? the lead man asked with a hand on his arm. Levi shook free and carried on walking. There were three of them and the mummers crowded close at his back and to either side. —Perhaps a bit of salt pork, sir? the man in the brin dress asked. —A bit of flour? A bit of cocoa or tea?

It was useless to run, he knew, so he turned to face them. The night so silent he could hear the mummers breathing raggedly under their masks.

—I don't believe Master Sellers heard you, a second mummer said. —Speak up for the good sir.

—A bit of salt pork, Master? the brin dress repeated, stepping in close. The others had circled around to hem him where he stood.

—I bid you a good night, gentlemen, Levi told them.

—He's ears do not work proper, the brin dress announced. —Perhaps you needs a operation, Master Sellers. Perhaps we'll have to fix 'em up for you.

The mummers were on him before he turned, his arms pinned to the ground while the brin dress drew a fish knife from his costume of rags. —Give ear, he said, to the words of my mouth.

Levi screamed bloody murder before he blacked out, a foul whiff in his nostrils as he went under. Servants alerted by the racket brought him inside. Newman was sent for and he swabbed the wounds with alcohol, clearing away the blood. Flossie and Adelina hovered near with a lamp, their breath catching in their chests. The lobes and half the cartilage sliced off both ears. Adelina fainted dead away and had to be carried to her bed. Levi came to while Newman was suturing and he struggled to sit up, trying to fend off the doctor. Mummers, Levi shouted, he'd been set upon by a band of mummers. —Hold him still, Newman told the servants at his shoulders.

Levi was up as soon as the bandaging was done, shouting orders. He took a pistol and four servants to Shambler's public house where he swore in a dozen drunken constables. They collected torches and rope, and every drinker at Shambler's followed them out the door, Levi leading the party over the Tolt Road. The stench that overwhelmed him still in his nostrils.

It was the second time in her life Mary Tryphena woke from the dream of a mob descending the Tolt Road into the Gut. The distant light of torches just visible as she went across to Laz's house to wake the men. She shouted at them to get up, the panic in her voice prodding them from their beds. She could hear Lazarus struggling with his wooden leg, fumbling with the straps, and she went into the room to help. — What is it, maid? he asked.

—Someone's coming for Jude.

Judah's face appeared at the door and Lazarus shouted at him to leave. —I'll be right behind you, he said, go on now.

By the time they'd gotten the leg attached the torches were moving in the yard outside. Mary Tryphena said, I'll go talk to them. She stepped into the red light, not able to pick out a single face among the crowd. —What is it you wants? she shouted. A figure detached itself from the mob of shadows and approached her, Levi's oddly accessorized head coming clear in the dim, white muffs at his ears. —You got no business here, Levi Sellers.

Levi waved a handful of men forward and they forced past her. Lazarus was dragged out in his shirtsleeves, his hands tied behind his back. Patrick came running from his house across the garden with Amos and Eli behind him. Levi turned to the constables. —Arrest them all, he said and he held Mary Tryphena as the Devines were wrestled to the ground and bound. —Where's the white bastard? Levi said. —The foul one, where is he?

—You've done enough to this family, Levi Sellers.

Levi put a hand behind one of the elaborate bandages taped to the side of his head. —Pardon me, Mrs. Devine, he said, I'm having a little trouble with my hearing.

The houses on the property were turned out and the neighbouring houses and the rooms on the waterfront, but there was no sign of the Great White. The Devine men were marched out of the Gut with halters around their necks, young Eli at the front of the column. Druce and Martha stood weeping in the yard with Mary Tryphena, watching the torchlight ascend the road and disappear over the Tolt. The night was windless and cold, the first glim of morning in the sky, and Mary Tryphena took them into the house where she lit a fire and set it roaring against the chill.

Before the day was fully gone to light Druce took Martha upstairs to bed and Mary Tryphena slipped outside, standing in the cold to listen awhile, testing the quiet. She made her way along the path to the outhouse and called to Jude from the door. His arms coming up through the hole like the pale shoots of some exotic winter plant.

She was surprised to think Father Phelan and his stories would sit so close to the surface of her mind and Judah's, these years later. Back in the house she knelt on the bare floor to pray for all her dead and gone, for Father Phelan and for Callum and Lizzie and for Devine's Widow, for Absalom and for Henley wasting in his shroud of salt in the French Cemetery. Druce came back down to the kitchen and she paused at the door, surprised to see Mary Tryphena on her knees, the woman crossing herself before getting up. Druce was embarrassed to

have disturbed her and uncertain what to make of the Catholic gesture.
—You were praying for the men, Mrs. Devine?

Mary Tryphena shook her head. —Prayers are no use to the living, she said.

For three days constables searched the Gut for Judah. Levi posted a reward of fifty dollars for information leading to his apprehension, though no one came forward. Eli Devine was only nine years old and Barnaby Shambler convinced Levi to release him, but the other Devines were held in the abandoned fishing room in use as a prison. Opinion on the shore was divided as to whether the attack was meant as payback for the burning of Strapp's barn during the campaign or retaliation for Levi's ruthlessness as proprietor of Sellers & Co. There was no shortage of people with a grudge against him, some of whom had threatened flesh or property, but no one else was questioned.

Newman visited Levi to change his dressings and he conducted a casual interrogation while examining the sutures. —They were disguised as mummers, is that right?

—Rags and bags and women's clothes, the works of them.

—They had their veils on, did they?

—Of course they had their veils on.

Newman straightened from his work. Levi's enormous nose was precipitous, his head unnaturally square. The loss of the ears wasn't going to do the man's appearance any favours. —How did you identify them, Mr. Sellers?

—The smell, he said.

—The smell?

—There's only one person on the shore with that stink on him, Doctor.

—You mean Judah?

—Of course I mean Judah.

—Hold still, the doctor said, and he worked in silence for a time. Newman had long ago figured out that Absalom Sellers was Henley Devine's father. He didn't understand Levi's particular hatred for Judah, the innocent cuckold in the affair. He seemed to despise the man for mirroring his own humiliation to the world so passively. —I don't mean to play counsel for the defence, Mr. Sellers, but what is your justification for holding the men you have in custody?

—You have just made a very close inspection of the justification, Doctor.

—But your evidence, such as it is, applies only to a man not yet apprehended.

—Birds of a feather, Levi said.

—None of this could possibly hold up before a judge.

—You forget, Doctor, that I am the judge.

Newman reported the gist of the conversation to Bride and she walked the Tolt Road after supper to speak with Mary Tryphena. Patrick's crowd had moved over from the house at the edge of the Little Garden to stay with her and they were all at the table, Druce, and Martha who was helping Eli with his letters, the boy copying Bible verses she'd written out on a scrap of paper.

—Dr. Newman thinks Levi's got no case, Bride said.

—Levi will see them hanged, every one, Mary Tryphena told her.

—Hush now, Druce said, nodding toward the youngsters.

Bride said, Levi couldn't sit as accuser and judge, is what the doctor says.

Mary Tryhpena waved off the technicality. —Then he'll have one of his merchant friends from St. John's sit the case. The result will be the same, mark my words.

There was an acrid undertone to the air at Mary Tryphena's that suggested Judah was listening in from the pantry or the upstairs hall. Bride said, Does Jude know what's happening at all?

Mary Tryphena glanced toward the stairs. —How would you tell?

He came down to them then, as if the mention of his name was a signal. Mary Tryphena said, I told you to stay in out of it, Jude.

Bride nodded up at him. —Hello Judah, she said. His strangeness was so familiar to her as a child that it barely registered, the smell of the man and his chalky skin, his fish eyes, his mute good nature that made him seem harmlessly retarded. But there was a strangely purposeful look about his face now, fear and resolve and an incongruous peacefulness. He stepped to the table to look down on the work the children were doing, moving the slate and shifting the lamp close. He turned Martha's slip of verses facedown and reached for the pen, dipping it into the inkpot. He glanced at the women sitting across the table and began writing.

Mary Tryphena stared at Judah as he worked. —Have Patrick been teaching this one his letters?

—He never mentioned any such thing, Druce said.

Judah blotted the ink with sand, shaking the excess onto the floor before extending the page toward the women. The letters were so ornate it took Bride a moment to recognize the verse. —Let the enemy persecute my soul, and take it; yea, let him tread down my life upon the earth, and lay mine honour in the dust.

— Gentle Redeemer God, Mary Tryphena said.

—It's from Psalms, Martha said.

—We know where it's from, maid.

Druce said, Where ever did he learn his letters, I wonder.

Mary Tryphena was staring at her husband who had retreated from the table to the centre of the room. —He've always known his letters, she said. —Haven't you, Jude?

But he refused to look at her.

—There's more, Bride said. —They that trust in their wealth, and boast themselves in the multitude of their riches, none of them can by any means redeem his brother, nor give to God a ransom for him.

Mary Tryphena was still watching Judah. —Are you sure this is what you wants, Jude?

He glanced at her and nodded.

She said, Do you think the doctor would bring a message to Levi for us, Bride?

—I'm sure he would.

—He's to tell Levi that Jude will give himself up if Levi lets the others go. Is that right? Mary Tryphena asked him. —Is that what you wants?

Bride looked down at the paper, reading over the verses a second and then a third time. —That's a lot to say from what he got wrote here, Mrs. Devine, she said. —Are you certain?

Judah was already out the door when she looked up and Mary Tryphena reached to take the paper she held, her hand shaking. —You see the message gets passed on, she told Bride and she left them all at the table then, walking up the stairs without another word.

Mary Tryphena went to her bed where she lay awake the full of the night, the Bible verses in her hands. That delicately belled cursive, those spiralling letters tilted at an acute angle. She thought of Judah following her to Jabez Trim's when she was a girl, standing by the door while she refused the hand of the one she thought had written the letter. She couldn't have imagined a second suitor on the margins of her life. It seemed a ridiculous joke, a mute competing with a helpless stutterer for her affections.

My sister, my bride.

Judah keeping his counsel as she turned down one proposal after another, through the decades of their marriage. For fear or spite, out of reticence or doubt or some murkier impulse, he chose to hide the fact she had married into love. As if it was her job to guess the truth. By the time the first hint of morning appeared at the window Mary Tryphena was angry enough to spit nails. She thought she'd never manage to wash the cold taste of metal from her mouth in all the years that were left her.

———

Patrick Devine was only three years married to Druce Trock when an English vessel bound for the Arctic wrecked on shoal ground off the Rump. Salvagers out of Red Head Cove and Spread Eagle had brought the crew safe ashore and ransacked the galley and cabins and most of the provisions in the hold by the time the Devines sailed down the shore with Az and Obediah Trim. The Trims stayed with the bully boat after setting the Devines aboard to collect whatever scraps remained. The hold was a deathtrap by then, already half filled with water. Lazarus and Jude picked through the remains in the galley while Patrick went off to see if anything had been overlooked elsewhere. The ship was tilted hard to starboard and Patrick spidered along the passageways with one foot on the floor and the other on the wall. The vessel rocked forward suddenly, pitching him face-first through a doorway and he fell into a pool of novels and books of poetry, tomes on botany and science and history, philosophy and religion, bound copies of *Punch*. Dozens tossed onto the floor by the storm and hundreds more behind the wooden barriers meant to keep them on the shelves.

Only Ann Hope and the Reverend Dodge had more books to their names than Patrick Devine. He was always searching for strays on the shore or in Labrador and he bartered away tools and clothes and food and alcohol to take home any book he encountered. Lazarus more than once threatened to blind him to keep their materials safe from his bizarre obsession. But the wrecked library Patrick had fallen into was unlike anything he'd ever imagined. Worlds within the world and he sat there a moment, trying to take it in. Just the smell of leather and binding glue made him dizzy.

The vessel shifted again, a tremor through the length of her, and Patrick pushed himself to his feet, slipping off his coat to lay it on the floor, stacking books side by side and tying them up by the sleeves. He crawled back to the passage and made his way toward open air, the vessel heeling on the shoals as he went. When he reached the rail off the breezeway he hailed Obediah and Az Trim and they eased near enough for him to throw down his jacket of books. On the way back he passed Laz and Jude pushing a green leather chesterfield toward the stern. —Give us a hand for jesussake, Patrick shouted, stripping out of his gansey as he went. He had tied up the neck and was already stuffing the woollen sack with books when his father appeared in the doorway. Judah's fish eyes agog as he took in the foreign sight.

—Come on then, Patrick said, this is all going under the once.

Patrick went at the job pell-mell, desperate to pack up as much as possible, and Judah took off his own sweater to mimic his son. But he seemed only to wander aimlessly among the shelves, tucking away one random book at a time. The vessel let go, slipping three or four degrees more to starboard before bringing up, and his father's retarded puttering was making Patrick furious. —You jesus idiot, he shouted, but Judah carried on as if he was picking the ripest fruit from a tree, all the time with the same terrified expression on his face. Once he'd stuffed his own, Patrick filled Judah's sweater in the same blind panic, shouting at the man to hurry. The two of them went back along the passageway then, dragging their improvised sacks behind them. All hands were off the wreck by the time they came out into the open, Lazarus with the chesterfield lashed across the bow of the bully boat. The Trims eased in over the starboard side of the stern which had slipped underwater and Patrick slid the books down to them from where he and Jude held to the aft rail. Judah made a jump for it then, grabbing hands to be hauled aboard the boat, and the men were waving for Patrick to follow after. But he turned back to the library, scuttling along with a grip on the rail, the decks awash below him. He sloshed along the passageway as it filled with water, hauling his shirt over his head. Patrick clung to the shelves as he grabbed at the spines and stuffed the books into the sleeves of his shirt, the sea sucking through the doorway and rising around the room behind him. The vessel let go a long groaning sigh then as its weight hauled free of the shoals altogether and keeled into the depths.

He managed to drag himself up into the passageway before a pintail of churning water swallowed him, the wild current turning and turning him until he lost track of up and down and east and west. His lungs burning in the black chill and he surrendered to the scald of it finally, taking in mouthfuls of cold salt just for the relief, knowing it was the end of him. A strange, narcotic peace flooding his limbs when he gave himself up to the notion. He wasn't a religious man but a vision of what Paradise might be came to him, a windowed room afloat on an endless sea, walls packed floor to ceiling with all the books ever written or dreamed of. It was nearly enough to make giving up the world bearable.

He saw a grey flicker of sunlight beyond that image and the last candle still burning in him clawed toward it, kicking for the sky. He was shirtless and still holding a book in his right hand when he surfaced into wind and rain, thirty feet from the Trims' boat.

The Bible was the only book the Trims had an interest in and they refused to take any salvage from the trip. —He'd as like crawl into the house of a night and slit our throats to have them back anyway, Obediah said. Lazarus insisted Patrick take the chesterfield as well, a green leather monument to his lunatic stupidity, and it occupied pride of place in the house ever after.

Druce was all of nineteen and pregnant for the first time. World within a world. Patrick sorting through the trove of books on the kitchen floor while Lazarus recounted the event. The ship pulled under in a matter of moments, Patrick breaking the surface with the book held above his head like a torch. Druce watched her husband pottering on his knees as if he were a toddler playing with blocks of wood. She said, Would you have done as much to save your wife and child, Patrick Devine? But he seemed not to hear her. She had never felt so helpless, watching her husband absorbed in the alien world on the floor, their baby moving under her hands, and an urge to violence took hold of her. After she killed her husband she planned to burn each and every book, feeding them one at a time to the fire.

It was a momentary impulse but it filled her with a sense of dread that would not lift. She went into labour four months premature and the baby died before it saw the light of day. Druce suffered late miscarriages seven times in the next five years, a little graveyard of nameless children growing in a corner of the garden. She began hiding her pregnancies from everyone but her husband who dug the graves and set the tiny failures into the ground. They never spoke of the affliction, out of humiliation or superstitious fear, and Patrick filled the darkening silences between them by reading aloud from his library of salvaged stories. Druce listened to him hours at a time, the sad facts of their own lives suspended while he led them through those foreign tales. The end of every book left them feeling melancholy and sentimental and they lay awake half the night in bed, the sex charged with loss and helplessness and a furious, unjustifiable hope they lacked the means to express any other way.

Amos was the first pregnancy Druce carried to term, followed quickly by Martha and then Eli. The children left her little time to sit still and Patrick seemed happy enough to have the library to himself. He could read through a gale, oblivious at the end of the chesterfield while the youngsters played puss-puss-in-the-corner, as the little ones rode Amos around the floor, squealing like donkeys. It was a private space he retreated to at every opportunity and Druce sometimes referred to herself as a book widow when company called, making a show of her grievance. But she never begrudged Patrick the pleasure, having spent the worst of the hard years there with him.

Locked away in Sellers' fishing room, Patrick passed his time reading the only book he'd been allowed and playing endless rounds of noddy with Lazarus and Amos. There wasn't a shred of real evidence against them, he knew, but he'd resigned himself to the trial and whatever followed. It was almost a relief to imagine what might come out in a forum so public, the sordid history of whispers and innuendo and scheming that had determined the course of their lives. But then Judah gave himself up to Levi's constables and the Devines were sent home. They walked over the Tolt without speaking a word, as if silence was a condition of their release. Once he reached the house Patrick took his seat on the leather chesterfield with the same Oliver Goldsmith novel and he'd barely moved in the time since.

Patrick was certain his mother brokered the exchange with Levi. Druce offered up some story of Jude writing out his surrender in a code of Bible verses, but he couldn't credit it. It was always the women at work in the back rooms of the family. He'd grown up in the shadow of the widow's legendary machinations, watched Lizzie and Mary Tryphena pulling strings to set their men left or right. Bride was just alike in her way and he couldn't avoid lumping Druce in with the lot of them. Judah given up like a sacrificial lamb and Patrick laid a portion of the blame at his wife's feet.

Still, he couldn't escape the galling conclusion the fault was their own somehow, he and his half-brother Henley, his uncle Lazarus and old Callum before them. The Devine men. All they had it in them to do was to catch fish and haul wood, to cut off the ears of their persecutors and marry the same woman over and over again. He was poisoned with the lot of them. He read his way through one book after another, getting up only to walk to the outhouse or carry in a turn of wood or go upstairs to bed. His corner of the room smouldering with a telltale shadow of his father's stink. The same fierce funk that seeped from him as he and Amos held Levi down, Lazarus flaying at his ears with the knife. Judah had been sound asleep in the Gut when it happened but he was paying for all of them now.

Mary Tryphena was the only person permitted to visit her husband and she walked into Paradise Deep each day with bread and breakfast fish tied up in a square of cloth. Judah never touched a morsel and seemed to survive on the salt sea air alone. Lazarus went straight to Mary Tryphena's to ask after news when he saw she was home but there was never any news. No official charges had been laid against Judah and Levi seemed in no hurry. He'd demanded a confession be part of the exchange and sent Barnaby Shambler with a written statement to read aloud to Judah. Shambler dipped a pen in the inkwell he'd carried with him before holding it out to the prisoner. He'd expected the man to place an X at the foot of the page, but Jude set the paper on his lap and affixed an elaborate signature. God's Nephew, it read. And nothing more had happened since.

Lazarus said, I've been thinking this year I might stay.

—Stay where? Mary Tryphena asked.

—Down the Labrador, he said. —Fly the fuck out of this for good. I've got people down there would take me in. I think Amos might do the same.

—Does Amos have people? To take him in?

—He won't be left out in the cold.

Mary Tryphena nodded. She said, Did Judah ever?

—Now maid, he said.

—I've a right to know.

Lazarus shook his head. —Jude's as true as the day is long, he said. His voice cracked and he pushed the heels of his hands into his eyes. —He's not ever coming out of there, is he.

—I don't know, Laz.

—And so you do, Lazarus said. —He got it in his head Levi will let us alone if he stays in that room and he won't leave it now for love nor money. You knows that as well as me.

Mary Tryphena nodded into her lap. —Jude's as true as the day is long, she said.

—I won't stay and watch him rot over there.

Laz started crying again and Mary Tryphena went away to her room for a moment. He'd pulled himself together when she came back into the kitchen with the tiny envelope in her hand. —I want you to take this with you if you goes, she said.

Laz held the envelope up, shaking it to guess at the contents. —What in God's name is it? he said.

Stories of Judah's biblical fast and his sudden gift for letters made their way along the shore. He'd taken to scratching verses from Psalms and Proverbs and Ecclesiastes into the rough plank walls with an iron nail and some claimed the Word was being transmitted directly to Jude's hand by the Lord. God's Nephew, he was said to be calling himself. Older tales of Jude's dominion over the fish of the sea, of the people healed by his presence, were revived and retold and the growing hagiography travelled on vessels heading north and south. Strangers made pilgrimage from outports around the island to stand vigil outside the prison and touch the walls on which the Testaments were being scribed.

Even Levi Sellers was made curious enough to visit Judah, sneaking to the shoreline after dark with a storm lamp. He set the light on the floor between himself and Jude who was lying under a blanket of canvas. The man was awake but wouldn't acknowledge him, staring at the black void in the rafters above the yellow glow of the lamp.

—So, Levi said. —God's Nephew, is it?

He stood watching awhile, wondering what was to be done with him. The confession was more or less useless, signed as it was by a relative of the Lord, and Shambler convinced him there was little hope of proving the case on the testimony of his nose alone. The whole affair had been hanging in legal limbo long enough that Levi had grown to like the arrangement. He thought for a time he might skip a trial altogether, to deny the Devines any hope of resolution. Let the man rot in his cell. But letters had begun arriving from citizens as far away as St John's demanding Judah's release in the absence of criminal charges. The governor had requested a complete report on the case. Even Shambler thought it inadvisable to hold Judah indefinitely. —Who catches hell, he asked, when Judah starves himself to death in custody? Hang him or let him go, Shambler said, those are your choices.

Levi stepped toward the pallet. —We haven't had the pleasure, he said, since our meeting Christmas last, Mr. Devine. Levi was wearing his black hair long to cover the sides of his head and used his free hand to reveal first one ear, then the other. —My wife tells me I look a little lopsided but none the worse, really, for that.

Judah glanced at him and then stared back up at the darkness. Levi was close enough to the wall to make out the verses etched into the wood. All cribbed from the Old Testament, a wild tide of quotations thrown helter-skelter at the boards. *For all our days are passed away in thy wrath We spend our years as a tale that is told A whip for the horse a bridle for the ass and a rod for the fool's back Thy way is in the sea and thy path in the great waters and thy footsteps are not known Whoso stoppeth his ears at the cry of the poor he also shall cry himself.*

Then in letters twice the size of any others on the wall: *They have ears but they hear not.*

Levi reeled away from the pallet to the far wall. Judah turned his back and pulled the canvas up around his shoulders, as if he'd made his point and was done. Only the preternatural white of his hair visible in the gloom. *They have ears but they hear not.* Levi shook his head to sidestep the sensation of being spoken to by some otherworldly voice. His heart hammering. He went to the door to leave but a line of verse scored into the wood at eye level stopped him. Even as he raised the lamp he tried to convince himself not to read it.

Their fruit shalt thou destroy from the earth and their seed from among the children of men.

He swung around to face the figure lying in the darkness. It sounded vaguely like the threat Devine's Widow cursed King-me Sellers with a hundred years ago and Levi felt the words had been placed there for him alone, that otherworldly voice announcing itself again. —You royal son of a bitch, he said.

Flossie was still awake when Levi came into the bedroom. He undressed without speaking and she waited for him in the same silence. She knew he'd gone to see Judah and expected he was in need of reassurance or comforting. But she was surprised to feel her husband sidle against her, his cock like a little brick heated in the oven and laid between them for warmth. They had three children in quick succession after they married and both Levi and Flossie seemed to feel they were released from their obligations in that regard. His foreign urgency frightened her and she kept her hands on his shoulders, willing herself not to think of his ruined ears under the long flaps of hair. She thought he might carry on rocking into the cradle of her thighs until daylight, her legs burning with fatigue and his forehead laid flat against her chest. She whispered the Twenty-third Psalm to herself but it seemed to goad Levi into more furious activity and she stopped. He was like a dog burying a bone out of reach of all other creatures, the same hunch and singleness of purpose, the same proprietary determination. He paused against her finally, holding his body rigid for so long she thought he might have suffered a stroke. Then he turned away and fell asleep.

Flossie was already at the table with Adelina when Levi came down to his breakfast in the morning. After he settled into his seat she said, I've been thinking, Levi, that perhaps it's time I move into a room of my own.

He raised his head from his plate, looking first at his wife and then his sister. He could see they had discussed the matter before he came down the stairs and the obvious collusion was too much for him. —Has everyone on the shore taken leave of their bloody senses?

—Now Levi, Adelina said.

—Tell me, he shouted, how a sensible man is supposed to deal with this insanity.

—We were only thinking, Florence said but she stopped there. Levi's face had gone blank suddenly, as if he was listening to a voice in another room. He went out the door and then came straight back to them at the table. —Adelina, he said. —Do you know if the good doctor is still interested in turning Selina's House into a hospital?

A meeting was arranged for the following morning and Newman was a self-righteous prick about the entire undertaking, as Levi expected. He offered his condescending American smile when Levi hinted the fate of Selina's House might be tied to whatever conclusions were reached. Newman insisted on examining the prisoner himself and implied he was above any incentive Levi might offer to sway him. Levi gave Newman the written confession with the lunatic signature as well as an affidavit freshly sworn out by Barnaby Shambler stating Judah Devine had threatened the life of His Majesty, the King of England, and claimed the throne as his birthright. —The governor has requested a full report on this case, Levi said, and I will be including the affidavit in that report. As I'm sure you know, Doctor, treason is a hanging offence.

—Unless the man is judged insane, Newman said.

—An open-and-shut case, clearly.

—In which instance he would be imprisoned indefinitely.

—It seems the only prudent course of action.

—And Mr. Shambler claims Judah made these threats in his presence?

—You have the affidavit, Doctor.

Newman nodded over the documents before folding them away. —Doesn't it seem strange to you, Mr. Sellers, that Judah Devine, who has not spoken a single word in all his years on the shore, would suddenly begin uttering threats to the Crown?

—No more strange, Doctor, than a man who was never known to read or write suddenly copying Bible verses from memory.

Levi offered an uncharacteristic grin and Newman turned his head away from the sight of it. —I'll have an opinion for the court as soon as I can, he said.

Newman had been asked to see Judah Devine early in his incarceration, when Mary Tryphena claimed he was refusing to eat. There was nothing written on the walls and no indication the prisoner was starving and he submitted to the examination with his typical passiveness. Newman didn't know what to expect this time around, given the rumours in circulation.

He opened the padlocks with the keys given him by Levi and waited for his eyes to adjust as he stepped inside. There was a rustle along the near wall, the head of white phosphor rising from the pallet. —Hello Judah, he said. Details slowly came into the clear—the open offal hole covered with an iron grate, bread and capelin untouched on the floor. Newman nodded toward the scored wall behind Judah. —You've been busy, he said.

He took out the confession and affidavit and he set them side by side on the lungers where Judah could see them, then looked up at the long lines of fragments on the wall. *To bind their kings with chains and their nobles with fetters of iron Deliver me out of great waters from the hand of strange children Happy shall he be that taketh and dasheth thy little ones against the stones.* It made Newman think there might be a case for madness after all, for the author of the Psalms if not for Judah. —Do you recognize the signature on this confession, Jude? God's Nephew? He pointed to the paper but Judah didn't glance down. —Barnaby Shambler accuses you of threatening the King and claiming the English throne. Is there any truth to that?

Jude pushed himself to his feet and shuffled by the doctor to piss through the grated hole in the floor. Which may have been a comment on Shambler's claims, Newman thought, or simply the call of nature.

The first patients of the day were waiting for him at the clinic—an ingrown toenail black with infection, a broken finger, a strained back. Bride had already prepped the toenail, the infected digit washed and stained with iodine, the scalpel and retractor and scissors in a porcelain bowl. Newman went to the office to change and he was helping himself to a quick cocktail of ethyl alcohol and juniper berries when Tryphie barrelled into the room, the door swinging against the wall. Newman set his glass under the desk. —Let's have a look at you, he said, turning the boy and pushing up his shirt.

He'd performed half a dozen rudimentary skin grafts across the shoulders and along the left side but he was reaching the limit of what he could do in Paradise Deep. And Tryphie was still bent nearly double by the scar tissue on his back. He travelled in a loping primate fashion, his hands swinging near the floor as he wandered through rooms to talk to patients, observing simple operations. He passed the hours of imposed bedrest by taking apart any gadget the doctor was willing to risk, a pocket watch, a gyroscope, a barometer, sketching each individual spring and screw before reassembling it. The youngster had the hands of a surgeon, the same distilled concentration and dexterity. He never failed to reconstruct any contraption and often in better working order than when he began. Newman's natural discomfort around children was swallowed up by his admiration for Tryphie's precociousness.

Bride knocked at the door. —Do you want me to do the toe, Doctor?

He glanced up at her. —I'll be right there, he said.

All the while he rooted after the rogue toenail, Newman tried to decide what to do about Judah. There was something in the whole affair that pricked at him, a sliver of some larger thing that he couldn't quite guess the shape of. Bride's hip grazed his shoulder as she reached for additional gauze and he lost his train of thought altogether. She wrapped the toe when he was done, offering the patient instructions on disinfecting and bandaging while Newman washed up under the window. He turned from the basin and the sight of her stole the wind from his chest. He went to his office, mixing another clandestine cocktail and sipping at it as he waited for the surge to pass. The innocent weight of her breasts against her blouse, the attention she lavished on the naked foot. Jesus loves the little children.

In the year since Henley Devine was carried home in his coffin Bride had insinuated herself into every facet of the clinic's operation. She managed the daily administration, organized fundraising teas, oversaw the volunteers who laundered and chopped firewood and set the hospital's vegetable garden. They spent most of their time in each other's company and she didn't give the slightest indication she felt anything for Newman but collegial admiration and a primly religious gratitude. He couldn't guess how a proposal would strike her but this much was certain— —propriety would force her to move out of the clinic if her answer was no. Marry her or let her go, these were the guillotine choices a proposal presented, and he abandoned the notion of marriage. He would never touch Bride as he dreamed of touching her, never so much as hint at how he felt. It was safer to live with the inadvertent nudge of her hip, with the purgatorial weight of her breasts, with the sudden tidal surges that threatened to choke him.

He drank the cocktail to the dregs and set his forehead on the desk with his eyes closed until Bride came for him. He splinted the broken finger and prescribed strict bedrest for the strained back and spent the rest of the morning dealing with the steady stream of patients as they arrived. That sliver of discomfort with him the entire time, its suggestion of some buried thing he couldn't guess the borders of. He'd just lifted his head from an impacted molar when Barnaby Shambler appeared at the door. The member opened his coat to reveal the neck of a bottle in an inside pocket. —You'll want a little pick-me-up, Doctor.

It was half an hour more of work before he was able to join Shambler in the office. He poured a tumbler of rum for his guest and mixed himself another cocktail of ethyl alcohol and juniper berries. —You prefer the medicinal drink? Shambler said.

—I prefer not smelling like a drunk while I work.

—Your Methodist inamorata disapproves, I imagine?

—Don't talk riddles to me this morning.

—Now Doctor, Shambler said. —Let's not be coy.

—Fair enough, Newman said. He took the affidavit out of a drawer and tossed it across the desk. —You are a disgrace to your office, Shambles.

—Without a doubt.

—You don't have a single shred of integrity.

Shambler raised his glass. —Preaching to the choir, Doctor.

—You are an absolute pig of a man.

Shambler drew his head back, a look of feigned hurt on his face. —I preferred you when you were being coy.

—Judah Devine is no more danger to the King than the ass you're sitting on.

—Undoubtedly so.

—Goddamn it, Newman said. —I don't understand how you can be party to such a farce.

Shambler raised his shoulders and dropped them in an elaborate sigh. —I live here, he said. He seemed genuinely exhausted. —Look, he said, play along and you'll have the hospital you want. No one ends his days with his neck in a noose. And Levi gets some satisfaction for the loss of his ears, among sundry other complaints. It seems a perfectly reasonable course of action to the ass I'm sitting on.

Newman finished his drink. —Damn it, he said. —Damn it all to hell.

Shambler looked into his empty glass, hesitating over a question. Glanced up at Newman finally. —Any regrets, Doctor?

The last of his patients was dealt with by mid-afternoon and Newman took his muzzle-loader into the backcountry, tramping through the first heavy frost of the fall. He wanted motion and silence, to let his mind skim out over the barrens like a stone across the surface of a pond. To see where it came to rest once it settled.

He crested a rise a mile beyond Nigger Ralph's Pond just as the sun was dipping behind the Breakers, three hills spooned one into the next like a run of waves curling onto a beach. He'd always loved those hills, the sculpted look of them mirroring one another precisely. They loomed on the horizon and regardless how far he travelled in their direction they always appeared the same distance off. The melancholy surge he'd felt in Bride's presence that morning came over him again, knowing he'd never get closer to them than this. And his mind dropped into the edgeless black of what had been worrying him all day.

None of this was his. He was being swallowed up body and bone by the shore and he didn't belong here regardless. The place he loved would never return his feelings as he wished. The irrefutable fact of it made him turn on his heel like a soldier ordered about-face and he made his way back toward the coastline. The sky startling alive with constellations as he went, an orange moon lifting off the rim of the horizon. When he reached the Tolt he took the road down into the Gut and stood at Mary Tryphena's door. There was a light through the window but he hesitated outside until she called him in. —You had no luck, she said and she gestured to the muzzle-loader under his arm.

—Didn't see a living creature out there, he said.

She sat him to a stew of cods' heads and potatoes and poured him a mug of tea. She asked no questions until he was done his meal and she'd cleared away the dishes, sitting across from him with her hands folded on the tabletop like she was awaiting some verdict. —I went to see Judah this morning, he said.

—So I'm told.

He said, I've been charged with making an assessment of your husband's mental state, Mrs. Devine. Mary Tryphena nodded and Newman guessed there wasn't a soul on the shore who hadn't heard this news by now. —Do you have any idea why he's covering the walls like that? With those scripture verses?

—I didn't even know the man had his letters, she said. There was a bitterness in her voice that surprised Newman. —Do you know the Bible well, Doctor?

—Enough to dislike it.

—I suppose I'm not as well versed in the Good Book, she said, being as I can't read. But I've heard it most the way through a time or two. Do you know Proverbs?

—I couldn't quote you.

—An open rebuke, she said, is better than a secret love. Now tell me, Doctor, why would a man keep such a thing from a woman?

He opened his mouth to defend himself but couldn't manage a word. He felt he'd been pulled wrong-side out like a wet sweater, that all his insides were in plain view.

Mary Tryphena said, It's the only thing the world gives us, you know. The right to say yes or no to love.

A memory of stitching Bride together came to him, how Mary Tryphena hovered at his shoulder to watch. She spoke as if she knew something where Bride was concerned that he did not and it occurred to him she might carry enough influence to swing things in his favour. His career, the hospital, his credibility, every shred of personal integrity, all of it seemed a fair wager for that kind of help. He tried to think how it might be worded to not sound like a threat. —Mrs. Devine, he said, if I determine your husband is competent. Treason is a hanging offence, he said. —On the other hand if I make a finding of insanity.

—Judah is never going to leave that room he's locked up in.

—That's one possibility. But if you could do something to settle things, he said and he shifted in his chair. —With myself and Bride, he said. —I could perhaps arrange to have Judah placed in the hospital's care.

Mary Tryphena nodded at him, not following. —Judah's mind is set.

—I'm sorry?

—They could take the locks off tomorrow, she said, and he won't be moved out of there.

Newman could barely hear her over the roar in his ears. —That makes no sense.

—And I suppose that makes your report easier to write, Doctor.

Mary Tryphena saw him to the door as he left, handing him his rifle from the corner where he'd laid it. He felt like a fool, like an absolute pig of a man. She said, I'll have a word with Bride if you like.

—No, he said, turning back to her. —Under no circumstances, he said.

She shrugged. —You're welcome any time, Doctor.

He was still trying to slow the conversation down in his head, to understand what had passed between them. Denial and silence were his only defence and they were useless to him now. He might as well have declared himself to Bride from the roof of the clinic while the entire harbour trooped past on their way to Sunday services. He went over the Tolt Road at a run, as if there was a chance the news of how he felt might reach the clinic before him. He came into the kitchen out of breath and wild-eyed, like someone chased over half the shore by Mr. Gallery. Bride turned from the stove, taking him in with a calm stare of appraisal. —You've gone and missed your supper, Doctor.

He raised his eyes to the ceiling to hide the emotion playing like a magic-lantern show behind them. He said, I don't suppose you'd marry me would you, Bride?

—I kept a plate warm for you, she said. —You'll want to wash up.

Newman ate the full of his supper a second time that evening while Bride was upstairs settling Tryphie for the night and he was still famished when he was done. He thought there was nothing in the world would fill him up. He could hear the crisp hammer-stroke of her heels overhead, each one a little explosion in his chest. He couldn't stay here, that much was clear. There was Alaska on the opposite end of the continent, still unsullied by his stupidity. South America, India, all the ancient histories of Asia to fall into if he chose.

Bride came back into the room and he swung around to face her. She let that appraising look linger on him. —You know you'll have to give up the drink, Doctor.

He had no idea what she was talking about.

—When we marry, she said.

—Of course, he said, nodding stupidly. —Of course I will.

They were wed in the Methodist chapel that spring and Newman took Bride to Connecticut for the honeymoon. They spent most of the summer in the States where Newman attended fundraisers to outfit the new hospital while Tryphie was guinea-pigged through skin grafting and physical therapy. Bride came home that fall with a set of false teeth and pregnant with a second child.

They moved into Selina's House and set about renovating the rooms for wards and an operating theatre and an office, for waiting and examination rooms and storage for equipment and supplies. Barnaby Shambler was on hand for the official opening and he toasted the new facility and the generosity of Levi Sellers who sold Selina's House for the sum of one dollar. He toasted the new couple and then led the local dignitaries in an assault on the tables of booze laid out for the occasion. He cornered Newman hours later, waving his glass of rum.

—She's a fine-looking woman with the teeth in, I'll grant you that, he said.

Judah Devine was officially placed under Newman's care at the same time the title to Selina's House was signed over. He arranged to move the patient to an outbuilding behind the hospital fitted with a proper bunk and a small woodstove but Judah could not be enticed or coerced through the door of the fishing room. Eventually he was left to Mary Tryphena's oversee and she was the only person to lay eyes on her husband in the years that followed. Newman relied on her for news of any change that might require his intervention but there was never any change. From the upstairs windows of Selina's House he sometimes caught sight of her on her daily pilgrimage to the waterfront, a solitary figure carrying her parcel of food. Widow in all but name.

Every two years, Tryphie returned to Connecticut to undergo additional skin grafting while Newman scrounged after money and medical staff for a northern practice. Tryphie's posture improved after each visit though he was never able to stand fully upright and his right shoulder was hunched at an awkward angle all his life. Twice Eli made the trip through Boston en route to Hartford with his cousin and he fell in love with the endless avenues of shops, the factories and train stations and opera houses, with the industry at the heart of the undertaking. It was a revelation to see that work could do more than strip a person of their health, that things might be created, that accumulation was possible. Tryphie grew up despising America for the pain it inflicted on him, but to Eli it looked like a fairy-tale kingdom.

The youngsters spent most of their time on the shore alone together. They holed up in Patrick Devine's library in the Gut, flipping through illustrations in the science and botanical volumes. At Selina's House they worked on one or another of Tryphie's inventions, a rotating contraption that toasted bread on two sides at once, a hand-held periscope fashioned from wood and mirrors that allowed them to spy around corners. Tryphie's affinity for material and the mechanical was at the heart of each design but he lacked Eli's nose for the pragmatic. The years of enforced rest had made him a bit of a dreamer. He spent months rigging canvas over a frame of intricate wooden hinges that he intended to strap to his back before launching himself off the Tolt. Newman confiscated the machine before Tryphie killed himself though it was too beautiful to destroy. It hung above the doctor's bed like a crucifix, the eight-foot wingspan nearly touching the walls on either side of the room.

When they weren't locked away with Patrick Devine's books or Tryphie's tools the boys tormented the goats in the meadow and tore up rhubarb gardens. They copied across the pans of sea ice that clogged the harbour each spring. They ran behind Sellers' barns at milking time, beating the walls with sticks to set the skittish cows bucking. They threw rocks at the fishing room where the Great White was shut away, hoping to rouse some response to confirm the man was still among the living. They wandered the backcountry to play out complicated scenarios involving pirates and English soldiers or cowboys and Indians. Occasionally web-fingered Hannah Blade or one of the younger Woundys was drafted into the action, but more often than not they were alone.

Increasingly their friendship felt like a straitjacket, an attachment cemented by obligation and guilt, and an edge of cruelty crept into it. Tryphie's hunchback made him an easy target, the livid skin stretched across his shoulders like a carapace. Ladybug, Eli called him, Monkeyman, Ape. They set tests of endurance to watch the other fail, holding their palms over a candle flame until someone surrendered, pushing the other's head underwater for the panic and choking, the snot and tears. Both boys felt diminished by their attachment but couldn't see how to escape it.

When they stripped out of their clothes to swim in the backcountry ponds the wind on their bodies stood their hairless pricks on end. They poked at one another innocently enough for a while, sword fighting they called it. And one afternoon Eli dared Tryphie to touch his cock, knowing Tryphie couldn't resist a dare. —Too chicken to put it in your mouth, he said a week later. For the rest of that summer they lay side by side on the moss to suck one another after swimming, a pale starfish surrounded by miles of wilderness. They never spoke a word about it and Eli sidled up to the act each time, looking for any hint of hesitance or judgment in Tryphie's manner. There was something shaming in the wariness it forced on them and eventually they avoided the backcountry ponds altogether to be free of it.

On Sundays they went to church together, sitting in a pew with Bride and Tryphie's two half-brothers. They never took in a word of Reverend Violet's interminable sermons, Tryphie's head full of gears, angles, torque, glue and bevels and sandpaper and ball bearings, Eli wandering the streets of Boston or Hartford or lying in the moss with a faceless man, the wind like a second skin on his skin. After the service he walked down the aisle with his coat buttoned and his hands folded in front of him while Tryphie rambled on about a watch that could predict the weather or a saw blade set into a table and powered by a foot-pump. There was no one else on the shore like himself, Eli thought, maybe no one in the whole of Newfoundland.

The cod fishery followed its tidal rise and fall with implacable regularity, seasons of relative bounty followed by years of poor catches or poor markets overseas. The annual hunt for seals on the Labrador ice was lost to larger, faster steamships out of St. John's and the bleak times made it hard to argue that anything less than Levi's ruthlessness could keep Sellers & Co. afloat. Patrick Devine began travelling to St. John's each spring in hopes of getting out from under the man's thumb, spending the summer months aboard a schooner fishing cod off the Grand Banks.

Eli lobbied to accompany his father on the bankers but Druce refused to surrender her youngest child, as if she knew Patrick was destined one year not to come home. Every spring mother and son descended into the same argument and found their crooked way back to the same conclusion. Patrick ignored the strife as best he could, though he sided with Druce when called upon directly. —There's no besting her, he confided to the boy. —You want to save yourself some grief, he advised, don't you marry a girl from the shore.

When Tryphie turned sixteen he left to attend college in St. John's in preparation for the inevitable medical degree. Eli was relieved to be free of his company but felt at a loss in his days without it. He knocked around on the waterfront and tramped over half the countryside, trying to fend off the hatred for the shore that grew in him like a black mould. It was a surprise to discover he despised the people closest to him simply for enduring their lives of want. The only venture on the shore not owned by or beholden to Levi Sellers was the Trims' sawmill and Eli took a job there over the winter months, squirrelling away nickels and dimes toward a way out.

He was seen in the company of Hannah Blade on occasion and people thought they were just odd enough to make a grand couple. But Eli was never known to set his cap for any girl in particular. There was a solitude about him, a whiff of secrecy that encouraged idle speculation. Every discussion of Eli eventually ran through his family tree, as if it were a list of symptoms. Devine's Widow begetting Callum who married hag-ridden Lizzie Sellers. Callum and Lizzie begetting Mary Tryphena and peg-leg Lazarus, raised from the dead and father to Jackie-tars on the Labrador. Mary Tryphena wedded to the stench of the Great White, and they two begetting Eli's father, Patrick, who all but drowned himself to bring home a stack of books.

Eli was a queer stick, no one could deny it. There's no escaping your blood, people said, and Eli Devine was saddled with more weight than most.

In the winter of his eighteenth year Tryphie brought his fiancée home to Paradise Deep for a Christmas wedding.

Newman had planned to send his stepson to school in the States but Tryphie refused. Even St. John's he had to be bullied into. He spent two homesick years at Bishop Feild College, miserable even while he fell in love with Minnie Rose, a kitchen maid at the house where he boarded. The two carried on a clandestine courtship for a year before Tryphie proposed.

The couple arrived at Selina's House mid-afternoon on Tibb's Eve. Newman was in surgery and didn't lay eyes on his future daughter-in-law until he sat at the supper table. A girl Tryphie had rescued from the life of a scullery maid, a seventeen-year-old with no education and less ambition, an attitude of congenital deference about her that set Newman's teeth on edge. He excused himself without taking tea and hid out in his office until he did a last round for the evening and went to bed.

—That girl wouldn't last thirty seconds into an appendectomy, he said to Bride.

—Tryphie isn't marrying a nurse.

—Well maybe he ought to be.

—Don't you say a word, she warned him.

—And what if I do?

Bride waited a moment, considering how far she was willing to push. —Tryphie's never wanted to go to medical school at all, she said. —You know that.

—And this is his way of getting out of it? Marrying a maid who can't manage a sentence without the word sir or ma'am tacked to the end?

Bride said, You're just like your father, Harold Newman.

—God*damn* it, woman.

—If you profane the Lord once more, Bride said.

Newman raised himself on an elbow, exasperated and furious and just the barest niggle of something sexual beginning to turn in him. —Are you going to wash my mouth out with soap, Nurse?

She turned away on her side to hide her smile.

—Kiss me, he said.

—I wouldn't touch those filthy lips to save my soul.

She tried to fend him off when he fell on her, slapping at his ears. He grabbed her wrists to pin her arms above her head. —You've ruined my life, he said, nuzzling her breasts.

—Sure you never had it so good, you foolish gommel, she said, falling back into an accent so thick he'd thought it a foreign language the first time he encountered her. There was something in hearing it that Newman rose to every time.

Bride had always been able to tell what men wanted that way. Even as a girl of twelve and thirteen she could suss it out. It was a kind of weakness in them all and men distrusted her for knowing so much about their private selves. Newman, at least, seemed not to despise her for it.

The chastity of her marriage to Henley Devine felt like a penance for her particular sins and there was nothing in lying with a man that Bride couldn't live without if God required the sacrifice. She'd resigned herself to a life of abstinence before Tryphie's accident set her squarely in the way of the doctor. Her son permanently scarred and her husband carted home in a box and she couldn't escape the thought it was God at work in her life. She prayed over the blasphemous notion for months and still it made no sense to her. The Lord was the only man Bride ever felt helpless to figure out and that helplessness was almost a relief. She set to work at the hospital as if it was her vocation and left the question of the doctor to Jesus.

She lay catching her breath after they made love, her face pressed against her husband's back. She never tired of it, the afterglow of giving and giving and being fed in return. And there was something in Tryphie that made her worry he'd never experience anything like it. He was different than her two younger sons, there was an insularity pushed on him by his long convalescence, an attachment to the mechanical world that seemed unnatural. She thought at times he might be incapable of recognizing love. —You won't deny Tryphie a chance for this, she whispered. —So help me, Harold Newman.

The wedding was set for Old Christmas Day and Newman didn't speak against it the rest of the season. There was a dry dance at the Methodist church hall that went on late into the night, drinkers slipping outside to nip at flasks before coming back into the crush of noise and heat. Eli sat with Druce and Mary Tryphena all evening, in a sulk. He was happy to see Tryphie married off, as if it relieved him of some debt. But there was a weight on his chest as the vows were traded and the rings exchanged, and the weight would not leave him. Druce was watching her son out of the corner of her eye. —It'll be your turn next, she said. —To get married, have a family.

—Perhaps it will, he said.

Druce nodded across the hall where John and Magdalen Blade sat at a table with Hannah. —I've always thought she was sweet on you, Druce said. —Why don't you ask her up to dance?

—I think I'll wander home out of it, he said.

It was after midnight at the tail end of the Christmas season and it was a surprise to everyone when the crowd of mummers came through the door of the hall, King Cole and Horse Chops and a retinue in rags behind them playing spoons and ugly sticks. They looked to have been on the move most of the night, drunk and rowdy to the edge of violence, shoving their way onto the dance floor, stealing women from their partners, yelling their fool heads off. Eli started for the door as soon as they came in but Druce grabbed his arm. —Don't leave me alone with those savages, she said, smiling and happy to see them.

King Cole made a proprietary round of the hall, shaking hands and begging drinks from teetotallers while people guessed at his identity. A Woundy, some thought, or one of the Toucher crowd. The King bowed low to the newlyweds before touching their shoulders with his staff as a blessing. Eli was in a chair behind his mother and the King almost passed by in the dim light. Raised both hands above his head when he laid eyes on him. —Horse Chops, he shouted in his high falsetto.

Eli bolted for the door but a handful of mummers fell on him, dragging him back to a chair set in the centre of the hall, the crowd urging them on.

—This one, this one, the King said, shaking his staff at Eli. Horse Chops stood at the King's side, draped in a brown blanket, the horse's head rough-carved of wood, one brown eye and one blue painted on the face, the jaws on a hinge of leather. —Is this fellow in love, Horse Chops? the King asked.

Clap.

—In love, he is, King Cole shouted to applause and whistles. —Now tell us, Horse Chops, is his love a secret love?

Clap.

—Undeclared, friends. Is his beloved in the hall, Horse Chops?

Clap.

—Aha, aha, the King said, circling to survey the crowd, a buzz in the air. He held his staff out as a pointer and he let it come to rest on one girl after another, Hannah Blade and Az Trim's youngest and Peter Flood's great-granddaughter, Horse Chops galloping to stand over each in turn before he offered his judgment.

Clap clap.

Moans of disappointment following every denial, names of other hopefuls shouted from all sides. Eli tied to his chair by the room's attention, wishing he was dead.

The King knocked his staff on the floor in frustration. —Horse Chops, he said, are you sure the beloved is in the room?

Clap.

—Then go, the King shouted. He sat in Eli's lap, an arm around his shoulders. —Show us, he said.

Horse Chops trolled slowly from table to table, passing the newly-weds once, then a second time, chased by whistles of impatience. The mummer stopped suddenly as he passed Tryphie's bride a third time, stepping behind her seat, the huge head swinging above her like a pendulum. She buried her face in her hands in embarrassment and the King jumped from Eli's lap. —No, he shouted, it's not our bride? Is the best man in love with the bride?

Complete silence in the hall as Horse Chops deliberated.

Clap clap.

—Stop teasing us, Horse Chops, the King begged. —Out with it, man.

Horse Chops wagged his head, as if catching a scent in the air. He shifted sideways to stand directly behind the groom, the hunchback, Tryphie Newman. Eli was out of his chair and aboard the King before another word was spoken, hammering at the man's head with a fist, half the crowd rushing the floor to pile on. Az and Obediah Trim and the Reverend Violet waded into the mess, shouting for calm, and nothing much came of the altercation in the end. The mummers slinking out the door without ever revealing their identities and the dancing started up again as soon as they left. Eli disappeared after the mummers and no one laid eyes on him the rest of the night.

The crowd escorted the newlyweds to the marriage bed when the dance ended, banging pots and pans and shouting behind the couple as they went. Eli heard the distant uproar from his perch on the Tolt, following the medieval wedding party along the harbour streets by the noise, the same as if they were carrying storm lamps in the dark. The well-wishers saw the couple through the door of Selina's House and a few minutes later their racket fell silent.

After the wedding party dispersed Eli walked back down into Paradise Deep, picking his way along the waterfront until he reached Judah's asylum cell. He had only the vaguest memories of his grandfather and the man had all but disappeared from their lives in his mute isolation. Eli listened outside awhile but heard only the ancient sish of ocean on the landwash. The progress of time barely registered on the shore, he thought, circling on itself like that endless conversation of water and stone. They were bearing down on a new century and everyone Eli knew was still sleepwalking through the Middle Ages. All of them lost to the larger world no less than Judah was, shut away behind an unlocked door, scribbling nonsense on the walls. If he wasn't half-frozen from standing out in the cold he would have wept at the thought.

There was a light in the Blades' window as he walked back through town and he let himself into the kitchen where John was sitting up with James and Matthew, a bottle open on the table. The two younger Blades were still dressed in the costumes they wore to the hall, Horse Chops's head on the floor at Matthew's feet.

—Is Hannah about? Eli asked.

John Blade stood to fetch him a glass. —She's gone to her bed, he said. —She and her mother both. Sit down, he said.

James was holding a piece of ice to the swollen side of his face and Eli nodded toward him. —You're all right are you, Jimmy?

—Hannah is some poisoned with us, he said.

Matthew said, It was only a bit of fun we were having, Eli.

John Blade brought Eli a drink and they all sat in silence awhile.

—I never meant disrespect to Hannah, Eli said. He was speaking directly to John, watching the girl's father in the light of the candle. —I never said anything meant to raise her hopes. She's a fine girl, Mr. Blade.

John Blade nodded and refilled glasses all around and they carried on drinking. Hannah came into the tiny kitchen an hour later, woken by the racket. Her presence in the doorway shushed them and Eli watched in silence as she took her drunken father by the elbow to help him to his bedroom. As soon as she was out of sight, James and Matthew crept to the door. They lived in houses to either side of John and Magdalen and were suddenly anxious to get home. Matthew pushed James out into the cold and turned back to the kitchen. —Hold her off for us, Eli, he said. —For the love of Christ.

When Hannah came back to the kitchen she was carrying a quilt. —You can lie out there, she said, pointing to the daybed near the stove.

—I was just on my way home, he said.

—That's a long walk this time of night.

He fixed her with a drunken look. Thick red hair, delicately freckled hands clutching the quilt. He'd held one of those hands an afternoon when he was ten, rescuing her from a pirate lair on the barrens, a simple childish affection between them. It was the first time she'd let anyone not her family touch the webbed skin between her fingers.

—What is it you wants, Eli? she asked him.

—Out, he said. —Elsewhere.

—And what do you expect to find elsewhere?

He gestured around the room, too drunk to censor himself. —Not this, he said.

—Well then, she said and she settled the quilt closer to her belly. —You watch yourself going home, she told him.

Barnaby Shambler died during an afternoon debate at the Colonial Building in St. John's. He'd gained a reputation as a napper in his latter years, snoring quietly through the business of government, and to all appearances the Legislature's most senior member had simply fallen asleep. But he couldn't be roused when it came time to vote on the tabled bill and was pronounced dead by one of the handful of doctors who served as elected members in the House. His body was shipped to Paradise Deep for what turned out to be the last funeral officiated by the Reverend Eldred Dodge.

Dodge was spry for a man in his nineties. He lived alone without an ache or complaint all the years of his widowhood but the wind of old age seemed to catch him broadside with Shambler no longer before him to bear the brunt. He took to his bed after the Honourable Member was laid to rest and never stood on his feet again. Adelina and Flossie Sellers attended him, the two women holding hands as they sat at his bedside. Adelina moved into the manse when it was clear he wouldn't recover, reading from the Gospels or simply keeping watch as the man slept. The morning of the day he died, she suggested a visit from Reverend Violet and Dodge shook his head on the pillow. —Send the other one round, he said.

—What other one?

—Reddigan.

The two men had little in common other than a shared distaste for the Methodist faith. It inspired a devotion too close to mania for the priest's liking, too close to sex for the Anglican. The congregation singing and rocking on their heels and praying to the rafters. It was appetite Reverend Violet was feeding with his Glory Hallelujah, with his Ye must be born again. And both Dodge and Reddigan distrusted appetite as a moral compass.

—Thank you for coming, Father.

—You've seen to more than a few of my flock in your time, Reverend.

Dodge lifted a hand. —I was all they had to look to, he said. He seemed to drift a few moments before he said, You never met the widow, Father. Devine's Widow?

—She was long gone by the time I got here.

—I went to see her before she died. A hundred if she was a day. Dodge closed his eyes. —She was a loathsome creature, Father.

—This wouldn't be the time, Reddigan said, to dwell on such things.

But it was too late to warn the dying man off standing one more time at the bedside to look down on that gaunt face, the bottomless black well of her eyes. —I've come to pray for you, he'd announced and the widow turned her head to the wall to dismiss him. —Pride goeth before a fall, he said.

—I'd watch my step then, she said, if I was you.

He was stung by the gall of her. —Don't you have the slightest concern for your soul, Missus?

—I don't remember being born, she said, and I won't remember dying.

He'd left the old woman there without a word of comfort, wishing her dead and gone as he walked back over the Tolt. The strength of that urge surprised him, it was animate and vital, a feral creature he dragged around on a leash, it kicked and clawed and kept him awake half the night with its racket. Reverend Dodge had never experienced a hangover though something akin to it afflicted him when he heard the news of the widow's death—a foaming sear of regret and a sick aftertaste in his mouth, the suspicion he'd made a royal ass of himself. That he'd been wrong about God or himself somehow.

Dodge looked up at the priest. —I hated that woman, Father.

—The Lord tests us, Reddigan suggested.

—The Lord is a miserable so-and-so, Dodge said.

After the priest gave a final blessing, Flossie and Adelina came to sit with him. They offered to read awhile but he sent them away. —You shouldn't be alone, Flossie said.

He shook his head. —I'm not alone.

God, they thought he meant. And he allowed them to think as much as they rustled their heavy skirts through the door. He stared up at the ceiling after they'd gone, left alone with the widow woman's shade. As was right and proper. He'd seen her at work through the years, sitting with the sick and dying. Not a comforting presence, but inexhaustibly patient. Days without respite sometimes before she could stand and weight the eyelids down. She was a little pool of darkness across the room now and he tried to raise a hand to greet her. But he'd left it too long and even that gesture was beyond him. When Adelina looked in an hour later he was gone, arms folded on the chest, the eyes drawn closed.

Dodge's death was the end of the Episcopalian Church in Paradise Deep, the congregation too small to warrant a new minister. The last adherents gathered for lay services a few months longer before they disappeared into the bosom of the Methodists, and Reverend Violet's congregation eclipsed the Catholic numbers for the first time. Father Reddigan continued to suffer occasional losses to the evangelist, prompting him to write the archbishop about his concern for the Church on the shore. *Monsignor, we are still celebrating Mass in a wooden chapel raised by an apostate more than half a century ago, one can hardly expect it to instill a sense of God's majesty within the congregation, and perhaps it is time, Monsignor, to consider building a cathedral commensurate with the beauty and glory of the Holy Roman Church.*

Every Catholic fisherman on the shore gave over his catch on the feast days of the saints to help underwrite the project, and the cornerstone was laid in 1892. The black granite for the church was quarried in the hills above Devil's Cove and shipped to Paradise Deep one half-ton block at a time, the stones dressed and raised under the supervision of two Italian masons recruited by the archbishop.

In December of 1894 the Union Bank and the Commercial Bank of Newfoundland collapsed under the burden of overextended credit to St. John's merchants and the entire colony descended into bankruptcy. Levi Sellers stopped taking fish altogether during the first year of the crisis and many Protestants joined the Catholic work crews on the cathedral for the single meal a day provided to volunteers. It was the largest stone building ever constructed outside St. John's and almost every soul on the shore had a hand in raising the sanctuary before it was done. There was a nondenominational pride taken in the height of the twin spires, as if the sprawling cathedral were a physical extension of their will, a testament to what they were capable of in the worst of times. Even the atheist doctor took an interest, setting up his box camera on the Gaze every few months to photograph the latest stage.

Three months before the church was completed, Obediah Trim fell from a five-storey scaffold while installing stained-glass windows behind the altar. His body was carted to the hospital where the doctor set the multiple fractures to make him look halfways human in his casket. Newman wired the misshapen jaw in place and he stared at the face from one side and then the other, testing it against his memory of the man. —There you are, Obediah, he said. He touched his finger to the faint line below the Adam's apple—the kinkorn, as Obediah called it—tracing the scar he'd left removing the egg-shaped fibroid in his first weeks on the shore. —There you are, he said again.

Azariah came to the doctor's office the day before the funeral, carrying Jabez Trim's Bible. He placed the ancient text on Newman's desk. —We thought you should have it, Az said. —Me and Obediah. Once we was gone.

—You aren't planning on leaving us are you, Az?

—I wanted to be sure it got to you, is all. You seemed so taken with it. It's not much for all you're after doing for us crowd, he said.

Newman nodded helplessly and the two men sat in silence a few moments. —I hear Tryphie's girl is going to sing at the service, Newman said finally.

—We're grateful to have her, Az said. —She's what now? Thirteen?

—Just turned fourteen.

—Where does the time go, Azariah said and the doctor shrugged.

Newman left the Good Book where it sat on the desk, refused even to touch it. He couldn't shake the sense that acknowledging the Bible's presence would mean losing Azariah to some misadventure as well. It was Bride who rescued the book from the clutter months afterwards, placing it on a shelf in the storage room they'd made of the servant's quarters off the kitchen.

Father Reddigan gave his congregation leave to attend the funeral and the crowd of mourners spilled out the doors, circling the Methodist chapel to listen at the open windows. Esther Newman sang "Amazing Grace," the hymn carrying all the way to the harbour where even the gulls fell silent to hear it. Old Callum and Martha Devine together couldn't hold a candle, people said. Esther herself wasn't always easy to take, but her voice inspired the same sense of proprietary awe as the new cathedral. As if it was the best of what they were, distilled into something elegant and pure and inviolable.

Esther was born precocious and brazen and generally made her parents' lives a trial. She avoided Minnie's preoccupation with manners and chores by escaping to the Gut to sit with Mary Tryphena, listening to the old woman prattle on about the courtships and epidemics and wild winters she'd seen in her time, walking her over the Tolt to visit with Judah in his cell. It was obvious to Esther that her mother had no time for Eli Devine, and she went out of her way to cultivate a relationship with him as well, just to spite Minnie.

Eli saw early on that Esther's talent was more than the shore could hope to hold to itself and he encouraged her nascent ambitions, as if some small piece of himself might escape into the wider world with her. She'd long ago outstripped what lessons Adelina Sellers had to offer and it was Eli's idea to find an instructor in St. John's, to have her board there several months of the year. Dr. Newman agreed to bankroll the venture and talked Tryphie and Minnie past their reluctance.

She was scheduled to leave for the capital city on the season's last packet boat two weeks after Obediah's funeral, and no one was surprised in the months that followed to hear Esther was singing at churches and concerts and weddings across St. John's, that she received invitations to perform in Halifax and Quebec City. Three years later the governor himself would request she be featured at turn-of-the-century celebrations on Signal Hill. And in the spring of 1900 she would sail for France with letters of introduction from the Newfoundland governor and the organist at the Anglican cathedral.

Soon enough, all the shore would hear of her would come from newspaper reports of her performances in the great opera houses of Europe, the London papers referring to her as the Northern Pearl, as the Nightingale of Paradise. The early letters would trickle off to occasional postcards and even that callous dismissal of their place in her life would seem inevitable and understandable. They would all remember her as she was at Obediah's funeral, when she made their grief seem regal and glorious, when she still belonged to them alone.

On the Feast of the Immaculate Conception, Dr. Newman gathered the work crews in front of the cathedral's main doors for a final photograph. One hundred and forty-seven men sitting on the steps of the building that was only days from completion, Eli in the back row beside Azariah Trim. Father Reddigan spoke to the doctor as the men wandered back to their work, asking for a print that could be framed and hung in the church.

No one could say who first took note of the anomaly and some who examined the picture in the vestibule dismissed the notion altogether. It was just a trick of shadow and light and wishful thinking, Newman said. But most swore they could see the dead man in the back row, his features indistinct but recognizable. Obediah staring out between the faces of Az and Eli. One hundred and forty-eight men on the steps of the cathedral they'd raised. Father Reddigan set a candle beneath the photograph that was lit all through Advent and there was a steady stream of visitors to see Obediah and bless themselves or whisper a prayer.

Eli had been at the foot of the scaffold when Obediah fell and he helped lift the shattered corpse into a cart. Every night since the accident the man appeared in Eli's dreams with his marionette limbs akimbo, his broken jaw flapping uselessly east and west. The thought of Obediah standing beside him whole and unharmed seemed a ridiculous notion, but it was too great a temptation to resist in the end. He went to the cathedral just after dawn on Tibb's Eve, hoping to find the place deserted. But Hannah Blade was there, standing at the photograph. He was about to slip out the door when she noticed him, backing away from the picture quickly, feeling caught out.

—Give you a fright, he said.

Hannah still had no man of her own. Eli heard of one or two fellows coming round to see her before Magdalen died but it seemed settled afterwards that she'd look out to her widowed father and wind up alone.

—First time in to see it? he asked.

—I been in a few mornings, she said.

Eli nodded. —Is it him there, do you think?

—Father will be wanting his breakfast, she said and she went by him with her head down.

—Say me to John, Eli called after her. He watched her awhile before he let the door close, turning toward the photograph across the vestibule, the candle alight beneath it. And without taking a step nearer it came clear to him why Hannah had been there. He leaned on the door, knocking his head against the wood, as if he might clear his mind of the realization.

He left without looking at the picture, making his way to Selina's House and walking to the workshop Tryphie had set up in an old barn. There was a forge at one end, benches along the other cluttered with tools and wood and metal, jars of screws and nails, blueprints and sheets of paper littered with sketches and dimensions. Tryphie's two half-brothers were both practising physicians, one working on the Labrador coast and the other in Montreal, which made it easier for

Newman to accept Tryphie's refusal to attend medical school. He eked a living from a stream of royal patents for new and improved wrenches, new and improved school desks, new and improved can openers, new and improved acetylene lighthouse lamps. Tryphie also made a few dollars as a carpenter, building small boats and puncheon tubs and other odds and ends. But all that activity was simply a way to avoid destitution. He devoted every moment he could afford to the fanciful creatures churned up by the endlessly turning gyre of his mind. Tools with arcane applications, many of them surgical in nature as requested by Dr. Newman; a method for fabricating and setting false teeth; coils of wire for conducting electrical current. The walls were hung with a dozen prototypes of his flying machine, one of which cost him a broken leg during a test flight off the workshop roof. —There are some things, Eli told him then, that are better left in your head, Tryphie.

Much of the floor space was occupied now by a great fish built of iron intended for underwater travel, the bowels of the creature just large enough to seat a man next to a series of levers and pulleys to operate the fins and rudder and ballast tanks. The Sculpin, Eli called it. They'd spent much of the previous year arguing the lunacy of the notion as the fish was framed out and took shape on the workshop floor. —You'll have yourself drowned in that goddamn thing, Eli said during his last visit two months before.

Tryphie had flung a screwdriver at him. —Fly the fuck out of it, he shouted as he reached for a hammer.

Eli hadn't come by the workshop since that argument and he had to make an effort even now not to ridicule the contraption. —How's Minnie keeping? he asked.

Tryphie leaned against a workbench, wiping at his hands with a rag. —She's after bawling herself to sleep every night since Esther left us.

Minnie had been dead set against sending her only child off to St. John's to be moulded and coiffed by some stranger. She was alone

in her opposition—Tryphie and the doctor, even Bride siding with
the girl's ambition—and she acquiesced in the end. But things were
said between Minnie and Eli in the process that cemented their dislike for one another.

—I expect it's hard for her, Eli said.

—You don't know fuck-all about it is the very truth of the matter.

Eli nodded, not up to a fight. There were moments when he felt
the weight of all that had passed between he and Tryphie on his shoulders. He was still waiting for something central and final to give way,
to set him loose or kill him. He gestured helplessly, casting his hand as
if he were throwing an imaginary line across the workshop floor. Tryphie
carried on wiping his hands, not willing to pick it up. —I just wanted
to look in, Eli said finally. —Wish you a merry Christmas.

—Same to you, Tryphie told him.

—That's a fucking coffin you're building there, he said as he left
and a wrench slammed against the door behind him.

He spent most of the day tramping aimlessly along the roads in the
backcountry, the spires of the cathedral rising up out of the harbour's
bowl as he walked back from Nigger Ralph's Pond. He saw Mary
Tryphena coming along the Tolt Road from her daily visit to the asylum cell and he walked down into the Gut with her. —You coming over
for supper tonight, Nan? he asked when they reached her door.

Mary Tryphena turned to look him full in the face. The blue of her
eyes glaucous, like water caught over with a film of ice. It was hard to
imagine what was keeping her alive. —Everything I eats these days, she
said, tastes like a bucket of nails.

After supper he set out over the Tolt again. There was a light on at
Hannah's place and John Blade waved him in from the table. Hannah
set about pouring a drink for them both as if Eli had made an appointment for the visit. John asked after Druce and Mary Tryphena and a
handful of other people in the Gut and he was only halfways into his
rum when he said, Matthew is expecting me next door. He got up for

his coat. —I might just kip down on the daybed if I has a few snorts, he told his daughter. —Don't wait up.

Hannah closed the door after him and turned back to the kitchen. —How's your drink, Eli?

He raised the glass still half full. —John don't mind leaving you alone like this?

Hannah walked to the stove, standing close for the heat, her hands hidden behind her. —If I had a mind for trouble I'd have got into it for long ago, she said. She was a plain-looking woman though the years of work in the gardens and on the fish flakes had made a virtue of her plainness. There was nothing delicate in Hannah's face to be ruined by time, just a mettle and vigour that looked more and more like beauty as she aged. She stared down at her shoes. —What is it, she said, keeping you on the shore all this time?

He laughed and shook his head. He stayed because Patrick hadn't come back to the Gut for years now and Druce had no one else to look out to her. Because Mary Tryphena was nearly as old as the century and bound to leave them before long. He stayed to spare Levi Sellers the satisfaction of seeing one more Devine pushed off the shore. He stayed because Tryphie . . .

—God knows maid, he said. —Why is it you never managed to get into trouble all this time?

She looked away, making a dismissive noise in her throat.

—It wasn't Obediah you were at the church to see, he said. —Was it, Hannah.

—What else would I be doing?

—You've been going over there to look at me in that picture.

Hannah shook her head. —You don't mind yourself, I know.

—Tell me I'm wrong, he said, and I'll be gone.

—Eli, she said, I've been waiting for you to leave here since I was a girl.

—Jesus Hannah.

She straightened where she stood. —I am not going to beg, that much I will tell you.

He watched her awhile then, that little cauldron of doggedness and impotent distress, reflecting his own heartache back to him. Shadows and light and wishful thinking was all there was to the world, that much he could attest. He lifted his tumbler and finished his drink. He said, I'd have another, Hannah. But she didn't move from where she stood next the stove. —If you can stand to have me, he said.

KERRIVAN'S APPLE TREE WAS STILL STANDING on the far side of the Gut when Eli and Hannah Devine's son arrived in the last year of the nineteenth century. The tree hadn't borne leaves or fruit for so long it was nearly forgotten and none but the oldest livyers on the shore remembered anything of Sarah Kerrivan who carted the sapling across the ocean in a wooden tub. The branches were gnarled and brittle and stripped of their bark and they stooped to the ground where even the stones of Callum Devine's rock fence had been scattered by generations of winter frost.

Hannah Devine was well on in her life to be carrying a baby for the first time and she was taken with cramps while working the garden in her fifth month. Druce sent Eli to borrow a horse and cart from Matthew Strapp and they clattered over the Tolt Road to the hospital with Hannah grunting through her teeth. The child was barely a child at all when it came into the world, a glove of translucent skin, dark clots of the organs showing through the flesh. The tiny cock like a thread unravelling at a seam. Newman clamped and cut the umbilical cord and handed the infant to Bride before he turned his attention to Hannah. She had still to pass the afterbirth and he'd all but forgotten the child when Bride called across the room to say there was a heartbeat.

A month later the infant weighed no more than a decent cod fillet and still wouldn't latch onto his mother's nipple to eat and few thought he would leave the hospital alive. Dr. Newman and Tryphie had fashioned a metal incubator with a glass cover, the little oven heated from below by cylinders of water suspended over kerosene lamps. A constant watch was required to monitor the temperature and the family took the work in shifts, Hannah and Eli, Druce and John Blade and Hannah's sisters-in-law, Tryphie and Minnie and Bride.

Even ancient Mary Tryphena took her turn beside the child. It had been years since the old woman showed the slightest interest in the world, but she'd fussed over Hannah during her pregnancy, pushing concoctions of bog myrtle and gold-withy on the expectant mother. And she carried on with her doctoring after the child was delivered, opening the incubator when she was left alone to smear his chest with liniments and poultices that could be smelled in every room of the hospital. Newman warned her away from tampering and barred her from the room altogether when she ignored him. —Keep that old witch away from the baby, he told Bride, or he won't live another week.

By his third month the boy was making a show of living through the ordeal when an infection took hold and even Bride was forced to admit there was no hope for him. —That's a sin now, she whispered. —The child's had enough torment.

There's no lack of that in the world, Druce said. She was thinking of the small garden of children she'd planted next her house, infants who'd never taken a breath before the earth stopped their lungs for good. And this one now in his metal coffin, waning under a pane of glass.

It was Mary Tryphena who suggested Kerrivan's Tree. Hannah hadn't left the child's side in three days but to wash her face and she was exhausted watching the slow ebb of his life. She was ready for something decisive to happen, one way or the other. —The doctor won't ever allow it, she said.

Mary Tryphena nodded. —You bring him by tonight, she said. —Once the house is asleep.

Eli considered himself an idiot to be humouring the women, but the child was lost regardless. Newman came in on his last round after midnight, listening to the tiny heart struggle through the noise of the lungs. He closed the glass cover and nodded to the mother and father in their chairs to say their time with the boy was all but gone.

After the hospital settled Hannah lifted the infant out of the incubator, wrapping him in a sheepskin blanket. He was paler than the palest Devine, the wisp of hair at the crown so blond it was nearly invisible. They carried him along the deserted roads and over the Tolt to the Gut. Mary Tryphena was sitting up when they came for her and she followed them back out the door. The tree shining silver in the moonlight on the far side of the cove.

Hannah and Eli had both been christened in the old way but the ritual had fallen out of use in their lifetime and they stood in silence when they reached the tree, unsure how to proceed. Mary Tryphena picked her way through the maze of branches and gestured for them to follow. They passed the nearly weightless package through the dead limbs in the dark, hand to hand to hand, the child silent the entire time. As she let him go Mary Tryphena said, A long life to you, Abel Devine. And Eli wept all the way back to Selina's House with the helpless infant in his arms, the last child ever to be welcomed into the world at Kerrivan's Tree.

There was no change in his condition the next morning but Abel survived the day. —Tough little bugger, Newman said each time he found the infant still breathing.

It was a sentiment that followed Abel through his childhood. He was smaller than other youngsters his age and prone to fevers and infections that packed his lungs with fluid and threatened to drown him in his bed. A raw smell of decay rising with his temperature, as if the death he'd cheated was leaching from his pores. Mary Tryphena refused to leave Abel's side when he was ill. Hannah was forced to wear a rag across her face against the smell. —I don't know how you can stand it, Mrs. Devine.

—The child's no worse than Judah, Mary Tryphena said.

There were half a dozen occasions when Abel's life hung in the balance and each time he pulled through when there seemed no chance of recovery. It was exhausting to live in hope until they gave him up, to live in hope and give him up, to live in hope. Druce eventually moved down the shore to Devil's Cove where Martha was married to a Tuttle, abandoning her garden of dead youngsters to be spared the torture of watching Abel teeter on the brink.

For years before they married Eli held Hannah at a distance and something of the habit stayed with him afterwards, though he wished it different. Hannah's pregnancy made him think they might find their way, that he could learn to properly love his wife through the child. But he was never able to wrangle his feelings for the boy into a manageable shape. For a time he shared Druce's sense of impending grief. But Abel's flirtations with death began to feel orchestrated, designed to pull them along in the youngster's wake. He stepped a little further back from the boy after each successive trauma, and a little further from his wife as well. They were never more than fitful lovers but what intimacy they shared slipped away in the ongoing crisis of Abel's health.

Hannah was increasingly protective of the improbable child. She barred Abel inside during inclement weather and through the entire length of the winters. She forbade activity that would overexcite or tire him. She refused to allow talk of politics or local gossip or the family's checkered history in his presence, as if he might catch something fatal from such topics. He spent much of his early years in his grandfather's library where he became a reader in self-defence, escaping his isolation in the worlds categorized and alphabetized and stacked on the parlour shelves. The youngster knew nothing of Absalom Sellers growing up ignorant of the most basic facts of his own life in Selina's House or Lizzie's years as a recluse wandering the backcountry, he'd never been told a thing about Judah Devine's biblical isolation in his asylum cell. But everyone else on the shore could see Abel was being raised in a solitude that was a peculiar inheritance of his blood.

Mary Tryphena was the only person who never doubted the boy would survive and she seemed to recover her appetite for life through the child's persistence. Hannah discouraged contact between the two, not wanting Abel exposed to the old woman's talk. She was forced to ask Mary Tryphena to watch him while she was on the flakes or working the garden but warned her to keep a tight rein on her inclination to reminisce.

Mary Tryphena was as ancient as Devine's Widow by this time, a meagre, emaciated figure. Her movements were deliberate, almost mechanical, as if she'd been designed and put together in Tryphie's workshop, and her reticence somehow enhanced that impression in Abel's mind. He thought her kin to the imaginary worlds of the library, a character out of *Gulliver's Travels*. There was something in her antediluvian bearing that made her seem immutable, and it never occurred to him that her place in his life was temporary. He was reading to her when Mary Tryphena took her turn, the ancient smiling oddly where she sat on the green leather chesterfield, as if she felt he needed encouragement. —Are you all right, Nan? he asked and she went on smiling in a surprised, pleading fashion. —Nan? he said.

By the time he'd fetched Hannah from the garden Mary Tryphena had found her voice and insisted there wasn't a thing wrong with her. —You scared me, Abel said and she laughed at him, as if his fear was a childish thing. She reached a hand to touch his face. —You loves your Nan, don't you.

—Yes, he said. —I do.

She said, I waited all my life for you, Abel Devine.

And there was something in the declaration that made the boy feel like bawling.

—We should get you to the hospital, Hannah said.

Mary Tryphena shook her head. —I'd kill for a cup of tea, she said. But she didn't touch the mug when Hannah set it on the table beside her.

—Do you want that tea or not?

—Can't move me arms, my love, she said. She shook her head and smiled at them in the same strangely apologetic fashion, the words gone again. Hannah sent Abel to fetch the doctor but the old woman was dead before they came back over the Tolt.

Judah Devine had been so long out of people's minds that no one thought to carry the news of Mary Tryphena's passing to his lunatic cell until after the wake. There was no sign of the man inside and he'd clearly been gone from the place a long time. Bald strips of sky showed through the roof and salt-spray rimed the gaps in the lungers underfoot. People felt foolish to have accepted the fact Judah was living out his days in the godforsaken hole and they denied ever believing such a thing. Some claimed to know he'd left the waterfront shortly after the locks came off the prison doors and spent the remainder of his days on an old trappers' line near the Breakers. Others that the escape was a recent one and Judah was still holed up in a woodland tilt near Nigger Ralph's Pond.

The greater mystery in it all was Mary Tryphena's custom of walking the Tolt Road to keep the appointment with her absent husband. If it was meant to cover Jude's departure no one could say why she considered such a thing necessary. Newman thought there was something mournful about the observance in retrospect, as if the woman was holding vigil at a gravesite. He tried to parse it out with Bride after the funeral but she simply turned to burrow into him on the bed. —She's gone to the peace of Jesus now, she said.

They fell into their oldest argument then, bickering back and forth. Bride's willingness to surrender human questions to mystery so blithely was a kind of laziness, Newman thought. He didn't understand why it appealed to a woman who despised sloth in any other guise.

—You can't bear the notion there's more to the world than what your little mind can swallow, Bride told him.

There was more to Bride than his little mind could swallow, that much he was willing to admit. He'd known from the outset that something of his wife would remain a stranger and his jealousy of that private corner kept his appetite for her keen. All their disagreements seemed to end with his face buried in her neck, his hands on her thighs to bring her close and closer again. Glory and mystery enough in those moments to shut him up awhile.

Levi Sellers had Judah's fishing room torn down after Mary Tryphena died. The rotten wood was tossed to a scrap fire on the waterfront—the pallet Jude slept on, the wallboards tattooed every inch with scripture as if the words offered some insulation from the cold. All of it set adrift on the wind, along with the ferocious smell that hung in the room until it came down, the unmistakable scour of blood and salt that Judah left behind him like a fingerprint.

Abel was listless and inconsolable without Mary Tryphena's company and his parents were at a loss to lift him out of his funk. Dr. Newman suggested that isolation and lack of activity was half the problem and Eli, who had been working one of Matthew Strapp's inshore crews since the Trims' sawmill shut down for lack of trees, convinced Hannah to let him take the boy out on finer days. Abel was surprisingly hardy on the water, cutting tail to identify the cod he jigged aboard, the marked fish set in store with his father's share at season's end. He proved himself a dab hand with a fish knife, though Hannah refused to let him stand in the cold and damp of the splitting room for long. The cod ran strong all summer which the fishermen credited to Abel's presence in the boat and it was hard to keep him off the water then, despite Hannah's misgivings. The Labrador crews came home with more fish than they'd seen in years and everyone on the shore was buoyant to see their fortunes turn.

The same fool's-gold story played out across the country, the same crushing disappointment. Prices collapsed with the glut of high-grade fish dumped on the European market and most hands were paid off

with less than they'd seen since the bank failures of 1894. It was a
bleak lesson, to be blessed with plenty only to learn that abundance
could be a tool of destitution, and all through that fall people abandoned the shore. James and Matthew Blade left for the Boston States,
and after three months at work they sent money to their families for
passage and a little extra to ensure their children arrived in half-decent
shoes. John Blade, who knew nothing but the ocean the length of his
life, left with them. Two dozen more set out for Halifax and Quebec,
for Boston and New York and homesteads further west. The sudden
groundswell of movement had the feel of a natural disaster, something
irresistible and ruinous bearing down on them. Tryphie was looking for
positions in furniture factories in Connecticut and Maryland. Even Levi
Sellers' youngsters were going off one by one to join kin who were
prospering in the milk-and-honey states of America. Given the shape
of things, people said, he'd have no need of an heir on the shore.

Eli and Hannah considered following after the Blades themselves
before Abel took sick over the Christmas season and Newman diag-
nosed him with tuberculosis. There was little chance of recovery, the
doctor said, and only a year of enforced rest offered any hope.
Everything in the old servant's quarters at the back of Selina's House
was shifted to an outbuilding, a small stove rigged up for heat. They
moved in a bed and Patrick Devine's library and Abel settled into the
exile he'd been rehearsing for all his life. There were periodic visits
from the doctor to take fluid off his lungs, and from Bride who brought
his meals and took away his filthy sputum box. But his mother and the
books his grandfather salvaged from the Atlantic were his only real
companions. A veranda was built outside the back door as far as the
southeast corner and Hannah set him up on a cot for the fresh air when
the weather allowed, Abel drifting in and out of sleep as she read to
him. He entered and left the stories by side doors and windows and
found it impossible to distinguish one book from another. The complications and disappointments and modest epiphanies of those disparate

lives seemed part of a single all-encompassing story that had swallowed him whole.

Eli went back at the fish in the spring, on the water before light six days a week, clearing the last of the cod in the whorl of seal-oil torches before walking gingerly home in the black, half-asleep on his feet. And no clue if there'd be a copper to show for it come the fall. Hannah already in bed and pretending to sleep when he came through the door, a plate of food kept in the oven. They never spoke of it directly, but he knew Hannah blamed him for dragging the boy out in all weather. And he supposed she might be right to think so. On Sundays he helped set Abel out on the veranda and then left them to the books, spending the duration of the visit in Tryphie's workshop.

The Sculpin still occupied the centre of the room. Tryphie declared it ready for a test voyage but his hunchback made it impossible to squeeze into the cockpit and no one else was willing to risk the job. Eli leaned against the Sculpin as they talked aimlessly about Tryphie's latest under-taking or the state of Abel's health. —He's a tough little bugger, Eli said.

Tryphie felt a particular empathy for the boy's predicament and he took exception to Eli's glib assessment. —You haven't got a goddamn clue, Tryphie insisted, you know that?

—That's quite a claim coming from the inventor of the Sculpin.

Tryphie reached for a screwdriver.

—I was just leaving, Eli said, backing away with his arms in the air.

Tryphie turned to the workbench to set the screwdriver down. —I've been meaning to tell you, he said over his shoulder. —Been offered a job in Hartford. Me and Minnie are heading up there come September month.

Eli was at the door and he leaned against it. —When did you hear? he asked finally.

—A few weeks back. I've been meaning to tell you.

Eli nodded over the news awhile, his eyes on his shoes. —You'll do well, he said.

Eli lay awake a good part of that night and woke early to the wind beating at the house like a sledgehammer. His heart hammering against his chest in the same wild fashion. He got out of bed and Hannah called after him. —You won't be going out on the water in this, she said.

—I'll just start the fire.

He knocked around the kitchen awhile but couldn't stay inside, pushing out the door into the weather. He walked into Paradise Deep while it was still dark, the wind so fierce on the Tolt he had to crawl on his hands and knees to stay on the headland. The sun came up a grey disc on the horizon as he walked to Tryphie's workshop behind Selina's House, the room empty but for the bulk of the Sculpin. Eli stood there as the day's slow rise brought the machine out of the shadows. He hauled himself up top and swung the hatch open to peer inside. The entryway as big around as an outhouse hole and he stripped out of his pants and shirt to slither through, settling himself nearly naked among the pedals and gearshifts and tackle. Through the starboard porthole he saw Tryphie come in the door and Eli lifted his head above the hatch.

—Jesus Eli, Tryphie said. —Don't mess around with her.

—Can't let you leave and not launch this thing, he said. He squiggled back into the seat.

—How does it feel in there?

—Snug as a casket, Eli shouted.

The Sculpin was wheeled to the shoreline the following Sunday. A huge crowd on the waterfront to watch the strange device being towed to the middle of the harbour on a barrel raft. Eli stripped to his skivvies and climbed inside, Tryphie leaning over the hatch to review the operation one last time. —You have to keep her trim when you let go the ballast tanks, he was saying. Eli looked up at his cousin as one esoteric instruction after another rattled his way, yaw and pitch, stern planes and rudder. —Shut up Ladybug he said.

Tryphie reached to shake his hand and Eli held on awhile.

—You'll do well, Tryphie told him, not to worry.

—I wish you were dead, Eli said.

Tryphie sealed the hatch and stepped off into a dory where he set about hammering holes in the barrels to scupper the raft. The iron fish floated clear into the bay, the sea around her boiling with escaping air and the vessel descending gracefully enough until she was halfway underwater. She started rolling aft then, Tryphie shouting correctional adjustments that seemed no help to Eli. The keel broke the surface a moment and the capsized vessel sank slowly into the black.

There was no plan for what in the aftermath seemed altogether predictable. Men scrambled to get boats on the water, half a dozen dories sculling to the spot where she went down. It was seven fathoms to the bottom and they tried to hook some part of the hull with grapples, casting where air bubbled to the surface. Two lines were rowed to shore and fifty men dragged the weight of the machine into the shallows where she lay on her side. A flood of seawater poured clear when Tryphie released the hatch, Eli extracted from the innards by the white of his hair. He was unconscious and his lungs waterlogged and the doctor worked him over for fifteen minutes on the beach before he could be brought to the hospital.

He didn't come to himself until the next morning, his eyes trolling slowly about the bed where Hannah and Bride and Tryphie stood watching him. Bride called for the doctor and Eli shook his head against the pillow. —This was all a mistake, he said.

—Don't waste your strength, Bride told him.

He was home the next day and back on the water with Strapp's crew two days later. But he refused visitors and never left the house except to work. He talked in monosyllables and ate his food with an apathy that verged on revulsion. No one spoke of the accident for what it was but Hannah could see that Eli was skewed somehow, as if his mind had capsized along with the Sculpin. For weeks she tried to pass Eli's listlessness off as a kind of hangover, as if the shadow on his heart was a physical bruise that would fade with time. But when she could stand it no longer she went to see Reverend Violet, thinking a dose of the evangelist's forcefulness and drive might be the tonic Eli needed.

The minister came to visit the house on a Sunday afternoon. —I thought I'd drop in, he said. —I'm not keeping you from something? He sat on the edge of a chair, hitching his pants up at the knee. Violet was past sixty and just as relentless as the missionary who appeared on the shore forty years before. His wife had raised a family of seven children while he proselytized the coastline and he had installed sons in the pulpits of new churches in Spread Eagle and Smooth Cove. Half the shore flew the Methodist banner as a result of his tireless campaigning. He had no time for prevarication. —Your wife is afraid there's some harm come to you.

—I'm fine, Eli said.

—You give yourself a good fright, he said.

—Never felt better.

They danced awkwardly back and forth the room this way for half an hour and neither man would surrender the lead. Violet stood finally and went to the door. —The Lord brings us low to lift us up, he said. —When you're stripped bare, that's the time to seek your true life, Eli. The minister pointed across the room with his hat. —Ye must be born again, he said.

Eli watched Violet walk across the garden and pass Mary Tryphena's empty house before he stood from his chair and set it carefully beside the table. He went upstairs and lay in his son's bed and he didn't budge before it was time to go out on the water the next morning.

In the middle of August word of a visitor passed along the shore. Eli heard of him from the other men on his fishing crew while they rowed out to the cod trap. A fellow named Crocker or Croker was calling a meeting of fishermen at the old Episcopalian church. Out of Notre Dame Bay, some said, though others claimed he was born and bred in St. John's, the son of a carpenter. Lost a merchant store in the bank crash and spent most of the years since running a farm on some island near Herring Neck. —A *farm,* Lord Jesus, Val Woundy said. The man had to be some sort of lunatic to persevere at the venture so long. He was supposed to have beaten his wife often enough to drive her away to St. John's with their only child in tow. A union he'd come to speak to them about, that and his plans to reform the country's fishery. From all reports Mr. Crocker or Cooker or Creaker—closet townie, failed merchant, crackpot farmer—had never caught a fish in his life. He'd worn the leather off his shoes gathering men in stores and church halls and kitchens across the northeast of the island. —Son of a carpenter, Val Woundy said, and fancies himself the fishermen's messiah.

It promised to be an entertaining evening and Eli's crew showed up at his house to drag him along, thinking the diversion might do him some good. Most of the men were away fishing on the Labrador which ensured a modest turnout, twenty or thirty scattered through the pews in the late-evening light. The hush in the damp church just enough to tamp down the undercurrent of ridicule they'd brought with them. At one minute past the appointed hour Thomas Trass suggested it was all a joke and no such man as Mr. Cracker ever lived.

The door to the vestibule opened then and he came up the centre aisle without looking left or right, leaning his weight on a cane. He turned below the pulpit to face them. —Thank you all for coming, he said. He was thickset though he carried the weight like a working man. Face falling into flesh and a trim little moustache, a receding hairline that made him appear older than his years. —My name, he said, is William Coaker.

He had the rhythm and demeanour of a preacher, the same bluff assurance. He began with an overview of the sad facts of a fisherman's life, the deplorable conditions they lived and worked in, the parasites in St. John's who bled them dry. A sycophantic tone to the presentation that made the men restless, the grievances so familiar they could have rhymed them off in their sleep. But Coaker paused at the end of the list, breeding anticipation with his silence, and they all leaned slightly forward in their pews. —You people, he said finally. He pointed with his sausage fingers. Grovellers, he called them. They were living the same miserable lives their fathers lived and their fathers' fathers before them. The wealth of the nation made on their backs and every one of them content to beg at Levi Sellers' door. They were backward and illiterate and happy to leave their children no hope of a better life.

A ripple of indignation stirred the room but there was enough truth in the harangue to keep them quiet. They knew nothing, Coaker told them. Not where their fish was sold or the price it sells for, not the cost of provisions they were paid with. They wouldn't even know how to go about asking. A decade into the twentieth century and they caught and sold their fish the way it was caught and sold when Napoleon ruled Europe. —And what is your excuse for this sorry state? Coaker asked. —That there's no changing the way things are because they've always been this way. The notion was so distasteful to him that it looked for a moment as if Coaker might spit. It was the only form of laziness, he said, that he'd ever observed in a Newfoundlander.

Eli felt himself pulled upright in his seat as the man went on, each new accusation ringing like a bell in the steeple. —Who among you gets their due from their labour? Coaker asked. —Do you receive your own when you have to work like a dog, eat like a pig, and be treated like a serf?

—No, Eli called out.

—No, Coaker confirmed. —You do not. Do you receive your own when your taxes pay for five splendid colleges in St. John's while your so-called schools lack teachers and books and equipment?

—No, Eli answered and others with him. Coaker threw out questions until half the men in the pews were shouting the same response. He stopped to pace a few moments, letting them stew. —I've signed up a thousand men across Notre Dame Bay and more joining us every day, he announced. —Men who were never taught to do a sum or read a word or ask for anything more than what was given them. But they are done with the world of ignorance and pauperism they were born into. *Suum Cuique*, Coaker said. —Let each man have his own. This is our motto in the Fishermen's Protective Union, one thousand strong and growing by the day. And I ask you now. Who here has the fortitude to join us?

—I do, Eli said, out of his seat with a hand raised high. He was ripe for it, the new life Violet prophesied for him, he felt ready to be born again.

Coaker asked those who wished to join to stay behind and a handful were still in the pews after the church emptied out, Val Woundy, Azariah Trim and his nephew Joshua, Doubting Thomas Trass. Coaker had one more night in Paradise Deep and they made plans to meet him again the next evening. —There's much to be done, he told them.

—Do you have a bed? Eli asked.

—I was about to ask if I might impose on someone.

—We've got room if you don't mind the walk.

Coaker said, A walk is just what I was wanting.

The three of them set out for the Gut, Eli and Val Woundy and the union man. It was almost an hour over the Tolt from the old church and Coaker talked the entire time, fish prices and overseas markets, competition and quality control, co-op stores and cash money in place of truck. The moon rising to light their way. Standards, Coaker harped on, standards and modernization. The fishery a shambles of dark-age technology and economics that had to be dragged into the modern world. Pricing had to be standardized, inspection and culling standardized, a minimum wage for labour legislated, compulsory schooling for all instituted, the quality of the cured product had to be standardized.

—Mr. Coaker, Val Woundy said, you aren't about to standardize the bloody weather.

—Perhaps not the weather. But why should we be dependent solely on the sun to cure the fish?

Val glared at him as if Coaker's lunacy was about to be confirmed.

—You mean dryers, Eli said.

—I mean let's question everything about how we operate. Where there are problems, we look for solutions.

—Hot-air dryers, Eli said. —Set them up in a warehouse. It could rain every day in August and it wouldn't make a peck of difference.

Coaker raised a hand. —Let's not get too far ahead of ourselves.

—I heard you was a farmer, Val said.

—Lay off him, Val, Eli warned but Coaker only smiled. Born on the southside of St. John's, he told them. Worked as a fish handler in Town as a boy, organized a two-day strike for equal wages when he learned a competitor paid more for the same job. Skipped school to listen to political speeches in the Legislature. —Shambler was your man for Paradise District, he said.

—He was, God rest him.

—He got plenty of that in the House, Coaker said.

Hired to run a merchant store in Pike's Arm when he was only sixteen, buying the operation outright at twenty. The bank crash buried the store and he purchased an island, set about farming it. Coakerville, he called the place. Taught himself the job of telegraph operator and worked at it through the winters to keep the farm from folding. Years of isolation to read and think, to pick apart the engine driving the country's corkscrew of toil and misery, to scheme and read.

—You don't seem old enough to have lived that much, Val Woundy said.

—All my living's yet to come, Coaker said. —This is the life I was meant for.

Val turned off to his house at the foot of the Tolt and the two men carried on past Mary Tryphena's. There was a light in Eli's window across the garden and as they drew closer they could see Hannah sitting up at the kitchen table, her lap full of crochet cotton. —Your wife, Coaker said, nodding ahead.

—My wife.

—And what else, Eli Devine. You haven't offered a word about yourself. You must have Scandinavian blood to get a shock of hair as white as that.

Eli shook his head.

—Well, your accent says Irish.

—We're neither fish nor fowl, our crowd, Eli said and he looked away across the cove. —We could walk on a little ways, he said. —Unless you're ready to call it a night.

They went as far as Kerrivan's Tree and stood among the silvered branches while Eli made a maze of Tryphie's scalding and his youthful obsession with America, his mother's family garden and James Woundy's mermaid and Hannah's webbed fingers, of Judah and his whale, of Levi Sellers and Patrick Devine's library and Obediah's crooked limbs at the foot of the cathedral. —Abel was christened in this very tree, Eli said. He'd never been called upon to set his story in order for a stranger and could not lay his hand on a straight line. It confirmed his suspicion he'd made a royal mess of his life. He leaned his forearms on a tree branch to get that much closer to Coaker, to the notion that all his living might be ahead of him. —All I ever wanted was to get the hell away from here.

—I thought about leaving myself, Coaker said. —Years ago.

—And what is it kept you?

—I figured I could change myself, he said, or change the country that made me.

Coaker reached to take Eli's scarred hand, running a thumb across the childhood injury a moment. There was a doctor's practised ease in the gesture, as if he was simply evaluating how well the wound had healed. —Let each man have his own, he said. —Would you stay for as much, Eli? If all you wanted was here to be had?

Eli drew his hand away and tucked it under his arm. He said, Have you really got a thousand men signed on to this union?

—You aren't having second thoughts already, Mr. Devine.

—Levi Sellers is a hard man, is all I mean. He won't just sit back and watch.

—You're afraid of Levi, is it?

—He burnt Matthew Strapp's barn years ago, to keep him out of Shambler's way.

Coaker nodded. —I don't think that's what scares you, he said.

Eli smiled to hide his confusion. —What is it scares me then?

—You think you're meant for something different than what you've got.

—It might be.

—But you're afraid to look a fool reaching for it, Coaker said. —That's what scares you.

Eli straightened and looked out at the black water of the cove. He could feel the blood in his face and was grateful for the darkness. To hell with you, William Coaker, he was thinking, but couldn't manage to speak it aloud.

—Perhaps we should get back, the union man suggested. —Your wife will be wondering where you've got to.

Hannah was half-asleep in her chair when they arrived. —We've got a stray for the night, Eli said though he seemed altogether poisoned by the man's presence. She set Coaker up in Abel's room and then went on to bed herself. Eli hadn't slept in the same room with her since Reverend Violet's visit and he lay on the daybed near the stove. He was up hours before light to fix himself a cold breakfast and was about to douse the lamp on his way out when he heard footsteps on the stairs. —Early to be up yet, Mr. Coaker, he said.

—I'm not much for sleep, Eli.

—There's bread and a few capelin in the pantry, help yourself.

Coaker had his jacket across his arm, his suspenders hanging loose at his sides. —I wanted to say, he said. —If I overstepped yesterday night.

—You were right about me, Eli told him. —About everything.

They watched one another and Coaker nodded encouragement. —Then I'll see you at the meeting tonight.

—Please God, I'll be there.

It was a week after Coaker left before Eli was able to get to Tryphie. He hadn't stepped inside the workshop since the accident, the Sculpin's carcass abandoned outside the doors. Tryphie was hunched over a diagram with ruler and pencil and didn't look up to greet his visitor. The walls above the workbenches were stripped clean of tools. Eli leaned in to watch awhile, trying to outwait him. Turned to stand against the bench finally. —If you were going to build a warehouse to dry salt fish, he said.

Tryphie glanced up, squinting. —A what?

—A warehouse for drying fish.

—Hot-air dryers, you mean.

—Could be.

—You'd want forced air.

—You think fans or what?

—You could rig it up with electric fans, Tryphie said. —But something that large you'd need your own power station.

—One bloody step at a time, Eli said.

Tryphie flipped the paper and began sketching a rough notion. Lost in the size of it, the technical issues that came piling one on the other. He was throwing out figures as he worked and the two men riffed back and forth on specifications and alternative designs, the exchange so fluid and singular it was almost sexual. They carried on another fifteen minutes before Tryphie paused in mid-stroke. —Who is it building a fish warehouse?

—You hear about William Coaker when he was here?

—The farmer? Tryphie said. —Jesus loves the little children.

—He've got a thousand men signed on in Notre Dame Bay, Tryph. Says another two or three thousand by next spring. I'm going up to

Herring Neck the winter. See how the union locals work, how the co-op stores are set up.

—Does Levi know anything about this?

—You should come with me, Eli said.

Tryphie laughed and walked across the workroom floor.

—This is going to change the country, Tryphie, top to bottom.

—That's a lot to ask of a fish dryer.

Eli picked up the sheet of paper and folded it. —We could be part of this, he said. —Me and you.

—Minnie's set on the States.

Eli nodded to himself awhile. He asked a few half-hearted questions about arrangements for travel and where in Hartford they'd be living and Tryphie answered with his back to Eli, picking at a trunkful of tools. —I'll go on then, Eli said finally but he didn't move from where he stood. He said, I rolled the Sculpin, Tryph. I sank her on purpose. He let out a long breath. —I thought you should hear it from me. In case there was a question in your mind.

—You're all right now, are you?

—Never better, he said.

Eli left for Coaker's winter quarters in Herring Neck a month after Tryph and Minnie sailed for the States. Hannah moved over the Tolt to stay at Selina's House while Eli was away doing God knows what in Notre Dame Bay. Bride set up a space for her in the upstairs room that Mr. Gallery had fallen into generations past, her cot set off from the hospital beds by a sheet hung from the ceiling. Hannah occupied her days with the tasks Minnie abandoned when she left, cooking and laundry and mopping floors. She read awhile to Abel each evening and drank a cup of tea with Bride while Newman carried out his last rounds. They discussed the day's patients and weather and the minutest details of Abel's condition. They talked often of the union, like everyone else on the shore. Coaker had passed through again at the end of October, speaking to three hundred men in the old Trim sawmill, making overnight trips with Eli to Red Head Cove and Spread Eagle and Smooth Cove where dozens more took the union pledge. Eli staying up half the night with Coaker to strategize, spending the days in clandestine discussions with fishermen, pushing the dream. It had been a relief to see him interested in the world again, if not in herself and Abel in particular. She thought he would come around to them soon enough. But there was a growing absence about her husband that was making her doubtful. —What do you think will become of it all, Bride?

Bride stirred sugar into her cup, set the spoon on the saucer. She'd heard people speak of Coaker as a tonic for the ills of the world. A visionary, they said. It made her squirm, that sort of church talk applied to someone flesh and blood. Coaker had the manner of a born pragmatist which made her suspicious of his lofty notions. As if she expected they would come to a bad end on the shoals of some trade-off down the line.

They could hear Abel coughing in the next room and both women turned their heads to the sound, waiting for the spasm to end.

—I don't know, maid, Bride said after the youngster went quiet. —I can't help thinking there's some lack in a man who would name a place after himself like that. Coakerville, she said. And the women laughed at the foolishness of it.

Coaker insisted that all F.P.U. members be able to read and write and he tasked Azariah Trim with arranging instruction on the shore. The union's night-school classes began at the end of November and forty-five men gathered in a lamplit room once a week to learn their letters. Az recruited Bride to teach and she nursed her students along with the same mix of temerity and charm that made her so invaluable at the hospital. By the time they left for the seal hunt in March most of the original forty-five were able to write their own names and read simple Bible verses and count by fives and tens.

The regular union meetings preceded the school sessions and without Coaker's guidance they degenerated into fractious free-for-alls. After those first heady weeks, a hangover of doubt set in. They had only Coaker's word that such a thing as the Fishermen's Protective Union existed. No one knew how the F.P.U. planned to outfit members for the fishery or sell their fish at the end of the year. Doubting Thomas Trass led a group demanding assurances, securities, but there were none to be offered. —We got nothing if we don't hang together, Az Trim told the room.

—Levi Sellers will see us all hang together if he gets wind of this, Trass insisted. —Make no mistake.

The numbers at the meetings dwindled as the season crept closer. Thomas Trass stayed on despite his vocal reservations and it seemed that the schooling was all that held him. He was one of Bride's slowest students, working at the lessons with a dull earnestness. He'd taken to tracing his name absently on the tabletop or his thigh during any idle moment, Thomas Trass, Thomas Trass, Thomas Trass, as if he had to continually remind himself who he was. Trass was past sixty and a lifelong bachelor. He was engaged to a girl in Smooth Cove as a young man and walked thirty miles down the shore the day before the wedding to find her dead. It was well after dark when he arrived, his fiancée laid out in the kitchen for her wake, and he'd turned to walk back to Paradise Deep without so much as taking off his jacket. There was something about Thomas Trass, people said, that was still out on that trail in the dead of night, somewhere between Smooth Cove and home.

After each night class he and Val Woundy accompanied Bride to Selina's House and saw her through the door. Val headed home to the Gut then and Thomas lay an hour on his daybed as he'd been instructed. Not a light on the shore when he slipped back into the cold, no sound but his footsteps over the snow. He walked along Sellers' Drung toward Selina's House, then beyond it to Levi's property where he circled behind the house to the barn. Levi sitting on a stool at the rear, among the heat of the animals. —I was starting to think perhaps they turned you, Sellers said each time Trass picked his way past the stalls to offer a report on the night's developments. It was all about to fall to pieces as far as Trass could tell and he'd be sorry to lose the schooling if it happened sooner rather than later.

Levi handed the man his two dollars and sat awhile longer after Trass left, avoiding his bed to spare himself the hours of lying there insomniac. He tried to think of the last proper night's sleep he had, sometime long before Mary Tryphena Devine passed on. Levi used to watch for her from his office window, the woman on her trek to the fishing room where Judah wasted away, and he developed a grudging admiration for the old woman's mettle. He'd had to keep reminding himself who she was to his father, but it all seemed so distant he barely felt it. She was just a marker in his days at the end, like a clock striking the hours.

It wasn't until she died that he learned Judah was missing and Levi felt a surge of the old poison in his gut. He burned the white bastard's crazy work scored on the walls of the fishing room, as if the absence of physical evidence might convince him the man had never existed at all. But he felt cheated of something by the disappearance. It was as if the old crone had made a cuckold of him. And that thought renewed his failing animosities.

He had Trass go along to Coaker's initial gathering at the old church out of idle curiosity. Sent inquiries to acquaintances in Notre Dame Bay and St. John's who reported Coaker was a loner and a fool, possibly delusional, addled by his years trying to conjure a farm out of rock and bog, by a marriage he was ill-suited for. The notion of him building a union was a joke, they said. Levi engaged Trass to attend the clandestine weekly meetings and he compiled a list of the local men who had taken the pledge. He was particularly gregarious when he crossed paths with them at church or on the streets, asking after their health and the health of their families, thinking how their faces would look when the union foundered and they came begging for credit. The spring promised to be as good as a concert.

He went to his bed after midnight and crawled out of it long before light. He was at the table when Adelina and Flossie came down to their breakfast. The women were virtually inseparable before the children left for the States and he never saw them but in one another's company now, walking the garden paths arm in arm, sitting together in the evenings to knit or crochet or read. He tried to send them to America with the youngsters and it was still a mystery why they refused. —I made a vow, Flossie told him, her eyes averted. As if it was a life sentence.

The women never spoke against him, but there were subtle acts of defiance he couldn't miss. Volunteering at the hospital after he bargained away Selina's House. Offering singing lessons to Tryphie Newman's daughter, cutting clippings from the *Evening Telegram* whenever there was a mention of the Nightingale of Paradise. Sitting side by side at Mary Tryphena's funeral in their best black mourning as if the woman were kin.

—How did you sleep? Flossie asked him.

—Adequately.

His wife set her knife carefully across her plate and glanced at Adelina. The two women were unfailingly demure in his presence, but there was an air of condescension about them, the residue of whispered conversations when his back was turned. —Have you thought of speaking to Dr. Newman? she asked.

—About what exactly?

Adelina said, It's been months of this now, Levi.

—You're exhausted, Flossie told him.

There it was, the one thing he could not abide, the reason they refused to leave with the children. They pitied him. He pushed his chair back from the table. —Sleep, he said, is the urging of the Devil.

In March the local men who'd secured sealing berths left for Harbour Grace and Brigus and as far as St. John's en route to the ice fields after whitecoats. No union meetings were held while they were gone and it was nearly a month before the sealers made their way back, wearing the clothes they left in, sleeves and pant cuffs crusted with blood, the lot of them haggard and punch-drunk and carrying trinkets from the Water Street stores for their wives and children. The sealers collected Eli Devine on their way through Notre Dame Bay and on the night of the union's first meeting back Levi went out to the barn as soon as the women retired, anxious to hear what Thomas Trass had to report.

It was a wild night, the rafters cracking in the wind and the cows restless. The foul weather made time crawl and Levi took out his pocket watch periodically to glare at it in the dark, trying to guess the hour. He'd all but given up on Trass when the door at the other end of the building opened and was hauled shut against the gale. The gust stirring up the smell of piss in the straw. —I was starting to think perhaps they'd turned you, Levi said and even before he finished speaking he knew it wasn't Thomas Trass coming toward him in the dark.

—Hello Levi.

—Not a very pleasant evening to be strolling about, Eli Devine.

—Thomas asked me to tell you he won't be able to make his appointment.

The thought crossed Levi's mind that Trass had been playing him all along but he dismissed it. The man didn't have the imagination.

—Val Woundy has been keeping a close eye on your Mr. Trass, Eli said, as if he could guess Levi's thoughts.

—Trass has been feeding me lies all along, I suppose.

—Let's just say the union meetings that mattered did not take place on the same night as Bride's classes.

Levi laughed out loud, slapping at his thighs. —Splendid, he said. —And this is the point where I claim to have a man attending the *secret* secret union meetings as well.

—You don't have the first clue what's coming, Levi. But I wanted to come by to tell you to watch for it. So you'll know I helped steer it your way.

Eli turned to leave and Levi followed after him. —You had an enjoyable time in the company of Mr. Coaker, he said. —Mr. Coaker wouldn't allow a man like yourself to go without the creature comforts. He took care of your needs while you were away from your wife?

The door swung shut and Levi pushed out into the weather, chasing Eli as far as the road. He was shouting for all he was worth though he could barely hear himself in the wind. He carried on yelling uselessly a while, the words whipped back over the roof of the house and scattered across the Gaze.

It was the Old Hollies that woke her, Flossie thought, the keening voices of some long-drowned sailors carried ashore by the storm, and she lay still in her room praying for them to pass. Heard the back door then, the entire house shifting to accommodate the weather's push. And the eerie voice rose through the wind's racket again, half-strangled and pleading, though she could swear now it was coming from somewhere inside the house. She rushed across to Adelina's room, shaking her awake. —Listen, she whispered. —Listen, listen, listen.

They went arm in arm down the hall, calling for Levi. The garbled voice going on as they reached the stairs and crept toward it one step at a time. —Levi? Adelina called again and the voice went quiet finally. They could just hear the muted sound of sobbing where Sellers lay helpless on the floor below.

Levi learned to scrawl a signature with his left hand after the stroke but needed assistance to perform the simplest tasks, to dress and eat and go to the outhouse. His eye was nearly closed on the dead side of his face, the invalid flesh so shapeless and drooping that he looked like a wax figurine set too close to the heat. Two hundred and seventy-six men came off his rolls that spring, taking provision sent by schooner from Notre

Dame Bay instead. The union members paid St. John's prices for their gear which led to complaints from the fishermen still buying at Sellers & Co., and Levi lived in a state of perpetual vexation.

It was only the intervention of the Catholic Archdiocese that saved Sellers & Co. from complete ruin. Father Reddigan had blessed the union's first steps on the shore with his silence, though he'd heard murmurs from the archbishop's office in St. John's. Before the men returned from the seal hunt in the spring, he received a letter of instruction dismissing the F.P.U. as a secret society that bound its members by an unlawful oath and was ipso facto condemned by the Church. *No Catholic can join it,* the archbishop wrote, *unless he means to incur the Censures of the Church. If he has taken any oath in the Society let him understand it is unlawful and not binding. Please act on this information to stamp out the Society at once if it has appeared in your Parish.* Reddigan made the announcement at Mass four Sundays in a row and by the time the Labrador crews set out in June not a single Catholic on the shore remained a member of the F.P.U.

Abel Devine spent part of each morning on the hospital veranda when the weather allowed. Everyone who passed would call or wave, as if it was bad luck not to acknowledge the Devine boy struck with consumption. The only person who ignored him was Levi, stilting his way past Selina's House toward the offices of Sellers & Co. His right arm in a permanent clench against the chest, the nearly paralyzed leg swinging from the waist like a pendulum.

Eli had been back in the Gut since March but Abel's mother chose to stay on at the hospital. The three of them spent part of each Sunday morning on the veranda before church and that was all there was to them as a family. Hannah refused to have Abel stirred up and she protected him from any talk of the union or politics in general, though even a shut-in could sense the tide of change rising on the shore.

Abel's condition improved through the summer and on his better days he wasn't content to lie in bed. He paced his tiny room or sat at the shelves to leaf through books he'd never opened before, just for the novelty of it. He stood on a chair to reach Jabez Trim's Bible tucked away on the highest shelf. He had no memory of seeing the book in Patrick Devine's library and didn't know what to make of the artifact. The pages were leathery and thick, the hand-lettered text archaic and blurred. It seemed a foreign language he was looking at and he wrote out lines and verses, trying to imitate the baroque bells and curves as if he was sketching a landscape. He spent weeks writing his way through Genesis and Deuteronomy and Psalms and Ecclesiastes, figuring one letter at a time, making the strange script his own through repetition.

There was a rush to join the F.P.U. in the fall. The union fish was sold in bulk in St. John's, fetching fifty cents a quintal above the price paid by Sellers & Co. A circular letter from Coaker announced that His Lordship Bishop McNeil of St. George's had approved a new wording of the union's pledge, and Father Reddigan said nothing when three dozen Catholic men took the oath a second time ahead of word from the archbishop in St. John's. Half the shore's population ordered their winter provisions through Coaker's wholesale outfit and Levi sold off a portion of his waterfront property to Matthew Strapp to keep the company afloat.

Eli left for Change Islands to attend the annual session of the supreme council of the F.P.U. in late October. He was due home the first week of November with Coaker in tow and there was a flurry of activity in preparation for the great man's arrival. The doctor pronounced Abel well enough to go home when his father arrived and he waited for the union boat with more anticipation than most. He browsed aimlessly through Patrick Devine's library, opened books at random to read a line or two. He stood on his chair to bring down Jabez Trim's Bible, to be sure it was a real thing and not just some figment of his consumptive imagination. Tracing the letters with an index finger as he mouthed the words.

Out the window of his sickroom he'd watched a new building being raised near the Episcopal church through the fall. The letters

F.P.U. painted a storey high over the doorway now. He was the only person on the shore ignorant of the acronym's meaning. Friendly Priests Unfrocked, he guessed. Furious Partisan Utopia. Forgetful Pastoral Undertakers. Free Parcels Untied. Bunting was pinned to the front of the hall, an archway of fir branches and wildflowers waited on the new union wharf just acquired from Matthew Strapp.

He woke one night to the flicker of red and yellow across the ceiling and he lay watching it shiver and drift there like the northern lights, thinking it was the fire in the stove. When the alarm was raised it went house to house all the way to the Gut, two hundred men and women standing in a line to pass buckets up from the harbour. They saved the hall though the facing and part of the roof had to be torn out and replaced, men spidered over the building to repair it before Coaker's arrival. Abel walked by with Hannah the morning the letters were repainted in red above the doors.

—Foul Plot Unhinged, Abel said.

Hannah jerked his arm. —Has your father been telling you stories?

—It's just a game, he said, pointing up at the acronym. —Funeral Pyre Unlikely, he offered. —Fallen Paradise Uplifted.

She looked at him a long time, as if she still had her doubts.

A flotilla of skiffs and dories went out that afternoon to meet Coaker's yacht, escorting the *F.P. Union* into harbour where the waterfront was jammed with spectators. The lungers of the wharf were laid over with woven mats in the F.P.U. colours and half a dozen sealing guns fired as the procession came to the docks. Coaker was led a walkabout like royalty, shaking hands and ruffling youngsters' hair. Abel stood among the crowd with Hannah, his head resting on her hip. —This is the boy can't be killed, is it? Coaker asked when he reached them.

There was a parade to the F.P.U. Hall and Abel sat in Hannah's lap at the back of the stage during Coaker's speech. He was overcome by the exertion of the day and the crowd's heat and he nodded off while

the man was speaking, startled awake to applause and glanced up at Eli
Devine leading the ovation beside them. His father looked half-starved,
Abel thought, and was staring at the union man like he was something
good to eat.

Hannah took Abel back to Selina's House before the dance began
and he slept awhile in the room behind the kitchen. The door stood
open and he could hear his mother and Bride talking in whispers at the
table as he dozed. He woke sometime after dark to the quiet of a
woman crying, the wet suck of breath as she tried to stifle her sobs. He
thought it might be his mother but fell asleep again before he could say
for certain.

After he was discharged from the hospital Abel walked the paths in
the Gut to regain his strength, wandering as far as the French Cemetery
where he strolled among the headstones, marking the names of family
laid there. When Mary Tryphena was still with them he'd peppered her
with childish questions, wanting to know where was she born, how did
her father and mother die, was there a church on the shore when she was
a girl. —I don't remember nothing about them old times, was all she
said. And he was still a stranger among his kin in the French Cemetery.

Before winter settled in he was spending hours a day on the backcountry roads, travelling beyond Nigger Ralph's Pond toward the
Breakers, trying to set the vast spaces to heart. Compared with the
densely populated world of Patrick Devine's library, the scrubland and
bog seemed virtually uninhabited, a place without history or memory,
a landscape of perpetual present. He knew it as his country but was at a
loss to say how and he walked the barrens endlessly, as if walking was
a way of courting a world he was barely acquainted with.

By the spring, Father Reddigan was instructed a second time to
threaten the censures of the Church if his parishioners did not forswear
the union. But even with that loss, the F.P.U. had an air of inevitability
about it. Ten thousand men across the country had taken the pledge and
not the old cabal of St. John's merchants or the Catholic archbishop's

disapproval, not Sellers' arsonists or God Himself seemed capable of bringing the movement down. Union stores opened in Paradise Deep and in Spread Eagle, stocked to the rafters with Verbena and Five Roses and Royal Standard flour, with salt pork and salt beef, molasses, sugar and kerosene, with creamery and Forest butter, with Ceylon teas and tobacco, all at wholesale prices. The stores offered a framed picture of President William Coaker that sold by the hundreds and hung in kitchens and parlours along the shore like a Protestant crucifix.

When Abel was thirteen years old he and his father sailed to the annual F.P.U. convention in Bonavista, sitting among two hundred delegates as they debated and presented motions. There was an election coming and the union planned to run enough candidates to hold the balance of power in the House. They hammered out a platform on fishery regulations and education and old-age pensions and a minimum wage.

Abel's ongoing recovery from tuberculosis was singular enough to be linked to the rise in the union's fortunes. He'd grown eight inches in the previous year and went out with one inshore boat or another when he could sneak away from Hannah, working a full day on the water with the strength and energy of any boy his age. His father had been taking him to local meetings since he left hospital, the union members making a point of shaking his hand or touching the white of his head for luck. Abel's story had reached all corners of the country with a union branch and he was brought to the convention as a kind of mascot. Coaker asked him to stand on the first morning and Eli pushed Abel to his feet when he hesitated.

The meetings went on into the evening by lamplight and Eli spent every free moment in Coaker's company, conferring over cigarettes, walking with him at the end of the night to analyze the day's events or discuss future projects. Abel joined them on those walks but there was something exclusive about their conversation that made him feel solitary in their company. They made monumental decisions as if discussing what they might like for supper. —A new hospital is what we need up our way, Eli said. —Something to show what the union can make of the place. Selina's House can't hold half what the shore needs anymore.

Coaker nodding as he walked, chewing it over. —You get a fund-raising campaign started when you get back, he said. —I'll write to the prime minister.

The union did nothing before it passed through the president's head, the ten thousand permutations and ramifications of every act played out in Coaker's skull before a course was set. —I want you to run in Paradise District next election, he told Eli, and even Abel could tell the decision was made. —Would you like that, Abel? Coaker asked him. —Your father a member of the House? His tone suggested he merely had to say as much to make it so, like God decreeing there be light in the world.

—I guess so, Abel said. He'd been sharing a bed with Hannah since moving back to the Gut, his father sleeping alone down the hall, and he couldn't avoid the absurd thought the union leader had arranged this as well. There was something in Coaker he chose to dislike, an expectation of deference, a proprietary assurance. Coaker had lately insisted Abel call him Uncle Will. As far as Abel could see, *Uncle Will* had no interest in him or children in general, and the false note made him distrust the man that much more.

He stood at the rail with Eli as they sailed into Paradise Deep after the conference. The cathedral's steeple and the F.P.U. Hall flying the union flag, the Methodist chapel and Selina's House on the Gaze rising out of the hills to meet them. Without looking at his father he said, I wants my old room back.

Eli looked at him for only a moment. —I'll talk to your mother, he said.

Paradise District went to the F.P.U. in the 1913 election, as did thirteen others across the island. Eli's first order of business was finagling government money to match funds raised by the union for the new hospital, which was already under construction. Father Reddigan led a Catholic campaign for the project and the entire population turned out for the facility's opening. There was an eight-bed maternity ward and a consumptive wing, X-ray and pharmacy, an operating theatre equipped with acetylene lights and its own power generator, a telegraph room in the basement. It was as if the modern world had arrived on the shore under one roof and official celebrations went on through the day, prayer services and a luncheon with toasts and speeches from visiting dignitaries. But the hospital's wonders were overshadowed in the minds of most by Esther Newman who had come home to commemorate the opening with a special concert, the Nightingale of Paradise performing on the shore for the first time since Obediah Trim's funeral.

An over-capacity crowd assembled at the hall, people standing four and five deep outside the windows for a glimpse. No one had yet laid eyes on Esther. She'd been holed up three days at the new hospital with a flu, they were told, though some claimed she'd never arrived, that she was delayed in London or St. John's or had changed her mind and cancelled. It wasn't until Adelina Sellers took a seat at the upright piano below the stage that their doubts left them. A rustle passed through the room as she adjusted the piano stool and the pages of her music. When the curtains opened the audience was faced with the sight of a young Mary Tryphena Devine in a gown of georgette and seeded pearls, her hair black as a crow's wing, curled and tied up in a style they'd never seen.

Abel Devine was having difficulty thinking of the creature on the stage as his blood, though he'd been told as much. She was wearing tight strings of pearls at her neck and wrists, the delicate line of the collarbone bare below the clasp. Applause drowned out the first lines of the song completely and when the noise finally settled the hair rose on the back of Abel's neck. The voice seemed too extravagant to come from the figure on stage and he looked behind periodically, thinking it was some sort of elaborate ventriloquism. The audience roared whenever Esther drifted into those impossible ranges and no one heard her falter the first time, though Abel saw her flinch as if she'd been stung under the bell of her skirt. Something in her face turned inward before the smile reasserted itself. Adelina Sellers glanced up at the stage and Esther waved her on impatiently. A hush fell in the hall as the Nightingale's voice rose and broke like glass. The flesh of Esther's neck flushed red and she asked for water and carried on a little while before she collapsed on the stage.

It was all anyone spoke of for days afterward, the shock of Esther's otherworldly voice failing her and the indecent outfit she wore before the entire community and the secrecy that surrounded her arrival. She'd been locked in a room at the new hospital before the performance to keep her away from liquor, people said, she'd fallen down drunk on the stage. The union had paid for her travel from Europe and she'd been booked to perform in half a dozen other F.P.U. districts, but Coaker cancelled the tour after her collapse. Everyone expected she would sneak off the shore the way she'd arrived. But two weeks later Esther Newman took up residence in the shambles of Selina's House.

The old hospital had the feel of a place evacuated during an emergency. The air smelled of formaldehyde and disinfectant and chloroform and rot. The margins of each room cluttered with the detritus of thirty years of frontier medicine, outdated equipment, empty glass bottles and stacks of paper, the shards of ten thousand teeth trapped along the baseboards. Esther made a bed for herself in the main room upstairs where an insistent leak had stained a medieval map on the ceiling, the misshapen outline of the continents drawn where Mr. Gallery had once come through the plaster in his ghostly boots.

She never appeared outside the house but she was drunk, the black extravagance of her hair in fits, her childlike face puffy and discoloured. She was supplied her liquor by Des Toucher or someone of the like and no one doubted how she paid for it. When she went out she wore as much of her wardrobe as she could layer, one outfit on top of another, ball gowns and skirts and blouses and sweaters and elegant robes, a tangle of jewellery about her neck. She bought a goat from Val Woundy and kept it in the parlour, taking it for walks on a leash or harnessing it to a wooden truckley and riding through the streets. Bride once or twice contrived to bring her granddaughter to church on Sunday mornings and they walked arm in arm to their pew, the younger woman unsteady on her feet, her eyes licked out and her head chiming like a steeple bell.

Hardly a soul darkened her door through the winter though her antics occupied everyone's idle time. They felt their good will had been abused and a merciless accounting was underway. There was talk that her storied career in Europe was a sham, that she performed only in dance halls and burlesque and worse. She had taken to drink in the aftermath of an adulterous affair or an abortion or some other European scandal and only their respect for the doctor saved her from open ridicule. They'd surrendered her gift to the wider world without complaint or envy and they couldn't forgive her coming home a fallen woman.

Early in the new year, Bride came to the Gut to speak with Eli and Hannah. Esther had left the hospital for Selina's House to be clear of Newman's meddling, Bride said. She'd been living in a home for indigent women in London much of the previous year and there was nothing to go back to in Europe. She asked Eli to write a letter to Tryphie.

Eli wanted no part of it, embarrased still to have talked Coaker into paying Esther's way home from Europe. —Perhaps you should be the one to do that, he said.

—I don't have the heart to tell him myself, Eli.

—Maybe Dr. Newman, Eli said and Bride shook her head. Her husband was useless in the face of any affliction that couldn't be stitched or splinted or removed with a scalpel. He refused to talk about his granddaughter except to rail and curse and throw whatever came to hand against the wall. —Tryphie will take it better coming from you, Bride said. —Tell him we'll send her down to Hartford in the spring.

—If she don't burn the house down lighting a lamp in the meantime, Hannah said.

Eli nodded. —She shouldn't be left alone over there.

—She won't hear of coming back to the hospital with us, Bride said.

Abel was on the green chesterfield, pretending to read while the conversation went on. He'd seen Esther Newman riding through the streets of Paradise Deep with an alder whip in her hand, caught glimpses of her behind the windows of Selina's House, standing in that unnatural stage posture and singing drunkenly to her goat. He'd snuck to the back of the house once, inching the door open to listen. Nursery rhymes mostly, children's songs and nonsense syllables when the words failed her. He could smell the stink of the goat stabled down the hall. The only thing Esther managed all the way through was a ballad he'd never heard before, a woeful profession of love for a dark-haired girl that was so tortured and graceful it made him wish he hadn't stood there to listen. There was a long pause when she finished and he could hear his own breath in the quiet. —Who's there? she shouted and Abel battered the hell out of it, running up to Tryphie's workshop to hide behind the rusting remains of the Sculpin while Esther cursed from the doorway.

He hadn't worked up the courage to go near the place since, though some bit of Esther Newman was what he woke to and what he carried to bed at night. The thought of her filled him with panic and dread and childish awe. He could feel the people at the table staring and he glanced up from his book.

—We could move Patrick Devine's library back into your room over there, Eli said.

—Just until we can make arrangements, Bride told him. —In the spring.

He could feel the vein in his neck jumping as the blood roared through. He was nearly fifteen and still sharing a bedroom with his mother. —I don't mind, he said.

Eli walked him over the Tolt three days later and they knocked at the door, letting themselves in when they got no answer. The goat wandered out of the parlour to greet them. —Who's the youngster? Esther asked from the top of the stairs.

—He's mine, Eli said.

Esther came down two steps and leaned against the wall. —I didn't think you had it in you, Eli.

He nudged Abel. —Go and put the kettle on, he said.

They sat together in the kitchen, Abel staring at his knees while the conversation between his father and the drunken woman juddered and jackknifed along. Much of their talk made no sense to him. Esther wept occasionally though Abel was at a loss to pinpoint the cause. —You love the music so much, she said, wiping away snot with her sleeve. —You love it and you think it must love you back somehow, she said.

Eli nodded.

—But the music could care less if you live or die, Esther said. She laughed at herself suddenly. —You don't have a clue what I'm talking about, do you.

—I know exactly what you're saying, Eli told her.

Esther never looked at Abel or spoke a word to him while he sat there, and it wasn't clear if she ever took in the arrangement his father proposed. —Who's there? she shouted every time Abel came through the back door of Selina's House. The same puzzled belligerence in her voice, as if she'd forgotten he was living in the old servant's quarters. —It's Abel, he called back and that was as close as they came to conversation. Esther ignored him, wandering the hallways drunk and talking to the goat in languages he didn't understand and singing her forlorn nursery rhymes. He felt as if he was eavesdropping at the back door still. He was given no specific instructions other than to make sure the house didn't burn down and he walked through the rooms at night to douse the lamps she'd left lit.

Each morning he emptied her honey bucket and made her bed and folded away the trunk of clothing she'd worn on her most recent jaunt through town. He cooked his own meals and left food in her way hoping she would at least pick at something. She took to leaving the goat in its harness after her drives and Abel put the truckley away in Tryphie's workshed, happy to be acknowledged as her kedger. She slept at all hours of the day and he made sure there was a pillow under her head and covered her with a quilt and he often stood looking at her awhile then, free to try taking her in without embarrassment. There was a simple prettiness in the face that the years of drink hadn't quite ruined, a veneer of refinement about her even in her cups, and he couldn't help but think of her as beautiful. He pulled the quilt higher around her neck to feel her hair brush against his fingers.

Esther could sleep for hours and he was at loose ends without her activity to occupy him. He pretended to read, half listening for the sound of her up and about again. He copied endlessly from Jabez Trim's Bible, he chopped firewood and hauled water and cleaned ash from the fireplace and the kitchen stove. He snooped through the rooms of the old hospital, picking through the clutter and junk, puzzling over the arcane surgical equipment or browsing through stacks of medical notes. Esther woke hungover and miserable and Abel boiled the kettle for tea, folding her hands about the mug to be sure she wouldn't drop it.

Hannah came by with meals on occasion, to satisfy herself Abel wasn't starving to death. Once a week Bride visited the house to ask after Esther. —She isn't causing you too much trouble?

—I don't mind, he told her.

—I could come for a night sometime to spell you off.

—We're fine, he said.

He resented these incursions into what he thought of as his territory. There had been no further word of shipping Esther off to Connecticut and by March month Abel had forgotten his station was intended to be temporary.

At the beginning of May, Esther's father came to Selina's House unannounced. Tryphie arrived with Eli and they knocked for fear of what they might barge into if they did not. —Hello Abel, Tryphie said when the boy peered out.

Abel slammed the door shut in the men's faces and stood behind it, the floor pitching beneath him.

—Open the jesus door, Eli shouted.

The goat looked out from the parlour, chewing placidly on a tuft of ancient case notes. Esther came to the top of the stairs and stared down at him where he barred the entrance. She was wearing a stage dress of black chiffon, backlit by sunlight through a window.

—You've the loveliest hair, he told her. He was struggling not to bawl, his pale face gone awry with the effort.

—You let them in now, Esther said. It was the first full sentence she'd ever blessed him with. —Tell them I'll be down the once.

Abel waited in the parlour with the imperturbable goat while Esther sat with the men in the kitchen. Eli appeared at the door finally, looking in at his son among the filth of the room. The youngster unable to hold his father's eye, his life hanging in the balance. —She says she won't leave with him, Eli said.

He only nodded at the news.

—Get that animal out of the house, Abel.

And he nodded again.

Tryphie stayed on in Paradise Deep a month, trying to cajole his daughter into coming to live with him in Hartford. He spent part of every day in the company of the Honourable Member, sitting in an office on the second floor of the F.P.U. Hall, staring out the window at Selina's House as Eli blathered on about the union. Twenty thousand men—a tenth of the country's population—had taken the pledge, fourteen union candidates elected to the House of Assembly in the last election. A monthly union newsletter to counter the fabrications in the merchant-run papers. Eli had a cot in a room behind the office and spent most of his nights there. Trade agents across Europe to sell their fish, Eli told him, an F.P.U. office in Greece. Levi Sellers reduced to pandering to the Catholics just to keep afloat. —We can't get enough warehouse space in St. John's to supply the operation, he said. —Mr. Coaker is looking for a place closer to the northeast coast. We're going to build every inch of this from the ground up somewhere, warehouses, drying rooms, cooperage, a shipyard. An electric generating station.

—I think I'll wander on, Tryphie said without looking away from the window.

—Elevators, Eli said, to shift the fish from the drying rooms to the warehouses at ground level. Things that have never been built before, things that haven't hardly been thought of.

—Is she going to drink herself to death over there? Tryphie asked.

Eli leaned back in his chair. —Abel will watch out to her, he said.

Tryphie glanced across at Eli, a portrait of Coaker on the wall above his head, the president's face appearing to float in the glare of light through the window. Tryphie considered it a fact that he hated Eli Devine and had done so for a long time. He looked back out at Selina's House. —You think there might be some work for me in all of that? he said.

—Down in Hartford, you mean?

—I figure it might be better if we came home out of it.

—I wouldn't have thought Minnie would want to set foot back here.

Tryphie stood from his chair to stop himself telling Eli to fuck off. —She'll want to be next her daughter where she can keep an eye on her. If you could set me up with some work.

Eli shifted forward to put both elbows on the desk. —I'll see what I can do, he said.

Tryphie left for the States in late June and all the talk that summer was about war in Europe, the flotsam of rumour and half-facts washing up on the beaches. Eli was away at Government House in St. John's all summer. Britain declared itself in August and Newfoundland carried along in its wake. Five hundred volunteers enlisted with the Newfoundland Regiment for service overseas. Coaker offered to resign to join up himself, only relenting when union locals flooded him with telegrams and letters urging him to stay on as president. The war inflated the price of fish and men were mad after the cod all season.

In October Tryphie and Minnie came home to Paradise Deep. Abel was afraid they'd move into Selina's House at first but Minnie wasn't prepared to live in close quarters with her daughter's misery and they settled into John Blade's old place instead. Tryphie went to work in the union office as an accountant though he spent most of his time blue-printing Coaker's elaborate fantasies, pulleys, gears and winches, electric motors, turbines, power lines.

Adelina and Flossie Sellers chaired the Women's Patriotic Association, hosting knitting bees to send scarves and socks to the troops overseas. Joshua Trim was among the first union volunteers to make it into action, and news he'd been killed reached the shore shortly before Christmas, the blinds down at the Trims' household all through the season.

Esther railed against the war with a drunken exuberance and Abel settled himself a pacifist out of allegiance to her. She seemed to have no argument with the conflict but that it was happening in Europe. As if the war was an escalation of the continent's appetite for sacrifice and waste. She greeted the young men on the streets with calls of *Hello Cannon Fodder* and they nodded warily. Watching after the woman and the pale youngster in her wake. Abel had grown to almost six foot and towered over his alcoholic charge, the pair like a carnival marriage on display, their strangeness a twinned thing.

After her first full sentence to him, Esther seemed incapable of shutting herself up. She talked endlessly of which roles she'd sung in what productions in which storied theatre, each opera's intrigue and backstabbing and doomed affairs mirrored in the dressing rooms and backstage halls and hotel rooms of the performers. The mad directors and absinthe-addled librettists, the aging Lotharios who lost their nature and the nose off their face to venereal disease, the pedophilic impresarios who bankrolled the productions. Esther was always drunk when she reminisced, breaking into scraps of arias or humming the orchestra lines, and there was no clear narrative to the diatribe. Abel had trouble keeping the details of one theatre or composer or horny, social-climbing tenor separate from all the others.

—Do you know what I am? she asked one afternoon and there was a belligerence to the question that made him wary of answering. —I, she said, striking a stagey pose meant to mock herself, am a mezzo-soprano.

The words meant nothing to him but he knew enough to let her carry on.

—Supporting roles, she said, that's what a mezzo gets. Servants. Mothers-in-law. I didn't go all the way to Europe for a life in the shadows.

She found a vocal instructor willing to stretch her range, an aging Swiss with an addiction to opium and few scruples, and she had to sleep with him before he consented to the undertaking. Esther mimicked his fussy accent. —You must sleep nine hours a night and drink only water, no coffee or tea, no alcohol, you must keep your throat covered at all times, you must never engage in Sapphic love.

—In what?

—He was a lunatic, Esther said. —But no one else would help me.

She pushed her way into lead roles with persistence and one judicious love affair after another. Criss-crossed the continent and left her audiences wet, roses thrown onto stages from Hamburg to Vienna to Paris, booking engagements a year ahead. —Then the voice started to go, she said. She shook her flask of gin and took a long pull. —I guess I should have steered clear of Sapphic love as well.

There was a man who did Esther wrong, a horny, social-climbing tenor with busy hands who swore his undying love to her. He practised his scales with his face between her legs, those muffled notes rising through her bones to strike in her head like pleasure's hammer. His father was German, his mother Italian, and he had confused the arts of love and war in his upbringing. He left her for a Frenchwoman with the breasts of a ten-year-old and a five-octave range.

The salacious detail aroused and appalled Abel. He was sorry to hear such things and hung on every word. Esther's tone was strangely light when she spoke of the man who discarded her for the bird-breasted soprano, when she ran through the long list of others she'd hurt or been scarred by, the whole merry-go-round of desire and flesh and betrayal and hope. A tinge of regret in her voice, to find herself beyond it all now.

In July of 1916 the name of a town in France arrived on the shore. Beaumont-Hamel. The desolate numbers whispered back and forth— eight hundred and two members of the Newfoundland Regiment ordered out of their trenches into the muck and wire and relentless machine-gun fire. A morning of blue sky and calm. It took all of half an hour to cut them down as they stuttered toward the German line, chins tucked into their shoulders against the hellish weather. Only sixty-eight men standing to answer roll call the next morning. There were three local boys among the lost and every family on the shore could claim a brother-in-law or nephew or second cousin dead or wounded or missing.

Hannah came to Selina's House to sit with Abel, just to watch him breathing across the table. Her mortal son, his eyes and teeth and hands. The numbered hairs of his head. —I never thought, Hannah said, I'd be thanking the Lord you had the consumption.

It was early afternoon and Esther was already halfways drunk. —Dr.

Newman says there's nothing wrong with him. Once conscription passes the House, she said, they'll be happy to take Abel as well as anyone.

—The union won't ever let a draft pass the House, Hannah said without the conviction she wanted.

—Why won't they?

Hannah made a feeble gesture with her hand. —Mr. Coaker, she said.

Esther threw her head back to laugh and she cursed the sham union and Coaker who ruled it like God Himself. She cursed the House of Assembly in St. John's and the war in Europe and then she cursed Europe itself, one country at a time. Abel had never seen her in such a state. She stalked down the hall and clumped upstairs to her room, still cursing.

—I don't want you alone here with that woman, Hannah said. —It isn't proper.

—You asked me to move in.

—When you were just a youngster that was, she said. —I never meant for. But she only shook her head.

Abel went upstairs when his mother left and stood outside Esther's room, trying to guess if she was awake. —Who's there? she shouted and he went back down without a word.

He sat with Jabez Trim's Bible, copying verses from the Song of Songs awhile. He wandered the servant's quarters like a prisoner exploring the nooks and crannies of a cell. Shifting furniture, trying mouldings around windows and doors as if he half expected to find some compartment secreted behind. Taking empty bottles from a high shelf to peer down their necks. There was a manila envelope sitting up there, a waterfall of photographs pouring onto his bed when he untied it, 10-by-14 and portraits all, though the focus was rarely on the sitter's face. It was a catalogue of injury, scars and misshapen limbs and heads swollen twice their natural size. Five wizened faces in a row, old turnips the lot of them though they were dressed in children's clothes, the incongruous stoop of age in their postures. A bald-headed man and woman who seemed to have no fingernails. There was a young girl he wouldn't have recognized as his mother except for the web of skin between her fingers, the camera focused on the hands splayed in her lap. A pale stranger with cloudy eyes and a shock of colourless hair, an expression of startled forbearance.

—You could almost be looking at yourself there, Esther said.

He turned to see her standing against the door jamb. He didn't know how long she'd been watching him. She nodded to the picture with her chin. —You're the spit of your great-grandfather.

—Who? he asked.

—The Great White, she said. —Mary Tryphena's man. Has no one told you a thing about yourself?

—I guess they haven't, he said.

The sheet of paper where he'd copied verses from the Song of Songs was on the bed and she picked it up. —What's this crazy writing you do? she asked and he told her how he'd found the Bible in Patrick Devine's library and deciphered it by copying one letter at a time. She said, You're a queer stick, Abel Devine. She was staring at him with an odd attention he'd never felt the weight of before. She sat next him on the bed. —Have you ever been kissed, Abel? A real kiss?

—I don't think so.

—That man there, Esther said—she pointed to the photograph—is your great-grandfather, Judah Devine his name was. She kissed him then, her mouth slightly open, the sweet and sour of gin on her breath. —He was born out of the belly of a whale down on the landwash, on the Feast of St. Mark. Her mouth again, a hand under his shirt against bare skin. —It was Devine's Widow cut him free of the whale's stomach with a fish knife, she said. —She was Mary Tryphena's grandmother, the widow woman, a witch is what some people said.

Esther carried on talking a long time, unspooling the family's tale as she undressed the youngster, navigating the complications of one generation and the next, rowing her way toward them where they lay together in the servant's quarters of Selina's House, blood on blood on blood. Abel lying silent through it all, willing to take every word as Gospel as long as her mouth came back to his, as long as her hands.

She was not drunk. Hadn't touched a drop since storming out of the kitchen to stew in her bedroom, staring up at the skewed continents. All those young men rotting somewhere in the irredeemable stain that was France. And she'd come downstairs to claim Abel before he was stolen away from her, kneeling over him now to bless his body and the soul it housed. A drunken notion though she was sober. Wanting to keep him safe from the world those few moments.

They lay nearly naked on the bed afterwards, silent under the weight of what had passed between them. Abel forced himself up on an elbow to look down at her. —Esther, he said, but she placed a finger against his lips. She said, Never tell a woman you love her, Abel.

He stared, his eyes filming over with tears.

—It will always sound like a lie, she said. —Better you let a woman figure it out for herself.

The sound of the front door interrupted them, a woman's voice calling down the hallway. They could hear the goat complaining as it was forced outside, the clatter of its hoofs on the wooden steps. Abel hustled into his clothes and went through the kitchen to find his mother closing the door on the animal, a bag set at the foot of the stairs. —We'll want to get that filth cleared out, she said. —You can put my clothes in the room next to Esther's.

You're too late, he wanted to tell her but decided it was best to let her figure it out for herself.

Eli left the shore the next morning and was gone for months, in St. John's for sittings of the House or travelling with Coaker to Catalina Harbour where construction was already underway on the union's base of operations. The entire project was scheduled for completion by the end of 1917, wharves, warehouses and offices, church, school, hotel, shipyard and seal-oil plant and branch railway. Fish stores with 135 feet of frontage and three electric elevators, a cooperage and sail-making room in the loft.

Most of the design work was done in St. John's or on-site, but Eli had enough piecework sent Tryphie's way to keep him fed. Dozens of small projects in the power plant and shipyard and cold-storage plant, telegraphs arriving from the project manager with requests and specs and alterations. Tryphie couldn't imagine any of it in the real world. The turbines in the power plant required the trenching of a twelve-hundred-foot canal, the installation of a nine-hundred-foot wood-stave pipe that was six feet in diameter and reinforced every six inches with steel bands. He expected the entire enterprise to falter at any moment. But the price of fish stayed at record heights as the war dragged on and the union had an endless supply of cash to keep the fantasy aloft.

He worked away at the plans in the F.P.U. offices through the summer and into the fall, the complex engineering problems and their clean mathematical solutions a relief from the mess he felt his life had become. Hours passed without a thought to Esther's condition or Minnie's lost Connecticut or Eli Devine.

Levi Sellers was sitting in a chair beside the window when Tryphie looked up from the desk one early December morning. A shiver ran through him at the sight—that box of a head and hawk nose, the mutilated ears hidden under a straggle of grey hair. One side of the face sliding earthward and making a slur of his speech. There was nothing in the fallen world, Tryphie thought, could kill the son of a bitch. Levi nodded toward Coaker's portrait on the wall. —You don't mind that one staring down at you all day?

—What are you doing here?

—How's your Esther making out?

—I've got work to do, Mr. Sellers.

Levi pushed himself to his feet with his cane. —You plan to spend the rest of your days sketching doodads for Eli Devine?

—I'm considering my options.

Levi started toward the door, his movements so exaggerated and awkward it was hard to believe he'd come into the room without Tryphie noticing. —My father, he said. —Absalom Sellers. He was your grandfather, did you know that?

—If you have something in particular you wanted.

—I'm not going to live forever, is what I mean. And you're the closest thing to blood I have in this country.

—Frig off out of it, Levi.

—I'm willing to sign over the portion of Sellers & Co. by rights is yours.

Tryphie straightened as much as his humpback allowed. —Out of the goodness of your heart, is it?

Levi laughed and shook his head. —We need something on your darling Mr. Coaker.

—We?

—Myself and others like me. Men with similar interests.

—Men of your interests, Tryphie said, are too goddamned stunned to see there's none but Mr. Coaker could put a stop to this now.

A flicker ran under the mask of Levi's face, something that made him look nearly human a moment. —I imagine you're right, he said and then pressed ahead. —We're after an affidavit that would hold up in court. It won't even have to be made public, just something to set in front of the man, make him listen to reason.

—An affidavit saying what exactly?

—The man's a sodomite, Tryphie. Everyone knows that.

Tryphie turned to the desk and leaned over it.

—One third of what I own, Levi said. —That's near enough to look after that daughter of yours, and maybe keep your wife from killing you in your sleep some night.

Tryphie turned to whip a paperweight across the room but Levi was already through the door.

He went by Selina's House on his way home that evening, found Hannah alone in the kitchen. They sat at the table with tea and talked briefly about the war and whether Esther was any better or worse.

—I had a visit from Levi Sellers today, he told her finally.

She said, He's turning into a social creature, that one.

Tryphie nodded, unsurprised. —What did he offer you, Hannah?

—A knife, she said and she smiled for just a moment, like the flame of a match lit and shaken out. —Why would he come to us, Tryphie?

—Only blood can make something like this stick. Otherwise it's just rumour. Are you going to tell Abel?

—Tell him what?

—About his father, maid. Him and Coaker.

A red spall rose on Hannah's neck and face. —I got no truck with gossip, she said.

—The boy's bound to hear of it sooner or later, he said.

—Not from me, he won't, Hannah said.

Eli didn't come back to the shore until after Christmas, travelling with Coaker on a winter tour to report on the progress at Port Union and to make a plea for volunteers to the Newfoundland Regiment. There was no sign of an end to the war. The Russians signed an armistice with Germany in November and tens of thousands of German troops were being transported to the Western Front. The regiment suffered heavy losses before Christmas and spent the holiday season licking their wounds in Fressen, waiting for new recruits to join them. Coaker addressed a public meeting in the F.P.U. Hall, the crowd respectful but unenthusiastic, like all the union crowds he'd spoken to. They had barely enough hands to crew the boats as it was and no one outside St. John's showed any appetite for the war.

Coaker worked the crowd afterwards, making a more personal pitch for volunteers. Eli stood with Abel and Dr. Newman, the three of them watching Coaker shake hands and plead and cajole.

—He seems worked up, Newman said.

—We might have to pull the regiment off the front lines if we don't shore it up, Eli said.

—It hardly seems the union's job to keep the regiment in soldiers.

—Be hard to hold off conscription if we don't meet the need with willing bodies.

The doctor pursed his lips. —And I suppose it does you no service in the House if the union looks like a crowd of shirkers.

—Perception is half the game, Eli said.

Coaker came around to them finally and he shook hands with the doctor and the youngster beside him.

—Mr. Coaker, Abel said.

—Uncle Will, Coaker corrected him. —You're looking well, Abel.

—He's in the blush of health, Newman said. —A miracle recovery, Mr. Coaker. I've never seen the like.

Coaker nodded and stared at him longer than Abel would have liked. He looked away, waiting for the appraisal to end. Newman excused himself to get back to the hospital and they watched him go, skeletal and stooped under his clothes.

—What is he, Coaker asked Eli, seventy-five now?

— Older, I'd say. And looking every inch of it since Bride passed away.

—Cancer, was it?

—She didn't last a month.

—Is he drinking again?

—He's heartbroken, Eli said. —A person's liable to do anything in that state.

Abel shifted his feet, feeling again like he was eavesdropping on a private conversation. Eli turned to him and said, Come see us over in the Gut tonight. Be good to catch up on your news.

The crowds dispersed by mid-afternoon and Abel helped take down the bunting and tables before walking back to Selina's House. He carted a turn of spruce from the shed as he let himself in the back

door, dropping the junks into the woodbox. Hannah was at the stove.
—Supper's almost ready, she said.

Abel nodded, brushing the bark from his jacket. —I'll go see if Esther's hungry.

—She's never hungry.

—I'll go see, he said.

He let himself into the gloom of curtained windows, the smell of her sleeping under the sting of frost in the air. He crossed to the bed and laid a hand against her face. —Esther, he said. Abel could hear the clank of cast iron on the stove downstairs, his mother letting him know she was there. They'd all three shared the house more than a year now with Hannah doing what she could to stand between them. Abel was forced to seek Esther out with pretend errands that gave him a few moments alone in her company. —Esther? he said again.

She muttered something guttural into the mattress. She'd been idly teaching him bits and pieces of all the languages she knew these last months and he'd picked up enough to sort one from another. —Guten Tag, he said and he asked in his broken German if she supper interested in was having?

Esther turned on the bed, covering her face with her hand. —Did I ever tell you how the widow died? Devine's Widow?

—Who was she to me again?

—She was Mary Tryphena's grandmother. Your great-great-great-grandmother.

Abel sat on the edge of the mattress. They hadn't slept together since the day his mother moved into the house and he'd had to satisfy himself with this, listening to the woman he loved tell him who he was. He suspected she was making most of it up as she went, but there was something intimate and illicit in the telling. As if she was undressing him one item of clothing at a time as she filled out the bare genealogy with courtships and marriages, arguments and feuds and accidents, the myriad circumstances in which his people left the world. —How did the widow die? he asked. Meaning her to know he was hers completely.

—She lay down, Esther said. —Went to her bed one afternoon and refused to get out of it. She said, I had enough of this. It was Lizzie looked out to her at the end, washed and fed her and brushed out her hair. You'll be happy enough to see me gone, the widow said to her.

—And what did Lizzie say?

—She said, I'll be happy to think something and not have you know it just looking at me.

Hannah interrupted from the foot of the stairs to say supper was on the table.

—Will you eat something? he asked.

—I'll be down the once.

It might be hours before she showed her face, he knew, or she might stay upstairs the rest of the night and he felt a new impatience bloom in his chest. He'd always assumed Esther was telling the stories to make company for his strangeness, to keep him close. But there were moments it seemed she was holding him at bay with the tale, hiding herself behind it. He went to the door and a sudden fear stopped him there. He said, You haven't had enough have you, Esther?

—Enough of what?

—This, he said. —Us.

—You go on, she said. —I'll be down now the once.

Abel sat alone at the table with Hannah. He knew his father had come by Selina's House when he arrived that morning though neither of his parents said a word to him about the visit. And they ate now without mentioning the afternoon's events or the union or Eli. He was nearly finished his meal when he looked up to see his mother crying. He put his fork and knife across the plate.

—She's twice your age, Hannah said.

—I knows how old she is.

—And you're in love are you?

—Maybe I am.

—Why let that ruin the rest of your life?

He got up to bring his plate to the pantry and when he came back into the kitchen Hannah had wiped her face dry. She pushed away from the table and stood there holding her plate. —Don't you go overseas, Abel.

—Why would I do that? he said, startled by the sudden shift.

—Promise me you won't.

—All right, he said.

She shook her head, fighting back the tears again, as if he'd denied her.

He left the house after supper without telling his mother where he was going. Clear and still over the Tolt and in the moonlight he could see the roof of Laz Devine's house had foundered, all the windows scavenged from Mary Tryphena's place. He found his father and Coaker in the house across the garden talking in the flicker of light from a damper left open on the stove. They took Abel's arrival as a signal to light a lamp and Eli set about making tea, asking after Dr. Newman and Azariah Trim and a handful of others without ever mentioning the women Abel lived with at Selina's House. They talked then about the war and about Port Union, picking up the conversation Abel had interrupted.

Coaker excused himself to go to bed an hour later and they could hear him settling into bed in Abel's old room at the back of the house. It was a private sound that embarrassed them both and Eli cleared his throat against the noise. —How's Esther getting along? he asked.

—She haven't changed much since the last you saw her.

Eli leaned forward in his chair to stare at his folded hands. —Your mother, he said. —She says you and Esther. She thinks it might be good if you moved out of Selina's House.

Abel watched the flicker of firelight on the wall above the stove, a lump of hot wax in his throat. Eli asked if he'd considered volunteering for the regiment now he was eighteen and Abel turned his head so quickly that his father held up a hand. —Uncle Will could make arrangements to see you get overseas right away.

Abel stretched his legs, kicking one heel off the toe of the other boot, trying to dislodge the ache at the back of his throat. He motioned toward the ceiling with his head. —Is this his idea?

—He asked what I thought of it.

Abel knocked his heel against his toe a while longer.

—You don't have to decide anything this minute, Eli told him.

Abel nodded. —Did you ever know Judah Devine? he said.

Eli sat back in his chair. —When I was a youngster. I hardly remember a thing about him.

—Esther says he was born out of the belly of a whale. And stunk like a dead fish.

—Esther, Eli said and sighed. —You know Esther isn't a well woman, Abel.

—I should get home, he said.

Abel started across the garden and halfway to Mary Tryphena's he stopped, turning back toward the house. Just the one lamp in the kitchen and he stood a long time in the cold, watching. He saw the lamp lift from the table finally, the brief glow of it at the turn of the stairs on the second floor as his father made his way to bed.

Esther spoke to him out of the darkness of the parlour when he came into Selina's House. —Where have you been this evening, Abel?

—Over to see father, he said and he paused a moment. —They want me to join up.

—Who does?

—Father, he said. He couldn't bring himself to say Uncle Will. —And Mr. Coaker.

There was only silence in the parlour's black. Hannah had scrubbed the floors and washed the curtains and aired out the furniture months ago but Abel could still smell the goat. He thought Esther might have fallen asleep in there. He said, How did Judah Devine find his way into the belly of that whale?

—How should I know?

Abel leaned against the door jamb. —That's the best you can do, is it?

—Maybe he was a fisherman washed overboard in a storm, she said. —Or a sailor drove mad by being too long at sea.

—That still don't say how he wound up swallowed by a whale.

—What does it matter, Abel?

She was drunk and he found his impatience welling up again. —You could care less if I join up, he said. —It wouldn't matter to you if I lived or died.

—Don't be a sook, Abel.

He walked along the hall and through the kitchen, pulling off his coat as he went. Certain it was all a lie, the life she'd given him, her mouth on his, her hands, the preposterous little history she'd spun to make him feel at home in the world. He felt he'd been made to look a fool.

Eli and Coaker rose early the next morning, both men all business over their breakfast. They discussed the general council at Port Union, the progress of bills in the House of Assembly, what would become of the price of fish when the war ended. —What did Abel say about signing up? Coaker asked finally.

—He's going to think about it.

Coaker looked up from the bread he was buttering.

—He seemed interested, Eli insisted.

Coaker set his food down and sat with his hands beside the plate. Eli turned to the stove so as not to see the panic Coaker was just managing to tamp down. They had so much to lose now, Port Union, Coaker's cabinet position in the coalition government, the new fisheries regulations that might save the industry from itself. So much the union had fought for on the verge of realization and Coaker already fearful it might slip away in the bog of the country's petty politics. —I know it's a lot to ask, Coaker said. —But he'd never see action, Eli, I promise you that. We can have him assigned a stretcher-bearer, he'll be safe as houses.

Eli couldn't help thinking Abel's volunteering to carry stretchers was a trifle in the grand scheme and he said as much. —It hardly matters one way or the other, does it?

—Everything matters, Coaker said. —Perception is half the game.

They were still eating when Tryphie put his head around the door. They'd both noted him absent the day before though neither had mentioned it. Coaker said, I was starting to think you were trying to keep clear of us, Tryphie.

Eli went to fetch him a mug but Tryphie waved him off. He refused even to take a chair. —I just come by to let you know, he said, if Hannah haven't already mentioned it. Levi Sellers come around to see us.

—When was this?

—Before Christmas. He was looking for something on Mr. Coaker.

—He only has to read the St. John's papers if it's gossip he wants, Coaker said. —Reprobate, abuser of the fairer sex, delinquent father, it's all in there.

—He was after something a little different than that, Mr. Coaker. Offered me a third of his estate to swear out an affidavit.

—An affidavit stating what exactly?

—Something that would implicate you—Tryphie made a motion with his hand—in acts. Unnatural acts.

Coaker was staring steadily at Tryphie, as if daring him to elaborate.

—He claimed he was acting on behalf of more than just himself, Tryphie said. —I thought you ought to know.

—I have nothing to be ashamed of, Coaker said.

—You'll want to watch out to yourselves, just the same.

—Levi went to Hannah? Eli asked.

—Right after he spoke to me.

Eli reached for the table edge and looked away out the window, caught sight of Abel coming across the garden at a run. Moments later the boy slammed through the door. —I wants to join up, he said. —Father says you can get me in, Uncle Will, is that right?

Coaker managed a smile as he stood from his chair. He seemed happy for the distraction. —I might be able to pull some strings, he said.

A series of telegraphs went back and forth between Paradise Deep and several government departments in St. John's and by mid-afternoon arrangements were all but made. There was a meeting of the local union executive that evening where Coaker announced Abel's intentions and made a show of him in front of the group. He'd be travelling into St. John's with them at the end of the week to sign up, Coaker told the assembly, and men lined up to shake Abel's hand and wish him well.

The news reached Selina's House before Abel walked the hundred yards back from the F.P.U. Hall. Hannah waiting at the door for him when he came in. —You made a promise to me, Abel Devine.

—I didn't know Mr. Coaker wanted me to join the regiment.

—And that's God's word, is it? What Uncle Will wants, he gets?

—You said yourself you wanted me out of this house.

Hannah grabbed a coat and pushed past him to the door. He watched her march down the path in the moonlight, an unfamiliar hitch in her step as she went, as if she was hobbled by some private grief, and he almost called out to her before he heard Esther moving above him. She was on the landing when he turned toward the stairs. —Hello Cannon Fodder, she said.

—What do you care? Abel said.

She turned away toward her room and he climbed the stairs after her. She had a fire lit and she waved him in to lie beside her. He stared up at the stained ceiling, trying to comprehend what he'd agreed to. It had happened so quickly it felt like an accident now, a fall from a rooftop. Regret funnelling through him at the thought of leaving Esther behind and he shook his head, fighting off tears. —This was all a mistake, he said.

—You don't have to go, Abel.

—Mr. Coaker is after telling everyone I'm joining up, he said. He moved to get out of bed but Esther pulled him back, lifting herself over him. She rocked slightly side to side and then steadied herself, Abel already hard beneath her. —Come on, she said, grinding into him.

—You're drunk.

—What do you care? she said.

It felt like a fight coming out of their clothes, as if they were each trying to keep something hidden while stripping the other bare. He turned her on her back and lifted his knee to pry her legs open but Esther wouldn't have it, twisting away to push her naked ass into him, reaching behind to guide his cock inside when he seemed at a loss. He fell across her after he came and held on until she turned underneath him, reaching up to pat his cheek. —A sin to waste that gear of yours, she said.

—I'm not wasting it.

—Go put some wood on the fire, she said and he stepped across the room, his legs rubbery beneath him. When he climbed back into bed Esther pointed up at the dimly lit ceiling. —There's France, she said.

—Where?

—Next to England there.

—There's nothing up there but a water stain.

—You can't see Italy? she said. —The one that looks like a boot?

—You can make anything out of anything, can't you.

Esther laughed. —I wouldn't be back here if that was true, she said.

He leaned up on an elbow to look at her. —What happened to you over there, Esther?

—Nothing, she said and she shook her head. —Everything, she said.

He watched her steadily.

—All right, she said.

She was in London the first time it came over her. Fifteen hundred people in the theatre and she stood in the wings listening to their murmur beyond the stage lights. All week the papers reporting how her voice had faltered in her last three performances on the continent. Her German understudy sleeping with the orchestra's conductor, the two of them leading a campaign to push the Northern Pearl off the marquee. She hadn't slept in days.

She walked on stage to polite applause but there was a whiff of blood about her and the audience could almost taste it. She felt like she was singing under water, she said, her own voice muffled in her ears, a sound as syrupy and thick as molasses. And she could sense something unfamiliar approaching in the middle of the first aria, a black tunnel that opened beneath her feet and she fell from the world in mid-note. She was in the wings when she came to herself, the bitch of an understudy already on stage. She could see faces gathered over her but couldn't move or speak for the longest time.

—Like Lizzie, Abel said.

—Just like Lizzie, yes. Esther rolled over him and out of bed, standing naked at the fireplace. An angry-looking scar on her abdomen. —Happened almost every time I went on stage after that. I spent every cent I had on doctors.

—What did they say?

—A kind of sleeping sickness. They think it travels through families. Not a thing they could do for me.

—I thought you made all that stuff up, he said. —All those stories.

—I can't help what you think, Abel.

He held a hand out to her. —Come back to bed, he said.

When Hannah left Selina's House she rushed across to the F.P.U. Hall only to be told Eli was already on his way to the Gut. By the time she caught sight of them the two men were crossing the garden to the house and she ran the last fifty yards to stand between them and the door, her chest heaving. —Mrs. Devine, Coaker said, and she shook her head as if denying the fact. He turned to Eli. —I might take a little stroll before I go in.

Eli stood within arm's length of his wife, waiting for Coaker to move out of earshot. —Abel volunteered, Hannah, he said. —He won't be anything but a stretcher-bearer, Mr. Coaker will see to that.

Hannah shook her head again. —You never give a thought to none but yourself, Eli, not once in your life.

Eli turned to stare in the direction Coaker had wandered off. —Tryphie says Levi Sellers come round to see you a while back.

—What does that have to do with Abel?

—I just wanted to say it wouldn't serve you to have any gossip come out in the papers or in the courts, he said. —It wouldn't reflect well on yourself or on Abel.

—I could kill you, Eli Devine, I swear to God, she said.

Eli stepped close so she could see every feature of his face in the pale moonlight. —I won't have anyone belonged to me hurt Mr. Coaker, he said. —I won't allow it.

Hannah covered her mouth with her hand, shocked to see so clearly something she'd tried to ignore all her life. She pushed past Eli, running back across the garden, and he stood watching as she went. Coaker ambled over to him once she was gone and they stood side by side in the dark. —Should we go in? he asked.

Abel left for St. John's en route to overseas at the end of the week, the wharf and shoreline crowded with well-wishers despite the cold. Union banners on the stagehead, Adelina and Flossie Sellers presenting him with woollen socks and a scarf from the Women's Patriotic Association, Reverend Violet offering a blessing before the boat departed.

Abel stayed at the rail of the *F.P. Union* long after his father and Coaker went below, watching the coastline slip by. Snow creviced in the headland of the Tolt, the nearly invisible entrance to the Gut snaking through the cliffs. Devil's Cove where the quarry cut for the cathedral's stones showed black through the drifts. Miles further on to Spread Eagle and Smooth Cove and the cold didn't touch him the whole way. Esther hadn't been on the wharf to see him off and he tried to tell himself he wanted no different. But by the time they sailed over the Rump his legs were watery and shaking and it was all he could do to keep from bawling. He wiped at his eyes and found the ridiculous socks from the Women's Patriotic Association still in his hand, bent down to shove them into his kit bag. Discovered Jabez Trim's Bible tucked away inside, tied up in its leather case. Only Esther could have stowed it there, he knew, to say something she was too goddamn precious or traumatized to speak, and in a fit of childishness he pitched the book over the rail. It floated alongside the boat awhile and Abel ran the length of the deck to keep it in sight, shouting at the water. He could just resist the urge to go over the rail after the book as it churned in the wake and sank below the surface.

Tryphie was surprised that Hannah stayed on with Esther after Abel left, though he guessed it was preferable to the company she might be forced to keep if she moved back to the Gut. He stopped by Selina's House every few days to see the women had enough wood in and to ask after his daughter. There was no word from Abel and they expected nothing for weeks if not months. Hannah had to make do with speculation in the St. John's newspapers and rumours passed on by Tryphie, or by Dr. Newman when he visited on Sunday afternoons.

At the beginning of April Tryphie came to Selina's House with news that Eli was back from St. John's.

—When did he get in?

Tryphie slapped at some invisible lint on his pant leg. —I saw him coming off the boat yesterday morning and he wouldn't so much as look at me, Hannah. He's holed up over in the Gut now. Haven't even been by the union hall.

—Did he hear something about Abel?

—I don't know what's wrong. I was thinking you might want to go look in on him.

Hannah shook her head. —I can't be the one to do that, she said.

Tryphie looked up at the ceiling and nodded.

He could see snow still drifted up the side of the house as he crossed the garden, a footpath kicked through to the front bridge. He leaned in and called, closing the door behind him when he got no answer. The fire had guttered to ashes and he stoked it up against the chill in the air. —I'm making meself a cup of tea, he shouted. He reached for the kettle where it sat on a small table beside the stove and startled at the sight of Coaker's portrait above it, as if it were someone flesh and blood in the room with him. —Jesus loves the little children, Tryphie whispered. It occurred to him that Eli could be lying dead up there and he forced himself to climb the stairs. Found him on the bed in Abel's room.

—Hello Ladybug.

—You just come up from St. John's, did you?

—Went through Port Union, he said, on the way along.

—Everything all right down there?

—How about that tea? Eli said.

Tryphie left an hour later without learning the first thing about what was troubling Eli. He packed the firebox with wood, thinking Eli didn't have it in him to keep a bit of heat in the house. —You know where to find me, he said, you needs anything.

Eli didn't get out of the chair to see Tryphie off. He sat and watched the portrait beside the chimney, half a mug of tea gone cold in his lap. He'd been held up in St. John's a week after Coaker left for Port Union and wired to say he would stop in on his way to Paradise Deep. Spent half an hour on the wharf when he disembarked to make the rounds, poking his head in at the office to shake hands and ask after this or that project. He walked up past the rows of union houses to the residence Coaker had built for himself. It was the only touch of ostentation in the town, a turret and gabled windows, a sun porch screened in at the back. Coaker had packed the rooms with lavish furnishings and every time Eli came through he found some new addition—a woollen rug from one of the union's European fish buyers, chairs from Harrods in London, a

South American dining table, Italian statues. Not a soul begrudged it to him, seeing he'd built the union and the town from nothing.

The Bungalow was the only house in Port Union where people knocked before entering and a youngster answered the door. Eli had seen him once or twice on the waterfront, Bailey he thought the name was. His hair combed back from a high forehead, wool coat and tie and a high starched collar. He couldn't be more than eighteen, Eli guessed. A mouth to make the angels jealous. —Uncle Will said to expect you, the boy told him.

There was an orphan's look about him, Eli thought, a hint of want so sullen it was almost predatory. He could hear Coaker's gramophone in the parlour, the music seeping past the boy into the open air.

—He's having a little lie-down, the boy said. —You can come in and wait if you like.

Eli considered that a moment before he said, Tell Mr. Coaker I stopped by.

He heard the door close as he walked down the long concrete walkway to the road and he stopped there, still trying to take in what he'd seen in the youngster's face. One more exotic trinket added to the Bungalow's comforts. Two men wandered along the path and they nodded to him there, courteous and a little wary. He could see them shake their heads when they'd gone past, as if the new arrangements at the Bungalow mystified them, though they couldn't begrudge Mr. Coaker even that.

Tryphie came by a second time two days later, standing just inside the door to tell Eli that Allied lines across the Western Front were overrun by a German offensive. Fifty killed in the Newfoundland Regiment, another sixteen unaccounted for, though the names of the dead and missing weren't known. Eli stood from his chair and picked up his coat lying on the green leather chesterfield. —I'll walk you back, he said.

They didn't speak until Eli dropped Tryphie at John Blade's house. —You're all right, are you? Tryphie asked.

—I'll be fine.

He went on to the F.P.U. office where he tendered his resignation from the union executive. He walked to the telegraph office in the hospital basement, cabling St. John's and Port Union to resign from the House of Assembly and the national coalition government. Back in the Gut he took his seat across from the president's portrait and waited for night to fall.

Late that evening Eli lit a lamp and stoked up the fire to boil the kettle. There was a basin on the table under Coaker's portrait that he poured full, shaving by his reflection in the glass. When he was done he took the frame off its nail and turned Coaker's face to the wall. He dressed in his best shirt and coat and set out for the Tolt under a cold flood of stars. He walked into Paradise Deep, past Selina's House and up Sellers' Drung to the merchant's house. Adelina met him as he let himself into the porch and he apologized for calling so late. —I wonder, he said, if I could talk to Levi.

On May eleventh the coalition government in the Newfoundland House of Assembly passed the Military Service Act with the full support of its F.P.U. members. The sudden reversal of the union's opposition to conscription was undertaken without warning, and local councils across the island passed resolutions condemning the act and Coaker's high-handedness in imposing the change without consultation. Responding in *The Fisherman's Advocate*, Coaker spoke of the torture he suffered making the decision to support conscription, how he neither slept nor ate in the days before the vote. But he never managed to explain his reasoning to anyone's satisfaction. In thousands of union homes the president's portrait was turned to the wall or smashed on the floor or taken down and put away for good. It was as if half the country had woken from a collective dream to find the world much the same as when they'd drifted off.

Abel's name wasn't among the list of the regiment's dead and missing published in the St. John's *Evening Telegram*. His letters to Esther began arriving belatedly, from England and then France. Esther never opened them in company and never reported their contents and Hannah was forced to read them on the sly, sneaking into Esther's room when she was gallivanting drunk through town.

Abel was marched around a parade square with a wooden rifle and a bayonet. He was granted two days' leave before being posted across the Channel and wandered over half of London to see the theatres where Esther made her name. The roads in France were frozen mud and his toenails had blackened and fallen off from the rough walking. There was a half-breed from Labrador name of Devine in the regiment, he carried a tooth he claimed belonged to Judah. Abel was assigned work as a regimental stretcher-bearer where he was least likely to get others killed. They were moved off the front lines while they waited for reinforcements and were living the easy life, assigned as guards to the commander-in-chief. All through that summer he complained he was bored to tears but he'd requested a transfer to the regular infantry and expected to be more than a stretcher-bearer when they moved back to the front. Each letter closed with a line in a hand unlike the writing in the body, a style so old-fashioned and baroque it was almost comical. *Behold thou art fair, my love, thou art fair, thine eyes are as doves. Thou hast ravished my heart, my sister, my bride.*

As the summer wore on Hannah began to catch glimpses of a change in Esther's figure, a rise in her profile under the layers she wore, a slight change in her posture that suggested a particular discomfort. Esther seemed determined to keep her condition a secret from the world, wearing even more clothes than was her habit, never leaving the house without a shawl or overcoat even when the sun was splitting the rocks. For weeks Hannah dismissed the evidence as her own imagination at work but by the end of August Esther's overcoat was barely equal to the task. Hannah finally mentioned her suspicion to Tryphie, talking in a roundabout fashion that allowed the word itself to go unspoken.

—I knew goddamn well, he said. —I knew it. Have you told Eli?

—I wanted to be sure, she said.

—Perhaps we should have Dr. Newman take a look at the girl, he suggested. —Before I bothers Minnie with it.

—Come by on Sunday afternoon, she told Tryphie. —We'll ask him then.

The doctor spent an hour at Selina's House every week, drinking cups of barky tea he fortified with rum when he thought Hannah wasn't watching. He was telling her the regiment was back at the front and fighting in Ypres when Tryphie stuck his head round the door. Tryphie looked from one to the other, tentative, trying to guess if there'd been any mention as yet of Esther. He sat to the table and fell into talk of the union to avoid the subject most on his mind.

—This conscription bill is the end of it, Dr. Newman predicted. —The F.P.U. is dead.

—Coaker won't let it go so easy as that.

—He'll keep it afloat a good while, Newman said. —But there's no one going to take him at his word again. He's just another politician now.

—The movement's finished, you're saying.

—No one will remember there even was a movement after Coaker goes.

—You sound more like Bride all the time, Hannah told him.

Newman nodded. —I have to keep her with me somehow, he said. He cast around the room, struck by the loss afresh and fighting for purchase. —I appreciate you looking out to Esther all this time, he said finally.

Hannah glanced at Tryphie. —We've been meaning to ask you, Dr. Newman. Have you noticed any change in her lately?

—She's drinking a bit less, I thought.

—I mean in how she looks. Her *shape*.

Newman squinted across at her. —I haven't really paid. He glanced down at the table as if trying to picture his granddaughter.

—I think before Abel left for overseas, Doctor, Hannah said. —Tryphie and me, we're fairly certain.

Newman was still staring at the table and she thought he'd never looked more like an old man. He glanced up at Tryphie and then Hannah. —You're sure?

—There's no mistaking it, she said, suddenly doubting herself again.

Newman shook his head and looked directly at his stepson. —She asked me not to tell you, Tryphie. She had a procedure in Europe.

—What kind of procedure?

—I tried cleaning up the scar tissue when she came home. A butcher's job they made of it.

Hannah turned away from the table, setting the teapot on the counter. She felt strangely disappointed to think she'd been wrong all this time.

—Perhaps I'll go up and talk to her, Newman said.

The stairs were almost too much for him and he stood on the landing a minute to get his wind. Ambushed by an image of Bride as the cancer dismantled her one organ at a time, the veins showing through her papery skin. The false teeth in her wasted face made her look a corpse in the bed and he'd wished he was dead, watching her leave in so much torment. —I can make it stop, he told her, knowing she would never consent to such a thing. —When you're ready.

Bride offering the slightest nod. —Now the once, she said.

It was the oddest expression he'd learned on the shore. Now the once. The present twined with the past to mean soon, a bit later, some unspecified point in the future. As if it was all the same finally, as if time was a single moment endlessly circling on itself. Bride forever absent and always with him.

Newman straightened his tie and knocked lightly at Esther's door, letting himself in when he got no answer. She was asleep on the bed dressed only in her nightshirt and even from across the room he could see the remarkable distension of the belly. The tumour at least the size of a cabbage, he guessed.

His presence in the room woke her and Esther glanced around until she found him there.

—Hello my love, he said.

She placed both hands on her stomach. —You told me I'd never be able to get pregnant again, Dr. Newman.

He shrugged. —Medicine is an inexact science.

—I didn't realize, she said, how much I wanted this.

Newman cleared his throat. — Sometimes that's all it takes, wanting something enough.

—You think I'm crazy to be happy about it.

—Are you having any pain?

—Nothing I can't manage.

Newman turned toward the door, put a hand to the frame to steady himself. —That's grand, he said.

—I used to think you were crazy, Esther said. —Staying here all these years when you could have lived anywhere you wanted.

—I thought the same myself some days.

She smiled across at him, unselfconscious, and looking for all the world like a child herself. —Any regrets, Doctor?

He shook his head. —Not a one, he said.

The regiment was held up by heavy fire from a farmhouse and six soldiers were sent into a stretch of bush to outflank the building. They were spotted as they skulked through the thin foliage and the relentless pendulum of machine-gun fire ripped through the underbrush. The others dropped around him one by one as he scrambled forward, running for his life. He was within shouting distance of the farmhouse when he heard the whistle of artillery incoming, covered his ears against an explosion he never heard.

Still light when he came to himself but the sun was almost below the trees, which meant he'd been out for hours. There was rifle-fire still though it was sporadic and stopped altogether as soldiers dug in or pulled back to support trenches for the night. Quiet, quiet but for the buzz in his head. He could make out the farmhouse through the bushes, watched a German soldier come through the back door to piss behind the building. He tried to crawl deeper into the undergrowth then but his legs would not move. Dead to the touch when he reached down, the flesh no more his than the tree roots or the ground itself. He heard a voice behind him, another soldier coming to and grunting helplessly against some grave injury. He dragged himself away from the sound till his arms could drag no further. Lay face down, trying to will the toes in his boots to wiggle or curl.

When the Germans came through the bush they were walking three or four abreast, whispering to one another. He lay with his face in the dirt as they moved past him toward the steady suck and moan of the injured soldier and the sickening sound of it went still suddenly. A voice called the group to another body a few yards further on. He could pick just enough from the talk to know they were stripping the corpses of their boots, turning out the pockets for coins and tobacco and ammunition, stealing rings and necklaces and keepsakes. He'd crawled away from his weapon in the panic to hide himself and he was too terrified now to move, the tramp of the trophy hunters circling closer in the woods. They would use the knife on him as well, he knew, and he'd likely never be found there in the bush. A mortal darkness gathering at his heart's heart as that anonymous death sidled toward him—dread and resignation and a searing, wistful longing that felt like homesickness, all of it rising in him like the stench of the fallen world.

A hand gripped his shoulder to turn him on his back and the German soldier pulled away in disgust, cursing under his breath. —Dead a long time this one, he told the others. He covered his nose and mouth with a square of cloth and kept his head turned away, rooting blindly at the pockets, gagging through the muffle of his handkerchief. No one else in the group would come near.

He stared blankly at the green canopy of trees as the German pushed a hand through the collar of his jacket. The dog tags yanked away and examined briefly before being tossed into the shadows. —Leave him, another voice said. —We should get back.

He spent the full of the night alone there, paralyzed and bored and terrified. He tried to choke back a suspicion the German soldier was right, that he was dead where he lay in the bushes. That death wasn't sudden and complete but took a man out of the world piecemeal, a little at a time. It was a relief to hear the artillery start up just before dawn, to feel it shake through him and ring his head like a bell. By first light hundreds of soldiers were crossing the field toward the abandoned farmhouse and he dragged himself into the open, waving at the legs as they passed. Hours still before stretcher-bearers carted him the half-mile behind the lines to the aid post.

—This one's lost a hell of a lot of blood, the medic said.

—He doesn't appear to be bleeding, Sergeant.

—Well what's wrong with him?

—Couldn't get a word out of him. Some stink coming off the man though.

The smell suggested an infected wound and they stripped him out of his clothes but there was nothing there to be found. The medic looked down at him again. —Even his eyelashes are white, he said.

— He wasn't wearing his tags?

—No sign of them. He's a Newfoundlander, that's all we know.

—What's your name, Private?

He opened his mouth to answer and then shook his head helplessly.

—Psych case probably, the medic said. —We'll have to transport him back to Casualty. He leaned over the man on the stretcher. —Don't worry, he said, we'll fix you up.

Two days later he was moved to a base hospital in Rouen. He was in a ward with twenty-three other soldiers until their complaints about the stench forced the orderlies to set up a tent where he could be kept on his own. He was bathed twice a day in a concoction of carbolic and lye but it did nothing to lessen the smell.

A girl from Belleoram in Fortune Bay was nursing with the Voluntary Aid Detachment and she made a special project of him when she learned he was a Newfoundlander. Morning and evening she came to the tent in a surgical mask to massage his dead legs and talk about home. Guild socials and hooking mats and berry picking on the barrens and painting her bedroom floor a shade of green she'd seen on Johnny Lee's boat. He followed her with his eyes and she could see he didn't know what she was talking about. —You don't remember home, do you.

He shook his head.

—But you miss it.

And after he'd considered this a moment he nodded.

The weather was already bitter before the German surrender in November but he never complained or showed any discomfort in his unheated tent. At the end of the month the nurse brought him a sheet of paper and a lead pencil. —Tell me something you'd like for Christmas, I'll see if I can't find it in Rouen.

He stared at the implements as if he'd never laid eyes on such things in his life.

—Do you not have your letters? she asked. She was embarrassed for him and made a move to retrieve the materials but he shook his head. He held the pencil over the page a moment before starting in. *Death and life are in the power of the tongue,* he wrote, *and they that love it shall eat the fruit thereof.*

She took the paper when he was done and held it toward the light through the tent flap, trying to make it out. —Whoever taught you to write like this? she said, scanning back and forth the page. —I can't pick out the half of it. You wants some fruit, is that what you're saying?

He stared at her blankly.

—Fruit? she said again and he nodded, though there was no conviction in his face.

After Christmas he was shipped across the Channel to a convalescent hospital in England where doctors stuck pins into his legs and feet, examined his throat and ears, performed a series of tests to assess his mental faculties. They held conferences at his bedside, speaking about him as if he were deaf. His muteness and the paralysis were clearly the result of shell shock and they prescribed fresh air and quiet along with electrical massage to slow the muscle atrophy while he recovered his senses. But as time passed with no improvement they began to suspect the debilitation might be permanent. And the smell of the man was a riddle they had no answers for.

In the middle of March a woman stood at the foot of his bed in a surgical mask. —Do you remember me? she asked. She was waiting in London while her repatriation arrangements were made, she said, and was looking up boys from home still recuperating. —Just to keep myself occupied, she said. She sat in a chair by the window. She was booked to leave on a boat sailing for Newfoundland on the thirtieth, she told him. Three years she'd worked in France and she couldn't wait for a home meal.

A doctor flashed by the door and backed up the hall to look in. —You know this man?

The young nurse stood up. —I was at the field hospital in Rouen. Does he still not remember who he is?

—Hopeless case, I'm afraid. Have you seen any of that crazy writing he does?

—A little, she said uncertainly, turning to look at the patient.

—We're trying to figure out how to send him home.

The girl from Belleoram imagined it must be a ring of Dante's Hell to remember not the barest scrap of the place you came from. As if all you loved, the world itself, had forgotten you existed. She turned back to the doctor. —You know I'm a nurse, she said.

He was booked on the steamer departing at the end of the month. The days were frigid and inclement but the girl wheeled him around the deck morning and afternoon. —Lots of fresh air for you, she said. —Doctor's orders. He seemed impervious to the cold and wet, preferring to sit outside in the foulest weather, and he spent most of April month near the stern wearing a hospital johnny under an overcoat. She sat with him as long as she could stand the chill, talking about her family and her trip to New York on the way overseas and a man at home with such a sore throat the wine ran out his nose when he took Holy Communion. Something in it might stick, she thought, some meaningless detail could tip him into his life. She threw random questions at him, as if she might trick him into remembering himself. Do you have brothers or sisters? Do you know the words to "Whispering Hope"? Have you ever been to Port Union? Are you Catholic or Protestant?

The day before they were scheduled to reach St. John's she said, Is there a girl waiting for you at home? He turned to her with a tortured look that she misread completely. —You remember her? she said. —You know her name?

But he only stared, as if pleading with her to stop.

He had no idea if there was a girl waiting at home and she could almost feel that absence yawing beneath him, the shadows flickering across blank space, nameless and unidentifiable. —I'll tell you what I think, she said. —Something will come to you. You'll see a face or a boat or hear someone's voice and that one thing will bring it all back to you.

He stared blankly out at the water and she patted his hand. —I'm freezing, she said. She stood up and wrapped her arms tight about herself. —Are you all right here awhile?

He nodded.

—Tomorrow's the Feast of St. Mark, she said. —Mean anything to you?

He smiled at her useless little ploy, shaking his white head. His life like something important he'd meant to tell someone and he couldn't recall now what he intended to say or to whom. He watched her skitter along the deck toward steerage and disappear inside, relieved to be left to himself. The nurse's endless questions served only to add depth and definition to what it was he lacked. Alone he could turn his back on the absence, look at the world as if there was nothing to it but surface, the endless present moment. A trick of shadow and light.

There wasn't another soul out in the drizzle and bitter wind when he spotted the whale steaming clear of the ship's wake, so close he could see the markings under its flukes, the white of them glowing a pale apple-green through seawater. The massive fan of the tail tipped high and disappeared as the whale sounded and he leaned forward in his wheelchair, expectant, as if he'd been told the humpback would breach, rising nose first and almost clear of the water, kicking up a wreath of foam as it fell back into the sea. The whale came full into the open air a second time and a third, it almost seemed to be calling his attention. And something in that detail turned like a key in a lock, a story spiralling out of the ocean's endless green and black to claim him.

The face of a girl waiting at home flashed below the surface and he pushed himself onto the deck, dragging his dead legs to the rail. He shed his clothes as he went, returning to himself naked as a fish. Even as he fell he pictured her watching from across the room the next time he opened his eyes to the light.

THANKS

Holly Ann.

Martha Kanya-Forstner.

Anne et al. at the McDermid Agency.

Nit-pickers: Holly Hogan, Stan Dragland, Martha Magor, Janice McAlpine, Larry Matthews, Lynn Moore, Alison Pick, Degan Davis, Mary Lewis, Shawn Oakey, God love the works of you.

There were dozens of community histories, journals and memoirs, academic studies, websites, archival documents, collections of songs, tales and folklore behind the geography, incidents and characters in *Galore*. MKF won't let me list them all, but here are some of the books I leaned on while writing the novel: *Family Names of the Island of Newfoundland*, E.R. Searey; *A History of Corpus Christi Parish, Northern Bay*, Edward Chafe; *Vignettes of a Small Town*, Robert C. Parsons; *A Heritage Guide to Portugal Cove–St. Philip's*, Robin McGrath; *Prime Berth: An Account of Bonavista's Early Years*, Bruce Whiffen; *The Irish in Newfoundland, 1600–1900*, Mike McCarthy; *Fables, Fairies and Folklore of Newfoundland*, Alice Lannon and Mike McCarthy; *Making Witches: Newfoundland Traditions of Spells and Counterspells*, Barbara Rieti; *Hope and Deception in Conception Bay: Merchant–Settler Relations in Newfoundland, 1785–1855*, Sean T. Caddigan; *A History of Health Care in Newfoundland and Labrador*, Stephen M.

Nolan; *The Labrador Memoir of Dr. Harry Paddon*, Ronald Rompkey (ed.); *Doctor Olds of Twillingate: Portrait of an American Surgeon in Newfoundland*, Gary L. Saunders; *To Be My Father's Daughter*, Carmelita McGrath, Sharon Halfyard, Marion Cheeks; *Theatre of Fish: Travels through Newfoundland and Labrador*, John Gimlette; *Your Daughter Fanny: The War Letters of Frances Cluett, VAD*, Bill Rompkey and Bert Riggs (eds.).

Parts of *Galore* were written during a stint as Writer in Residence at Memorial University in St. John's. Thanks to everyone in the English Department—in particular Danine Farquharson and Jennifer Lokash—for looking after me. Thanks as well to the staff of the Provincial Archives and Mark Ferguson of the Provincial Museum at the Rooms, and to Larry Dohey at the Archives of the Roman Catholic Archdiocese in St. John's.